OF LEGENDS & DESIRES

OF LEGENDS & DESIRES

SOUL OF THE DRAGONFLY
BOOK ONE

ABIGAIL R. SCHIEBER

Cover Design by Moonpress | www.moonpress.co
Map by Rena Violet | www.coversbyviolet.com
Editing by Noah Sky | www.noah-sky-editing.com
Proofreading by Norma Gambini | normasnookproofreading@gmail.com

Library of Congress Control Number: 2025907643

ISBN: 9798992386325 (hardcover)
ISBN: 9798992386301 (paperback)
ISBN: 9798992386318 (ebook)

First Edition

Dear Reader,

Please be aware that *Of Legends & Desires* contains content that may be triggering. For a list, please see the *Content Warning* page at the end of the book.

For every Riley out there—keep planting the seeds of hope.

CHAPTER 1

R iley Hayes shrank further into the shadows of her corner booth, trying to make herself as invisible as possible without possessing a drop of magic.

She abhorred the Ivory Pearl. The small, dilapidated tavern was far from the alluring elegance the name suggested. Tiny, glowing faeries fluttered in glass jars strung from the ceiling, testing the resistance of their prisons. They bathed the tavern in playful shadows, their pleas for help unheard while the band played from across the room. The foul stench of death lingered in the air, blending with blood, stale food, and cheap liquor. And one was lucky if they didn't receive a splinter upon sitting down.

Only those with a lifestyle of depravity and mayhem would come to a place like this—and why Riley inwardly cringed every time she had to step foot inside and triple-check her weapons. Or would have, if she had remembered them.

After Riley had been kept up most of the night by an insatiable merman, her captain had barged into her cabin, ordering her to meet her at the Ivory Pearl. Half-asleep and in a hurry, Riley had forgotten to strap on her dagger and sword. Fortunately, she'd never taken the knife sheathed inside her boot out the night before. It wasn't much, but it would do.

Unfortunately, the Captain of the Roaring Tigers was running late, as usual. Riley assumed wherever Mara was, she had become distracted and was gambling away whatever money she had left.

Shifting in her seat, taking care to avoid a splinter, Riley subtly adjusted the candle wax she'd stuffed in her ears before walking through the doors. A human couldn't be too careful in the proximity of a faerie playing an instrument. The likelihood it was enchanted to enthrall one, such as herself, into doing sensual acts without their knowledge was far too great.

Despite the wax, she could still hear the din of the other pirates in the tavern. She wondered if shoving the wax farther down would make the pounding at her temples disappear. The riotous laughter was obnoxious. The tavern vibrated with a hunger for violence, but it wasn't toward one another as it usually was. It was a rare sight to see rival pirates getting along, but it was all owed to the tavern's late-morning entertainment dancing atop the bar.

A human presented all sorts of fun for faeries.

All faeries, of status or even a lowly pirate, had two things in common—they couldn't resist a bargain and they loved entertainment, especially of the *human* nature. If they weren't being used to keep a faerie occupied, they were forced to become mindless servants. It was almost unthinkable to come across a human living freely in Erithena. They couldn't all be as lucky as Riley. But that didn't mean she was always free.

There had been a time, years ago, when her fragile heart had shattered. When she had found herself alone, defeated, and without a seed of hope. It had been a long path to stability, but even after putting the pieces back together, she still had the cracks from the time she had given up—and the scars to prove it.

Absently, Riley ran a pale thumb over the puffy flesh on her right arm. The old scar ran the length of her inner forearm and was covered by a dragonfly tattoo. The abdomen of the insect was inked over the long scar, the geometric wings wrapping around her wrist where they met on the other side. On her left forearm, she had a matching scar to go with the right, but the head of a roaring tiger above a compass covered it.

Riley tugged the sleeve of her sweat-stained shirt down farther, conscious someone might notice the tiger. The Roaring Tigers' insignia was well-known among pirates, but with the crew's reputation, having it on your skin put a target on your back. And they only had their captain to blame for it.

Despite what they tricked the humans into believing, faeries were more than capable of lying—and Mara was exemplary at it. She stole from everyone and anyone, racking up debts and threats from the other pirates. It was only her crew who remained untouched by her thievery, abiding by her own moral code. There was no *honor among thieves*. The only honor Mara showed was toward those who happened not to piss her off that day.

Atop the bar, Brock—a goblin known to Riley for his love of *playing* with humans—had joined the poor girl, guiding her around as a dance partner might. He slipped his clawed, moss-green hand free from the girl's, and everyone watched as she spun until there was no bar left. Her body pitched forward, and she landed on a nearby table, breaking glasses filled with liquor before rolling onto the filthy wooden floor. Shards of glass protruded from the girl's pale chest and neck, staining her coral sundress with her blood. After days of being forced to dance, her nightmare had finally come to its inevitable end.

Riley blew out a shuddered breath, her chest aching as a new mark etched itself into her heart. The girl couldn't have been more than sixteen.

At the other end of the tavern, across from the bar, the band stopped playing. Laughter turned into grumbling as the faeries looked at the broken girl. Brock nudged her with a pointed boot. "It croaked," he said, disappointed. He scratched his jaw with his right hand, the last two fingers stumps from where a rival had chopped them off. He looked around the dimly lit bar, past the others, searching.

Riley took that as her cue to leave. She had no desire to play his games again.

Keeping to the shadows, Riley left the Ivory Pearl by the rear exit, out into the alley. She removed the balls of wax from her ears, squinting into the sunlight, letting her eyes adjust.

The outside was just as glamorous as the inside. The painted white wood was flaked and warped, rats made use of the varying holes, birds nested in alcoves—and just like the inside, splotches of blood decorated the walls.

Breathing in the fresh air, Riley crinkled her nose in disgust. She tossed the wax aside and grumbled to herself, her boots squelching in the mud as she slogged through moldering scraps of food and bones of a gremlin.

When Riley was almost free of the alley, the air less pungent, two faeries stepped in her path, blocking her exit. She recognized the one with dark skin and dandelion-seed hair and the pale, silver-haired elve as two of Brock's crew members—Cloud and Lux—as the back door of the Ivory Pearl opened and closed.

"Where are you going, sweetmeat? I need a new dance partner."

Brock's snarly voice grated on Riley's bones as she balled her hands into fists.

She sized up his crew members before glancing over her shoulder at the goblin. "You're going to have to find someone else," she said. "I forgot my dancing shoes at—"

With the silent grace all faeries possessed, Cloud and Lux grabbed Riley by the arms. She struggled against their hold as Brock stalked toward her. "I said *no*," Riley all but snarled like a feral wolf.

Standing before her, Brock tilted his head back to look her in the eye. "I wasn't asking, sweetmeat." The corner of his mouth lifted as he commanded, "*You will dance for me.*" The compulsion was so stark in his voice, you could almost taste the magic singeing the air.

Just as all faeries had the capability to glamour themselves and fool a human into believing they were harmless, they also possessed the magic to compel them. They needed to voice their commands to the human, who had to obey no matter how hard they fought. It was why the girl in the tavern had danced upon broken glass for days without so much as a wince.

And if it wasn't for her dragonfly tattoo—painted on with

enchanted ink—Riley would already be dancing in the alley, taking the deceased girl's place.

Brock's magic bounced off an invisible barrier as Riley thanked the gods Mara had taken her to get the tattoo three years ago.

Riley arched a brow at the goblin. "Is that so?"

Brock's dark, wayward brows rose to his receding hairline. His mouth opened, closed, then opened again, as if he couldn't quite process that his magic had failed him. "Impossible," he snarled, his green skin paling.

"It's all right," Riley said, smiling sweetly, "I hear performance issues aren't uncommon." As a growl emanated from the back of his throat, she basked in his frustration, if only for a fleeting moment.

Brock curled his lip back, baring his teeth once more before he turned it into a cruel smile. His laugh sent a shiver down her spine, making her heart race more than it already was. "I don't know how you resisted my magic, sweetmeat," he said, "but one way or another, you will dance for me."

Riley barely heard a word coming out of his mouth; the smell of his breath was horrendous: the strong odor of cheap liquor and sweet faerie wine. She scrunched her nose in disgust. "I'm sorry," she said. "I didn't catch a word of that. You should really invest in some breath mints."

At this, Brock snapped. He pulled out a dagger, lifting it to her chin and digging the point in enough to draw blood. She sucked in a sharp breath, and Brock's smile was all pointy teeth.

"You might as well get all your little jokes out now," he said, "because once you start dancing for me, you won't stop until your feet fall off."

Riley's heart hammered against her chest.

She might've had her enchanted tattoo to ensure she could see through any faerie's glamour and resist their compulsive commands, but it couldn't protect her from other enchantments. All Brock had to do was find a bewitched instrument and she would dance for him until her body burned itself up from the inside out, as humans always eventually did from their magic. It was why she had gone to the tavern with balls of wax in her ears; if she couldn't hear the music, she couldn't lose control of her body—but she had thrown that precaution into the mud.

It didn't mean she was helpless.

Riley thrust her knee up into Brock's groin. He dropped the dagger and fell to the ground, groaning in agony with his hands between his legs.

Before Brock's crew members realized what had happened, Riley stomped her heel onto Lux's foot and quickly drove the back of her head into Cloud's nose. They lost their grip on Riley, Cloud clutching her nose and Lux staggering on one foot.

Riley kicked Lux in his stomach then spun, bringing her fist into Cloud's jaw, her braided hair whipping the air. She collapsed in the mud, her eyes rolling into the back of her head.

Riley's brows rose. *Lightweight.*

With Brock still immobile, Riley whirled on Lux as he got to his feet. He unsheathed his dagger. Taking a deep breath, Riley drew her own from inside her boot.

The corner of Lux's mouth lifted. "You sure you know how to use that thing, human?"

"Only one way to find out," Riley said. She mirrored his crooked grin. "Unless you're too scared."

Lux's half-smile vanished. He thrust the dagger forward. Riley ducked to the side, dodging the blade, and plunged her knife into his belly. She twisted it for good measure before pulling it out.

He fell to his knees as he swiped at the air wildly. Riley knocked the blade from his hand before it cut through flesh.

Lux breathed heavily, his hands desperately trying to staunch the bleeding, but it was no use. He was losing blood faster than he could use his faerie magic to heal.

Crouching before the elve, Riley remarked, "I guess I do know how to use it." She adjusted her grip on the handle, readying to put him out of his misery—

Clawed hands gripped her by the back of her shirt. Her eyes widened as she was whipped back from the dying elve and into the wall of the tavern. Her teeth knocked together and air flew from her lungs. She slumped forward in the mud, trying to gather her breath, but before she could, the clawed hands found her braid.

Brock dragged her backward, back to the rear entrance of the Ivory Pearl—toward the music she could not resist.

"While I find someone to play you an enchantment," Brock said, breathing heavily, "I'm sure the others would *love* to keep you company."

Her heart reared up her throat, pounding furiously. She thrashed and clawed at his flesh as the goblin dragged her back into a nightmare she had worked so hard to forget.

"It's all right to be afraid, sweetmeat." Brock was too close for comfort. The words tickled her ear, and a shiver shot up her spine, bringing every survival instinct she had screaming into existence. "I like it when you are." The tip of his pointed, wet tongue slithered up the column of her neck, Brock tasting the beading, fear-induced sweat as he ground his arousal into her back.

With that scream of survival lodged in her throat, Riley struck, hoping she would rip out his tongue with her bare hand. Instead, she found the golden hoop in his ear. She tore it free from his earlobe. Brock cried out, releasing her enough for her elbow to find his chin. He stumbled backward, falling.

Before he could recover, she crouched over him. And with fear, adrenaline, and blinding fury, Riley beat her fists into his face again, and again, and again, until her knuckles were coated in both of their blood. It thundered in her ears, blocking out the birds squawking overhead, the loud laughter of the pirates in the Ivory Pearl, the water lapping on the shoreline beyond the alley. She could not hear her own screams of rage or the goblin's wheezing breaths before her. All she heard was the drum of her heart beating in time with her fists slamming against the goblin's broken and battered face.

Riley raised her fist in the air, ready to drive the bones in his nose into his brain, but before she could, a hand caught her wrist. She resisted, needing to end the goblin's worthless life, but it wouldn't let her. It wouldn't let her know the pathetic creature before her would never be able to hurt her or another human again.

"Riley!"

A familiar voice found its way through the blood thrumming in her ears as someone screamed her name.

"What the fuck have you done?"

CHAPTER 2

"What are you doing here, Jasper?"

Riley glared at the merman, not letting her features betray the shock washing over her at the sight of him. His bare, sun-kissed chest hovered next to her in the alley. She came eye to eye with the flaring sun tattooed over his heart, surrounded by others covering his defined chest and arms.

His grip tightened on her wrist. "I think *I* should be asking *you* that."

Riley kept her mouth clamped shut. Being an unessential part of the crew—or rather, just another mouth they had to feed, since all she knew how to do was get in everyone else's way while they did their jobs—she didn't want to drag Jasper into her mess. He had enough of Mara's messes to clean up already, being her second-in-command. It was that or hope another pirate came along and wiped it up for him.

Jasper surveyed Riley closely with golden eyes, the outer rims the same ocean blue as his hair. He waited for her to break and tell him why she knocked out Cloud, gutted Lux, and beat Brock until his face was unrecognizable. But even with Jasper's gaze boring into hers, she couldn't. The words wouldn't work their way to the surface, not when she had been burying them for so long.

She arched a withering brow. "You want to let me go?"

"That depends," he said, his voice hard. "You good?"

Riley nearly snorted, keeping her eyes from rolling. She had almost been thrown to a mob of hungry monsters, while a goblin went in search of someone to enchant her to dance for him—and gods only knew what else. And that was if the monsters hadn't dealt with her before he returned.

She gave Jasper a smile as sweet as sugar. "I'm fucking fantastic."

A moment ticked by before he sighed and released his webbed hand from her wrist. Offering her the same hand, he helped Riley to her feet. She took a few steps back from Brock, letting what she had done sink in. Her hands clenched and unclenched at her sides; the sting in her bloody knuckles slowly became a dull irritation as her adrenaline faded, but the urge to finish it was still pulsing through her veins. Her fingers twitched.

"Shit," Jasper muttered, drawing Riley's focus. His dagger was unsheathed from where it had been strapped across his tattooed chest. With a quick flick of his wrist, the blade, made from a narrow, spiked tooth of an angulper—sea monsters deadlier than any sea wyrm—sailed through the air. The scaled hilt shimmered through the light before finding Lux's neck. The elve went still, his fingers just shy of the dagger he had been silently crawling through the mud for.

Riley's brows shot to her hairline as she stared at Lux. "Huh," was all that came out of her mouth. She could've sworn he was dead, but then she remembered Brock slamming her into the side of the tavern before she could put the elve out of his misery. It occurred to her if Jasper hadn't shown up when he had, stopping her, she might still be beating her bloodied fists into Brock's broken face, unaware of the remaining threat. Her mouth became a tight, thin line. Running off of fear and anger had almost gotten her killed.

Watching him withdraw his dagger from the elve's neck, she repeated her earlier question. "What are you doing here, Jasper?"

"Mara sent me to come get you," he said distantly, scrutinizing the scene around them, making sure Cloud was still out cold—she was and snored deeply. He frowned at the flaking, white walls of the Ivory Pearl behind him. Inside, faeries sang a sea shanty as loudly and off-key as they could.

Riley crossed her arms over her chest. "Why?"

Shrugging, he said, "All I know is now she wants to meet somewhere else."

Irritated, Riley sighed, eyes going to the blue, cloudless sky. That explained why Mara hadn't shown at the tavern. But was she so drunk, or high, or both that she'd had to send Jasper in her place? "Where are we meeting her?"

Jasper sighed heavily. "The fighting pit."

RILEY WALKED with Jasper through the mud-laden streets of Obsidian Island, trying to keep a low profile from the other pirates.

The island was located in the middle of the Gorsium Sea and was home to most, if not all, pirates after they'd relocated from the kingdoms of Erithena. Deemed too reckless and a danger to everyone, including themselves, pirates were hunted by the High Crown Guard, who'd originally been ordered by High King Idris and now by his son and heir, High King Darrow, to arrest any pirate on sight. They would be hanged with no trial nor an opportunity to make a plea for their lives. Pirates were ruthless toward everyone, not just their own. They didn't listen to those begging for mercy when they robbed, raped, and murdered—but not all were as ruthless as most. Some had nowhere else to go or simply craved adventure.

"Are you ever going to tell me what happened?" Jasper asked, low. It wouldn't be wise to have one of the pirates they passed overhear them.

Riley frowned, turning her head to the sky. "Not if I can help it," she answered, squinting from the brightness. It was miserable out—hot and humid—and if she wasn't careful, her fair skin would burn from being in the sun too long.

Sighing, Jasper said, "If you've gotten into some trouble, I'm sure Mara would be more than happy to get you out of it. Gods only know she can't get *herself* out of trouble, but she's good at getting her crew out of it." His fingers brushed against hers, sending her stomach fluttering, as he lifted his hand to his hair, running it through the short cerulean mohawk. "And if you didn't want to get Mara involved, I can always—"

"I can take care of myself," she snapped, cutting him off. She really didn't want to hear the end of that sentence. He pursed his lips, arching his left brow and the gold hoop in it. It matched the ones going up the length of his finned ears. "What, you don't think I can?"

He shook his head. "It's not that—I've seen what you can do with a blade—but . . ."

"But, what?"

He shrugged. "You're human," he said simply. As if this statement explained everything.

And it did. In this world, it was known humans were weak, filthy, lowly creatures who were easy to manipulate and deceive, deserving nothing more than to become pets or playthings.

Riley halted her footsteps, and Jasper stopped a couple of steps ahead after realizing she was no longer walking beside him.

She glared at him, her arms shaking with the urge to swing her fists right into his face. It was bad enough she already had these thoughts swirling around inside her mind, but to have Jasper come out and say it made her want to . . .

Cry? Scream? Give up and never face the world again?

All of that, she admitted to herself. *It makes me want to do all of that.*

But she didn't do any of those things.

Instead, Riley kept her mouth shut, shoving it all down where the shadows lived within her soul, and if Jasper noticed, he didn't say a word.

Pushing past him, she kept going, passing over one of the many bridges built where the water rose too high to walk through.

The island had been formed from the skeleton of the first dragon ever created by the Mother of All and was once the god of fire, Beldir. He had perished during the Battle of the Gods, and the land had grown through and around Beldir's body, forming Obsidian Island.

Riley continued past the different stalls in the market. She narrowly avoided a pirate spearing different meats onto a skewer at a kebab stall, the smell making her stomach grumble in protest for having skipped breakfast. She didn't stop until Jasper caught her hand.

"What?" she snapped, whirling on him.

His dark brows rose in surprise at her outburst. He pointed to the tall metal walls ahead. "We're here."

She recognized where they were and suddenly felt guilty for snapping at him.

The fighting pit was located on the skull of the island, inside the eye socket. The large arena was embedded deep within with seating wrapping around the inside, stretching high above it, halfway up the walls. It was always packed with faeries begging to catch a glimpse of bloodshed. Daily competitions were hosted, and once a week were tryouts, where faeries were allowed to show off their fighting skills and hopefully earn themselves a position on a crew. It always overflowed with pirates on the day of tryouts—and today was like any other week.

Jasper tugged Riley off to the side, away from the crowd. "Before we go in there," he said, his hand going behind his back, "I wanted to give you your birthday gift."

"But my birthday isn't for another week." She didn't mention that in the three years they'd been friends, he had never given her a birthday gift before, and she knew it wasn't because they were sleeping together. Their not-courting-just-having-fun relationship had started two years ago, but he'd always claimed to have forgotten a gift and would have something for her the next day. He never had.

"I know," he said, "but I'll be leaving for home after we meet Mara, for my rejuvenation."

The rejuvenation was vital for all water faeries; they could be on land for only so long before they needed to submerge themselves in water. If they missed rejuvenation, the wilting would begin, causing them to dry out and shrivel up—both inside and out.

Riley had seen the wilting more than once. Pirates were notorious for being cruel to water faeries. They would spike them to the bows of their ships and use them as figureheads, leaving them to perish from the sun's rays.

Riley laced her fingers with Jasper's one hand still in sight. "Stay.

Don't go home to rejuvenate. You could do that in a bath full of hot water, and I could stay in there with you."

"As much as I would love to stay and do naughty things with you"—Jasper grinned, the blue waves around the gold in his eyes rippling with sinful delight—"I need to return home for my rejuvenation or else my mother would send an army to drag my ass back by my fins."

He might have been making light of the situation, but Riley knew what he said was all too possible. When your mother was the Sea Queen —and terrifying from what Jasper had mentioned of her—an army of water faeries could come knocking down your door at any given time just because the mood struck her.

Riley opened her mouth to tell him not to joke about his situation, but he unlaced their fingers, placing one over her mouth, mistaking what she was going to say with an objection to his departure. "We both know I made a bargain with my mother," he said. "My five months of freedom on land have passed, and now it's time to go home for two months to rejuvenate." He tucked a loose strand of her curly chestnut hair behind her ear. "But before I go, I'd like to give you your gift and see why Mara thinks we can find a new cook for the crew at the fighting pit."

Riley snort-laughed. "Okay."

Jasper untied a small pouch from the back of his belt, handing it to her. She lifted it up and down, weighing it in her hand. Whatever was inside, it had a little bit of weight to it.

"You know," Jasper drawled, the corner of his mouth lifting, "you could just open the damn thing and find out what's inside that way."

"Smart-ass." She smacked him playfully in the shoulder with the pouch, hoping whatever was inside wasn't fragile, then quickly pried it open. Jasper chuckled as she pulled the gift free.

The muscular, shirtless man on the cover of the romance novel, small enough to fit within her hand, stared back at her with intense, smoldering eyes—ones that were all too familiar. She remembered bringing the book back from one of her trips with Mara to the mortal world and she wondered if Jasper hadn't, giving her a different copy of the same book. Or if he had forgotten her birthday, as he always did, and scrambled for something to give her, picking up the first book he knew was hers.

There was only one way to find out—and it wasn't by simply asking him.

Flipping through the book, she found the title page, where it was addressed to the previous owner and signed by the author. Her heart sank. It was the exact copy from the little, used bookshop in the mortal world. She had taken the book because she'd thought it deserved to be cherished by someone who not only saw its worth in the value of the author's signature, but also the flaws of the water damage and the broken spine. It had once been loved by the previous owner, but something had happened to cause her to give it away. To allow Riley to pick it up and love it just as much and more than the previous owner.

"Do you like it?" Jasper asked, bringing Riley out of her thoughts.

She looked up from the small book and into his hopeful golden eyes and gave him a small smile, nodding. "Yes, thank you." But on the inside, her heart made of glass added a new crack to it, despite the stone she had laid down around it, protecting it—even the strongest barriers had vulnerabilities. She tried to remind herself that he had at least given her a gift this year, and that had to mean . . . something.

A grin broke out across his face, and the crack in her heart widened. Leaning in, he cupped her face and kissed her, quick and soft. "I'm happy you like it," he murmured against her lips.

The book felt like it weighed a hundred pounds in her hand.

He pulled back, still smiling proudly. "Come on." He gestured to the side with his head. "Mara's waiting for us."

Removing his hands from her cheeks, Jasper walked into the throng of pirates spilling through the doors of the arena. Her eyes tracked the blue mohawk and the roaring tiger inked on the back of his neck, until he disappeared completely.

Pirates pushed and shoved at each other, trying to get in first, hoping to get the best seats for the entertainment that followed.

Riley took deep breaths, willing herself to move forward, and rolled her shoulders. She hadn't noticed when the tension in her body began. The heavy book was all her mind could focus on. She curled it in her hands.

It wasn't that she didn't like crowds; she just didn't like this particular one.

Taking one last deep breath, she plowed ahead.

Riley mimicked the others around her, still holding her book, and shoved her way through the masses. She bit the inside of her cheek when her right arm grazed a faerie with sharp scales, but the sting didn't last long. She was lucky the scales hadn't drawn blood or the smell might attract unwanted attention.

She made her way through the crowd, and—

A hard elbow knocked into her sternum. The air was punched from her lungs for a second time that morning, and her legs quickly became unsteady. The world tilted on its axis as she teetered backward.

CHAPTER 3

Everything slowed around Riley. The shouting and grumbling of faeries faded away, but the crashing waves of the nearby shore roared in her ears, nearly outweighing the drumming of her heart. She cradled the sound and smell of the water close to her—there would never be another opportunity to do so.

The moment she connected with the earth would be the end for her. Faeries surrounded her, and none cared if they trampled a weak, little human to death.

Cherished memories and moments flashed before her eyes, replacing the blue sky, as she waited for the impact to come and the pain that would follow.

But it never did.

A steady rhythm accompanied the rolling waves in her ears as warmth spread through her from the back of her head and under her arms. Her skin tingled, as if from static electricity.

The world began to right itself, and Riley with it.

After a moment, she realized, amidst the haze of her fear, the warmth under her arms were someone's hands, and they were lifting her onto unsteady legs. She became aware that the prominent rhythm in her ears was that same someone's heart beating strongly in their chest—that her head rested upon.

Adrenaline raced through her veins as she sucked air into her lungs raggedly, but the warm hands remained on her arms, an assurance that they would be there to catch her.

With her breathing slowly coming back to normal, the waves receded into the background where they'd once been and the faeries' shouts and grumbles returned. But the steady rhythm of a heart remained.

"Are you all right?" rumbled a baritone voice. Through the back of her head, she felt the vibrations within his chest, sending a shiver down her spine.

Nodding, Riley turned around, her legs steadying with each passing second. "Thank y—"

Her breath hitched. She didn't know which she was more surprised by—the elve being kind enough to ask if she was all right or his eyes that were a vibrant mixture of rippling green and blue with golden streaks branching out from the center. They looked like lightning striking over green waves.

The elve bent down, retrieving something from the mud, and Riley's gaze snagged on his dark, curly hair. It was much shorter on the sides, the tips of his pointed ears unable to hide within the luscious, tight curls.

Gods, I would love to run my fingers through that, Riley found herself daydreaming. Her fingers twitched at her sides, aching to live out that dream. His strands were well-behaved and appeared to be softer than the brush of a feather against one's skin. Nothing at all like the frizzy, heavy mass braided midway down her back that not even a bird would find suitable to nest in.

Bent over, he came to her waist, and when he stood, brushing mud off Riley's forgotten book, he towered at least a foot taller than she was.

He held out the book to her, its small size exaggerated in his large, calloused hand, but she was too busy gawking to notice.

If one looked closely enough—which Riley was absolutely doing—a small scar from a blade could be spotted on his jaw beneath a sprinkling of facial hair. And there wasn't a single freckle on his smooth bronze skin. She mentally cursed him. After all her time in the sun, she wished she could say the same for herself, but freckles dotted her nose, cheeks, and shoulders.

When she didn't take the book and the staring became borderline creepy, he arched a dark brow, frowning. "Are you sure you're all right?" he asked. His black cloak brushed against her fingers as faeries shoved their way past them. If she didn't have the solidness of his body shielding her from the crowd, she would already be trampled.

Before she had time to say anything, she heard Jasper yell her name, turning in the direction of his voice. The top of his blue hair could be seen weaving through the crowd toward her. She breathed a heavy sigh.

Turning back around to thank the elve, Riley found the space empty. He had vanished, as though he had never existed, along with her book. And once again, Riley found herself alone.

SEATED in the first row with her leg resting on a ledge above the pit, the Captain of the Roaring Tigers peeled a faerie apple with her favorite knife, the curved blade resembling the claw of a cat. Hidden blades lined her battered and muddied pants, while one was sheathed within each boot. Riley knew of two particularly small knives hidden within the tight, cropped leather top she wore, the sleeves removed to reveal a beautifully intricate tattoo covering the entirety of her left arm: a sea wyrm readying to strike a ship caught in a storm. At her wrist was a compass identical to Riley's and Jasper's.

Her straight raven hair stopped just below her chin, the ends curling inward as though her square jaw were luring them, and hid her subtly pointed ears. They were the only indication she wasn't full-blooded elven and considered an imperfection among her faerie kin. But Mara never minded them. She embraced them, along with the other features her human mother had given her—like the boldness to ink the Roaring Tigers' insignia on her throat.

"Nice of you to finally join me," Mara said as Riley and Jasper sat down next to her.

Riley rolled her eyes. Mara could go kiss a toad's ass for all she cared.

She was just happy to be alive. "Nice of you to manage to get a spot in the front row," Riley retorted. "You might actually be able to see everything without sitting on my shoulders."

Slowly, Mara's narrow teal gaze slid to hers. She was only a few bites into her apple, but her eyes were already beginning to glaze over from the effects of the fruit.

Faerie fruit was a popular euphoric drug in Erithena—especially on Obsidian Island—and coated with pixie dust. Pixies preferred to feast on fruit, and while they ate, their magical dust would find its way onto their meal and those surrounding them. It was so potent, one bite of the fruit would have someone hooked on it for the rest of their lives.

"Funny," Mara said dryly. She arched a dark, manicured brow. "Did Jasper's short jokes rub off on you?"

Jasper looked over Riley's head at Mara. "That's not the only thing that rubbed off on her," he added, winking. Riley's face fell into her hands as she groaned, and Mara gave the merman a withering look.

"Anyway," Mara drawled, saying to Riley, "we both know I could see just fine, even if we were in the top row, but you wouldn't see a damn thing—and not because of your human eyes, but because you would be too busy passed out after pissing your pants from fright."

The corners of Riley's mouth curved down, even though Mara was right. She glanced to the top of the walls and felt lightheaded. Facing the front again, she leaned forward with her head down. A small, thin hand came to her back, rubbing circles. Riley breathed, inhaling and exhaling, until the vertigo subsided, and she straightened.

Mara's hand disappeared, reappearing in front of her, holding a slice of apple. Riley looked from it to Mara, giving her a stern look.

"It'd take the edge off," Mara said. Riley shook her head, and Mara shrugged, tossing the slice into her mouth. Her pupils dilated more, the teal shrinking away.

Pirates were still filing into the arena, trying to find a seat for themselves. Riley heard someone cry out in pain, and she wondered what the cause of it was.

Riley scanned the crowd for the answer, only for her gaze to land on a menacing faerie's glare. He had the appearance of a lizard with thorns sticking out from his head, face, and bare chest beneath his dark blue coat; two thorns—the largest of them—grew right above his black, beady eyes. Sitting a few rows higher than them, he was tall enough that Riley could see the desert-striped scales covering him and the scars stretching over his chest and mouth. She considered for a brief moment if it had been his thorns that had scraped her arm outside the walls. She swallowed, asking, "Why is that faerie staring at us?"

"You'll have to be more specific," Mara drawled, peeling another slice of apple, just as Jasper mumbled under his breath, "Who isn't giving us a death glare?"

Glancing over her shoulder, Mara looked around for the faerie and found the thorny devil lizard. She gave the pirate a saccharine smile and a salute before turning back around to keep working at her faerie apple. The pirate didn't look pleased as Mara sliced off the last piece.

"That's just Grimsley," Mara said, chucking the core into the pit.

"Why is he pissed at us?"

"He isn't pissed at *us*," Jasper said, crossing his arms. "He's pissed at Mara because she cheated him out of a bargain in a game of cards last night."

There wasn't a single part of that sentence Riley was surprised by. She whirled on Mara, hissing, "Did you cheat?"

Mara gave her a look that said *of course, I did*, and Riley shook her head, frowning.

"I'm not giving him what he wants," Mara said, raising her chin.

"He doesn't look happy, Mara—"

"Understatement," Jasper muttered.

"—and what if he tries something?"

"Don't worry about him, Leyley," Mara said, waving a hand dismissively. "He's got the memory of a goldfish. He'll forget about it in a few days."

Riley glanced back at Grimsley; the anger rolling from him indicated otherwise.

Mara smacked the side of Riley's leg, gaining her attention. "The fights are about to start."

Two faeries emerged from doors on either side of the pit. The crowd buzzed with anticipation. All around the arena, bets were placed on who would win.

The two rules of tryouts were very simple—no weapons, no magic. Of course, there were always rule breakers, and although they would be disqualified and the fight would end immediately, they were always the first ones to get job offers.

"Unless someone magically whips out a stove and ingredients and starts cooking," Riley said to her captain, "how do you expect to find a new cook in the fighting pit?"

Mara arched a brow, smirking. "Who said we're here for a new cook?"

"But I thought we needed—"

A bell sounded, cutting Riley off, the chimes echoing around the arena and beyond. Riley could just make out the cheers from outside the walls; even if they couldn't make it inside to see the fight, the pirates still thrummed with the energy of one.

"Who do you think will win?" Jasper asked, leaning in so Riley could hear him above the crowd.

She gestured with her chin to the redcap. "One of his arms is the size of that porcupine."

Jasper laughed.

It wasn't that she was being rude. The faerie truly looked like a porcupine, quills and all. He wore no shirt, the quills on his back rendering it difficult, and his pants had more quills poking out of the back.

"Want to make it a bet?" Jasper asked.

"What would I win?"

A wickedly sinful smile spread across his face. Whispering in her ear, he said, "One hell of a memorable goodbye."

Her teeth pulled on her bottom lip. "And if I lose?"

"One hell of a memorable goodbye," he repeated, nipping at her earlobe.

Her body heated. "You're on."

The fight didn't last long. The redcap charged while the porcupine faerie remained where he was. Once the redcap was within distance, the porcupine faerie plucked quills from his back and threw them with precision at his opponent. The redcap made it two steps before his eyes rolled into the back of his head and he fell into the mud, unconscious.

The crowd roared with a mixture of cheers, from those who won their bets and were heckling to those who didn't like the outcome, claiming the faerie had cheated.

The quills wouldn't be considered cheating—fighters were allowed to use what they'd been born with as long as it wasn't magic. It wasn't uncommon for a faerie's claws, fangs, or, in this case, quills to possess a toxin.

"Looks like I owe you 'one hell of a memorable goodbye' when we're done here," Riley said to Jasper, smirking.

He grinned. "Let's hope tryouts don't last long then."

Glancing at Mara, Riley found her best friend with half-lidded eyes and not impressed in the slightest by the fight. Riley leaned over, asking, "Am I going to have to dump water on you later to wake you up?"

Mara's eyes slid to Riley, and her smile faltered. There was barely any teal left, they were so dilated from the faerie fruit. Riley's breath caught in her throat, and she prayed to the gods she wouldn't have to find a physician. If something happened to Mara in this crowd, she didn't want to imagine trying to get her out, and if Grimsley didn't make sure Mara stopped breathing, there were plenty of other pirates here who wanted to see her dead.

"Only if all the other fights are this boring," Mara slurred.

Two hours later, Riley pondered where to get a bucket of water and sun-repellent cream without losing her seat—if she remained in the sun much longer, she would burn.

Mara played with the tiny gold beads woven within the teal and silver threads of her bracelet and the golden tiger charm dangling at the center of her left wrist—a birthday gift Riley had made her last year—looking as bored as ever. But her eyes weren't nearly as dilated as before. She was coming down from her high thanks to her elven metabolism breaking down the drug quickly.

The fights dragged on after the first hour. Bets were still being placed, but not as many as there were at the beginning. Pirates who had been waiting outside came and took the seats of those who had left after fighters had accepted their offers.

Riley's back hurt. She had been sitting in one spot too long, and her muscles were tighter than when she'd first made her way through the crowd to get into the arena. She rolled her neck and shoulders, for what could've been the hundredth time, and twisted her back from side to side, cracking it. Jasper noticed and kneaded the knots. She sighed from the slight alleviation.

Her leg bounced as she watched another unconscious faerie dragged away by their ankles. Huffing, Riley asked, "How much longer are we going to watch? I'm going to be as red as a lobster soon." Jasper chuckled softly beside her. She ignored him.

Mara's hand stretched, resting over Riley's legs, trying to get them to stop bouncing—they didn't. She couldn't help it; she was restless.

"We should've just posted fliers for the position at the taverns," Riley grumbled. "Even the jobs board at the docks would've been better than sitting here for the last—"

"Stop," Mara said, placing her other hand on Riley's legs. "I beg of you. Your bouncing is driving me insane." Riley's legs stilled, but once Mara removed her hands, they started up again. She sighed. "Just wait a little longer, Leyley."

Riley threw her hands up in the air, exasperated. "For what?" she demanded.

But Mara was no longer paying attention. She stared at the pit, her eyes alight with new interest.

Standing on one side was an orc. The muscles of his putrid green skin pulled at the leather bands wrapped around his biceps, and a long scar crawled from his right eyebrow straight down into his copper beard.

Riley grimaced. She had seen fights against orcs. The contender always left with their skull crushed, only to be tossed into the sea. Her stomach churned. "I don't want to see this, Mara," she said, standing.

Jasper stood next to her. "Let's go have that memorable goodbye. I can feel the magic of my mother's bargain beginning to tug me home."

"Sit down," Mara commanded, tugging Riley's hand and planting her ass back in her seat. "Both of you." She gave Jasper a look that held a warning of reprimand if he chose to disobey, despite the magic of the bargain. Gesturing with her chin, she pointed out the challenger. "This is the fight we've been waiting for."

Finding the contender, Riley eyes widened.

It was him—the elve who had caught her before she could be trampled—and he was about to be fish food.

"This bastard isn't getting out of here alive," Jasper murmured. "It's a godsdamn shame the pretty ones always die too soon. Could've had some fun with him, right, hazel?"

The nickname Jasper had given Riley for her eyes—a rare color in the faerie realm—always sent a flutter through her stomach, causing her worries and doubts to subside.

But not this time.

With her stomach in knots, Riley glanced at him out of the corner of her eye, seeing disappointment on the merman's face. She knew what fun he referred to. The last—and only—time Jasper had brought another to bed with them had left her feeling not as she had wished. She had been satisfied, yes, but wistfulness had overwhelmed her senses. As though she would never be enough.

Leaning in, Jasper shouted over the others in the arena, "Fifty silvers the elve faints within five seconds of the bell."

Disgusted, Riley ignored him. Or at least she tried to, but it was difficult when all around her pirates were voicing how short this fight was going to be. They changed their bets from who the victor would be to how gruesome the elve's death would be. The only one who wasn't convinced of the outcome of the fight was Mara.

Her legs joined Riley's and began to bounce. No longer inhibited by faerie fruit, her eyes were bright and focused on the cloaked elve. She leaned forward in anticipation, nearly going over the ledge.

What did Mara know that everyone else didn't?

Clouds gathered in the sky, blocking out the sun, as the elve's cloak fluttered to the ground. He removed the leather straps crossing over his chest.

Unfurling from his back, large, black, feathered wings stretched wide, revealing the long and pointed shape of them. Sharp ivory talons curved at the apexes. They were wings made for speed and acrobatic flight, known to all across Erithena.

A murmur erupted throughout the arena as a grin settled on Mara's face. Riley's eyes went wide, her mouth agape.

He wasn't elven—he was aileron.

The reputation of the ailerons was not far from the orcs. They were known for their brutality during the Terra War—a dispute that had been started by the giants to protect the last land they'd possessed after High King Idris had wanted it for nothing more than greed. Rumor was King Torryn, ruler of Dormirrius, had used magic to create the winged elven himself, carving them with his own hands. But he'd forgotten to give them the most important piece—a heart.

The aileron stretched his arms and legs, clad neck to boots in a form-fitting, armored leather suit, as new bets were being made. No longer were the pirates wondering how long before the aileron shit himself or what limbs would be missing before he took his final breath. Some argued about who would win, while some didn't have a clue whom to bet on.

Behind Riley, a faerie voiced, "I changed my mind. My money is on the aileron."

Hearing this, Jasper said over his shoulder, "But all the stories are of how gruesome they are with weapons, and this one has none. I think the orc is going to rip him apart with his bare hands."

Riley pinched her eyes shut as Jasper made a bet with the faerie, seeing the imagery unfold behind them, and shuddered.

Abruptly, she stood again, unable to watch the aileron die when he had shown her a kindness many faeries weren't capable of. But Mara pulled her back into her seat.

With wild eyes, Riley stared at her captain. "Why do you insist I see this?"

"Because this is who we came to see today," she answered, her grin still plastered on her face.

Riley's brows furrowed. "How did you know he was going to be fighting?"

If anyone had known there was an aileron on Obsidian Island, it would've gotten around. It was big news, and word traveled fast on the island. Unless you lived in Paladon, no one had seen an aileron since the Terra War. They were King Torryn's pets, and he liked keeping them all to himself in his golden city.

Mara's mouth was clamped shut, as if she didn't want to answer the question, but Riley was ready to pry it out of her—until the bell sounded, signaling the start of the fight.

CHAPTER 4

With the bell ringing in his ears, Roth wished he were anywhere else. Across from him, he watched the orc crack his knuckles, his smile displaying the jutting bicuspids from his lower jaw. And unfortunately, due to his keen eyesight, he could see the flesh stuck in the orc's teeth.

"I've never killed an aileron before," the orc said, his words a gnarled mess.

Not many have the skill or luck, Roth thought.

Ailerons were feared for a reason.

Roth tilted his head. "Funny," he said, an amused half-smile playing at his lips, "I've never heard an orc form a sentence with more than two words before."

The orc snarled, charging at the aileron.

Good.

It was what Roth had hoped would happen. He wanted to get this over with—he had a deal to uphold.

Roth took deep breaths, willing the crowd to fade and the warrior to come to the surface. It didn't take long. That part of him was always ready for a fight—and he hadn't gotten one in months.

His smile turned deadly as his legs guided him forward, into a sprint.

The orc lunged, and at the last second, Roth slid past him. He hooked his wing out, dragging the sharp talon at the apex along the side of the orc's rib cage. But unlike most opponents, the orc didn't cry out; he gritted his teeth as the crowd's cheers roared throughout the arena.

Roth and the orc went back and forth, the former jabbing with his fists and talons, and after several minutes, the orc breathed heavily, his body covered with puncture marks and slices.

After jabbing the orc in the shoulder blade, Roth tucked his wing back in tight as he kicked out with his leg, knocking into the back of the orc's knee. It gave out, but he caught himself before he could go down. With unexpected speed, the orc whirled around with his fist outstretched. There was a resounding *smack* as he made contact with the side of Roth's head.

Roth fell to the ground, dazed. He felt a trickle of blood slip down his temple just as the orc grabbed him by his right wing and yanked.

Roth's eyes flared from the pain, and he inhaled sharply as he went careening through the air. He flapped his wings, slowing himself, before he collided with the wall of the pit's ledge with a loud *thud*. His head bowed, he slumped against the wall, unmoving.

He tilted his head back, his eyes closed. *That hurt like fucking hells.*

It didn't help that Roth was out of practice. It had been a while since he had been home to train with his brothers and sisters—but that shouldn't make a difference. He had fought against deadlier foes during the Terra War. One minor tug from a giant could take your arm from its socket.

Around the arena, the pirates hummed with anticipation. They wanted to see violence, and they were getting it.

The blood from Roth's temple slid down the side of his face to his neck, disappearing under the collar of his leathers. His head pounded, and with his eyes closed he could feel the world spinning.

As a part of the warrior slipped back into the shadows, Roth had the faintest notion the orc was approaching him, getting the crowd to cheer louder. Was this the end for him? After everything he'd gone through in the last two centuries, this was going to be his end?

Get up, a feminine voice said, soft. Distant.

Roth's brow furrowed.

Rise, the woman added. The word was crisp and loud, as if it were in his head.

The crowd's shouts were deafening, but it didn't prevent Roth from hearing the woman's voice again. "Get your ass up!" she shouted.

He blinked his eyelids open, focusing on the human above him. He realized then she hadn't been inside his head, but shouting at him from over the ledge.

He recognized her. Although their meeting had been brief, what he had seen in her eyes outside the arena would forever be engraved within him. And it wasn't the fear of what should've happened, but the shock that someone had had the heart to save her. It was seeing that surprise that made him hesitate to damn his plan to the hells.

She looked away from Roth to the orc stopped in the center of the pit, still egging the crowd on. Worry etched across her hazel eyes as they found Roth again. "This isn't over yet!" she shouted at him.

Overhead, a low rumble was heard as water droplets began to fall from the sky.

Ignoring it, Roth gritted his teeth as he pulled himself to his feet, letting the human's words stir new strength within him. His wing hung limply, dusting the pit's floor, and pain shot through him when he tried to move it. Muscles were torn; it was something he could heal on his own with his faerie magic, if not for the rules of tryouts. But, thank fucking hells, his bones were intact—it was the only part of him faerie magic couldn't heal—only those blessed by Medyssa, the goddess of healing, were capable of mending bone and others too wounded or without magic to fend for themselves.

He took quick, sharp breaths, balling his hands into fists before he forced himself to lift his wing from the ground, never letting the pain past his tight-sealed lips.

Through the reverberating shouts in the arena, Roth heard a heavy sigh of relief from the human as she mumbled, "Thank the gods."

Roth glanced over his shoulder, making eye contact with her. He nodded his thanks, and she responded with her own nod. *This makes us even.*

He turned back to his opponent, still taunting the crowd. "Hey, asshole," he said, gaining the orc's attention. He held his arms out wide. "I'm waiting."

The orc turned his full attention on Roth, chuckling. "You want to know something?"

"I'm guessing if I say no, you'll tell me anyway," Roth muttered under his breath.

"I was disappointed when you went down as easily as you did," the orc said, "but this is better. I was hoping you'd feel the moment I rip your fucking wings from your body, when I tear you apart limb by limb. I'm going to enjoy knocking your godsdamn teeth out and making you eat your own tongue. And then—"

"There's more?"

"—I'm going to squish your skull like a grape."

Roth rolled his eyes. "Are you done?" he drawled, wiping mud from his leathers. "I don't want my muscles to tighten up after that warmup."

The orc smiled. "I'm just getting started."

He advanced on Roth as another rumble of thunder sounded. Light rippled through the gray clouds, and the sprinkling rain came down heavier.

With his injured wing, Roth needed to be smart about this. He couldn't heal, otherwise he would be disqualified, and if the orc got ahold of his wing again, there was the possibility he would be left with only one.

Once the orc was upon him, Roth sidestepped him, using the momentum to push him into the wall. While the orc was dazed, Roth grabbed him by the ankles and pulled him through the mud. The orc tried digging in his fingers, but it was no use; he couldn't stop the aileron from dragging him to the center of the pit.

Twisting, the orc threw a fistful of mud at Roth's face, and Roth shielded himself with his uninjured wing.

He lowered it as the orc's fist flew at him. He ducked beneath the outstretched arm, driving his fist into the side of the orc's knee just as a ripple of light flickered above.

The flash illuminated the sky as the orc's bellowing cries were drowned out by another rumble, followed by a crack of lightning and shuddering thunder.

The orc fell to the ground, clutching his knee, seething as he watched Roth circle him. He kicked out at the aileron's groin with his uninjured leg, but it never made contact. Roth caught it easily, as if the orc had merely been stretching the limb.

Holding on, Roth said, "I realize I might not be strong enough to tear your limbs apart, but I promise you this—I know how to break them." The orc's eyes widened, and Roth jerked the leg to an awkward angle.

The orc's screams weren't muffled by the thunder this time, but the roar of the crowd. They drank up the entertainment, as if a thirst for violence were being quenched.

One by one, Roth broke the orc's limbs and left him in the mud as the rain washed the blood from his body.

The flash storm dispersed, the rain subsiding back into a sprinkle.

Roth wrapped an arm around the front of the orc's neck while his other hand rested on the back of his head, placing him in a chokehold, and lifted him into a sitting position. The orc thrashed against Roth, but with his broken arms, he wasn't able to lay a finger on the aileron. Roth's grip remained tight around the orc's neck until his thrashing eased, but his chest still rose and fell shallowly.

Roth loosened his arms around the orc, hesitating.

Lifting his head, he found her in the crowd. The Captain of the Roaring Tigers leaned back on her hands with her legs stretched out, crossed at the ankles. Her brows were arched as she patiently waited for the deed to be done.

His shoulders slumped.

"I'm sorry you got caught in the middle of this," Roth whispered to the unconscious orc. "Even though you were kind of an asshole."

With the wrenching of his hands, Roth snapped the orc's neck.

The cheers of the crowd ricocheted through the arena as Roth took a step back from the deceased orc. His hands clenched and unclenched at his sides as he stared at the creature before lifting his head back to Mara, arching a brow in question. A satisfied grin stretched across her face.

Overhead, the clouds parted just enough for the sun's rays to shine through, onto the center of the pit. Roth squinted from the sudden brightness as the walls of the arena began to shake from the stomping of feet.

The crowd began to chant one name over and over again, their fists pumping in the air in time with the words.

"Crimson Knight! Crimson Knight! Crimson Knight!"

Roth didn't have to look to know the sun illuminated the true color of his wings. Unlike other ailerons, his weren't the shade of a raven's, but the dark color of blood—so dark it could only be seen in the brightest light.

He surveyed the crowd—his fans—in a slow circle, stopping once he found Mara again. She had joined in, chanting his earned name from the war.

As his eyes left the captain's, he found the human nearby. A blue-haired merman pulled her along, away from the arena, and judging by the rush he was in and the wild look in his eyes, Roth knew what they were hurrying to go do. It was all they had done since he'd arrived on the pirate island three days ago. His jaw popped from grinding his teeth too hard.

Where had he been when she'd needed saving?

The chanting grated against Roth's bones as he turned back to the dead orc. Dipping his chin, he closed his eyes. His injured wing drooped in the mud.

I am not who they say I am.

Clenching his hands into fists, Roth took deep breaths, willing his faerie magic to heal the cut on his temple and the torn muscle in his wing, and snatched up his cloak and leather straps. He stretched his wings, and with no sign of pain, he shot into the air as fast as a raging storm.

CHAPTER 5

D rowning out the smell of fish, the sweet scent of pears blended with the earthy one from the recently fallen rain. The clouds dispersed, leaving no trace they were ever there. The only visible signs it had rained were the puddles and Roth's damp cloak.

He hadn't wanted to put it back on, let alone the leather straps to flatten his wings to his back, but it was the only way he could get around the pirate island unnoticed—especially after his performance in the fighting pit.

Although the afternoon heat was in full effect, Roth felt chilled down to the bone.

Crimson Knight! Crimson Knight! Crimson Knight!

He hadn't heard that name in two hundred years, outside of Dormirrius, and would have willingly given up his wings never to again.

Roth had thought about it—giving up his wings.

Ailerons cherished their wings almost as much as their children. It was seen as dishonorable to lose them. He couldn't imagine what his people would think if he had taken his own, but they were partially to blame for the tales that had arisen in the wake of the Terra War. All of the theories regarding their color were wrong, of course—especially the one claiming he'd bathed in his enemies' blood. He might be known for his brutality during the war, but he would never do something so appalling.

While he strapped his swords back at his sides, Roth shifted on his feet as he glanced at the alley beside the Land Drake Inn from the shadows of a fisherman's stall, checking to see if the human and the merman were done yet. They weren't.

Roth immediately looked away, turning his attention to the small inn. The docks were the perfect location for the popular Land Drake Inn. It was the first sign of drinks and a cooked meal after pirates docked their ships inside the mouth of the dragon's skull. The inn was carved from one of the dragon's teeth by dwarves, and grass grew on the high slanted roof, where a mountain goat munched on the green blades.

Roth observed the Captain of the Roaring Tigers leaning against the outside as she sliced off a piece of her faerie pear. If she was supposed to be keeping watch for the two in the alley, she was doing a lousy job of it.

From where he stood a few shops down the street, Roth could smell the fruit and the promises of false euphoria. Even if he had missed the scent of it on her breath during their first meeting, it would've been hard not to notice the glaze in her teal eyes.

Roth looked toward the alley again, and when he saw they still hadn't finished, his patience wore out. As he walked toward Mara, who was enjoying her pear a little too much, he reminded himself he'd given the couple plenty of time to finish fucking, but as he neared, the soft grunts growing louder and louder, he regretted his decision.

Clenching his hands at his sides, he urged his blood to cool to a low simmer and the shade of pink on his cheeks and ears to go away. Faeries weren't shy, himself included, but . . . fucking hells, it had been too long.

He stopped in front of Mara, and her eyes slowly slid to him. She stared at him, unblinking. She had no fucking clue who he was, as if they hadn't struck a deal that morning.

Roth cleared his throat. "I held up my end of the bargain," he said. "Now, it's your turn to hold up yours." Slowly, her eyebrow rose in question. He sighed, exasperated. "I killed the orc like you wanted, and in turn, you said you'd give me a position on your crew."

"She did *what*?"

The human emerged from around the corner, buttoning the top of her mud-splattered pants. There was a slight flush to her cheeks and her lips were swollen. Behind her, the merman looked as pleased as could be with himself, not a hint of embarrassment in his smug, satisfied half-smile. Whereas the human looked as if she wanted to crawl back into the alley and away from Roth's knowing gaze as she wrapped her arms around her middle.

The merman looked Roth up and down with a scrutinizing eye, sizing the aileron up. Roth would have done the same—if he had the need. The merman's half-smile grew, as if he knew something the aileron didn't. "Nice fight," was all he said.

Roth stared at the merman, trying not to let the shame he felt from the statement show.

Looking at Mara, the merman's smile fell, and he sighed heavily. "Try not to get into too much trouble while I'm gone, half-pint," he said to her, but the captain didn't hear.

Now that she was no longer staring at Roth, her attention wandered to a faerie with brown skin and monarch butterfly wings. More specifically, to her large breasts.

Roth turned his gaze away from the faerie before recognition could show on his face.

The merman sighed again, longingly this time. Roth noted his eyes were, too, on the faerie's breasts, and he wasn't the only one. The human watched the merman, as much longing in her eyes as there was in the merman's sigh.

When she felt Roth's attention on her, she glared at him. Doing what no other was bold enough to do. And for the first time in nearly a century, he felt the prickling of a true smile on his face.

Tearing his eyes away from the faerie, the merman turned back to the human—the woman, Roth thought, he should've been staring at all along. "I will see you when I get back, hazel," he said, placing his hands on her hips. His eyes met Roth's for the briefest moment before he kissed her thoroughly and unabashedly.

Roth held the curling of his upper lip back. It wasn't the display of passion that set him on edge, but the way this merman treated the woman he was courting with such utter disrespect. He was a breath away from snarling just that, but he pulled away before Roth could, leaving the woman red-faced and breathless. A muscle ticked in Roth's jaw.

They watched the merman make his way to the shoreline. He stripped himself of his boots and pants, leaving the dagger strapped at his chest, and dove into the rolling waves.

Roth's eyes slid to the human; she still stared at the spot where the merman had disappeared under the sea, her shoulders sagging slightly at the sight of a gold-speckled, blue tail splashing in the water. Roth had the sudden urge to place a hand on one of those shoulders and tell her she would see her merman again. But he couldn't, not when he—

Abruptly, the human whirled on Mara. "You said you would hire him if he killed that orc for you?" she demanded, pointing at Roth. All thoughts of comforting her leapt from his mind as he stared at that accusatory finger. "Well?" she asked impatiently.

Mara was doing a fine job of ignoring her. She was too invested in her fruit, and that made the human all the more frustrated with her. She tore the pear from Mara's hand, throwing it into the dirt.

Slowly, Mara turned her head from Roth to her faerie fruit in the mud, and lastly to the seething human. Her eyes might have been glazed over, but it did nothing to hide the rising anger. "What. The. Fuck. Leyley?" Mara said through gritted teeth. "Why do you always have to be such a fucking thundercunt?"

Roth's brows rose.

The human's hands balled into fists. "That's just the drug talking," she said under her breath, as if reminding herself. "You don't actually think that about me."

"Do you really want to know what I think about you?" Mara pointed the knife in her hand at the human, taking a step toward her.

Eyes on the blade, the human took a step back, keeping her distance, but Mara took another step forward.

"I think," Mara said, "I should have never saved your ass. I think I should have let you bleed to death—"

Stopping her from advancing toward the human, Roth wrapped his hand around the one holding the knife. "I would stop now, if you don't want to regret something later," he said, his voice low. "You wouldn't want to poke someone's eye out with that thing, and making the assumption that pear wasn't the first faerie fruit you've had today, that eye might very well be your own."

Mara stared at Roth, but he wasn't going to let go of her hand until the knife dropped—and if it didn't, he was prepared to use force.

Blinking slowly, Mara dropped it into the mud, and the human snatched it up before Mara could. She cleaned it off with her shirt and tucked it through her belt. Mara gave her a look.

"Don't worry," the human said. "I'll give it back when you're not threatening to stab me with it."

Roth didn't know Mara—he had only just met her that morning—but judging by how quickly things had escalated, he didn't think she had any intention of sobering up anytime soon.

Mara curled her upper lip back. "Fine," she snarled. She stormed to the door of the Land Drake.

"What do you think you're doing?" the human asked. "You aren't going to sober up in there."

Standing in the doorway, Mara turned to her. "I have to hire a new cook," she said, sweetly, "or did you forget we needed one?"

Before the human had time to snap back, Mara turned her gaze on Roth. "You're hired," she said, her words clipped.

She shifted her eyes back to the human before entering the inn. "If you want answers so fucking badly, interrogate him while he gets officially inducted into the crew."

With raised brows, Roth looked at the human. Her nostrils flared as she stared at the empty doorway of the Land Drake. "What exactly does getting 'officially inducted' entail?" he asked.

The human whirled on him and poked him in the chest. "Why did you get involved?" she snapped. "I was perfectly capable of handling that on my own." It didn't matter she had called them even during the fight with the orc; her gratitude from before was gone.

Roth's eyes slid down to the finger poking his chest. No one ever dared lay a finger on an aileron, especially him. The only ones who ever tried were folk like the orc, but he had never met a human who didn't fear the consequences of the action.

Arching a brow, Roth tilted his head, noting the welling tears in her eyes. "You sure about that?"

Her mouth curved downward and her eyes darted away, blinking away the tears before they could fall. Taking a deep breath, she fixed her gaze back on him. "I don't know who you think you are, *Crimson Knight*," she said, tapping the tip of her finger against his chest, "but whatever—"

"Roth," he said through his teeth, cutting her off. He caught her finger before it could poke him again. "My name is Roth, not Crimson Knight. Don't ever call me that again."

She stared at him, and he could tell from the gleam in her eyes she wanted to call him by that foul name again just to spite him.

Before she could do so, he said, his tone clipped, "Mara mentioned something about an induction."

He had no idea what he had to do for this "induction," but at this point, he didn't care if he had to sing naked while he balanced a bowl of fruit on his head for an audience of mountain goats. He just wanted to get everything he had to do over with and go home.

Her eyes narrowed at his tone. She mumbled, "Ass," under her breath before she began walking inland, telling him, "Follow me."

CHAPTER 6

The human led him over a bridge connected to the spine of the dragon, past vendors and taverns, and over another bridge, leading to one of the ribs of the skeleton. The taverns and shops disappeared along with the bustling of pirates as she led him down a small, sandy path inside a dense tropical forest.

They didn't make it far before the human made a left turn, into the thick foliage between two tightly spaced trees. For once, Roth was glad his wings were constricted against his back as he squeezed through. They ducked under wayward vines and stepped over fallen trees, all while dodging large palm fronds and thick branches. Or rather, Roth was doing all the dodging.

Every time the human batted at what stood in her way, it caused it to snap back at Roth. But she didn't seem to care. She was too preoccupied grumbling to herself.

"'I have to hire a new cook.'" The human imitated Mara's saccharine tone, dripping with all the disdain Mara's eyes had held. Slapping a fern leaf away from her face, she snorted. "I'm a fucking thundercunt? You're the one—"

A yelp escaped the human as her foot caught on an exposed root. Before she knocked her head into the boulder in front of her, she caught ahold of the tree next to her. Her shoulders rose and fell with her rapid breaths as she held on, her knuckles white.

Without a word, she pushed off the tree and continued on her way, leading Roth through the jungle. Her grumblings ceased, but Roth didn't doubt Mara's words proceeded to cut through her mind.

Once they reached the top of the steep hill, they slid down the other side, careful not to go tumbling. At the bottom, the human stopped, turned, then turned again, until she came full circle. She chewed her lip.

Roth swatted at a mosquito buzzing in his ear. "You're lost, aren't you?"

The human ignored him, closing her eyes. She took a deep breath.

Roth leaned against a tree, crossing his arms, as he watched her stand as still as a statue. He tilted his head away from whatever plant was tickling his ear—at least, he hoped it was a plant. If it was a snake, he was flying out of the forest immediately. He didn't care if he had to climb a tree first in order to have enough room for his wings.

"What are you doing?" Roth asked when the human hadn't moved. But again, she ignored him.

He sighed. "At least tell me where we're going."

Her hands clenched into fists at her sides as her eyes opened, and she glared at him. "We're going to see Ambrose so you can get your tattoos."

"You're taking me to get tattoos?" he asked incredulously.

"Yes, but if you keep talking, I won't be able to hear the water running from the river we need to cross."

"You mean the river over there?" Roth pointed behind her. She glanced over her shoulder before looking back at him in question. He tapped his ear. "I can hear it. It's straight ahead."

Glaring at him again, the human began in the direction Roth had pointed them in.

"So, about these tattoos," Roth said, catching a branch she moved aside before it slapped him in the chest, "they're necessary to be a part of the crew?"

The human nodded.

"And what do they look like?"

What Roth really wanted to know was how much he was going to regret not sticking with his original plan when he had docked on Obsidian Island.

Stopping, the human turned to Roth. She pulled up the sleeve covering her left arm. He noticed the roaring tiger and compass inked there for all of one second before his gaze narrowed on the long, thick scar beneath, leaving a bitter taste in his mouth.

He had often seen similar scars on those he'd fought with during the war, but more often than not, they had been self-inflicted. And some hadn't survived, their choice leaving behind loved ones to pick up the pieces of their shattered hearts on their own—that was, if they had any loved ones left after the war.

Roth wondered what had happened to her to make her choose death over life. But he could only imagine, her being human in a world like this, that held no shred of mercy. He would know; it was how he'd earned his *nickname* after all. And it was how he'd lost—

Breath snagged in his airways, as if a boulder crushed his chest.

"All new members of the Roaring Tigers get these tattoos," the human continued, pointing to hers. "The tiger is our insignia."

Roth shook off his disgust, trying to focus on the ink covering the scar. "Do I have to get it there on my arm?" he asked.

"No, you can get it anywhere you'd like. You could get it on your forehead or your ass for all I care. But the compass is supposed to go on your wrist."

"No, it won't."

"Yes, it will," she argued. "That's where it's supposed to go. You can get it on your other wrist, if that's more natural."

Roth crossed his arms. "No."

She closed her eyes, pinching the bridge of her nose. When they opened again, the golden flecks sparked with frustration. "Excuse me?"

"Be happy I'm getting the tiger," Roth grumbled. "I don't want a tattoo at all."

"If stubborn is what you want to be," she said, throwing her hands up, "then don't get the compass."

She began to climb over a series of low-hanging branches with white flowers as she mumbled, "Stubborn bird," under her breath.

Wanting to get this over with, Roth ignored the jab, and with a sigh, he uncrossed his arms and followed her to the river.

There was no bridge or fallen tree to cross the rushing water, only a serpentine path created by slippery rocks.

Before the human had taken the first leap, Roth had thought for sure he would have to pull her from the water halfway, but it was as though he were watching a dance with the way she glided from one slick stone to the next, the tips of her toes barely landing on a rock before she was onto the next.

On the other side of the river, the human's lips curled into a half-smile. "You coming, or are you just going to stand there gawking at me?"

Roth rolled his eyes. He chose not to point out that she had done exactly that to him earlier. Instead, he was off, leaping from stone to stone. His feet didn't glide as hers had, and he realized the stones were more slippery than he had originally thought. But he made it across without causing a splash.

After walking through more brush, they came upon a shanty house in the middle of the jungle.

The human knocked on the door. "Ambrose?" she called out, stepping inside. "You in here?"

Ducking his head, Roth followed her through the doorway. The inside was even smaller, more of a studio than a home. It was cramped, packed to the brim with everything Ambrose needed. A wide table rested in the center, and lanterns illuminated the space. A desk lined the left wall, drawers most likely filled with inks and needles, and the opposite wall had shelves upon shelves with sketchbooks.

In the back corner, taking up the rest of the space, was a bed with a burly human who snored loudly. He was bald with a full, auburn beard, and tattoos covered his olive skin head to toe. Through the gaping hole in his earlobe, Roth saw a small symbol behind his ear; whatever language it was, he had never seen it before.

The human approached the sleeping, snoring man and rested a hand on his shoulder. "Ambrose?" She shook him lightly. "Ambrose, wake up."

Ambrose jerked awake, his large arm knocking into her. She fell on her rear, nearly smacking her head into the table.

Clambering to her feet, she said, "Nice to see you, too."

One of her hands rubbed her backside absently before she glanced over her shoulder at Roth, remembering he was there. He caught the flush in her cheeks before she glanced away from him, and he felt the sudden, foreign sensation of the corners of his mouth twitching in amusement.

Running a hand over his tattooed scalp, Ambrose blinked away sleep. "Riley?" He said her name as if he were still dreaming. Realizing she was truly there, he said, wincing, "Sorry for knocking you on your ass."

The human waved a hand through the air, the incident already forgotten.

"You here for another tattoo?" he asked. "Maybe the one you were talking about the last time you were here?"

"We're not here for me," she said. She hooked a thumb over her shoulder, pointing at Roth. "Roth's getting one. He's our new recruit."

As if just noticing him for the first time, Ambrose looked past the human and stood. He approached Roth, tilting his head back, and gave him a once-over. "He doesn't look like a chef," he mused. To Roth, he asked, "Can you cook?"

"Cooking isn't my specialty," Roth said. He didn't have to say *killing* was.

He could feel the shift in the air as Ambrose went to the desk, opening drawers and pulling out jars of ink. "Have a seat on the table," Ambrose said.

Roth fought against a grimace as he imagined getting a tiger, its maw opened wide to reveal its sharp canines, inked on his flesh. But the sooner all of this was over, the easier he would be able to breathe.

Stiffly, he walked to the table and sat down.

"He's going to get the tiger like usual," the human said to Ambrose. She swept her gaze to Roth, adding dryly, "but not the compass."

Roth rolled his eyes.

He pulled a small book from beneath his cloak, handing it to her. He was going to give it back to her earlier, but she'd been in a foul mood

—and it appeared it wasn't going away, despite the short reprieve at the water. He hoped offering it to her would at least get her off his back about the damn compass.

The tight smile she had been giving him curved downward. She stared at the book, unmoving. Emotions swept across her eyes before she reluctantly took it from him.

"Thanks," she mumbled, but she didn't seem as grateful as he'd thought she might be.

After she opened the cover and turned the first couple of pages, her frown deepened.

He had the sudden urge to ask her what was wrong. Sadness had settled in her eyes—the words *I am not worth the effort* plainly written in them—and the urge intensified with the need to simply wrap her up in his arms and wings to comfort her. It prodded at him, where he thought it could never reach.

"Where are you getting the tiger?" Ambrose asked, bringing Roth out of his thoughts.

Roth pointed behind his right ear, never taking his eyes off Ril—*the human*, he chastised himself. He needed to remember why he was there —why he couldn't allow himself to get too close.

"Lie back and turn your head to the side," Ambrose ordered.

Roth did as he was told, exposing his ear to the tattooist. He waited for pain to strike against his skull, but it never came. Instead, the light, cool touch of a paintbrush stroked against his skin. His brow creased.

The human looked up from her book, seeing the confusion on Roth's face. "He doesn't use needles," she explained. "The ink is enchanted to seep through the skin. It allows him to do more intricate art."

Roth grunted in answer.

She tilted her head to the side, her eyes narrowing. Roth mirrored her but kept his head still for Ambrose.

"What?" he asked. "Am I doing something wrong?"

"I don't know," she said. "Are you?"

Roth frowned, confused.

"Why did you strike a bargain with Mara?"

"I can already see where this is going," he said, rolling his eyes. Irritation settled in his gut, making itself comfortable for the foreseeable future. "This is the 'interrogation' Mara mentioned earlier."

"Well?" the human prompted.

He sighed. "Tell you what, I'll answer one question and one question only," he said. "So, decide if that's what you really want to ask me."

Her mouth opened, closed, then did it again. Her eyes simmered with the question: *Is he serious?* But she didn't want to waste asking that if he was.

"I'm quite serious," he told her. "One question—that's all you get. I don't like interrogations."

She glared at him like she had in the jungle, waiting for him to flinch, but he wouldn't. Seeing that, she huffed, crossing her arms over her chest.

Questions flashed across her eyes as she tried to determine which one she would deem "the right one." Minutes ticked by, and Roth thought she wasn't going to ask any, until she blinked and only one remained.

"Was the bargain you made with Mara worth a position on this crew?"

He blinked, not expecting that, and the truth was he honestly didn't know. He'd needed a position on this crew and had been willing to do anything for it—or at least, he'd thought so. But in the end, had killing the orc been worth it?

"I guess we'll find out," Roth answered.

CHAPTER 7

The ship rocked gently with the motion of the water beneath the early morning sky, lulling Riley into a tranquil state.

Blinking sleep away, she tried to keep herself awake. She leaned her arms against the wooden rail of the ship as she kept an eye on the small dot in the sky over the water. The aileron stretched his wings in the distance.

Has he been flying all night? Riley wondered. When she had gone to bed late the night before, he had been flying under the cover of stars.

"Can I join you?"

Riley glanced over her shoulder, sliding wayward hair behind an ear.

Hands tucked into her long coat's pockets—and for once without faerie fruit—Mara stood behind her. She looked like a child playing dress-up in her parent's clothes. With her petite size, the too-big maroon coat brushed along the ship's deck. Her sleeves were rolled up to her wrists, hiding the silver embroidery on the cuffs identical to the stitching around the buttons going up the length of it and around the collar.

Riley nodded.

She knew why Mara was there. They had gone through this for what felt like the hundredth time in the last few months. Mara would say something while she was high on faerie fruit, hurt Riley's feelings, and then, hours later, would apologize. And just like every time before this, Riley would forgive her, giving her another chance.

Each time this happened, the stone constricted around Riley's glass heart, feeling heavier and heavier, to the point she began to wonder how she was still afloat and not at the bottom of the sea.

Crossing her ankles, Mara leaned her back against the railing and propped her elbows on the wood. She was silent, as she always was before she apologized. She liked to gather her thoughts, formulate the right words before she said anything.

Looking at the deck beneath her boots, Mara inhaled deeply. "I want you to know I never intended to threaten you with a knife. I never know what I'll do while I'm . . . in that state of mind. But I never want to hurt you," Mara added quickly. "I need you to know that."

She sighed through her nose, her eyelids fluttering shut. "And yet," she said, her voice small, soft, "I always seem to show you the worst side of myself." She brushed away a tear sliding down her cheek.

That was new—the tears. She had never cried during one of her many apologies, but she had never pulled a knife on Riley before, either.

Placing a comforting hand on Mara's shoulder, Riley said gently, "It's okay, Mara."

But Mara shook her head, her lips pursed. "It's not, Leyley. You shouldn't forgive me this time."

Riley's brows lifted a fraction of an inch. That was new, too.

"The knife was not okay," Mara went on, her voice shaky, "but it still wasn't the worst of what happened." At last, she faced Riley head on. "Everything I said about you wasn't true. I'm so, so sorry I didn't stumble upon you sooner three years ago, and I will be forever grateful I found you when I did."

A sob rocked through Mara, and Riley couldn't take it any longer. She wrapped her arms around Mara, holding her close. It wasn't long before her friend's arms wrapped around her waist. Riley stroked a hand down the back of Mara's head as she wept freely on her shoulder, her tears soaking through the light fabric. Mara's whole body shook against her.

"I need your help, Leyley," Mara said between sobs. She pulled her head back enough to look at Riley. "I want to stop eating the fruit, but I can't do it on my own."

Fresh tears streamed down Mara's face as she buried her head against Riley again.

They stayed that way for some time. Mara's sobs eventually subsided as the minutes passed, turning into the occasional hiccup.

Riley didn't know when it had happened, but she found her gaze back on the aileron flying over the water.

Roth must have been getting tired because he circled back toward the ship. With her human eyes, Riley barely made out the tucking of his wings before he dove toward the sea. She sucked in a breath as he kept diving, never letting up. But before he hit the water, his wings shot out. Riley released a deep exhale as he glided over the waves.

"How did it go with him yesterday?" Mara asked.

Riley blinked, realizing her friend was no longer tucked tightly in her arms. She leaned against the railing, facing the water as Riley did, her attention, too, on the aileron. Her eyes were bloodshot from the many tears shed.

Was I really that distracted by Roth? Riley wondered briefly to herself.

When Riley remained silent, looking as if she were in a daze, Mara asked, "Did you make a friend?" Amusement danced along her lips.

Riley rolled her eyes. "Oh, yes," she said flatly. "We're the best of friends."

Mara chuckled. "Okay, what's wrong with him?"

"He's stubborn."

Mara snorted. "Being stubborn doesn't mean he can't join the crew. If that were the case, you wouldn't be here."

Riley shot her a look, and Mara grinned.

"What about the tattoos?" Mara asked. "Does he like them?"

"The damn bird refused to get the compass," Riley said, crossing her arms over her chest.

"Did you tell him what it does?"

Riley shook her head. She did not tell him the enchanted ink allowed those with the compass to find anyone with the Roaring Tigers' insignia tattooed with the same enchanted ink. "If he didn't want it," she answered, "it was his loss." He'd been so godsdamned stubborn about it. She added, "I don't trust him anyway."

No one sought out Mara for a position on the crew unless they had nowhere else to go, and even then, most tried to avoid the Roaring Tigers at all costs.

Sighing, Riley tucked her loose curls tickling her cheek behind her ear. She would find out what the aileron wanted with Mara, one way or another.

She heard a soft snort behind her and glanced over her shoulder at Nathair, the helmsman. "Have anything to add?" she asked the serpent faerie.

His forked tongue flicked out, tasting the air. "You don't trust anyone after you first meet them," he hissed.

Riley considered this, her head tilting side to side. "True, but I really just don't *like* anyone at first."

Nathair's venomous fangs glinted in the sun as he chuckled softly, the sound coming out as a series of hisses.

"I would also like to add," Mara interjected, "that we're pirates, Leyley. All of us are up to no good—it's part of the code we live by." She closed her eyes, soaking up the sun like a cat. "It would do you some good to uphold and honor that."

"Like you?" Riley questioned, arching a brow.

"Well . . ." Mara considered the question as Riley's thoughts went straight to Mara's debts and enemies. Slowly, Mara's eyes opened. "Maybe not like me," she said after a moment.

Riley watched Roth glide past the ship, beating his wings against the air. He lifted high into the sky, the sun's rays showing off the true color of his wings. She'd wanted to ask him why they were red the day before, but she hadn't wanted to waste her one question—and she was a little scared of the answer. The stories about them were all gruesome, but however they came to be that shade of red, she thought they were beautiful.

"Oh, I see it now," Mara said, drawing Riley's attention. She gestured to the aileron in the sky. "You're attracted to him."

Nathair glanced over his shoulder at the change in topic.

Riley's jaw dropped. "What? No, I'm not!" But even as the words left her mouth, she knew they were not true.

Mara arched a brow, the corner of her mouth lifting as she heard the lie settle between them. "Even I can see he's attractive," she said, placing a hand on Riley's shoulder, "but I'm not gawking at him every chance I get."

Riley's face fell slack. "Is it that obvious?" she asked, feeling her cheeks go hot.

"Yes," Nathair said, chuckling softly at the helm.

Riley shot him a glare promising pain. He turned back around, but she didn't miss the shaking of his shoulders.

Mara's hand went from Riley's shoulder to poking her in the cheek. "You think he's a pretty bird," she cooed.

Riley swatted Mara's hand away as Nathair broke into uncontrollable laughter, and Riley swore to the gods that if he drew the attention of the others to the wretched conversation, she would shove his fangs down his throat. *Maybe*, she considered, *the venom would paralyze him, too.*

Thankfully, for Nathair's sake, the rest of the crew went about their duties.

Mara laughed, as if she knew what Riley had begun plotting.

"He's not pretty," Riley said—another lie.

Amused tears were in Mara's eyes as she questioned, "Devilishly handsome? Drop-dead gorgeous?" Riley groaned. "Wait," Mara said, a shit-eating grin on her face. "I've got it. Realm-shattering, sky-splintering, wish-upon-a-shooting-star—"

"Stop."

"—beautiful."

"I will tie you up and gag you."

"Sounds like a wonderfully kinky time," Mara said, a mischievous shine in her teal eyes, far from the sadness that had been there not long ago. "You should know my safeword is pineapple."

Riley gave her a glare that would make any faerie think twice before they tried to have some fun without her consent.

Mara laughed. "Okay, okay," she said, holding up her hands in surrender.

Silence stretched between them for all of two seconds before Mara said, "So, speaking of Wyne—"

"We weren't," Riley muttered.

"—I was thinking we could"—she glanced at Nathair—"get lost in the mazes while we're there for your birthday."

Nathair looked over his shoulder, a crease on his forehead. He might not be able to read between the lines, but Riley knew what Mara meant. There wasn't much Mara kept from her crew, but for one thing—and she trusted only Riley and Jasper with the information.

Mara was obsessed with the dead, famous pirate, Lothaire, and his treasure. He was notorious for the amount of money and valuables he had acquired over centuries, and rumor claimed it was worth more than the kingdoms combined.

But the one thing that was said to be the most valuable was a magical scroll—the Scroll of Desires. It's said the scroll grants any wish your heart desires, and if it truly existed, it could turn kingdoms to ash and ruin.

For Mara, the scroll could give her a new start—no more debts, no more enemies. Just a happy, shiny, new life surrounded by all the riches in the world.

But like all famous treasures, Lothaire's had been lost. There were rumors he'd left clues behind to the location before he'd vanished— believed to have transcended his soul to the Elysian Fields, leaving his body behind to become one with the land—but none had been found.

Until a month ago.

While under the influence of faerie fruit, Mara had followed a glowing, floating blue light—a wisp—into the mountains on the skull of Obsidian Island, finding drawings and a riddle carved within a small cave.

Once lost, now buried.
They walk among the stars and bathe in their glory.
Join them, ye of fortune, and seek your destiny.

Since then, Mara had been convinced it was the first clue to Lothaire's treasure and the scroll, due to the drawing of his insignia above the riddle of a dragon breathing fire. It had been Jasper, though, who had recognized the drawing of a sun with lilies as the kingdom of Avernii's emblem, and it hadn't been long before Mara had concluded the riddle pointed to the star maze in Wyne, its capital. But after searching said maze for the past month with no luck, she'd decided to reevaluate the words—and two nights ago, she'd had a breakthrough.

She'd barged through Riley's cabin door on the ship with wild eyes, saying: "*It's the fountain! It's the fucking Fountain of the Lost in the royal garden!*"

Riley would've been excited for Mara—if Mara hadn't walked in while she'd been riding a tied-up, moaning Jasper.

Riley frowned. Looking for Lothaire's treasure wasn't what she'd had in mind for her twenty-first birthday. She wanted to eat fancy food until she couldn't anymore and get drunk on wine. But mainly, she wanted to spend the day with her best friend—no treasure, just Mara.

"I thought we were going to drink and eat until we fell into comas," Riley reminded Mara with a pointed look.

"Oh, don't worry," Mara said, waving a hand through the air. "We're still going to do that. But think about how much fun it would be to try to solve the mazes wasted."

"I don't know if I want to go through the mazes," Riley said, knowing Mara didn't want to mention the fountain in Nathair's presence. She hoped the message of what she was really saying got through to her: *I don't want to look for Lothaire's fucking treasure on my birthday.*

"But it'll be so much fun," Mara begged. "Please, Leyley." She gave Riley her best big puppy eyes, pouting. She mouthed: *Please.*

This treasure had been Mara's goal for years. Her quest. Of course, she would want to see if her new theory was correct, even if it had happened to come to her near Riley's birthday.

Looking up at the sky, Riley sighed. "Fine." She held up a finger, stopping Mara as she opened her mouth. "But only if you get me a mound of apple roses. And I'm not just talking about the ones I want for my birthday." She loved the desserts to the point they had become a necessity; they were as important to her as the air she breathed. Mara was addicted to faerie fruit, and Riley was addicted to those. She could never turn down anything cinnamon, and the mini pies made to look like roses were always glazed with caramel. Just thinking about them made her mouth pool with saliva.

"I'll get you all the apple roses, in all the worlds, for the rest of your life," Mara said, grinning as she bounced up and down on the deck.

"Good," Riley replied, "because I'll agree to those terms and those terms only."

Mara wrapped her arms around Riley's waist, squeezing tightly. "Thank you!"

Riley smiled, patting Mara's back. "You can thank me with the first of many apple roses."

A gust of wind blew their hair back and a shadow blocked the sun as they separated from each other. Roth landed gracefully on the deck in front of them.

Riley admired his windblown hair, and out of the corner of her eye, she caught Mara wiggling her eyebrows at her, grinning. Mara might as well have been cooing *you think he's a pretty bird* at her again. Riley rolled her eyes, but she couldn't stop them from going back to the *pretty bird*. Her skin tingled as their eyes met, but not because he could feel her stare—his eyes were already trained on her. His mouth curved down.

Riley arched a brow in question.

Slowly, as if realizing he was staring, Roth blinked, turning his gaze from Riley to Mara. "There's a fleet of pirates heading straight for us."

Mara went rigid beside Riley.

"What!" Riley whirled around. She scanned the waters behind them but saw nothing except the never-ending sea and a whale rising out of the waves, leaving behind a cloud of mist as it dove back under the surface. "I don't see anything," she said.

"They're a long ways off," Roth explained, "but approaching fast."

Mara looked around Roth at Nathair, holding out her hand. "Spyglass," she ordered. Riley had almost forgotten he was there as he retrieved his spyglass from his belt and held it out to Mara. She took it, lengthening it, and peered through. "Fuck, it's Grimsley," she said, lowering it. "That shithead is coming for his prize, and he's brought the entire Thorny Devil fleet to get it."

Nathair took his spyglass back and peered through it.

Riley could make out the shapes of ships in the distance. She glanced back at Roth; he stood there with his arms crossed, looking at her again.

"Why do you keep staring at me?"

"I'm thinking," he mumbled.

Mara twisted to him. "What are you thinking, Crimson Knight?"

Riley expected him to snarl at her not to call him that, but it never came. The only sign he disapproved was the slight tick in his jaw.

"I think," he grumbled, "I picked the wrong time to join this crew."

Mara's expression turned to stone. "So," she said, voice hard, "do you think we should tuck our tails and run?"

"I never did during the war," he answered, "and I'm not about to start now."

A smile broke through Mara's stony exterior, one of admiration, and she turned it on Riley. "This is why he's on the crew." Roth was a warrior—loyalty was carved into his bones—and although Riley assumed Mara was just using him because he would be handy in a fight, he would fight until the very end for her.

Mara focused on the situation approaching rapidly. "Leyley, tell the gunners to ready the cannons, and make sure everyone is armed." Riley turned to do so, but Mara added, "Oh, and take whatever whiskey we have onboard. Tear some linens."

"Am I thinking what you're thinking?" Riley asked, grinning wickedly.

Mara smiled, mirroring Riley. "Let's light these thundercunts up."

The two women bounced excitedly on their feet as Roth turned his eyes up to the sky with his arms still crossed. As if he were praying to the gods to strike him down and put him out of his misery.

"Wouldn't it just be easier to give Grimsley what you owe him?" Nathair asked, interrupting the women's wicked delight.

Mara pointed a finger at him. "The next time an idiotic thought pops into your head, just keep your mouth shut and steer the fucking ship."

"My apologies, captain," Nathair muttered. "I only thought it would be in the crew's best interest if you just paid Grimsley."

Mara opened her mouth, ready to snap at her helmsman, but Riley interjected before an argument broke out. "Are we going to wait until they catch up to us?"

The Captain of the Roaring Tigers glared murderously at her helmsman before slowly sliding that gaze to the approaching fleet. "If Grimsley wants a fight," Mara said, her hand going to the hilt of her sword, "we're going to bring him one."

CHAPTER 8

The burning ship sank to the ocean floor as smoke billowed toward the sky. Flaming bottles of whiskey had been a *very* bad idea. It hadn't taken long before Mara's ship had caught fire when one of the crew had been struck with a cannonball while holding one. It had ignited the deck, along with some of the crew, and while trying to jump into the water, the scurrying, living torches had spread the embers to anything—or anyone—they'd come into contact with.

While the rest of his fleet had surrounded him and the burning wreckage, Grimsley had taken the opportunity to bring the remaining Roaring Tigers aboard his ship, strip them of their weapons, and bind their wrists and ankles in iron shackles. He'd lined them up in front of the rail, facing the half-sunken wreckage. At the ankles, a small cannonball had been tethered to their chains.

The shackles scraped against Riley's wrists as she struggled with them in front of her. The rocking of the ship caused the small cannonball at her ankles to roll slightly; she felt the weight trying to pull her with it, but she leaned in the opposite direction, hoping to balance it out.

"That could've gone better," Riley muttered, watching the ship sink.

To her left, chains clinked as Roth shifted from one foot to the other. He was shackled, like the others, in iron at the wrists and ankles with a small cannonball, but he also had his wings wrapped in iron chains, a padlock keeping them there. Like all faeries, ailerons were not immune to the effects of iron, and his wrists and wings burned from the metal.

Smelling the scorched flesh, Riley's stomach churned. For the first time since she'd been brought to this world, she was grateful to be human.

Roth mumbled a string of words in a language she had never heard before, and she arched a confused brow. He was covered in Thorny Devil blood. The stubborn bird had put up one hell of a fight, but it hadn't been enough to escape one of the many nets made of iron chains they'd shot at him. If it were anyone else, they would be crying out in pain from the iron, but Roth looked simply inconvenienced by the entire situation.

Catching her eye, Roth translated for her, "That went as smoothly as Grimsley's thorny ass."

Riley chuckled softly. "I think I liked those words better in your mysterious language." She caught the corners of his mouth twitching before it went back to impressively annoyed.

"I really thought lighting them up was a good idea," Mara said on the other side of Riley.

"No," Roth grumbled, "you thought it would be *fun*."

Glaring, Riley whipped her head to him. She opened her mouth to give him hell, but a Thorny Devil with the nose of a vampire bat shoved her, saying, "Face the front." The push sent her forward, the cannonball rolling with her.

Eyes wide, she thought she was going to go overboard, but her body ran into a solid mass leaning in front of her. A feather brushed her parted lips, silencing a scream at the back of her throat. She stared at the broad shoulder and muscular arm covered in black, armored leather. Roth didn't move until she wasn't in danger of going over the railing.

The look Roth gave the vampire bat faerie promised pain. "When I get out of these chains," he growled, "I'm going to kill you first."

The pirate smiled, showing his fangs.

Is he faerie or actually a vampire? Riley wondered. Although it had been difficult twelve years ago to come to terms with the fact that faeries were real, she wouldn't be surprised if vampires were, too.

Amused, the pirate said, "Good luck getting out of those chains when I have these." He dangled a set of skeleton keys in front of Roth.

Roth's smile was equally amused. "I don't need luck."

"Says the aileron in chains."

"Shut up, Alonzo," a raspy voice said, cutting through the tension.

Riley quickly turned away before anyone could see the smile forcing its way onto her face. Snickering came from the right of her, and she glanced over. Mara's lips were wobbling as she kept them sealed tight. Her cheek twitched with the same amusement Riley was trying to contain.

Mara mouthed: *Alonzo.*

Riley bit her tongue to keep the uncontrollable laughter from escaping, but it did little to keep the soft snort inside. Roth's arm brushed against hers in warning. If she couldn't contain her amusement, she might actually go over the railing this time.

Grimsley's clawed feet clicked against the wood as he came over and smacked Alonzo across the back of the head. He ignored his crew member rubbing the spot as he paced down the line of remaining Roaring Tigers, his unbuttoned, long, dark blue coat floating behind him. His bare torso, covered in tiny desert-striped scales, displayed the scar on his abdomen that drifted below the red sash tied around the waist of his gray pants, where two swords were strapped.

Grimsley stopped behind Mara, and the amusement faded from her eyes. He leaned in, and his thorns scraped against her skin, leaving trickles of blood running down her cheek. His black tricorn hat covered the thorns atop his head but did little to hide the ones poking out of the sides. "Where's my payment, kitten?" he snarled.

Riley's lip curled back as Mara said sweetly, "This is quite a lot of trouble you've caused." She glanced at Grimsley, adding with a purr, "And it's tigress, not kitten."

"Who said this was just a debt collection?" Grimsley questioned. Mara frowned. "I'm not the only one you owe. A lot want you dead."

"Tell me something I don't know," Mara quipped, rolling her eyes.

His lips curled into a cruel smile. "You have a traitor among your crew."

Riley paled, her gaze sliding to Roth. She'd known there was something off about him. She'd fucking known it. He'd betrayed them and was working with Grimsley.

Roth's eyes flicked to her, and he gave her an almost imperceptible shake of his head.

On the other side of Riley, Mara became preternaturally still. She stared ahead, unblinking, at what was left of her ship: the bowsprit and figurehead of a leaping tiger. "Who," she said, voice low, dangerous. She wasn't asking, but demanding to know who had betrayed her trust.

"I did," a slithery voice said as chains clinked.

Riley forgot how to breathe as her face fell slack.

"You fucking snake," someone in the line spat, but she didn't know who.

A dull ringing began in her ears and the world became nonexistent. She didn't want to believe her eyes as the helmsman of the Roaring Tigers stepped out from the line. Her nails dug into the skin of her palms, creating crescent moons. She wished she had torn out his fangs and shoved them down his throat when she'd had the chance.

Nathair had been on the crew before Riley and had been one of Mara's first recruits. He'd had Mara's back countless times, and yet he'd betrayed her—he'd betrayed all of them.

Standing with his chin held high, Nathair's golden, slitted eyes watched Mara carefully. Her gaze was on him, unfocused, her mind no doubt replaying every interaction she'd ever had with him leading up until this moment, trying to decipher when he'd made this decision.

Riley couldn't fathom why Nathair would do this. Her throat burned with the bile she worked to keep down.

Something must have sparked in Mara's memory. "You told me to just give Grimsley what he wanted," she said. "Would anything have changed if I had?"

"You mean if you had handed me over like you were supposed to after cheating in the game of cards the other night?"

Riley's eyes widened as she sucked in a sharp breath. She whipped her head in Mara's direction, seeing her mouth become a tight, thin line.

Nathair chuckled low. "That's right. I know about your bargain. Nothing could ever change my mind after Grimsley approached me, telling me everything. You always choose yourself above the rest of us."

"That's not true," Mara said, practically snarling. "You're my family. I value each and every one of you. If I didn't, I wouldn't have had to cheat in that game of cards to ensure you remained a part of the crew."

"Family." He snorted. "Except for the human and your mer-bitch, you never gave a shit about the rest of us." He gestured to the line of Tigers. "We're not a family, Mara. If we were, you wouldn't have made that bargain with Grimsley to begin with. We're just here because you need bodies."

Mara shook her head. "I have never thought any one of you as invaluable."

Nathair's shackles clanged to the deck, further proving his captivity was a lie. "Exactly," he said. "Valuable, but not irreplaceable."

Some of the Tigers voiced their disapproval, but some were silent, reevaluating their views.

"For those who agree," Nathair said to his former shipmates, "step up and join a crew worth fighting for." No one moved at first, but after a moment, Riley watched in horror as some stepped out of line; the corner of Nathair's mouth lifted. "For those who don't believe me, then let me prove it."

Nathair pulled Alonzo's sword from its sheath, and the Thorny Devils went for their blades, not quite ready to trust a Tiger, but with one shake of Grimsley's head, they stayed their hands. He was interested in what the snake had planned for the kitten.

Nathair pulled Lyra—a thin, long-limbed faerie with translucent moth wings and bright turquoise hair—from the end of the line. He held her against the front of his body with one arm wrapped around her waist while holding the blade against her ebony throat. Lyra's golden eyes were wide, showing true terror. Her lower lip wobbled as her body went rigid.

"Nathair, please," Lyra begged. "I thought *we* were family."

"We were, once," Nathair said, his grip on the sword loosening. "When I still believed the lies Mara spewed to make us believe she cared about us by giving us a false sense of belonging in exchange for what she's truly craved the most—our undying love and devotion."

Hatred hardened his slitted eyes as they met Mara's. "But I was reminded that we're pirates. We all stab each other in the back eventually. It's inevitable." His grip on the sword tightened. "Isn't that right, Mara?"

Nathair's words settled heavily over his former crew while Mara stood motionless, never denying his accusation.

A knowing smile crept over Nathair's face. "See?" he said to Lyra. "It's nothing personal."

And then, he slit her throat, right down to the spine. Someone screamed as Lyra collapsed. Riley stared at Lyra's lifeless body bleeding onto the deck, staining it. With little effort, Nathair threw Lyra overboard, the sound of splashing water following.

Riley tried to swallow but couldn't get the muscles to work as she stared at the pool of blood.

"I'm going to keep killing your *family* until you admit the truth," Nathair said to Mara. "Either way, my point will still be made."

He waited, giving Mara time to say he was right and her crew didn't mean anything to her, before pulling another Tiger from the line, but Mara kept her mouth shut. She watched impassively as Nathair slit another throat, causing more Tigers to defect. She never said a word as he cut throat after throat. Never blinked as he threw body after body into the water, letting the blood attract the unwelcome company of sharks, where they feasted on the flesh of dead Tigers.

Riley shook with each new victim Nathair claimed. She dug her nails into her palms, hoping to wake from this horrendous nightmare, but deep down she knew this wasn't a bad dream—it was very real. She couldn't stop what was happening, but Mara could.

She looked at her captain, her best friend, for some sign she cared about what was happening, but found nothing there. There was no emotion, no grief lining her face.

Feeling a new kind of betrayal, Riley realized everything happening proved Nathair was right, just as he had intended.

Nathair reached Roth. His forked tongue flicked against Roth's neck, causing the aileron to look as if he wanted to crawl out of his skin.

"Does the legendary *Crimson Knight* have any last words before your wings are stained with *your* blood?" Nathair asked.

Roth's teeth were bared, but it was Riley who answered, surprising everyone, including herself. "His name is Roth, you traitorous fucking sack of shit—"

Riley never saw the hand coming. One moment, she was snarling at Nathair, the next Mara was on her knees beside her, saying her name in a shaky voice. Blinking stars away, Riley lay on the deck with a welt forming on her cheek, watching the snake fall on his back with a bird on top of him, strangling him.

Even in iron shackles, Roth was still the apex predator. It took Alonzo and two other Thorny Devils to pull him off Nathair. Murder seeped from Roth as he struggled against his captures.

Nathair coughed. "You defend her?" he wheezed, holding a hand to his neck. "A *human*?"

"Just because she's human," Roth growled, "doesn't mean I'll let you toss her around so you can prove to your new crew that you're not weak and pathetic like you actually are."

"I am neither of those things," Nathair spat, his golden eyes flashing.

"If that were true," Roth said, staring the snake down, "you wouldn't have stabbed your captain in the back, you wouldn't have killed your friends to make a point, and you wouldn't have hit a woman —chains or no chains." He spat at Nathair's boots. "She's right—you're nothing but a fucking sack of shit."

Nathair got to his feet, prepared to run Alonzo's sword through Roth's chest, but Grimsley's clawed hand on his shoulder stopped him. "I'm keeping that one," he said. "He still has a lot of fight left in him. He just needs a new master to teach him some manners."

"I bow to no one," Roth declared, his voice dangerous. It sent a chill down Riley's spine.

"We'll see about that." Grimsley chuckled.

Roth's legs were kicked out from under him, and he landed on his knees before Grimsley. Lightning streaked across his sea-green eyes as he stared down the Captain of the Thorny Devils.

"Looks to me like you're plenty capable of bowing," Grimsley said, but Roth kept his chin held high. To Alonzo, the captain said, "Break his wings. That'll show him who his new master is."

Riley's eyes went round with horror. She didn't want this to happen to him. It was all her fault. If she had kept her mouth shut, this wouldn't be happening.

But if I had, would he be dead already, just like everyone else?

"No more," Riley whispered.

Grimsley turned to her, his skin lifting where his eyebrows should have been. "No more, little one?"

"Don't call me that," she snarled. There was only one soul allowed to call her that, and if they were here, it would be Grimsley on his knees, begging for his life.

"What would you do for him?" Grimsley asked, crouching before her. "What would you do to save his wings?"

She looked at Roth. There was something in his eyes as he shook his head once, but she couldn't read what it was.

"There's an opening on the crew," Grimsley went on. "My men could use a way to release some tension out at sea."

Riley blanched as a low rumble came from Roth.

Mara blocked Riley's body with her own from Grimsley. "She will do *nothing* for him," she snarled. "She will not bargain with you. She will not be your slave to be raped over and over again. I won't let that happen. I don't care what you do to him, but you will not harm her."

A sick feeling settled low in Riley's belly. Where had this ferocity been when the rest of her *family* was being slaughtered right in front of her?

"I guess the snake was right after all," Grimsley said, coming to the same conclusion as Riley, and he snapped his fingers.

But before Alonzo could break Roth's wing, Riley shouted, "Wait!" She had no idea what was going to come out of her mouth next, but it better be good.

Slowly, a smile spread across Grimsley's face as he halted Alonzo.

Never taking her eyes off Roth, Riley blurted, "I'll tell you where to find Lothaire's treasure."

"Riley," Mara warned.

"The treasure is in Wyne somewhere," Riley said, ignoring Mara.

Her breaths were heavy and uneven as Roth's eyes grew in astonishment.

Water splashed against the hull of the ship and birds circled above as all went silent, until Nathair said, "That's why we've been going to Wyne so much." He clenched his teeth, baring his fangs. "You've been searching for Lothaire's treasure and didn't tell anyone but your darling *human*." He spat the final word.

"That's not true," Mara said, holding her chin up. "Jasper knew, too."

Nathair shook his head. "And here I thought you just liked trying to figure out the star maze while you were high off your ass, but you were actually looking for the treasure," he said. "That's where it is, isn't it?"

"Yes," Mara confirmed.

Riley searched for a sign on Mara's face that showed the lie, but there was none. If there was one thing Mara was good at, it was lying in the face of danger.

"Is that enough to save Roth's wings?" Riley asked. She was barely breathing now.

"It is," Grimsley said. Riley sighed in heavy relief—until he added, "But I'm not going to."

A sickening crack was drowned out by Roth's screams. He panted through clenched teeth while his nostrils flared; his wing hung limply, feathers brushing the deck.

Riley gaped in horror. *I'm sorry*, she tried to say, but she couldn't speak. Nothing would come out no matter how hard she tried.

About to snap the other wing, Alonzo stopped when shouts were heard coming from another of Grimsley's ships—and then another and another. Soon, the entire fleet sounded their alarms.

Grimsley's crew ran to the other side of the deck, including Alonzo and the two Thorny Devils holding Roth.

Mara got to her feet, too, narrowing her eyes as she tried to discern what the commotion was about. She shuffled forward, dragging her cannonball and chain with her.

Booming began as cannons were fired, followed by splashes and an ear-splitting roar. It scraped against Riley's eardrums, sending a shudder down her from head to toe, and goose bumps broke out across her skin.

Wood shattered across the sea and large splinters came raining down on them. Riley closed her eyes, pressed her face into the deck, and covered her head, praying to the gods. There were scrapes on her skin where the wood had torn through her clothing, but she was still breathing, unlike some of the others on board. She opened her eyes to a Thorny Devil impaled to the deck through his chest. Others screamed from the shards protruding out of their bodies. The metallic stench of blood filled the air. It was everywhere and all-consuming.

Too much, Riley thought. This was too much.

"Holy fucking gods," Mara breathed.

Riley looked up in time to see a flash of shimmering green-blue scales.

A sea wyrm—half the size of the dragon that made Obsidian Island, but it was no small creature. Its mouth was almost the size of one of Grimsley's ships, and it was taking out the fleet as cannonballs and harpoons bounced off it. Around the monster, ships sank and pirates tried to scurry away, but they were quickly swallowed up. Blood seeped out between the beast's sharp teeth.

A cannonball came careening through the air, hitting the deck and creating a hole behind her. The ship rocked back as it was struck by the sea wyrm—

Riley slid toward the gaping hole. She caught a loose board poking out, but it snapped beneath her momentum, her cannonball pulling her toward the opening. She heard someone scream her name as she went through it, into the water below.

Sucking in a large breath, Riley plunged under the red waves filled with debris from the ship. She sank, the cannonball dragging her down. She waited for a shark to sink its teeth into her flesh, but the bite never came; all the sharks were gone, scared off by the sea wyrm.

Riley wrestled with her shackles as the cannonball pulled her closer to the ocean floor. Pressure built in her lungs, against her skull. She was too deep. Black crept in all around her, and it wasn't long before it consumed every part of her, down to her withering soul.

CHAPTER 9

"Riley!"

Roth shouted her name as he watched her disappear over the ship, into the water. His heart was in his throat, stuck. He couldn't fucking think.

Too many names, too many faces flashed before him. All of them about to die because he'd failed. He had one simple task to accomplish and he had hesitated. He could've been on his way already, but his heart had gotten in the way.

Fuck, fuck, fuck.

A cannonball whizzed by his head, nearly taking it off. The screams, the smell of blood, piss, and shit, it all came flooding back to him. Slowly, his heart began to make its way back to where it belonged in his chest.

The ship rocked, and he moved against it, staying upright. He couldn't let himself be dragged into the waters below, not before he got his damn chains off.

Tucked within him, waiting to be set free, the warrior said in a calm, cool voice: *First the chains containing your wings, then find the faerie with the keys for the shackles binding your wrists and ankles. I'll do the rest.*

Taking a deep breath, Roth nodded, knowing this was going to hurt like fucking hells. With his one wing broken, hanging limp, it took some maneuvering, but he managed to slip the chains free from them, grunting, his teeth bared in a snarl as he bit down on his agony.

Just as the iron chains fell to the deck, a cannonball hit nearby, sending wooden spears flying. He rolled out of the way of an incoming board before he could be impaled, like many of Grimsley's crew already had been. He gritted his teeth against the pain shooting from his broken wing through the rest of his nerve endings. Once upright, his eyes searched the living, still running around frantically.

There, on the other side of the deck, cowering behind a crate, was Alonzo—and Roth's only path to saving hundreds of lives.

Roth stretched his neck, cracking it. "Time to go to work."

Every time the warrior came out—the Crimson Knight—a sick feeling would settle with a heavy weight in Roth's chest and stomach. But this time, there was no sick feeling, no heavy weight. This time, the faerie who was about to be dealt a gruesome death deserved nothing less. He felt no regret for what was about to happen to Alonzo; he only wished he had more time to make it as painful and slow as possible. But the knight within made do with the time he had.

Alonzo cursed, seeing the aileron approach with death in his eyes, and he stood, drawing his sword. Using the chains between his wrists, the knight blocked the incoming attack and tangled Alonzo's sword, allowing him to drive his elbow into the faerie's nose. There was a sickening crack, but the knight was already moving his feet, tripping the faerie.

Alonzo landed on his back with a *thud* and a yelp as he clutched his nose with one hand, blood coating his fingers and face.

Seconds—that was all the knight needed.

While Alonzo was falling on his back, the knight was taking the keys from his belt and unlocking the shackles at his wrists. He took Alonzo's sword and sliced through the faerie's other hand—the one that had dared to touch Riley. Blood splattered, but the sight, the smell, the taste —it didn't bother him; the knight had lived and breathed it day and night during the war and, to Roth's dismay, after.

With dead eyes, the knight swiped the sword across Alonzo's belly before the faerie finished his first cry and disemboweled him. He shook with the urge to drive the sword through the faerie's gaping abdomen, pinning him to the deck, but Roth reminded the knight there wasn't time for this.

Strapping the sword to his waist, Roth came back to the surface, tucking the Crimson Knight away once more, and unlocked the shackles at his ankles.

"Knight!" Mara screamed nearby. "Fucking help me already!"

Clenching his hands into fists, Roth glanced at the Captain of the Roaring Tigers as he made his way to the spot Riley had fallen overboard. Mara was fighting for her life, still shackled, as Nathair came at her with all he had, his fangs bared. She glanced at Roth, seething, but he didn't care, even as he knew that was going to be her final mistake—she wasn't the one he was there for.

Nathair pushed through her defenses, sinking his fangs into her neck, tearing through flesh. Mara's eyes widened in shock and betrayal—from Nathair's or Roth's, no one would ever know. She collapsed to the deck, her life seeping from her body.

Nathair crouched over her, but Roth didn't wait around to find out what he was saying to her.

With one final deep breath, Roth dove into the crimson waves.

CHAPTER 10

R iley woke in a bout of coughs, spurting saltwater from her lungs onto the sand. It tore at her throat, leaving it sore. It felt like someone had punched her in the chest repeatedly.

With her eyes closed, she rolled onto her back. Grains of sand and strands of damp hair clung to the sides of her face. She buried her fingers in the sand, feeling the grains slide through them. A soft breeze stroked her skin and rustled through the nearby foliage. The smell of the ocean mixed with the trees as the wind brought the faint stench of smoke. She crinkled her nose as she swallowed, licking her lips and tasting salt.

A droplet of water fell onto one of her closed eyelids.

Was it beginning to rain?

A featherlight touch brushed away her damp hair before cupping her cheek. They were large, calloused hands, but ever so soft against her skin; she leaned into the touch, and a thumb stroked her brow.

"Riley?"

She knew the voice but couldn't place it; her mind was still drowning as her body had been not long ago.

Blinking back the sand and water, Riley first saw striking green eyes, the golden cracks of lightning lined with concern, watching her intently. His damp curls were matted to his brow, and droplets of water ran down his bronze skin. One fell from his nose into her eye. She blinked rapidly until her vision cleared. There was a flutter, a rustling deep within her as she focused on the aileron hovering over her. "Bird?" she croaked.

The concern vanished from Roth's eyes, turning into a withering glare. "Here I was," he said flatly, "worried about you, but I'd say you're just fine." He sat back, giving her room. She groaned as she slowly sat up.

Seeing the smoke in the distance over the water, creating dark clouds in the sky, Riley looked behind Roth, and when she didn't see Mara, she peered over her shoulder. But all that greeted her was sand, palm trees, and the rising, tree-covered slope of a hill.

Where is she?

Her heart began to beat faster within her aching chest, her breathing becoming rapid. "Where's Mara?" she rasped.

Roth was silent. His mouth became a thin line as he shook his head once.

Riley looked at the billowing smoke far out at sea again. Tears pricked her eyes as she shook her head. "No," she breathed. Mara couldn't be dead. She was a survivor. She could still be out there, wading in the water—or worse, drowning.

Panic set in.

Without Mara and Jasper, she would be alone.

She didn't want to be alone again.

Standing, Riley strode toward the sea with her jaw set with determination, her hands clenched into fists at her sides. She would find and save Mara, and if she lost her own life in the process, then so be it. She didn't give a damn if she was breathing or not; Mara—*her family*—was all that mattered.

"What are you doing?" Roth's concern was back.

"What does it look like? I'm saving Mara."

"No, you're not," he said sternly, placing a hand on her shoulder.

"Yes, I am." She shrugged out from under him. "She needs me." He stepped in front of her, blocking her path. "Get out of my way, Roth. I don't want to hurt you, but I will if I have to."

There was a twitch of a smile before it disappeared just as quickly as it had appeared. "Riley, I need you to listen to me," he said. "Mara's gone, and she isn't coming back. I'm sorry," he added, his face softening. He reached a hand out to hers—

His eyes widened as she gripped his wrist, pulled him to her, and used her hips to drive him over her back, into the sand. He swore, his broken wing crushed beneath his body.

Riley took off running toward the water, kicking sand into his face as she heard his protests to stop. But she didn't—not when her boots hit the water, not when it reached her knees, and not when she heard splashing as Roth came after her. He gained on her faster than she could wade; she cursed her damn genetics for making her so much shorter than him. When he caught up to her, he wrapped his arms around her and lifted, carrying her back to the beach.

She thrashed against him, screaming, "Let me go! I have to save her!" He was a solid, warm mass against her back, and although he had her arms pinned to her sides in his iron grip, her legs were free. She kicked wildly behind her, trying to make contact with any part of him, and she smiled when her foot connected with his shin, hearing him grunt.

"It isn't nice to kick the ones trying to help you," Roth growled.

How was he helping?

The kick didn't deter him, and Riley snapped at his hands with her teeth as he carried her out of the water. A hiss escaped through his clenched teeth. Tasting blood, she knew she broke the skin, but it still wasn't enough to loosen his hold.

If she didn't reach Mara soon, her best friend would be gone forever, and Riley didn't think she would be able to close off the overwhelming flood of emotions. They would take her, drown her, never letting her come up for air.

Feeling nothing was so much better than feeling *everything*.

Riley kicked and snapped her teeth at Roth until he had enough, and they collapsed, backward, to the sand. There was a sharp gasp from Roth, his body going rigid beneath her, but whatever pain he was feeling, he pushed it aside. He wrapped his legs around her, pinning them. Arching her back away from him, she tried to get any leverage against him, but it was no use; his hold on her was too strong, and she couldn't escape him.

With his arms around her, her breathing began to slow, along with her heart, as time passed, but Roth's grip never loosened. The dam keeping the emotions at bay was threatening to collapse, threatening to drown her in their flood, but she needed to know. "How?" she rasped. It was all she could manage to get out, but Roth didn't need her to elaborate.

"After you went into the water," he said gently, "things got . . . intense. It all happened so fast, Riley. You went over, and while I managed to get free of my shackles, Mara was fighting Nathair. He sank his fangs into her throat. It was the last thing I saw before I went in after you."

No, Riley thought. *No, no, no.* Mara couldn't be dead. Her best friend had a knack for getting out of dangerous situations. Like a cat, Mara had nine lives, and Riley refused to believe she'd spent her last one.

"I don't believe you." There was an edge to Riley's quiet voice. A determination to prove Roth wrong and a promise that if he was lying to her, she would find a way to end the infamous Crimson Knight's bloody reign.

Without an ounce of fear from Riley's unspoken promise, Roth said, "I'm telling you the truth, Riley. Mara is gone. Nathair killed her."

"I don't believe you!" she repeated. She began to squirm again, but with new purpose this time. "I can prove it to you! Release my left arm!"

"How is that going—"

"Just do it! Now! We're losing precious time if I'm going to save Mara from Grimsley!"

Sighing, Roth released Riley's left arm and that arm only, holding it above them, the tiger inked there snarling at them. It was as if it were roaring at Riley to move faster before all was lost.

Throwing every ounce of authority into her voice, Riley said, "Find Mara." At the sound of her command, the compass on her wrist, below the tiger, began to glow with the magic it was laced with. An arrow shimmered into existence within it and began to spin.

"Well, I'll be damned," Roth muttered beneath her, causing the corner of her mouth to lift in smug satisfaction.

"I bet you wish you had gotten the compass now," she said,

watching the arrow spin faster, the compass glow brighter, "instead of being a stubborn bird."

Roth grumbled something in that foreign language again, as he had on Grimsley's ship, but before Riley had a chance to ask what he'd said, the arrow suddenly vanished and the glow of the compass with it. Riley's brows knitted together.

"Is that supposed to happen?" Roth asked.

Riley didn't answer. She commanded the compass once again to find Mara. And like the first time, the arrow spun until it suddenly vanished. She tried four more times, her hope dwindling until it vanished into nothing as the arrow did for a sixth time. Her arm dropped limply into the sand beside them.

She began to shake. The compass couldn't locate Mara because she no longer existed. Her best friend was truly gone.

Roth's hold on Riley turned into a comforting embrace. "I'm sorry," he said softly.

The two words nearly shattered her glass heart. Tears spilled over as sobs worked their way up from her chest. She couldn't breathe; she was drowning all over again. An ache started in her center, working its way through the rest of her.

Too much.

She was feeling too much.

"Let me go," Riley said between sobs. His grip tightened. "Let me go, Roth!" she cried, but he wouldn't.

"I can't risk that," he said, his voice low and thick.

"Please," she pleaded, "let me go. I won't do anything stupid. I just need . . ." Gods, she didn't know, but she needed to get away from him. She needed to be able to stuff everything she was feeling back down where it belonged, and she couldn't do that with him reminding her *he's sorry*. "I just want to walk," she finished. "I *need* to walk."

After a long minute, Roth let out a deep breath. "Okay," he said, releasing her.

Riley scrambled out of his arms, starting down the beach, until she broke out into a sprint, running away from all she had worked so hard, over the past three years, to seal away behind the stone encasing her fragile heart. She ran until her lungs begged for air, until her legs threatened to give out on her, until the throbbing in her head was as overwhelming as the feelings inside. She ran until the moon and stars came out and it was only her and the welcoming darkness.

RILEY WANDERED into the tropical forest on the island, finding bananas, mangos, and leaves pooled with fresh water. Her stomach grumbled at her; she hadn't realized how hungry she was. The emptiness was annoying yet welcoming. Hunger, she could handle—could use to push all those unwanted feelings aside for a short time.

Making her way through the forest, she left a trail of banana peels and mango skins. A lemur leapt through the trees as she explored, finding trees and sand and more trees, until she came out on the other side of the island. There was no one else there with her; the land was deserted save for some animals. She saw a flash of silver and dark spots under the moonlight, but the seal waddled away. Riley wondered if it was truly a seal or if it was a selkie—water faeries used to deliver messages quickly and more reliably than the best-trained manatee.

Riley's eyes widened.

Jasper.

She would have to tell him what had happened but would wait until the two months were over. This wasn't the kind of news one delivered in a message, especially knowing he wouldn't be able to leave his mother's side because of their bargain. Riley would tell him in person and witness the grief and guilt firsthand. She knew him well enough to know he would feel responsible for Mara's death because he hadn't been there to save her or realize what Nathair had planned.

Riley's hand came to her mouth as the fruit threatened to come up with the images of Lyra's and the others' slit throats. Nathair had killed his friends and dumped them into the sea as if they were nothing.

Swallowing the bile, Riley ignored the tiny voice in her head saying, *It's all your fault. This wouldn't have happened if Mara had left you to bleed to death.* She urged the encroaching feelings back down.

Riley turned around and walked back into the forest, picking more food to eat. And that was when she saw them: yellow-capped mush-rooms with what appeared to have a smattering of white clouds.

She'd heard tales of what this mushroom was capable of. The lure of what it could do sang to her now, and yet she was hesitant to let it guide her down a path of bliss—or death.

She had been here once before, at this very crossroads. Then, she had been nothing more than an empty husk, years of isolation leaving her desolate. Yearning for her deliverance to another life. And now . . .

She wasn't sure anymore. She was tired, yes, but was she beyond caring if she breathed any longer? Was she so sound in that knowledge to take the leap of faith?

Plucking one, she frowned, studying the magical mushroom while she pondered her next move. Flashes of her family from the mortal world appeared in her mind. Cracks, large and small, zigzagged their way across her glass heart, but it wasn't enough to break her. Not this time. The faces of the Roaring Tigers flew by her, each one cutting her open. But it was Mara's that made her suck in a shaky, aching breath, pushing everything back down as it tried to worm its way up from her barren soul.

Mara. That name alone was all it took. She knew what to do next, but which path of the crossroads it would lead her down was yet to be discovered.

Without another thought, Riley shoved the mushroom into her mouth and chewed, leaving the Fates to write her destiny.

CHAPTER 11

R oth scratched away a tickle on his nose, the scent of citrus and vanilla lingering in the air. But it wasn't sand he swept away.

Blinking sleep out of his eyes, he focused on the source: Riley hovered above him, kneeling behind his head with her face immeasurably close to his, her finger lingering over his nose where she had been poking him.

He nearly jumped out of his skin. "What are you doing?" he asked, his voice rough with sleep.

"Did you know you snore?" she asked.

"Excuse me?"

"You snore. Well, it's more like a soft purr, like a kitten."

Roth hadn't known, nor did he care.

There was something off about Riley, and while he hadn't known her for more than two days, he didn't think this was normal behavior for her, or for anyone. He observed her dilated eyes and could hear her heart beating rapidly inside her chest, mirroring his own.

She poked him in the nose again.

"Stop poking me," Roth demanded, swatting her finger away.

"If you didn't have wings," she said, pulling her finger away from his nose, "I would've sworn you were feline, not avian."

Despite taking her finger away, she was still hovering above him, unblinking. "Can I sit up now?" Roth asked irritably. "Or do you want to poke me some more?"

Riley leaned back, letting him sit up. He could feel her stare on him the entire time he struggled to sit up, his broken wing shooting pain through his body. He sucked in a breath, wishing he hadn't let his exhaustion catch up to him before he mend it.

"Fucking hells," he cursed, his arms trembling as he finally managed to sit up.

He needed to set the bone in his wing before wrapping it, but would have to find something to use first.

Dreading the movement, Roth forced himself to stand. He winced as Riley scrambled in front of him, grabbed his wrists, and pulled him to his feet.

She beamed at him, proud of herself for helping.

"Thanks," Roth mumbled, arching a puzzled brow at her.

He moved to retrieve Alonzo's discarded sword. Roth had kept it, figuring it would come in handy, but now he considered himself lucky Riley hadn't seen it while she'd run laps around the island. He had felt everything she'd been feeling leaching from her soul. All the pain and sorrow and anguish—it was a miracle she hadn't drowned in it already.

Sword in hand, he trudged into the forest, looking for anything to wrap his wing, and Riley followed. She ran past him, arms outstretched, trailing her fingers along white-petalled flowers with pink, heart-shaped centers. She giggled as a child would as she plucked one and brought it to her nose.

Grinning, she darted over to Roth and jumped on him. He stumbled back a step, dropping the sword in surprise. His eyes went round. She giggled, tucking the flower behind his ear, and wrapped her arms around his neck and her legs around his waist. He swallowed, fighting the instinct to cup her ass.

The pain in his wing was forgotten as she leaned in closer. The sweet scent of the flower swirled with her citrus and vanilla scent, and he could see the gold flecks in her eyes. They reminded him of tiny, golden wildflowers in a field. His breath hitched as she grinned from ear to ear.

"Mara was right," Riley said softly. "You are a pretty bird, and with very pretty eyes."

Roth blinked—not only from surprise, but from the familiar smell on her breath. His brain was cloudy as he waded through memories, trying to find the source of the familiarity but coming up empty. Every time he tried to think, he got distracted by the warm caress of her breath against his lips and the beating of her heart against his chest. She was so close, it could have been her lips brushing against his. Swallowing, he asked, "What did you eat, Riley?"

"I don't remember." She shrugged. "But it was good." She dragged the word out as she slid down the length of his body. Her ass hit the sand with a new fit of giggling.

Abruptly, it stopped. Her eyes just about bugged out of her head. She was poking him again, wrapping both of her hands around his thigh and squeezing. A hiss escaped between his clenched teeth as she kneaded the muscle.

Blood heated and rushed through Roth's veins, flowing to the same destination. His cock hardened.

Fucking hells, get ahold of yourself, Roth chided himself. But they were a poor choice of words. The scene flashed before him: Riley's hand gripping him, running up and down his length, coaxing every pleasurable sensation from him until it was too much.

His hands balled into fists at his sides as he forced his eyes shut, picturing anything else. But it wasn't working as she continued massaging his thigh, making him harder.

Roth's eyes snapped open, and he stepped clear of Riley's hands and out of the circle of her legs, nearly taking her with him. Her hands froze in the air, fingers curled as if she were still gripping his thigh. Her eyes were wide and mischievous. Until her arms stretched to the sides and she fell backwards, giggling. She ran them up and down in the sand, making wings.

Roth breathed heavily, his blood going down a degree—but only a degree. He picked up his sword, reminding himself he had a broken wing to tend to, and began his trek through the jungle again.

The farther he traveled inland, the denser the forest became, almost enough to block out the sun. Gone were the banana and mango trees, replaced with ferns and thicker, taller ones covered in moss. Fallen branches littered the grassy dirt, and vines traveled from one trunk to another, making the trek difficult.

Slicing through vines in his way, Roth grumbled; they weren't what he was looking for. Too thick and not flexible enough. If all the vines proved useless, he would have to resort to weaving bark. He'd already passed trees with small enough trunks that would work if it came down to that, but even if it took him into the dead of night, he would search the entire island for the right vines before weaving bark. He hated the tedious, repetitive process, but not only that, he needed to keep an eye on Riley.

The scent of what she'd eaten, causing her to behave this way, remained a mystery to him.

The pain in his wing was back and made it harder to think about anything else. It became difficult to continue walking instead of lying on the ground, wishing he were dead in the belly of the sea wyrm.

"Isn't he cute?" Riley cooed. She stopped a few paces behind Roth in front of a fern, her knees bent. A tree frog with two tiny horns above its red eyes rested on one of the leaves, watching Riley as she watched it. The frog made a croaking sound, and she did her best imitation.

Roth rolled his eyes and went back for her. "Tremendously," he said dryly, wrapping his hand around hers. He dragged her along and resumed chopping down vines and foliage in his way. He kept his hand in hers; he didn't need her wandering off on him, not when there were probably snakes twice *his* size out there.

After an hour, Roth's stomach growled. He regretted not taking a banana or mango before he'd gone as far inland, but he wasn't going to turn around now.

Glancing at Riley, he saw she had a growing bouquet of flowers in her other hand, and unfortunately for Roth, so did he—but in his hair. Every once in a while, she stopped to pluck a flower and weave it through his curls because, "*A pretty bird deserves a pretty nest.*" He had rolled his eyes, keeping his mouth shut, and had let her put flowers in if it meant she wouldn't wander off, but the strong floral scents were beginning to tickle his nose.

Roth sneezed before pushing a large fern leaf aside. Behind the plant, long, sturdy vines hung from a tall tree. They were exactly what he was looking for.

Reluctantly, he let go of Riley's hand and checked that none of the vines were snakes. Finding none, he went to work cutting down as many as he could carry; he didn't know how many he would need to wrap his wing.

As he chopped down the vines, he kept an eye on Riley, watching her tangle herself within them. She giggled the entire time, never letting go of her flowers. He shook his head, the corners of Roth's mouth twitching. She looked ridiculous. But he didn't care as long as she wasn't getting into trouble.

Soon, Roth had more than enough vines. He untangled a giggling Riley and sheathed his sword. Wrapping his hand around Riley's, he led them out of the forest, onto the beach.

On the other side of the island, the forest was lined with palm and more banana and mango trees. The tree-covered hill was steeper than it had appeared on the other side of the island and dropped off into a sharp, rocky cliff. Waves crashed against jagged rocks at the bottom of it, where a small cave cut a path into the hill.

Roth sat down in the sand, letting go of Riley's hand. She took off running to the water, removing her boots as she went. He sucked in a breath, remembering the previous day. Ignoring the jolt of pain his wing sent through him, he bolted to his feet. He was prepared to drag her back from the dangerous waves, but she stopped, ankle-deep, splashing around. He blew out a sigh of relief, sitting back down, and attended to his broken wing, trying to keep one eye on Riley as she played.

Ailerons weren't able to wrap their own wings, but Roth was determined to do it on his own. He wasn't going to be asking Riley anytime soon, nor did he want to even if she wasn't high off her ass. Ailerons tended to lash out at those who tried to help them while they were injured. If Roth hurt Riley, he would never be able to forgive himself.

"Pretty bird!" Riley shouted. "Come fly with me!"

The vine slipped off Roth's wing. "Dammit," he grumbled.

"Pretty bird!"

"Later, Riley." He finagled the vine around his wing another way but failed again. "Why does this have to be so fucking difficult?"

"Meet me in the sky, pretty bird! I have wings to stretch!"

"Sure, whatever, Riley," Roth mumbled, brows knit in deep concentration. He was finally getting somewhere, and the vines were cooperating—albeit very poorly, but it would have to do. He didn't want to lose his wing.

During the Terra War, ailerons had broken their wings all the time in battle—being shot out of the sky did that—but not all had recovered as well as they would have liked. Sometimes the wing had to be amputated to prevent further injury or a liability in battle. If it came to that, most didn't want to live—but they were bred to be fighters and couldn't take their own lives willingly. Instead, they turned to dreamshade, hoping it might accomplish what they could not—

The vines slipped from Roth's hand. His face slackened. He knew the scent of her breath was familiar.

Fucking dreamshade, Roth cursed to himself. *She ate fucking* dreamshade.

Dreamshade was dangerous and reckless; it didn't guarantee death, but most who ate the mushroom died. It was unpredictable, and things could turn deadly. Fast. It was like having a dream turn into a nightmare, but instead of jerking yourself from sleep, more often than not you never woke up again.

Roth scanned the beach, the water, but Riley was missing. He took off to the shore, ready to jump in after her, but her words came drifting back to him: *"Meet me in the sky, pretty bird! I have wings to stretch!"*

Slowly, Roth turned to the hill and rocky cliff. There, amongst the trees, Riley raced up the hill to meet Death.

"Shit," Roth said sharply, turning on his heels.

He sprinted after her, not knowing if he would make it in time, and shoved foliage out of his way, his long legs nearly leaping to cover more ground.

Almost to the top, Riley stretched her arms out wide, mimicking wings.

"Riley!" Roth shouted. "Stop!"

She couldn't hear him. He wasn't going to make it in time.

The wind picked up as he leapt over a fallen tree, ducking under branches from another. Birds circled in the sky at the edge of the cliff, as if showing Riley how to use her wings. Her laughter was bright and excited over the pounding of Roth's heart and the gasps of air he tried to inhale—but he couldn't breathe.

Fucking hells, he couldn't *breathe.*

What am I going to do if I don't reach her in time? Roth panicked. He couldn't fly with a broken wing, and if by some miracle she survived the fall, he would have to reach her before she drowned—

Fucking hells, she was going to die.

Roth needed to get her attention; he needed to slow her down enough to allow him to catch up to her. He sucked in as much air as his burning lungs would allow.

"RILEY!"

Her name boomed through the trees and up the slope as loud as thunder. Birds took to the sky from their nests.

Riley glanced over her shoulder and grinned. She turned around, facing him, and slowed to a walk. "Come on, pretty bird!" she called. "You're lagging!"

He didn't need the reminder.

She turned around again and ran to the edge of the cliff, but slowing her pace was enough for Roth to gain on her.

Reaching the edge, Riley stopped, turned, and waited—she actually fucking waited for him—grinning from ear to ear. "Stretch your wings with me, pretty bird."

Roth stopped a safe distance away from her, afraid if he got any closer, she would jump. He doubled over, out of breath. Between breaths, he said, "I . . . can't stretch . . . my wings . . . Riley. One's broken . . . and you . . . don't have any."

"Yes, I do." She frowned, her brows knit in confusion. "See?" She held out her right arm, lifting her sleeve, showing the dragonfly inked there. "I have wings, pretty bird. Like you."

That's why she thinks she has wings? Roth realized, bewildered.

Shaking his head, Roth said, "That's a tattoo, Riley. It isn't real." He closed the gap between them and lifted her other sleeve, showing her the tiger and compass. "It's a tattoo, like these."

"But I'm a dragonfly. The deer said I was."

Roth was confused as much as she was. Was she hallucinating?

"What deer?" he asked. "Riley, there's no deer."

She looked around, her frown deepening. "I-I," she stuttered. Her wild eyes fell back to Roth. "I'm telling you, I'm a dragonfly," she insisted. "I can prove it."

Riley whirled to the edge of the cliff. She was faster than Roth expected, but not fast enough. He caught her by the back of her shirt and pulled her to him. She slammed into his chest with an *oof*. Riley struggled against him, but Roth held on.

"I have wings!" she shouted. "Let me fly!"

Roth tightened his grip. He couldn't let her out of his arms, not while the dreamshade remained in her system, without risking her life. He wouldn't be able to wrap his wing if he had to keep an eye on her at all times, but he couldn't wait any longer or it would be permanently limp. He needed to do something with Riley until the dreamshade wore off.

He willed magic to flow through his veins, onto his tongue. "*Go to sleep, Riley,*" Roth commanded, compulsion in his voice.

She thrashed harder. "Let me fly!" she shouted over and over again.

Frowning, Roth's brows narrowed, confused. That should've worked—but compulsion wasn't the only way he knew to get her to sleep.

Applying pressure, he pinched the nerve between her neck and shoulder. She slumped in his arms, unconscious.

His legs gave out beneath him as he relaxed, and bringing Riley with him, he sat down, finally able to breathe again.

He watched the birds flying and dipping into the water, catching fish in their beaks. Closing his eyes, he soaked in the sun, deep into his bones and further.

The wind calmed with Riley's steady breathing, her face serene under the brightness of the sun. It was the first time Roth had seen her look at ease, peaceful. No misery burdening her weary soul.

CHAPTER 12

Warmth tickled the soles of Riley's feet and crawled up her legs. It caressed her arms, her face, sending soothing strokes to stamp out the pounding in her head. Her neck was sore from her chin resting against her chest. She lifted her head and winced, the back hitting something rough and solid.

Opening her eyes, she saw Roth sat on the opposite side of a fire, wood popping from the heat. His back was to the sea, but his poorly wrapped wing was as stark at night as it would have been during the day. Remnants of flower petals remained in his hair; she remembered weaving a crown for him but not much before that. He grumbled under his breath about . . .

Bargains?

I guess he does regret his bargain with Mara, Riley mused. She had a distinct feeling it wasn't only due to being deserted on an island, but because he was deserted with *her.*

Bits and pieces of the morning and afternoon remained with her; she had done some ludicrous things—the flowers the biggest of what she could remember—but nothing topped the reckless flight she would have taken if Roth hadn't stopped her. After reaching the cliff's edge, everything went dark, but she knew she was alive because of him. And she didn't know if that was a good or bad thing. The way she was feeling, it was most certainly not good.

In addition to the pounding in her head, Riley's stomach was queasy, and if she sneezed, she would wet her pants.

She tried to stand, but quickly realized she was tied to a tree. "Are these vines?" she asked, her voice groggy from sleep. There was a sour taste in her mouth.

Without looking at her, Roth nodded.

"Can you untie me?"

"No."

"If you don't, I'm going to need a change of pants."

Roth looked at the stars, mumbling, "I'm probably going to regret this," but he stood and cut her free with a sword she hadn't noticed before.

Riley darted into the trees before she had an accident and Roth would have to deal with her grumbling. On her way back, she listened to the crickets chirping within the forest.

She smiled.

Mara had loved listening to crickets. They'd always kept Riley awake at night whenever they'd stayed on Obsidian Island in their cave, but the insects had always relaxed Mara into slumber. She would awaken refreshed, while Riley had looked like a feral raccoon with dark circles around her eyes and was crabby for the entire day.

An ache built right in the center of Riley's chest from the memory. She rubbed at it, hoping it would loosen. That it would vanish.

It didn't.

She placed a hand over her belly; her stomach twisted into knots. Gods, she felt like she was going to vomit. She doubled over with her hands on her knees, waiting for the contents to come up, but nothing happened. She started to make herself gag, hoping that would help move things along, but still nothing.

Two seconds away from shoving her fingers down her throat, Roth shouted, "If you keep making gagging noises, I'm going to vomit."

Riley rolled her eyes.

There was a horrendous smell in the air; it mixed with the scent of burning embers. *Gods, what in all the fucking realms is that?*

A moment later, she vomited.

Wiping her mouth, she sauntered back to the warm fire and the grumpy, stubborn bird turning a fish spiked to a stick over the flames.

So, that's *what made me sick.*

"Feel better?" Roth asked, glancing at her.

"From not wetting my pants or vomiting?" Riley shook her head, holding up a hand, keeping him from clarifying. "You know what, it doesn't matter; the answer is yes to both."

She sat down close to the fire, crinkling her nose at the fish. "Tell me that isn't dinner."

"It isn't dinner," he said flatly. She gave him a withering look, and he gave her one right back before directing his attention to the fish again.

A tense silence stretched between them like a yawning chasm. Stretching that ache in the center of Riley's chest wider and wider, until she couldn't take it any longer. She needed to ease it before it split her apart.

Tilting her head, she asked, "How did you manage to catch a fish?" His lips curved down, but before he could answer, she added teasingly, "It's because you're a bird, isn't it?"

He gave her a sidelong glance, and it only made her barrel on. She needed to be rid of the pain inside her.

"Do you secretly have a beak, too?"

Roth jerked his head to her. "Are you done?" he snapped.

At his tone, a muscle in her jaw popped. Her skin prickled with a sudden burst of anger, vanquishing the pain within her chest. "Why do you have to be an ass all the time?" she demanded through her teeth. "I just lost my best friend because of someone I trusted, and all I wanted to do was forget about that—if only temporarily. Why can't you just play along?"

He huffed, snorting. "Really? Did you seriously just ask me that?"

"Yes?"

"Fucking hells, Riley." He shook his head. "I was so— And if I did what you're asking—" He shook his head. "I understand to a point, but —" He raked a hand through the dark curls at the crown of his head. "*How could you be so fucking* reckless?"

"What are you—"

"The dreamshade, Riley!" he shouted. "The fucking dreamshade! Others are depending on you, and here you are being as fucking reckless as you possibly can!" She gaped at him, at the haze of frustrated fury in his eyes, as he continued shouting at her. "And you want me to just *play along*? You're un-fucking-believable!"

Riley froze, stunned. "I don't know who you think is depending on me, Roth," she said, voice small. And she didn't; she had no gods-damned clue who he could be referring to. She lived in a world that continued to prove over and over again how completely *human* she was. "*I* depend on others—not the other way around."

"*I'm depending on you*," Roth said thickly, his eyes boring into hers, trying to make her understand the depths of what he was telling her.

Riley's lungs stopped functioning for a moment.

Could that be true? Was he depending on her?

She couldn't fathom why, but then it hit her—maybe he had no one else. She knew it was strange for an aileron to be away from Paladon, let alone wanting to join a pirate crew. Maybe he had nowhere else to go.

What if everyone he loved had died in the war? Riley suddenly realized. His friends, his family—all gone. Her heart sank; she knew all too well what it felt like to lose the ones you loved so fiercely. It shattered your heart, and you were left to pick up the pieces and place stone around it to guard it from future damage.

"I'm sorry I ate the dreamshade, Roth," Riley said softly, her shoulders scrunching.

He scoffed. "No, you're not. You said it yourself. You wanted to forget about Mara and the pain it's causing you. If you happened to die doing that, oh-fucking-well."

She flinched. She might not have said all of that, but clearly, she didn't have to. He'd heard everything that had gone unsaid.

She glanced away from his judging eyes. "Yes," she admitted, her voice whisper-soft. "I didn't care if the dreamshade killed me. Either way, I would've gotten relief from the pain, temporary or everlasting." She met his stare again. "But I am sorry. It never crossed my mind that someone might be . . ." She sighed, unable to voice what she was still having a hard time wrapping her head around.

Roth was depending on her.

Looking away, Roth rolled his right shoulder and winced; his wound was bothering him. The vines tangled around his wing, another wrapping around the appendage and torso, keeping it in place.

Gesturing to it, she offered, "I can redo that for you. That is, if you want."

He rolled his shoulder again. "You've done enough already."

He might as well have come right out and said, *I don't trust you after the shit you've pulled.*

"I can do it," she told him, determined. And just too godsdamned stubborn for her own good to let it go.

Deep down, just beneath that ache in her chest, she felt the urge to make things right between them. *But only because I'm stuck with him on this dreadful island,* she told herself. Not because she cared if he was angry with her or not.

"It's no problem, Roth. I can see what you were trying to do." She reached out to untangle the loosely tied vines.

He flinched away.

Exasperated, she said, "I don't bite." He arched a brow, holding up his right hand where her teeth marks were embedded in the curve between his thumb and forefinger. "I don't bite *much*."

He rolled his eyes.

"Don't roll your eyes at me," she said, placing her hands on her hips. "In a different situation, you would be begging me to bite you some more."

The moment understanding dawned on him was clear; his cheeks flushed, spreading to the tips of his ears and down his neck below his leathers. She grinned, finding his reaction *very* intriguing.

Riley reached for him again, but he jerked away, grounding out, "Don't."

Gods, he was infuriatingly stubborn.

She crossed her arms over her chest. "I thought you were depending on me?" she reminded him.

The flush from his ears to his neck was gone, replaced with tightly scrunched brows, as if he were debating whether or not he should let her touch him.

Or maybe he doesn't like people touching his wings.

The thought appeared and grew.

He does have a broken wing and must be in all kinds of pain. She mentally facepalmed. *I'm so stupid.*

Her face softened. "Roth, I promise I'll be gentle. There will be no biting. Only wrapping your wing so gently you won't even notice I'm doing it, and I'll be done before you know it."

Roth's eyes searched hers for a long moment, darting back and forth, reading the truth within them. He looked to the stars again, sighing, but nodded.

Riley attempted untying the vines with her fingers before giving up; the knots were too tight. She took the sword, and Roth watched as she carefully cut through the vines. His eyes weren't on guard as she expected, but bright and curious.

"What?" she asked.

"Biting? Really?"

Finished cutting through the vines, Riley placed the sword down next to her as she smiled. So, she had caught his attention with this tiny detail. Interesting.

"It's not really biting," she told him, noting he gave her his undivided attention. "It's more of a . . . love nibble."

He remained perfectly still as she picked up a vine and began wrapping it around his wing, making an *X* formation, the talon peeking through at the top, but she didn't miss the hint of color coming back to his cheeks or the way he swallowed.

"Love nibble," he echoed distantly. The flush to his bronze skin deepened in his silence before he cleared his throat and rasped, "And you think I'd beg for more?"

She chuckled softly. The words "love" and "nibble" coming out of his mouth in succession didn't fit with the warrior he was known to be. "Okay, I don't know if *you* would beg for more, but Jasper does."

The corners of his mouth dipped before going back to impassive so quickly, Riley thought she'd imagined it.

"Jasper's the merman?" Roth asked, a hint of tightness to his voice.

Her brow furrowed in confusion before she remembered. "Oh, that's right. You didn't get introduced to him before he left for his rejuvenation." She nodded. "Yes, that was him. He's . . ." A tiny chink scraped across her heart, bypassing the stone walls. *He's the only one of the crew to live through Nathair's betrayal.*

"That's not true," Roth said gently. "We made it. We're still alive."

Riley's hands stilled halfway through the knot she was tying.

Can he read minds? she wondered. As rare as they were, there were those who could read and control minds, but she hadn't considered Roth might be one of them.

"No," Roth said, "I can't read your mind." Her eyes narrowed. "You just have a very difficult time keeping your thoughts from your eyes," he explained.

Clicking her tongue, she replied, "That's not true. I have an excellent poker face. Just ask anyone I've ever played cards with."

"I'm sure you do, but you've never played with me." His voice was as smooth as decadent chocolate.

Heat pooled low in her belly, sparking and crackling like the beginning embers of a fire. His words took her by surprise, and by the slight widening of Roth's eyes, she wasn't the only one.

He cleared his throat. "You almost finished?" he asked roughly. His hands tightened around his knees.

"Yes," Riley answered thickly, finishing the final knot, her hands shaky. "I just have to"—she cleared her throat—"I have the final vine to wrap."

Roth nodded and lifted his arms, allowing Riley to wrap the makeshift bandage around his wing and torso, holding the appendage in place. She held her breath as her fingers brushed against his chest, the leather smooth under her skin.

She knew he watched every move her fingers made. His face was inches away, and it took every ounce of willpower to keep her mind on the task at hand instead of moving the small distance it would take to look into those sea-green eyes she wouldn't mind drowning in.

With his breath warm against her exposed neck, a chill skittered down her spine and goose bumps rose along her arms, despite the heat from the fire. For all she tried, she couldn't remember why she had been angry at him only minutes ago. Or how she had gotten herself in this position, so close to him and nearly in his lap.

She wondered what it would be like to straddle those thick thighs and feel all that hard muscle against her soft skin.

She shook her head lightly at the slow, pulsating ache growing between her legs.

That's it, she thought. *When I finish helping the bird, I'm going to walk straight into the water and dive headfirst.*

She hoped her head hit a rock. Maybe that would knock some sense into her.

Ignoring how hot she felt, Riley tied off the vine around Roth's torso and sat back. She observed her work while he did the same.

"Not bad," he said with raised brows.

She raised her own. "'Not bad'? I'd say that's pretty damn good compared to your attempt."

He grumbled something in the same language he'd spoken on Grimsley's ship, and she didn't have to understand his native tongue to know he was griping about her, determined not to tell her she was right.

Rolling her eyes, she muttered, "Stubborn bird." But she made sure he heard. Loud and clear.

Roth sighed through his nose, his mouth becoming a thin line. "Well," he grumbled, not meeting her eye, "I suppose I owe you again."

"Again?" She reared her head back, surprised. "What was the first thing?"

"You tried to save my wings."

"You don't deserve to lose them."

Sorrow appeared in his eyes before vanishing just as quickly. "But no one else tried," he explained thickly. "Mara certainly didn't. She didn't care what Grimsley did to me."

Riley frowned as she remembered Mara's words. "*I don't care what you do to him, but you will not harm her.*"

Her stomach tightened.

No, Riley thought, *she didn't*. Mara had only cared for Riley's well-being, no one else's. But she was thrust into a horrible situation. Deep down, Riley knew there had to be some part of her that had cared.

Riley tried to explain, "Mara isn't"—she swallowed—"*wasn't* a bad person. She just . . . had a rough past."

Rough didn't come close to describing what Mara had gone through growing up. She had told Riley everything one drunken night.

Her father had wanted a son, not a daughter, to take up his mantle, and no matter how much he'd tried to produce another heir with Mara's human mother, it had never happened. During one of his fits of rage, her father had killed her mother, leaving Mara to deal with him on her own.

He had been determined to make Mara suffer for the failures of her mother. Every day, she'd endured the wrath of her father. He'd never cared who saw him lay a hand on her, nor had it mattered. It hadn't been her father's rage that had terrified her the most—it was when he'd been silent, turning a blind eye while he'd let his crew have their way with her night after night.

Faerie fruit had been Mara's salvation all those years—until one night the beast within had finally had enough of her father's torment.

"My father left his quarters with my blood dripping from his knuckles, just like any other day," Mara had told Riley. *"I lay on the ground, curled in on myself, holding my ribs. Across from me was his letter opener. It had fallen from his desk when he had thrown me at it. I stared at the letter opener, trying to work up the strength to crawl to it to end my life— but the Fates didn't allow it."*

All Mara had remembered was a high-pitched ringing in her ears before she'd blacked out.

"When I came to, there was blood everywhere, Leyley. On my tongue, down my throat. It covered my chin and neck, my bare body. They were all dead—the crew—torn to shreds. Bits of flesh were caked under my nails and stuck between my teeth. And my father"—she had taken a long swig of wine—*"that bastard's entrails led a path from the deck to his disemboweled corpse on the bed."*

After that, Riley had begun to feel a deeper kinship with Mara. They'd told each other things they hadn't dared whisper to another soul.

They might not have gone through the same nightmares, but they had endured enough that could leave them wondering most days why they'd bothered to continue breathing.

"I wish she were here," Riley said in a too-small voice.

Roth's hand came to her shoulder. "I know, but she's gone. You can't wish her back to life."

A tear ran down Riley's cheek. Everything she'd shoved down was slowly creeping its way back up. *Gods, if I could wish Mara back to life, I'd—*

Her thought ended abruptly.

"But there is a way to wish Mara back to life," she said distantly, a bit breathless.

"What do you mean?" Roth asked, leaning forward. "How?"

Riley's laugh burst from her, startling Roth. "Holy shit." There was a wild, gleeful feeling coming to the surface, and for once, she didn't try to stop her feelings from overwhelming her. She welcomed this new excitement, this elusive happiness.

Joy.

"Are you going to tell me this revelation you're having?" Roth prodded. "Or are you going to keep cackling like a madwoman?"

"Lothaire's treasure," she told him with a wide grin. He stared blankly at her, as if she had spoken another language and her words had no meaning. "I can use the Scroll of Desires to wish Mara back. It's supposed to be hidden with Lothaire's treasure," she added when he remained confused. "I just need to get my ass off this island and to Wyne." She stood and paced, thinking.

"Okay," Roth said, holding up a hand. "Even after my wing heals and I can fly us off this island, Grimsley will have beaten us to the treasure."

Riley jolted to a grinding halt. "Grimsley's alive?"

He nodded. "While the rest of his fleet were fighting for their lives, he managed to sail away. The sea wyrm was so distracted with feasting, it didn't notice. Your treasure and scroll are probably already gone."

Riley grinned. She held up a finger. "Not necessarily." He arched a brow, waiting. "Grimsley thinks the treasure is in the star maze, but it isn't."

"It's not?"

"No," she answered. "It's—"

She cut herself off, clamping her mouth shut tight.

"It's . . . ," Roth prompted, his hand circling.

"What happens if I tell you?" she started warily. "We get off this island, and there's nothing stopping you from killing me and going after the treasure yourself."

He stared at her as though he waited for her to laugh and say she was joking. When she didn't, he said flatly, "You can't be serious."

She crossed her arms over her chest. She was deadly serious.

He sighed. "Riley, I can assure you, my intentions are not to kill you. Especially after I've saved your ass—what was it?—*three* times now."

Well.

Someone was keeping count.

"Ass," she mumbled under her breath.

Hearing her, Roth said pointedly, "Trust goes both ways, Riley."

With her arms still crossed defensively over her chest, she stared at him, not giving an inch.

Roth rolled his eyes. "You're as stubborn as I am," he muttered, then reminded her, "You still have to get off this island before Grimsley discovers the true location, and like I said, I can't fly until my wing heals."

She waved a hand through the air, dismissing the notion. "I'd never let you fly me anywhere. I'm terrified of heights."

"Not on dreamshade, you're not."

She ignored the jab, but it still hurt. "If only we could get word to someone to come get us . . ."

Roth snorted. "Good luck with that."

But he saw the moment her eyes lit up with an idea.

"Okay." He leaned back. "How?"

She opened her mouth to explain, but—

She sniffed the air, a slow grin spreading across her face.

Dinner was burning.

"Shit," Roth swore as he removed the forgotten fish from the flames. It was blackened on both sides.

Riley crinkled her nose. "I'm definitely not eating that now."

CHAPTER 13

After a week of coaxing the selkie Riley had spotted to the shore with fish, she was more than ecstatic to bathe in the stream with a little waterfall she'd discovered while picking mangos and bananas.

The pile of fish, thankfully, had qualified as payment. The selkie had been delighted to deliver Riley's message for her after seeing the mound, and after eating, she had taken to the water with the shell in her mouth, waving goodbye to Riley while Roth watched on with disdain. The bird had hoped there would be leftover fish for himself later—Riley had explained the night he'd burned their dinner that she didn't eat or like seafood—but the selkie had eaten them all, her belly big and round.

"What do we do now?" Roth had grumbled, watching the selkie swim away.

Riley had simply replied, "Wait."

With nothing to do but argue whether Riley would become desperate enough to eat fish when she "inevitably grew tired of mangos and bananas"—Roth's words—patience wasn't easy to come by.

"If I ever do, in fact, grow tired of mangos and bananas," she had explained, "I will just make a bargain with you to make a heaping pile of apple roses appear." But Roth had snorted at her idea and delivered the sad news that his magic couldn't make food appear out of thin air, even if she did make an offer he couldn't refuse.

Pulling her sweat-drenched shirt over her head, Riley sighed longingly, wishing Roth were a god with magic that could make all her favorite foods appear whenever she wanted. She would never admit to him how much she *was* already growing tired of mangos and bananas. She took one look at the pile of fruit in the grass beside her and crinkled her nose.

She stripped from the rest of her clothes, tossing them aside on a large rock beside the stream. The water was cool against her skin, and she hissed from the sudden chill. But it wasn't long before she was sighing, waist-deep in the stream, ducking her head under the cascading water flowing over the boulder.

She hummed while she threaded her fingers through her hair, washing away the sand and grime from the last week. Losing herself as she scrubbed away all the horrors she witnessed on Grimsley's ship. After she was clean, she remained in the water, her skin becoming pruny, but she didn't care. She didn't want to leave the its soothing presence.

With her eyes closed, Riley floated on her back, soaking in all the comfort she could absorb with the ache still at the center of her chest. It took all of her concentration not to feel it, and later she would tell herself that was the reason she didn't hear the brush rustling or the approaching footsteps. It was only when he cleared his throat loudly, as though it weren't the first time, that she saw him standing at the edge of the stream awkwardly with the slightest hint of color to his cheeks and neck.

A cry of awareness tore from Riley's throat as her eyes went round with surprise. She flopped around in the water, trying to right herself while hastily covering herself with her arms.

"Roth! What the fuck are you doing?" she demanded when she was finally able to stand on both legs without slipping on a slick stone. Water and fury dripped from her chilled skin. "I'm naked!"

A sardonic brow arched. "Thank you for that observation," he said dryly. "I never would've noticed on my own." But his eyes didn't waver from hers. Even when he blinked, they didn't stray lower for that short beat.

"Why are you lurking while I bathe?" she asked through clenched teeth.

A thought struck her, and the angry tightness in her muscles loosened. "Is she here?" she asked hopeful. "Are we getting off this island?"

Roth's uninjured wing dropped an inch. "No, that's not why I'm here."

"Oh." Riley's shoulders sank, the small seedling of hope drying out before it could grow and bloom. Her brow furrowed in question and her body stiffened again as anger rolled through her once more. "Then why are you lurking?" she repeated.

He crossed his arms over his chest. "Just to be clear, I'm not 'lurking.' I had been here maybe a minute before you finally heard me."

She glared at him, waiting for an explanation for his intrusion.

He sighed heavily and pointed to the sky, as though that were answer enough.

Looking up, she noticed the sun had disappeared behind gray clouds, and in the distance, they grew darker with flickers of light within, sweeping across the expanse at a high velocity.

"Storm's coming," Roth said, drawing her attention back to him. "I found shelter near the cliffs on the other side of the island. It'll be a tight fit with my wings, but it'll work." He gestured behind him. "We need to go now if we want to make it before those clouds reach us."

Riley glanced back at the roiling dark clouds and knew Roth was right. If they wanted to get to shelter in time, they would have to go now. She grimaced at the thought of getting caught in the storm, but her feet remained planted where they were in the water.

"Do you mind?" she said pointedly, raising her brows at him.

Despite the rolling of his eyes and the wry tone of his voice when he said, "I'll go wait over there," the slight color to his cheeks and neck grew brighter, spanning to the points of his ears.

FLASHES OF LIGHTNING lit up the earth, followed by crashing thunder, setting Roth's entire being on edge. Every crack and boom made him want to flinch and jump out of his skin, but he wouldn't—not in front of Riley. He settled for tight muscles and a clenched jaw instead, listening to rain pelt against the outside of their shelter as if it had a vendetta.

The opening at the base of the hill Riley had decided to take her leap of faith from was small, and they had to crawl through it. Once inside, though, the animal den was just large enough to fit them and a small fire Roth had managed to start when the temperature dropped.

Riley's teeth had begun to chatter from the sudden chill, her clothes still damp from having to hastily put them on before she could dry herself. And when the chattering hadn't faded with the heat of the embers, Roth had considered tucking her under his uninjured wing—but one look at her and he knew she was still seething that he saw her without a stitch of clothing on.

Hours after coming upon her, Roth still couldn't shake the image of her floating nude in the stream. And knowing what her hands felt like on him, from when she massaged his thigh, he couldn't get the fantasies out of his mind. He wanted to know how those hands felt wrapped around him, the wet slide of her tongue. But most of all, he wanted to know what she sounded like when she came with him inside her, clenching tight around his—

"Okay," Riley said, bringing him out of the daydream he knew would only make things difficult for him . . . and certain appendages harder than they were already becoming. She sighed heavily. "I've been thinking about this a lot—there's not much else to do in here—and I think the only way to make myself feel better is to make things even."

Roth arched a brow. "And how, exactly, do you plan to do that?" He clenched his jaw tighter, a muscle popping. His voice was huskier than he would've liked, and he hoped she hadn't noticed.

"It's time to show me yours," she said, lifting her chin. "You saw me naked, and now it's time I see you. Tit for tat."

He kept his eyes from flicking to her breasts, but his mind had a better idea. Her bare breasts appeared before him, water lapping at the plush flesh he wanted to sink his teeth into.

Shaking his head, he cleared the image from his thoughts, never hating his vow so fucking much before. But how could he have predicted being alone in a tight space with . . . *her*?

"Oh, come on, Roth." She groaned. "*Tit for tat.*"

He pinched his eyes shut, bringing his thumb and middle finger to them, rubbing. "Please, stop saying that."

"If you strip, I'll stop saying *tit* for *tat*."

"No."

"Tit for tat," Riley said again, her teeth no longer chattering. The rise of her frustration warmed her more than the fire.

Roth shook his head, grinding his teeth. Trying not to let his mind conjure any more naked images of her. She said the words again, and he covered his ears. If she said it one more time, he would start humming to drown her out. Or maybe throw her outside into the storm that sounded just as annoyed with her as he was. Bargain be damned, he couldn't take this much longer.

"I can do this all night, bird," Riley said with all the stubbornness Roth was discovering she possessed, "and by the sound of the storm, we have all night."

He nearly groaned, not needing the reminder. The images his mind was determined to sear into his retinas and his cock hardening at the mention of *tit* over and over again were doing that for him already.

Opening his eyes, Roth looked at her then. Staring her down with an intensity that would've made anyone else shrink from his gaze. But she just put her chin in her hands, rested her elbows on her legs, and never broke eye contact. The corners of her mouth lifted in smug satisfaction when his curled into a grimace at the sight of her *settling in*, as though she were truly prepared to do this all night.

They stared at each other for some time, never uttering a word. This could go on forever, Roth realized, both of them determined to be the victor, and eventually, after what felt like hours, he sighed and looked away.

A squeal of victory came from Riley, her arms shooting in the air, her fists pumping. With gleeful eyes, a smile stretched across her face. "I win!" she declared, her voice as loud as the raging storm outside. She did a small victory dance from where she sat on the other side of the fire, snapping her fingers in time with her torso's movements. It ended with her pointing at him, shouting, "Strip and show me your dick!"

Roth groaned, rolling his eyes. "Let it go, Riley."

"But I won," she said, jabbing a finger in her chest before pointing it back at him. "And now, you have to take off your ridiculously tight leathers and show me the goods you're hiding under there."

"I never agreed to do that."

"It was implied when we started the staring contest."

Face scrunched in annoyance, Roth mumbled under his breath in Scyathan, the language of his people, "*I'm getting too old for this shit.*"

"What was that?" Riley asked, leaning in while cupping her ear.

"Nothing," he grumbled, picking up a stick. He poked at the fire before he could do the same to her with it.

Shadowed light danced across Riley's face, revealing her mouth to be a tight, thin line and brow to be knit in irritation. She shook her head slowly, her teeth chewing on her bottom lip.

"I don't understand what the big deal is. Why won't you just let me see you—" She cut herself off abruptly, sucking in a sharp breath. "Unless," she said, a knowing eyebrow inching higher while an amused smile played on her lips, "it isn't a *big* deal."

Giving her a withering glare, he drawled, "I think from my 'ridiculously tight leathers' you know that's not true."

Despite actively trying to keep her eyes on his face, they dropped to the clear outline of his hard length, widened, then found his eyes again. Her cheeks flushed pink in the flickering light, and smug satisfaction washed over him.

It was about fucking time she felt a hint of what she'd made him feel since they'd arrived on this hellsforsaken island.

"I don't know, Roth," she said, slow and thick. But there was a spark of mischief in her hazel eyes, as though she sensed he liked seeing her flustered for once and was determined to throw it back at him, hard. "How am I supposed to believe you when you won't show me? Trust goes both ways, remember?"

Roth stared, surprise washing over him from having his words used against himself. "I walked right into that one, didn't I?"

The amused smile that had played on her lips stretched wide when a bolt of lightning struck the earth too close for comfort.

They jumped from the sudden deafening boom; the animal den shook all around them, dirt sprinkling on top of their heads.

With his pounding heart in his throat, Roth clenched his hands into fists, digging them into his lap. Trying to keep his body from shaking as the overwhelming smell of burnt flesh stung his nostrils. He squeezed his eyes shut, hoping that would help keep the nightmare away.

But behind his closed eyelids, he saw the flashes of light above him as rain fell from the heavens into his eyes. Sharp, jagged stone dug into his back and wings, but he couldn't feel it. All he felt was a numb, tingling sensation dancing over him. But he knew what horrendous pain would follow.

His breathing quickened inside the animal den as another whip of lightning struck nearby. The winds picked up the pace, and he could just make out the crashing of a tree.

He waited and waited for the paralyzing agony to take hold of him again, but . . . all he felt was warmth seeping into his side. And he knew it was her. That the soothing heat washing over him, calming the chaos stirring within him, came from her presence beside him.

Slowly, Roth opened his eyes. Across from him, the spot on the other side of the fire was empty. He'd never heard her shuffle to where she sat now, her legs scrunched so she could fit in the small space beside him.

Bit by bit, air filled his lungs again and his heart slowed to as calm a pace as it could handle with the storm outside.

She didn't say anything, didn't touch him as she sat beside him. She closed her eyes and took a deep breath, her chest rising. She held it for one beat, two. After five, she released her breath in a slow stream. Without looking at him, she repeated, taking another deep inhale, but this time he mimicked her, inhaling and exhaling when she did.

They remained that way through the night, watching the fire flicker and listening to the wood pop. Letting their heartbeats sync in a harmonious rhythm while the hells raged and sought to destroy everything around them.

CHAPTER 14

Riley decided no one was coming for them. That the selkie had become distracted and never delivered her message or, more likely, Mara's selfishness had cost them their chance of ever being rescued.

A little over a month had passed since Grimsley had attacked, and they were still stuck on Devil's Paradise—a name given to the island after Riley had hallucinated the devil himself, reveling in the heat while drinking margaritas with his toes in the sand. But it wasn't until after she'd tried to tackle him for his margarita that she'd realized it was all in her head.

Sitting on the beach, Riley watched the waves, as she'd been doing after that night in the animal den, while Roth was off doing whatever he did every day. He was always gone from the time she awoke to when she would rest for the night, leaving her to do nothing but stare at the water, alone with her thoughts. And if she wasn't careful, she could wander into a pit of despair, something becoming more difficult to avoid the longer she was on the island without any distractions.

Sighing, she stood from her usual spot and began to run. She *loathed* running, but if the distraction wasn't going to come to her, then she would have to go to it—she just had to find him first. And although hard to admit to herself, she missed the bird's presence. Or anyone's, for that matter.

But she remembered the struggle not to place her head on his shoulder while the tropical storm had threatened to wash them away. She had wanted comfort as much as he had needed it.

Making it to the other side of Devil's Paradise, she stopped in her tracks. There, on the beach, she finally discovered where Roth went every day and why.

"Are you doing *yoga*?" Riley asked incredulously, her breathing heavy.

Roth glanced at her. His feet were bare, but his leathers remained on, even under the sweltering sun.

The weather hadn't cooled once during their time there. The humidity had spiked the week before, and Riley was feeling the effects of it in full force.

With some difficulty, she had used the sword to cut away the long sleeves of her sweat-stained shirt and the legs of her ripped pants, the latter barely hiding her ass now. One of her shirt sleeves was used to keep her thick, frizzy hair from her face, wrapping around her hairline. And every inch of bare skin was the shade of a lobster. Blisters morphed on her shoulders and the sunburnt flesh peeled and flaked. Every time she moved, it hurt tremendously.

With her bright red skin, frizzy hair, torn clothes, and boots, she looked ridiculous—while Roth remained flawless.

Unaffected by the weather or the sun, Roth was a deeper shade of bronze and his hair was as pristine as the day they'd met. Still, not one freckle dotted his nose and cheeks. There wasn't even a sheen of sweat on his brow, whereas Riley was drowning in her own.

She smelled like a Calydonian boar; he smelled like wet earth. She was burning to a crisp; he was realm-shattering, sky-splintering, wish-upon-a-shooting-star beautiful.

It was not fair.

"What's yoga?" Roth asked, shifting into a new pose.

"What you're doing," Riley answered. She wiped sweat from her brow.

"No, this is my meditation routine."

"And your routine is yoga."

"I don't know what *yoga* is, but I'm not doing it."

"You're literally doing the second warrior pose." He arched a brow in disbelief, and she crossed her arms over her chest stubbornly. "It's okay to admit I'm right. I am occasionally." He didn't budge. "My mom loved yoga, Roth. I learned a little of what you're doing from watching her."

Riley inhaled a shaky breath. Her heart threatened to shatter—stone or no stone—at the mention of her mother. She hadn't thought about her or her father in three years. Forced herself not to in an attempt to save herself from the pain. But when she'd seen how scared Roth had been from the lightning, it had reminded her of the times when she would climb into her parents' bed while it had stormed during the night, her brother, Liam, already there or soon to follow.

It had been over a decade since she'd seen her family—and would never see them again—but she could still picture them. It blurred as the years wore on, but the feeling of safety and comfort never vanished when she pictured them.

Riley blinked back tears, and Roth was no longer in the second warrior pose. He stood, watching her with gentle eyes. As if those eyes read everything she was feeling. Thinking. From what he'd told her before, he probably could see everything through them.

"How old were you when you were taken?" he asked gently.

Breathing became difficult. No one ever said *taken*. They asked when she was *brought* here. But she wasn't brought here. It hadn't been her idea to jump on a ship and travel through a magic portal to another world, away from her family.

No, she'd been taken.

Stolen.

"Nine," she answered roughly.

His mouth became a tight, thin line and his hands balled into fists at his sides. They clenched, unclenched. "I'm sorry you had to go through it, especially at a young age. And I know it must be even harder with the difference in how time passes between here and there."

She snorted. That was an understatement. After nearly nine years of finding her way back to her world, she had found out her entire family

—father, mother, brother—were all gone. Dead. Passed away after living a long life without her. "It's too bad I had to find that out three years ago. I didn't take the discovery too well."

Almost imperceptibly, his eyes flicked to her forearms before darting back up. The tight, thin line of his mouth dipped down. He opened it, as if he were about to say something, but thought better of it, closing his eyes momentarily, shaking the thought from his head.

Silence stretched between them, and Riley considered going back to her side of the island, leaving him to do yoga in private. As he had apparently been doing for the past two weeks. She assumed it was because he thought she would tease him about it—and he was absolutely right; she would find any and every way possible to tease him with this.

Later.

Right now, all she wanted was to keep watching him stretch his muscles and show off his thighs some more.

The corner of Roth's mouth lifted. "Or you could meditate with me. It's not *yoga*," he added before she corrected him again. She considered doing it anyway, but if she did, they would be going back and forth all day. They were both too godsdamned stubborn to quit.

Riley rolled her eyes as she considered his offer. She sighed through her nose; it was better than running.

"Show me what to do, stubborn bird."

———

"YOU'RE PUTTING TOO much pressure on your hips," Roth said, his hands on his own. The sun shined on his wrapped wing, revealing the true color.

Riley clicked her tongue. "My hips are fine."

They were not fine, and she wobbled, balancing on one leg in tree pose—a name Roth refused to call it.

She had asked him, when he'd taken up his first pose, where he'd learned yoga. While glaring at her, he'd explained it had been passed down through generations of ailerons. When it started or where it came from was unknown. After she'd broken the news to him his "meditation" had come from her world, he'd just rolled his eyes and shifted into downward facing dog, causing Riley to immediately forget what they were talking about.

"This one," Roth said now, placing a hand on her left hip, "is jutting out. That isn't correct." He applied pressure, making her inner thigh press against her right foot resting against it. "It should be square with the rest of your body like this."

All of Riley's nerve endings zoned in on that hand. She felt the same static shock she had when he'd caught her from being trampled. Her skin tingled and warmed, and that godsdamned pulsing ache between her thighs was back.

His eyes found hers and his pupils dilated. Feeling his fingers dig in ever so slightly, she tried to arch into him, but his hand grounded her there. Her lips parted and breaths quickened. The gold flashed in his eyes as they flicked to her parted lips—

Roth's hand disappeared. He cleared his throat. "Hold that position for five breaths and then switch to the other side." Riley counted her breaths, never taking her eyes off him. Once she reached five, she switched to the other side, making sure her hip was in line with the rest of her body. "Good," he said, "that's much better."

Riley counted her five breaths again. "What's next?" Her voice had noticeably dropped an octave.

Roth's hands clenched and unclenched at his sides. "Let me show you." His voice was low, rumbly, and it did nothing to make the ache between Riley's legs go away. Beside her, he took up the same pose as her and shifted slowly into the next. His bent leg stretched back as he clasped his fingers together, his forefingers pointing straight, while he bent forward, bringing his back in line with his outstretched leg.

Riley watched before duplicating the third warrior pose. But instead of counting her breaths, her eyes roved over him, admiring the strength and balance he held standing on the one leg. His leathers showed every curve of muscle and just how thick his thigh was. Her hands felt an invisible firmness as they were clasped together, beginning to dampen. Her cheeks flushed from a memory trapped in fog. Her eyes drifted to the curve of his ass, partially hidden by his wing. She leaned forward slightly on her toes to get a better view—

Riley gasped, her eyes widening.

The world tilted on its axis, and she tipped forward into the sand next to Roth. Her jaw smacked against a stone and pain lanced through her. She spat grains of sand from her mouth as he towered over her. His hands were on his hips again. He shook his head.

"Someone needs to work on their balance," he said, lips twitching in amusement.

She wiped sand from her face. "My balance is fine. It's not my fault someone has a distracting ass." Her lips pinched shut as she blushed.

That was not meant to come out.

Slowly, his mouth curved up into a smug grin. "Did you just call my ass 'distracting'?"

The blush on her cheeks spread to her neck and chest, and she reacted without thought: her leg swept across the sand and knocked into his ankles. He fell on his left side, facing her. He grunted on impact.

"Was that really necessary?" Roth groaned.

"Right now, in this moment—yes, it was. Later, I don't know."

"You could have done more damage to my wing if I landed on it."

She cringed. "Sorry."

Roth sat up, sighing. "I guess meditation—"

"Yoga."

"—wasn't going well, anyway."

Riley sat up next to him and shrugged. "It was better than staring at the water like I've been doing," she said, tacking on, "Gods, and running. I hate running."

"If you hate running, then why were you?"

Unable to admit she'd craved his company, she said instead, "I needed to do something to get rid of all the energy."

He hummed, understanding. "Without being able to fly, it's as if, no matter how much I stretch my limbs, there's this incessant thrumming. It's been happening for a long time, even when I could fly, but lately—"

He blew out a breath, dragging a hand down his face. "Fucking hells, it's as powerful as an encroaching violent storm, and I'm just waiting for it to consume me." He stared at the sand for a beat, his hand in his hair, before clearing his throat, adding quickly, "Or something."

He loosened his fingers from his curls. "It's why I meditate." He placed a finger to her lips just as she was about to correct him. "Don't."

She smiled beneath his finger, and when he removed it, it didn't go back to his side as she thought it would. It hovered for what felt like the longest second of her life before his knuckle dragged along her jaw, over a small forming bruise. The touch was whisper soft. Painless. Her breaths became uneven as she watched his eyes follow that knuckle.

Gods, I wish it were his mouth, she thought. His tongue. His teeth. She would even settle for the tip of his nose.

Roth's throat bobbed, and she knew he saw everything she wanted through her eyes. His own had turned dark and hungry.

The knuckle traveled from her jaw down her neck, then it was replaced with the tips of his fingers. He reached the curve between neck and shoulder and dipped. The pads of his fingers traced her collarbone over her shirt and followed it back to the center before tracing the other side.

Her mind grew thick with fog, and all that was known to her were the soft touches.

She shivered.

Without any coherent thought, she moved to straddle him. Her hands landed on his chest, and her thumbs brushed over the soft leather he wore.

His hand went from her collarbone to her calf and lightly drew tiny circles on the tender, burnt flesh. The sensation made her skin tingle where a pulsating need was building. It would only take a shifting of fabric, the slide of a finger down her center, for him to know how much she wanted him.

Tentatively, Riley leaned in, waiting to see if he would lean away, and when he didn't, her lips brushed featherlight against his. She kept her eyes open, as did he, searching for a sign if this was all right. That she wasn't misinterpreting the buildup to this moment. But he didn't balk from her, didn't push her away, and she deepened the kiss. Her eyelids fluttered shut as he kissed her back tenderly and felt his lashes tickle against her skin as his eyelids closed.

Heat pooled and spread, all the way from the tips of her fingers finding their way into his soft, silky hair to her toes curling in her boots. It dove deep, deep, deep within her. Past the feelings chipping away at the stone guarding her glass heart and finding the slithering shadows roaming a barren field at the edge of a chasm, where monsters with fangs and sharp claws dwelled below.

The shadows converged on the warmth—the trespasser—and when they collided, the shadows jumped back, screeching and yelping. They were no match for the heat, the unwelcome guest.

They circled, waiting. Biding their time until the warmth vanished so they could reclaim their home.

Riley hummed against Roth's lips, wanting more.

His hands went to her wrists, traveled up her arms, and she shivered. His gentle, calloused, and warm hands found her shoulders and—

—there was pressure against her shoulders. Light at first, becoming heavier, more forceful.

They broke apart.

Riley's eyes snapped open. Roth leaned away from her, his mouth a tight, thin line. His body was stiff, rigid beneath her as he reached up, gripped her wrists, and removed her hands from his hair. He placed her arms at her sides gently.

"I can't do this," he said roughly. The want in his voice contradicted his words.

Unless . . .

Oh, gods, he didn't feel the same spark I did, Riley realized, mortified. Her stomach dropped and her body became impossibly warm—the kind of warmth that made her cold while she sweated profusely. *He doesn't want me.*

"I'm sorry," Riley whispered, even as a small, bitter voice in her head asked: *Why are you sorry? He's the one who pulled away. He's the one making you feel stupid and ashamed. You have nothing to be sorry for.*

She told herself to move, to get up, but was frozen, still straddling him. In his eyes, there was an emotion growing there.

Oh, gods, is that disgust?

She waited for him to move her himself, but he never did. As if, he, too, were frozen.

His mouth parted but nothing came out. Not one sound.

"Do you two need some more alone time?" a light feminine voice asked. "Or would you like to leave this island first?"

Riley and Roth blinked, turned their heads in unison.

The faerie with warm brown skin and monarch butterfly wings—the one Mara and Jasper couldn't tear their eyes away from—leaned against a small rowboat on the shore. Her arms, defined from hard work, were crossed over her sleeveless golden shirt, and a smirk had settled on her triangular face.

Aurora had gotten Riley's message after all.

Behind Aurora, in the distance, a large ship was anchored offshore. The *Mariposa* was the grandest ship known to the residents of Obsidian Island and Erithena, and it was paid for legally—something no other faerie on Obsidian Island could say themselves without it being a lie.

Aurora was more businesswoman than pirate, importing and exporting goods for the lords and ladies of Avernii, earning a sizable amount in payment. But overall, she was an admirable faerie, and one who had respected Riley and shown her kindness from the moment they'd met over two years ago.

Riley had considered Aurora would make an exceptional privateer for the High Crown—or any royal as open-minded as King Jorah of Avernii—but with the laws enacting arrests and executions on pirates, she didn't think privateer would work out for her after all.

The instant Aurora's words sank in, Riley bolted from Roth's lap. She walked briskly to the rowboat, mumbling her thanks to Aurora.

"You look like shit," Aurora said. She pinched her nose shut. "And smell like it, too."

Riley's cheeks heated further. *Oh, gods, that's right,* she thought. *Why did I kiss him before having a chance to bathe?*

Another, more logical voice in her head answered: *Because you didn't know Aurora was coming. You were bored and alone and in need of a distraction from your thoughts. His rejection is nothing to be embarrassed about. It would have meant* nothing.

She nodded to herself. "Nothing," she muttered under her breath, trying to convince herself. "It would have meant nothing." But it did little to vanquish the stark embarrassment she was feeling.

"What was that?" Aurora asked. "What's nothing?"

Riley stood ramrod straight. "What?" Her eyes flicked to Roth quickly and she saw the concern on his face, just as quickly looking away. "Nothing," she said to Aurora, her voice pitched an octave too high.

"I know. That's what I'm asking you." A brow arched high over the eye patch covering Aurora's right eye. It nearly reached the rim of her black tricorn hat with white and turquoise feathers sticking out of the back; it was failing miserably at taming her dark brown, coiled hair. "What's nothing?"

"Nothing."

It was the only word Riley knew at the moment.

She climbed into the rowboat and sat down. She didn't look at Roth as he rose to his feet, snatched up his boots, and sat next to her. The feathers of his unbandaged wing brushed against her arm, tickling her skin. There was a question in the touch. *Are you all right?* it seemed to ask.

Feeling his eyes on her, Riley refused to look at him as she fought a shiver. Her embarrassment was climbing every second, and she didn't need it to overtake her completely.

But even as Aurora climbed in the boat after them, rowed them to the *Mariposa*, and the cool breeze sent a chill down Riley's spine, the warmth remained deep within her. It swirled and swirled, kicking up dust from the barren land. Inside the circle of warmth, grass grew, and at the center, a bud poked through the earth.

CHAPTER 15

After days at sea and healing Roth's wing and Riley's sunburn, Aurora dropped them off on Obsidian Island instead of the port in Wyne. She insisted she was on a schedule, and getting them off Devil's Paradise had taken up enough of her time. Riley thought it best not to tell Aurora she was also on a schedule—determined to find Lothaire's treasure before Grimsley—and instead thanked her for her help. If it hadn't been for her, Riley would still be stuck on Devil's Paradise with the one person she did not want to see.

Thankfully, Riley couldn't see Roth at the moment. She stood in the dark, damp cave of the mountain made up of the dragon's horn and felt, rather than saw, the aileron hovering behind her. She could feel his eyes on her and, even in the dark, knew his arms were crossed as he waited for her to do something.

But she couldn't do anything because she couldn't *see* anything.

She had been in this cave hundreds of times, but Mara had always lit the oil lamps for her, knowing her human eyes couldn't penetrate the dark as faerie eyes could.

With her hands outstretched, Riley stumbled forward, searching for the lamps. She bumped into something hard and stubbed her toes.

Her hips hit a hard edge, and she heard shattering as something fragile tipped over.

"Fuck," she muttered, exasperated.

Roth sighed, and Riley heard footsteps coming up behind her. Inhaling sharply, her eyes widened as she felt the hardness of his body against her. He reached around her to light the oil lamp on the table her hips rested against. His breath brushed against the top of her head as light flickered to life in front of her, displaying the pieces of a broken wine glass splayed over photographs her and Mara took with a camera they'd found in the mortal world.

Just as quickly as it had pressed against her, Roth's body was gone, striding from lamp to lamp, making them come to life around the cave Mara had found and claimed as her treasure trove.

The cave was small and couldn't fit the entire Roaring Tigers crew —until now—and it didn't house what faeries would claim as treasure. Trinkets from the mortal world littered wooden tables and the cave floor. A cabinet held liquor with a bong Mara had stolen resting atop it. Books were piled high on tables, chairs, and the ground—any space large enough to fit one. Riley had put it there knowing she would one day be buried alive beneath the lot of them. Within the piles was Jasper's growing collection of graphic novels. Riley had read through a few of them and decided they were reading material she could appreciate, the handsome male characters with thick thighs being the cause.

Roth observed all of it with curious eyes as he glimpsed into another world—Riley's.

She watched as he picked up one of her books from a table where it had been left open where she'd left off. She narrowed her eyes, trying to remember what she had been reading last, and upon seeing the cover, the color drained from her face.

THE BOOK WAS FILTHY. Roth's eyes moved along the words of the page, reading about a couple pleasuring one another inside a bath that wasn't a bath. They stood and the water flowed freely from above, running down their bare skin. It didn't make any sense, but he continued on, even as he saw a flash of movement in his peripheral.

Riley lunged at him, and he easily lifted the book out of reach of the jumping, snarling human.

Turning the page, Roth read: *He came with me, releasing into my hand, against my ass. Our cries were cut off by his hand still covering my mouth and his face buried in the crook of my neck.*

Filthy indeed.

Slowly, Roth turned his head down to Riley with raised brows and a wickedly delighted smile. "This is what you read?"

She bared her teeth. "Give. Me. Back. My. Book," she spat, holding out a hand.

He shook his head. "I'm never letting this go. It sounds so very interesting and *stimulating*." He grinned at her, waiting for her to snarl at him some more, but it never came.

Silently, Riley turned to gather a bag—but not before Roth saw the look on her face. Saw it turn a shade of red in anger or embarrassment, maybe both.

Roth closed the book, setting it back down on the table where he'd found it.

He observed the rest of the cave.

There were tiny-paintings-that-weren't-paintings scattered on the table. They weren't canvas but a type of parchment, the top glossy. They didn't take up the entirety of the space, but rather a square, leaving a thin white border around it, except for the bottom where it was thicker. In the center of most of them were lifelike images of Riley and Mara. Roth had never seen anything like them and didn't understand any of it.

Picking up one, Roth peered at a series of small images stacked on top of each other. The background was all of the same gray curtain, each image of Riley and Mara in a small, enclosed space. At the top, Riley and Mara grinned, their arms wrapped around each other with their cheeks pressing together. In the middle one, Riley's eyes were crossed with her tongue sticking out of the side of her mouth, while Mara bared her teeth, holding up only her middle finger. On the bottom, Riley's head was thrown back, eyes pinched shut in hysterical laughter, as Mara stood bent over with her bare ass front and center, a shameless grin on her face peeking over her shoulder.

Roth chuckled quietly to himself.

He picked up another book from a chair, this one much thinner. Opening it, he found it was not like any he had ever seen, filled with drawings and very little dialogue.

A flutter caught his eye.

Clenching his jaw, Roth stared at the tiny-painting-that-wasn't-a-painting. Lounging in a bed was the merman—*Jasper*—who had made a show of thoroughly kissing Riley for anyone to watch. As if fucking her in an alley, for any passersby to see, hadn't been enough.

Acid slid down Roth's throat as the merman stared back at him, smirking, with an arm around a sleeping Riley. They were both naked, and Riley was pressed tight against Jasper's side, nearly lying on top of him.

Roth couldn't stop the jealousy sparking and crackling through him, even though deep down, he knew it was unfair. He had been the one who'd stopped him and Riley from going any further, and after he'd seen the hurt and embarrassment on her face, his insides wouldn't stop twisting.

It was clear she'd enjoyed the kiss just as much as he had, but he'd had to stop. A vow had been made, and he intended to do his damn best to uphold it—no matter how much he wanted to hoist her over his shoulder, take her to bed, and let her give him as many *love nibbles* as she wanted.

He wanted more than that, though; he wouldn't be satisfied until he discovered the taste of her. The feel of her as he moved inside her. And even then, he didn't know if that would be enough—if *once* would be enough.

Nothing can happen between you.

Roth pushed the intrusive thought away, even as he knew it was right.

Glancing over his shoulder, Roth saw Riley crouching in front of a trunk, her shortened pants riding up and exposing her further. It wasn't hard for him to imagine what it would be like to sink his fingers into her plump flesh from behind, to slap her ass.

The parchment with an image of Riley and Jasper crumpled in his clenched fist. He swallowed, his throat suddenly parched.

In Scyathan, Roth muttered, *"I'm so fucked."*

CHAPTER 16

R iley listened to Roth going through her things behind her as his words replayed in her mind on a loop: *"I'm never letting this go. It sounds so very interesting and stimulating."*

She could throttle the godsdamned bird.

She was still mortified at the memory of what had happened between them on Devil's Paradise and hadn't said much to him since. He'd tried speaking to her on the ship, but she hadn't been ready to face him yet. She'd locked herself in a spare cabin, not leaving until they'd docked on Obsidian Island—all the while, she'd tossed and turned on her cot until she'd screamed into a pillow.

A flash of light and Roth's snarl filled the cave while Riley rummaged around for the flashlight she had taken from her world. She glanced over her shoulder. Roth covered his face with one hand and the other held a camera outstretched before him.

Riley snatched the camera away from him. "What are you doing?" she demanded. "Stop messing with my stuff."

"What the fuck is *that*? It tried to blind me."

"It's a camera," she said, rolling her eyes. "It does that." She pulled out the picture sticking out from the front and waved it through the air.

"Why would you keep that *thing* around?" Roth asked, blinking rapidly.

Stilling her hand, Riley watched as an image came to life on the blank, glossy paper. She clamped a hand over her mouth, her shoulders shaking with laughter. An image of Roth with his eyes half-closed and the start of his snarl with his lip curling back appeared before her. "This," she said, holding up the picture, "is why I keep that thing around." She handed Roth the picture.

Brows furrowed, Roth pointed to the image of himself. "How did you do this?"

"I didn't do that. You took a picture of yourself all on your own."

Roth peered at her above the photograph, brows bunched so tight it had to hurt. His mouth formed a tight, thin line as he flipped the picture over, seeing nothing on the back, and flipped it over again.

Roth was so confused, and Riley was enjoying every second of it.

He waited for her to explain what the camera was, but her eyes focused on the table behind him. On the crumpled picture. She reached around him, smoothing out the wrinkles, and looked at herself in bed with Jasper.

When did he take this? she wondered.

Riley glanced at Roth and saw a muscle tick in his jaw.

"Did you crumple this up?"

Roth's wings twitched, the only sign he did crumple the photograph.

"Unbelievable," she muttered, shoving the camera into his chest, and searched the remnants of the cave for clothes to replace her ruined ones she still wore from Devil's Paradise.

He caught the camera easily before it could smash into pieces on the cave floor. "What?" he asked innocently, brows raised.

Finding a semi-clean outfit, Riley turned her back on Roth and stripped from her tattered clothing. There was a sharp inhale behind her and the scuffing of boots as he turned around to give her privacy. She nearly snorted. It wasn't like he hadn't seen everything already.

She shoved on the leggings she'd found and slid her arms through the shirt's sleeves and over her head. "You can't reject me, Roth, and then act jealous when you see a picture of me lying naked with another man.

"I'm done changing," she said while her eyes shot daggers into his back.

Roth tensed, as though he felt the imaginary blades sinking into his flesh, before facing her.

"You're wrong," he said matter-of-factly, but his wings were tucked in tight. As if they braced against what was to come next. "That's not why I stopped us from going further."

She scoffed, rolling her eyes. "Sure, whatever you say." She pulled on black, fingerless gloves from the mortal world that went to her elbows to hide the tiger on her arm a tad too aggressively. "I'll just forget about the disgust I saw."

Frowning, he drew his eyebrows together.

"But I get it," she barreled on. "I would've been disgusted with me, too. I smelled terrible, looked horrible. I can't even imagine what my breath must have been like. I can see why someone like you—someone who doesn't have one single, godsdamned flaw—wouldn't want to be with someone like me. Someone riddled with them—human."

The following silence was palpable. A living, breathing creature. One that sucked all the oxygen from the cave.

Slowly, Roth took deliberate steps; he didn't stop until they stood nose to nose. He took her chin gently and tilted her head back, making her look him in the eye. "Listen closely because I'm only going to say this once—I have never, nor will I ever, have a problem with your humanity, Riley." His voice was steady, confident, but as tender and gentle as a caress. He spoke only truth.

"You think you're the only one with flaws?" He shook his head. "I have made my fair share of mistakes over the past four centuries"—her eyes widened—"and those I cared about paid with their lives and freedom because of them."

Riley's breaths became shallow. If it wasn't her humanity, then— "What was it about me?" she asked quietly.

"Nothing," he answered. "There is nothing wrong with you. I wasn't disgusted with *you*, but *myself*. If things were different, you can trust me when I tell you that I want to have my way with you on that table over there." He pointed to the one behind him with the crumpled picture of her and Jasper.

She inhaled sharply. The image of her legs on either side of him as he stood over her, thrusting into her, flashed in her mind. Her thighs squeezed together.

With his jaw clenched, no doubt seeing what she wanted, Roth ground out, "But I made a vow, and being with you would've broken it."

"What vow?" she rasped, her throat suddenly dry.

"One of abstinence I took long ago."

Her mouth fell open. She gaped at him long enough for him to clear his throat.

"You're abstinent?"

"Yes."

"*Why?*" she blurted, and regret immediately followed. "I'm sorry," she quickly added. "You don't need to answer that." She resisted the urge to bury her face in her hands.

"It's all right. You're not the first woman to ask, and I doubt you'll be the last."

Riley had felt jealousy before. Every time Jasper's eyes had wandered to another woman or man, she'd felt it eating away at her. But she'd never thought she'd feel it burn through her as quickly as it just had.

What made Roth so different from Jasper?

"And you shouldn't be the one apologizing," Roth said. "You didn't know about my vow, and I had plenty of opportunities to tell you—fucking hells, you gave me time to stop the kiss before it began, but I didn't. I wanted to kiss you, so I let it happen. I should've been more considerate of your feelings. I'm so sorry, Riley."

There was her answer.

Jasper never apologized for anything, including the others she knew he was fucking. And he never tried to hide it because he didn't have to. They weren't together in the way she wanted them to be.

The corners of her mouth curved down slightly. Why did she want to be with him again?

"Riley?"

She flinched, her eyes snapping back into focus.

"Are you okay?" Roth asked gently.

Too quickly, she nodded her head. "I'm fine." But she didn't sound fine as the words squeaked out of her.

He took a step toward her, and simultaneously, she took a step back, needing to keep some distance between them. Inwardly, she cursed her eyes, knowing he could probably see all she was trying not to feel.

She had to change the subject. There was a tightness squeezing inside her chest, and she didn't want to find out what would happen if it squeezed too tight.

"So, four centuries, huh?" She threw the question out as if it were the only thing that could keep her afloat.

Roth arched a brow, and in that one gesture, she knew he was aware of what she was doing.

She held her breath, waiting.

He cocked his head. "Of course, that's what stuck out to you," he said after a moment.

All the air rushed back into the cave, and Riley could breathe again.

Thank you, she told him through her eyes.

Her lips twitched with a ghost of a smile. "Four hundred years." She whistled. "That's old. I have to admit, though, your skin is flawless. Tell me, what is your secret, old bird?"

Rolling his eyes, Roth groaned, straightening. "You're going to make this a thing, aren't you?"

"Yes. Yes, I am."

"Fucking lovely," he drawled, grabbing her discarded boots and handing them to her. "I'm really going to enjoy our time together."

"I know."

He gave her a withering glare, and she grinned.

Riley put one boot on, losing her balance momentarily, and Roth steadied her before she could fall. "Thanks," she said. She put her other boot on, still using Roth to steady her.

"So, what's next on the to-do list?" he asked after she was standing on two feet, her boots back on.

"Look, Roth," she began, the corners of her mouth dipping, "I don't think we should—"

Roth lifted a hand, stopping her. "Before you go any further," he said, "my answer is no. I know you've been wary of me accompanying you to Wyne to look for the treasure, and I know my vow might make going our separate ways seem like an even better idea, but it's not going to happen."

"It's not?"

"No, it's not. If we find the treasure, you can have it all to yourself. I don't care about it."

"You don't?" She eyed him skeptically as he shook his head. "Then, why go with me?"

"I have my reasons," was all he said, shrugging, not bothering to elaborate.

Her skepticism broached wariness as he picked up Riley's bag, slinging it over his shoulder.

"What's next?" he asked again.

It was a moment before Riley answered, turning over the possibilities of why he wouldn't answer her question. And while she eventually believed him when he said he didn't care about the treasure, the only plausible reason she could think of was the loyalty bred into him. That just as he wouldn't run from the fight with Grimsley, he wouldn't leave her alone to find the one thing that could bring Mara and the others back.

Sighing heavily, she finally told him, "Weapons and a ship."

Roth nodded, hands on his hips. "Okay, easy enough." Riley cringed, and Roth's shoulders slumped, his wings dropping an inch. "Not easy?"

"The weapons we'll have to get from the blacksmith and hope he's willing to trade for them."

"And the ship?"

Riley chewed on her lower lip. "That's where things get tricky. We'll have to steal one."

Getting a ship was going to be one hell of a risk, and it would mean she could never show her face on Obsidian Island again without someone trying to kill her—not that it would make her life much different from now. No one stole a ship from another pirate. The only way to lose one was through a game of cards, and even then, the pirate stupid enough to bet their ship would have to be shit-faced drunk. And if Riley could somehow manage to find someone shit-faced drunk enough to bet their ship, she didn't have the time it would take.

"Asking for one would be too easy?" Roth joked, a smile playing at the corners of his lips.

Riley snort-laughed. "No. Everyone knows Mara, and they know a human is on her crew. They would attack first, talk later."

Her stomach dropped. *Fuck, what am I thinking?* she asked herself. *Maybe I should forget about this bullshit plan and go back to Devil's Paradise. How many dirty books can I fit inside my bag?*

Roth straightened, his wings tucking in tight again. "Anyone lays a hand on you and they will wish for a swift death—I promise you that." His voice was dangerously low and his face stark with the violence he'd spoken of. It was intimidating. Anyone who dared challenge him would be a fool.

Riley felt some of her building stress melt away, but she still considered packing a book or two . . . or ten. All of them would be an excessive amount to try to carry. *Can I fit a small one in my boot?* She pondered how many filthy books were too many as a smirk spread across Roth's face. *Can he see my thoughts through my eyes again?*

"Yes," Roth said, and her cheeks pinked.

He set down Riley's bag in front of her. "Pack the books you want to take," he said, snagging the one he'd read from earlier and dropping it on top. "If you know what to trade for weapons, I'll take it to the blacksmith. Meet me at the docks when you're ready."

"Do you have a plan?" Riley asked, shoving the book on top of her bag inside. She ignored the smirk he gave her and searched her stacks, deciding which ones to take.

"No," he answered, shrugging. "I'm making it up as I go."

The corners of her lips twitched. "I guess you could say you're *winging* it."

Rolling his eyes, Roth groaned while Riley laughed at her own joke. He turned around and began walking out of the cave, but in the reflection of the mirror propped on a nearby table, she saw his small smile.

CHAPTER 17

Riley listened to the seagulls circling overhead in the afternoon sun and the dinging of a bell signaling the end of tryouts.

Ships large and small, wide and thin, bobbed and rocked in the water. She looked for one capable of being manned by two people and getting her to Wyne in a timely manner. It was a tricky task finding the perfect one amongst hundreds of pirates all ready to kill her if they saw her looking at their ships.

Across the mud-laden street, the physician moved from one patient to another, his long black beak almost puncturing his patient's sternum as he observed a nasty gash. The physician's stand was busy, as it was every day of the week, but today was another tryouts day, gaining extra patients to treat. By how many filled the beds, how many waited in line —those who could—it was a day with few deaths. The cart behind the stall with few corpses proved as much.

Riley groaned and dropped her bag, resting it between her feet. She rubbed the crook between her neck and shoulder, wondering why she'd packed as much as she had—books included.

I should make Roth carry that thing around, Riley thought. *It could be payment for letting him come along.*

She couldn't help but feel Roth thought he had to look after her.

Babysit her. After he'd saved her from being trampled, drowned, and jumping to her death, all in the span of a month, she didn't blame him for that—but the thought cut deep. As if she weren't capable of doing this on her own.

Her chin rose slightly. "I can do this," she told herself. "I don't need a stubborn, old bird to look after me."

Leaning against a cart filled with hay, Riley set her sights on the lone skiff nestled between two large ships in the middle of all the hustle. "Why can't one thing be easy?" she mumbled.

She scanned the area, looking for any semblance of a plan to strike a full-fledged idea. She chewed on her lower lip. *How can I steal that skiff without getting caught and prove to Roth I don't need his help?* she wondered.

Riley shook her head.

Who was she kidding? She couldn't do this. She couldn't steal the skiff without getting noticed. Not even Roth could—

There was a sharp pinch on the side of her neck. Assuming it was a mosquito taking a large bite out of her, she brought her hand to the spot—but she didn't find a mosquito. A long, thin object protruded. She tried pulling it free, but whatever it was came out with difficulty; it pulled on her skin until it popped out—

Pinched between her fingers was a porcupine quill.

Riley's brows scrunched; her eyes narrowed—

Her vision blurred and she shook her head, trying to clear the fog closing in fast. She teetered to the side and threw out a hand, but found only air. The side of her face splashed with mud as she collided with the ground—she was lucky her head didn't hit the cart on the way down.

A shadow loomed over her, blocking out the halo of the sun—but the shadow had moss-green skin and its right hand was missing the last two fingers.

"Shit," Riley rasped, her throat suddenly dry. She should have killed him when she'd had the chance. Had known sparing his life would only make him want her more.

"Shit is right, sweetmeat." Brock's remaining sharp teeth gleamed in a smug smile, stretching the remaining splotches of yellow-tinted bruises. "You owe me a dance."

CHAPTER 18

Roth walked out of the blacksmith's shop with a dagger strapped to his thigh; it was the only weapon he could trade for Riley's trinkets from the mortal world, and it was hard enough to get the dwarf to trade for the dagger.

There was only one item the dwarf had been interested in—Roth's armored leathers. But there was no way in fucking hells he was going to part with them. Even after his death, he would make sure whoever stole them from his corpse was cursed for the rest of their life.

So, Roth accepted the dagger—after he tried intimidating the dwarf into giving him more weapons but with no luck—in exchange for the trinkets. He would figure out another way to get weapons, but first, Riley was waiting for him—or she was still determining which books to bring with, as she had been when he'd left the cave.

A smile tugged at the corners of Roth's mouth. He hadn't had the faintest clue what type of books she preferred, and having found out, it delighted him to know he had one piece of information *he* could tease *her* with. Although he hated to admit, her teasing was growing on him. But her red cheeks, after he'd read a passage from one of her books, was a sight he never wanted to forget.

Roth arrived at the docks with a small smile on his face and searched for Riley; he couldn't wait to see how many books she'd managed to stuff into her bag. *I wonder if she can carry it?* he mused to himself.

Walking up and down the docks and back again, Roth's smile slowly vanished. After checking one more time and then the nearby physician's stall, he couldn't find Riley anywhere.

Could she still be at the cave? he wondered.

He turned in a circle, scanning the stalls. His brow narrowed as his mouth curved down. He shook his head. "Something isn't right," he muttered. "She shouldn't be taking this long—"

Roth froze, his face falling slack. Panic settled deep in his soul, stirring.

There, by a cart of hay, was Riley's bag, left in the mud. Forgotten.

The panic spread through his veins, his bones, as he picked up the bag and saw the drag marks. And a . . . *Is that a quill?*

Ignoring the quill, he followed the drag marks, gripping Riley's bag tighter and tighter the farther the marks led him away from the docks and the other pirates. They went down a side path.

Roth looked around. Observed the other pirates going about their business as if nothing had happened. But he knew they'd seen who'd taken Riley—but they didn't care. She was just a human, nothing more than entertainment. It was normal to see one in that predicament. Roth balled his hands into fists, and his jaw ached from clenching it tightly.

"Fucking pirates," he muttered.

But it wasn't only on Obsidian Island that this would happen; it wasn't only pirates who thought nothing more when they witnessed a human being used for entertainment. It was faeries all across Erithena who didn't give a damn what happened to them. Roth's lip curled; if he ground his teeth any harder, he would chip a tooth.

Following the marks to the base of the largest mountain on the island, Roth scanned the hillside, past the trees and brush.

Nothing—Riley was nowhere to be seen.

Roth's heart pounded against his chest; it threatened to break through bone, muscle, and skin. Right through his leathers. "What did you get yourself into, Riley Hayes?"

Fog began to settle in, slithering between trees, curling around

Roth's legs. It grew denser by the second and inhibited his keen eyesight down to mere feet in front of him.

I'll never be able to find her in this fog from here, Roth thought and took to the skies.

"I NEED TO TAKE A BREAK," Cloud said, gripping Riley by the ankles.

Riley had woken up some time ago, finding herself bound at the wrists and dragged by two of Brock's crew members, but she'd never let on. She needed to formulate a plan to get herself out of the situation.

Brock had parted ways with them at the base of the mountain, instructing Cloud, the faerie with dandelion-seed hair from the alley behind the Ivory Pearl, and Spike, the porcupine faerie from the fighting pit, to take Riley up the mountain for gods knew what. Riley had felt a sense of relief when Brock had vanished and she only had these two bumbling idiots to deal with. But the fog had set in, making things more difficult for her—and not just her.

"I can't see shit," Spike said. He sat down in the grass as Cloud rested on a boulder covered in moss. "Where did this fog come from?"

Cloud shrugged her shoulders, dropping Riley's ankles—*they really were idiots*—and stretching her back. "What does Brock plan to do with her anyway?" she asked, gesturing to Riley.

"I thought *you* knew," Spike answered.

Riley was *this close* to slapping her forehead and giving away the element of surprise. Listening to them talk was giving her a headache.

Brock had told her, "*You owe me a dance*," and she assumed he was going to get someone to play an enchanted instrument. The real question was: why were they going into the mountains for this?

Maybe he's going to have me dance right off a cliff, Riley mused to herself.

She cracked an eye open, barely enough for the faeries to notice. She waited for them to turn their backs; that was when she would make her move. She didn't have a weapon, but she wouldn't let that stop her from running. If she got out of this alive, she hoped Roth was able to get weapons from the blacksmith without difficulty.

"Why can't we just kill her?" Spike asked.

"Because Brock said we can't," Cloud answered.

"But Brock isn't here. What if she had an accident? With the fog, we could make it happen."

The silence from Cloud confirmed she was considering it.

I need to make my move soon, Riley thought, *or I'm going to get thrown over the cliff.* Fog be damned, she needed to get away from them.

"I don't want to face Brock's wrath, do you?" Cloud asked, shivering.

"Brock doesn't scare me."

The two began bickering back and forth, and Riley knew this was it. This was her chance.

Slowly, quietly, she rolled away from the faeries. She couldn't see if she was moving toward a tree, a bush, or anything else that might be in her way, but she didn't care. As long as she was moving away from her captures.

Once they were engulfed in the fog, she got to her feet and ran, side-stepping near collisions with trees, jumping over large stones, ducking beneath branches, and following the slope of the hill, hoping it would take her to safety—

Riley gasped. She willed her legs to stop pushing her farther before she went careening off the cliffside. With the dense fog, the edge had come out of nowhere. As she took careful steps back, shouts came from higher up.

The pirates had noticed she was missing.

Riley chewed on her bottom lip, debating whether to take her chances and follow the cliff's edge and hope she would see any gap that appeared or go back within the trees and take her chances with the pirates, hoping she was heading in the right direction.

But before she could decide, music began to play behind her. The melancholy notes took hold of her, its song enchanting her into mind-less bliss.

CHAPTER 19

The fog threatened to choke Roth; it became denser every passing second he was in the air. Every passing second he didn't find Riley.

Where are you, where are you, where are you?

He repeated the words until they were all he knew. They were an improvement from the images his mind conjured. The possibilities of what she was suffering through for every moment he couldn't find—

Music floated on the wind, the tune sorrowful.

Familiar.

Roth followed the sound, his wings beating against the air. The fog swirled around him, and as he drew near, he remembered.

The city of Paladon—where Roth had ended up spending the majority of his life training and guarding—housed more enslaved humans than the other kingdoms. He had seen a human enthralled by an enchanted instrument on many occasions, and each time it didn't get any easier bearing witness to the atrocities they were forced into.

As the solemn notes of the enchanted flute reached him, his wings beat faster and a weight dropped in Roth's chest. That was why Riley had been taken. Her suffering was all for the faerie's pleasure.

When I find this pirate, Roth thought, *I'm going to shove that fucking flute down his throat. And then, I'm going to—*

The fog thinned. Roth spotted Riley immediately. Her limbs moved fluidly as she danced, toying with a cliff's edge. She still wore her clothes, and he knew it was because the tune the flautist played didn't command her to take them off—yet.

Two faeries danced on their own nearby, but Roth didn't give a damn about them; they weren't the ones playing the flute—and neither was the goblin.

The heavy weight that had dropped in Roth's chest began to boil with simmering fury. Every cell in his body urged him to tear the goblin away from Riley as he danced with her, hand in hand. But that wouldn't stop Riley from dancing over the cliff's edge. So, he kept searching until he found the one that truly held Riley's life in their hands.

Roth's eyes locked on the flautist, on his gilded skin. On the elve's nimble fingers moving over the flute as he produced the enchanting song only mortals could not resist.

He flew into position, tucked in his wings, and dove.

The wind whipped past him; it roared in his ears. But then it all faded away. His surroundings vanished, and all he saw was the elve and that fucking flute.

He waited, his timing needing to be perfect—

Roth's wings shot out. He used the wind to drift forward as he swung his body. His feet connected with the flautist's chest, and the elve soared backwards into a tree. On impact, the flute slipped through his grasp, landing in the dense fog, lost.

Once the music ceased, so did Riley, her feet stumbling to a halt, but she swayed as if she were dizzy.

Using his element of surprise, Roth spun, propelling his massive wing into the two gaping faeries. The shock washed off their faces a beat too late for them to dodge the incoming feathered battering ram, and they were flung into the fog as the flute had been.

Roth turned his violent gaze on the goblin. And at the sight of a dazed Riley sluggishly struggling against the arms that tried to hold her, he let all the simmering rage boil over. He stalked toward them, pulling his dagger free, ready to flay the goblin alive.

The goblin's black eyes widened, and he—

Fucking hells, he shoved Riley away from him, toward the cliff's edge, and ran.

Riley's and Roth's eyes widened in unison as she fell backward. Her arms flew out, windmilling, as if it might stop herself from plummeting to her death.

Forgetting about the fleeing coward, Roth lunged, flapping his wings, giving him the push he needed, as Riley was disappearing over the edge—

His arms found her just as her feet left solid ground.

They soared through the air, and Roth adjusted her, tucking her close to his chest. His heart beat wildly, matching her own. Her body trembled against him.

"Roth?" His name was barely more than a whisper, one full of disbelief.

"I'm here," Roth reassured her gently, nestling her even closer. "I've got you."

She sagged against him in relief. Without opening her eyes, her hands searched along his chest until she found his neck. They wrapped around him, holding on tight. Her head rested against his chest where she buried her face against the wind and, no doubt, the flight.

Even though the fog remained, the sensation of flying, knowing they were in the air, must have terrified her. He brushed his chin over the top of her head, reassuring her he was there and she was safe.

They were quiet as Roth tried to navigate through the fog; it thinned enough for him to know he was moving away from the mountain and the goblin.

"I'm going to kill Brock," Riley declared, the words almost lost to the wind. "I'm going to kill that fucking goblin—but not before I take the rest of his hand and make him pay for what he did. To me and every human he's ever touched."

Her declaration would've sent a shiver down Roth's spine if he hadn't already been conjuring up all the different ways he was going to make Brock suffer if he ever saw that fucking goblin again. "I am all for that idea," he said close to her ear, "but it's going to have to wait."

Her head jerked back, and her eyes snapped open. "What do you mean, 'it's going to have to wait'?" she asked, shooting daggers at him.

"I don't know where he went," Roth admitted, a muscle popping his jaw. He wished he did know where Brock was, wished he had gotten to him before the goblin had been lost in the fog, but he'd had to make a choice—kill the goblin or save Riley.

Some time ago, in the past, he'd been faced with a similar ultimatum. Never again would he make the same mistake.

"He could be anywhere on that mountain," Roth said. "I'm not going to waste my time searching for him."

"But he needs to pay for what he did."

Roth met her dark gaze with his own. "You think I don't know that? I want him to die a slow death for what he made you do, but we're never going to find him in this fog."

"Then, we wait for it to clear."

"And risk Grimsley finding the treasure while we wait on our asses to kill a goblin?" he asked, brows raised. "Do you really want to risk your chance to have Mara back?"

Jaw clenched, Riley closed her eyes and sighed through her nose. "No," she ground out, "I don't."

"I know this is hard for you, Riley, but I promise you—you will have your revenge on Brock."

She nodded, leaning her head against his chest again. "Do we at least have weapons to do that when the time comes?"

Roth grimaced. "I was able to acquire a dagger but nothing more. That dwarf wasn't interested in the items you gave me to trade."

"So," Riley said, her grip tightening around his neck, "we have a dagger and a sword—or more accurately, *you do*."

"The sword and dagger are yours. Once we land, I'll give you them. I'd prefer you have them."

"I can protect myself just fine without them," she snarled into his chest. "Brock got the jump on me. If he hadn't, I could have handled him on my own, just like before."

"Before?"

"Where are we going to get more weapons from?" she asked, as though she hadn't heard him over the wind. "And we still have to steal a ship!" she added, her nails digging into his skin.

They punctured flesh, and at the first bead of blood against her fingertips, she mumbled an apology, loosening her nails from his skin. Almost absently, her thumb rubbed over the crescent moons she'd made. There was a calming in his chest from the touch.

"I know we need more weapons," he said gruffly. "I know we need a ship, and I know that it all seems impossible, but we'll—"

An idea struck him as fast as a flash flood.

"What?" Riley asked, her thumb stilling. "What is it? Do you have a plan?"

Roth's smile was back. "I have a plan."

CHAPTER 20

Roth stepped onto the deck of Brock's ship, carrying a bottle of wine and a large platter with an assortment of food. He made his way over to Riley where she sat, leaning against the rail of the enchanted ship, behind the helm. In her lap was a book she'd brought with.

Riley had whistled when Roth had enchanted the vessel to sail on its own, taking them to Wyne. *"You can make a ship sail on its own, but you can't make an apple rose appear?"* she had said, and Roth had rolled his eyes in reply.

Sitting down next to Riley, Roth crossed his legs at the ankles, offering her the bottle of wine.

Riley set her book down and gladly took it from him. Popping the cork, she took a sip, giving the bottle an approving look before passing it back to him. She bit into a slice of cheese from the platter in his lap and hummed, closing her eyes as she chewed.

"I love cheese," she said to no one in particular.

Roth smiled softly at her declaration. "Which is better: cheese or apple roses?" he asked.

"Apple roses," she answered without hesitation. "Anything cinnamon, really," she added, opening her eyes. She looked at him, her expression serious. "But cheese is a very close second."

His smile turned into a grin, and he felt the corners of his eyes crinkling. He could have sworn he'd heard Riley's breath hitch.

The wind sent a soothing caress against Roth's feathers and stroked through Riley's loose chestnut waves; it drew her hair away from her neck, showing the bright red circle from the quill, compliments of Spike. Riley had briefly told Roth what had happened while he'd been at the blacksmith's shop, and even if she hadn't, it wasn't difficult to put the pieces together.

He brushed a thumb over the wound, wishing he could heal her. Save her the reminder of what she'd endured. Instead, it would heal in time and most likely scar. "Are you sure you're all right?" he asked.

She stiffened beneath his touch. "I'm fine," she answered curtly, moving out from under his fingers and picking up her book. "Thanks for the food and wine, old bird."

Ignoring the new nickname, he lowered his hand and resisted the urge to draw her near and comfort her. He didn't have to see her eyes to know she was lying.

He took a sip of the wine. "You mentioned if Brock hadn't taken you by surprise, then you could've handled him like before." Her gaze slowly slid to him. "When did you deal with him before?"

"The day we met," she answered hesitantly. "Not long before you caught me outside the fighting pit."

"What happened?"

Sighing, Riley set her book down again. "Brock tried to compel me to dance for him, and after he realized he couldn't, he threatened me instead. But my instincts took over before he could force me and gods know what else. Lux died and I knocked out Cloud before I beat Brock's face until he was unrecognizable. I would've killed him if Jasper hadn't shown up and stopped me."

Roth stared at her with raised brows, his mouth slightly ajar, as she picked up her book once more and began to read. He was stunned. This woman—this *human*—stunned him into awe-induced silence.

Throughout his four centuries, Roth had not met many humans who weren't under a faerie's influence, but none had ever been as capable as the one who sat beside him. Who'd endured being taken to a foreign, cruel world. Who'd lost her entire family, only to gain a new one and lose them, too. The evidence of the time she felt weak had been left behind on her forearms, but she'd survived. She was still here—fighting. And Roth knew—could see through her eyes—there were still pieces of herself in need of care, but she was strong and fierce and resilient. With time, she would be whole once more.

CHAPTER 21

Twilight faded with the remnants of the sun, leaving behind only the moon and starlight to guide them.

Hooking a lantern above Riley to the rail of the ship, Roth sat down beside her. After he caught her squinting into the darkness to read the words on the page, he disappeared below deck in search of a light source.

"Thanks," Riley said as the words became visible once again.

Quirking his mouth, he asked, "How's the book?"

She knew he was trying to make her blush, but she wouldn't give him the satisfaction. "It's good," she answered. "I'm about halfway and clothes are coming off, so it's getting even better now."

He chuckled, and she glanced at him, catching the crinkling of his eyes before it vanished. The sight made her feel that same warmth she had while kissing him.

"I'm glad I saved it for you before it got completely ruined in the mud," he said.

Riley leaned her head back. She had all but forgotten it was *that book* she was reading. "I got this from my world," she said, "and Jasper decided to give it to me for my birthday." She frowned, not understanding why she'd told him this.

"He gave you a book you already had?" Roth asked, confused. "That's understandable, considering the collection in the cave."

"No, he found the book in my stacks and gave it to me," she clarified.

"He forgot to get you something," Roth reasoned, understanding.

She sighed. "I know he was probably preoccupied with the thought of going home to rejuvenate, and I want to give him the benefit of the doubt, especially since this is the first year he got me anything, but . . ."

"But what?"

"Try harder?" Riley threw her hands up, exasperated. "We've been having sex for the past two years. I wouldn't be upset if he got me a duplicate book, but to just grab from my stack and say, 'Here you go, hazel. Happy birthday. Let's go fuck behind that tavern over there before I have to go home to Mommy Dearest and possibly never come back.'"

With raised brows, Roth was silent.

Shit, that was too much. Riley inwardly cringed. *He's going to think I'm being childish or stupid or both or—*

"Did he say that?" Roth asked incredulously. "He's not coming back?"

Shocked he didn't roll his eyes at her, she shook her head. "No, but it's . . ." She sighed, thinking how to answer but coming up empty. "It's complicated," was all she said.

"I'm sorry, Riley," Roth consoled gently. "You deserve to be respected. Tell me if this isn't my place, but if this is how he chooses to treat the ones he courts, then he's not worth a single drop of the misery you're feeling."

Beneath her breastbone, her heart did a little somersault, despite whether she believed him or not. But that was before everything he'd said sunk in.

Without turning her head, Riley's eyes slid to Roth's. "Jasper and I aren't courting," she said bitterly. "Never have and never will."

"Oh?" There was a hint of hope mixed with curiosity in Roth's voice. His wings seemed to relax, but as he studied her, they drooped slightly. "But you want to," he said quietly, the hint of hope gone, but there was a new edge to his voice.

Did she want to court Jasper? She'd thought so, but was she just lonely? Did she just want companionship? *If that's the reason,* Riley thought, *Jasper is not the right man for that.*

"I once thought I did," Riley said. "Not too long ago." She shrugged, trying for nonchalance, but Roth wasn't fooled; he could see right through her, down to her very soul, just by looking into her eyes.

She sighed heavily, taking the bottle of wine from him. "Jasper is nice," she tried to defend, her voice small as she clutched the bottle to her chest. "He's always been kind to me in his own way and has never looked at me with disgust or like a shiny, new toy to play with as most faeries do, but I'd like to be more to someone."

Silence stretched between them, and deep within her, the shadows grew stronger, louder. They screamed: *You are nothing!*

The words echoed in Riley's mind as she took a large gulp of the wine.

I am nothing.

Roth stiffened, and his wings tucked in tighter than should have been possible. Riley knew he was reading those three words in her eyes, and she couldn't look at him. Couldn't bear to see if all her thoughts, her fears, were confirmed.

I am nothing.

Holding back the tears threatening her, Riley flinched as Roth's hand gently took her chin and turned her to him. To lay bare everything within her.

Riley sucked in a breath, her lungs constricting. Everything was tight: jaw, limbs, heart. She couldn't face the truth of what Roth thought about her. Her body began to tremble. She didn't want him to see every feeling—every shadow—she had shoved down deep within her soul, where it had turned everything to rot, a barren wasteland.

She shoved Roth's hand away, willing the trembling to cease. Forcing out a breath, Riley asked, "What would you do with the treasure if we found it?" But all the emotions were crawling their way to the top. She kept going, hoping if she continued deflecting—distracting herself—then everything could stay buried where it belonged. "I know you said you weren't interested in it," she said, her voice cracking, "but there must be something you would use it for."

Roth was quiet, and Riley could feel his eyes on her, studying her. Wondering if he should go along with the change in subject.

Please, Riley willed silently. *Please*.

The shadows closed in on the warmth. They were no longer susceptible to the heat as they once were, as a chill swept in. The bud in the center of the swirling warmth began shrinking as the shadows threatened to overwhelm her, throw her over the cliff into the chasm she would surely never climb out of. The monsters dwelling within would sink their fangs into her, sucking out her essence. Everything that made her who she was, who she'd been, until there was nothing left but a husk—a mere shell of the person she used to be.

Roth's eyes drifted to Riley's lap, to where her arms lay. To the scars she bore beneath the tattoos she used to cover them. She folded her arms against her abdomen, away from the keen eyes of the aileron beside her. She didn't need the reminder of what she had endured. It all seemed trivial when there were others enduring through worse.

There were others who needed saving more than she did.

"Everyone," Roth said, taking Riley's right arm in his hand, "during their lifetime needs saving." He ran a thumb over the dragonfly, down the long, thick scar. "Some will only need it once, while others will need it often—but that doesn't make them weak. It doesn't make them unworthy of saving or less important."

Riley felt the first of many tears fall as she listened to the words she'd never known she needed to hear. They were hard to believe, as feelings she had worked so hard to keep within her came rushing to the surface. If she wasn't careful, they would drown her in their never-ending flood. She clung to the words like a sailor drowning at sea did to a lifebuoy.

How could he possibly know that? Riley thought.

"Everyone," Roth went on, thumbing a tear from her cheek, "is worthy of saving—of being reminded they are important and they are loved—despite thinking they don't deserve it or don't want to be more of a burden than they already believe themselves to be."

Riley had no words—couldn't form any—as he brought her arm to his lips, brushing them against the tattoo. Against the horrendous, puffy scar.

"You are worthy, Riley," Roth said against her skin. She shook her head, not believing the words he spoke. Squeezing her arm lightly, he said, "No matter what you believe—*you are worth saving.*"

The sob that tore from her throat echoed across the waters, and Roth tugged her close, tucking her into his side. He rested his chin atop her head and rubbed soothing circles on her back as she cried against him, her body shaking with the force of her sobs.

Worthy, every pass of his hand said against her back. *You are worth saving.*

AN HOUR PASSED, and Riley's tears were gone, but her body shook every now and then with the force of soundless sobs. Her eyes remained open, marked red and puffy.

Roth still held her in his arms. Still rubbed circles across her back as he looked up at the stars, thinking of home. He hadn't seen the glittering dark like this since the Scyathan Mountains.

Fucking hells, he missed home. Missed seeing black wings stretch out across the star-filled sky, flying so high they could touch the moon if they dared. Missed seeing the children learn to fly for the first time, the mothers fretting while their children took the leap of faith off of Mount Kyem, and hearing the laughter, whoops, and hollers of the exhilarating new experience.

Yawning, Riley shifted in his arms, stretched, and recoiled back into his embrace, nuzzling her head against his chest. She stared at the sky, reminding Roth of simpler, happier times.

A warm breeze tickled his face as his mouth stretched into a soft smile.

"Close your eyes, Riley," Roth said gently against the top of her head. "You should get some rest. It's been a long day." A long month, he didn't add.

Riley shook her head. "I don't think I can," she rasped, her throat used up from crying.

Expecting her stubbornness, Roth sighed. He spotted the forgotten book on the deck. "Would you?" He trailed off, embarrassed and, to be honest, a little nervous.

"Hm?" Riley hummed.

He swallowed, gaining the courage he needed. "Would you like me to read to you?" he asked before he lost his nerve. "Would that help?"

Riley shifted, looking up at him incredulously. "You're offering to read to me?" she replied, stunned.

Roth nodded. "If it will help you to fall asleep, then yes."

She considered his offer while he held his breath, wondering if it had been foolish. He had never proposed such a thing to anyone before and was guaranteed he would come to regret it. But it was the only thing he could think of to help her. He couldn't take away the thoughts, the memories, but he could read to her to help keep them at bay.

Riley picked up the book, handing it to him with a look that, for once, he couldn't read.

Roth swallowed. *I am going to regret this.*

He started from where she'd left off, her finger pointing to the paragraph.

Eventually, he got into the story, reading the characters with different voices. The first time he read the words of the female character in a high-pitched voice earned him a surprised laugh from Riley, and the sound made him want to hear it more. He continued in different voices, making a fool of himself no doubt, but the woman nestled in his side, following the words on the page as he read aloud, made it all worth it.

Her *smile* made it all worth it.

Roth read page after page into the night, Riley still awake nestled into his side, engrossed in the story. She didn't want to miss a single romantic scene.

Considering the content he was reading, Roth thought he held himself together quite well during the steamier parts of the story. Riley snickered into her hand the whole time as Roth read: *"His cock was huge; my hand couldn't wrap around the whole of it."*

Unable to help himself at times, he burst into laughter, causing Riley to laugh, her head thrown back against his chest, and other times, he would forget to read aloud, becoming so immersed in the story, until Riley would flick his nose.

Roth read until he couldn't anymore, the filthy words becoming too much. The bulge stretching at his leathers proved as much.

Yes, he was coming to regret his offer.

"Do you need me to fetch a bucket of ice-cold water?" Riley teased, but the red in her cheeks suggested she might need it dumped on her as well.

Roth didn't think a bucket would be enough to douse the pulsating heat. "I think a swim would work better," he countered.

Riley snorted. "Can I join you?"

Her eyes widened; she hadn't meant for that to come out.

Yes, Roth wanted to say, but before he could say anything, Riley got to her feet.

It took all of his willpower not to take her in his arms and jump overboard for that swim.

But he let her go.

If they started down that path, would either of them be able to stop?

Roth had a vow to keep and didn't want to make her feel worse than the last time they'd kissed.

So, he kept his hands to himself as Riley turned to him with her flushed cheeks and said, "Goodnight, old bird. Thanks for the bedtime story." He kept his mouth shut as he watched her go below deck, and he kept his leathers on, hands fisted at his sides, as he heard her muffled moans drift out from the cover of the hand she held to her mouth to stifle the enchanting sounds.

Trembling, Roth took to the skies. He flew out of earshot of the ship. Stretched his wings, focusing on the beat, the sound of the wind whipping by him. But nothing tamed the taut feeling of the fabric against the pulsing through his veins.

Without thought, Roth made the dive. He plunged into the water below, letting the cooler temperatures soak through to his bones, and stayed there until his lungs screamed at him for air. And after he shot above the water into the sky, he took one look at the ship, heard Riley's moans in his head, and dove back into the sea.

He surfaced and dove back into the water three more times, reminding himself of all the reasons why they couldn't go down that path, before landing on the deck, shivering. Frozen down to the bone and his soul, where ice slowly encased it.

He would need that ice to make the decision he dreaded.

But there was another option—he was sure of it.

If only he knew what it was, because Riley was so damn *worthy*.

CHAPTER 22

"Have you ever been to Wyne?"

Riley shielded her eyes from the sun reflecting off the water.

Avernii was a welcoming kingdom to all species and trades, even piracy—as long as they behaved themselves. If a pirate stepped out of line, they didn't find themselves hanging from a rope by their neck, as they would in Bilyndria, or their heads on a pike in Valrath. From the treaty struck between King Jorah, ruler of Avernii, and the Sea Queen, a pirate would be taken to the Trenches—a prison at the bottom of the sea in the Abyssal Court.

The buildings crept closer as they sailed to the eastern side of the port. Riley couldn't see the flowers climbing up the sides of the shops and houses along the waterfront, but she knew they were there.

Although High King Darrow had the magic to control the land over all of Erithena and resided in Kararhys, Wyne was known to be the most breathtaking city on the continent. Its gardens and mazes drew visitors to the

"City of Canals" from other continents.

The city resided on a branch of river deltas coming from the Drave Mountains. Bridges spanned waterways, and while sometimes it was easier to travel on foot, many preferred boats to get to their destinations.

Riley had only ever traveled by boat through the city once—Jasper's ingenious plan to get her in the mood, but all it had done was make her hungry for every dessert she'd smelled from the bakeries they'd passed.

Riley's mouth watered at the prospect of getting her hands on one of those desserts.

"No, I've never been to Wyne," Roth answered, standing a good distance away from her, never taking his eyes off the approaching city.

It had been days since Roth had soothed Riley and read to her. He hadn't offered to read to her since, nor had she asked him to. She had been so aroused from the words on the page—and the proof of Roth's own—she couldn't stop from pleasuring herself below deck in the first cabin she'd found. And ever since that first night, she'd found herself with her hand between her legs, trying to fulfill the overwhelming need, but it remained unquenchable.

Riley felt her cheeks flush as she squeezed her thighs together. She glanced in Roth's direction. He focused on her like a hawk watching its prey, and she knew he could read exactly what was going through her mind.

She cleared her throat. "Well, brace yourself," she said, ignoring the heat rushing through her body, "because you've never seen anything as beautiful as Wyne before."

"I'm sure I have," Roth replied huskily.

"I'll bet you an apple rose you haven't," Riley retorted. Her body vibrated, begging to close the distance between them.

"You're on."

After their first night on the ship, they had kept a respectable distance between each other. Nothing could happen between them. Roth had made a vow of abstinence, and she wouldn't help break it. Not when it would be nothing more than satisfying a physical need. She would be treating him with the same respect Jasper had treated her with. Roth deserved better. If he broke his vow, it should be for someone he loved and returned that love in kind.

Riley willed her blood to cool as she turned away from him and looked back at the city.

Ships, small and large, sailed in and out of the largest port on the western side of the continent, carrying shipments of anything from food to clothing to tonics. The buildings were larger and the flowers, varying in every shade imaginable, crawled up the sides of colorful buildings with red-slated roofs. The scents of them drifted by on the wind.

The city reminded Riley of a rainbow, and somewhere at the bottom was a pot of gold waiting to be found.

"Grimsley's here," Roth said, catching Riley's attention. She looked where he pointed at a large ship anchored near the port. The flag with a thorny devil lizard waved at them as if taunting them to come and play.

Roth crossed his arms over his chest. "On the island—"

"Devil's Paradise."

"—you said the treasure wasn't in the star maze, like Grimsley was led to believe, but you never said where you thought it actually was."

"And?"

The corner of Roth's mouth lifted. "*And* I'm wondering where we're going once we dock." She narrowed her eyes. "Do you really not trust me with the location?" he asked incredulously, a hint of disappointment in his voice. "I assumed by now you would trust me."

Riley chewed on her bottom lip. It wasn't that she didn't trust him. She just . . . didn't want the crack in her glass heart to widen further. "Don't take it personally," she told him. "I don't trust anyone—not completely, anyway. There was only one person I trusted wholly, and I'm afraid I'll never see them again."

Roth's face softened. "We'll get Mara back, Riley," he said, adding. "I promise."

She nodded and turned away from him before he could see in her eyes she hadn't meant Mara.

After a minute, Riley answered, "The Fountain of the Lost, in the royal garden—that's where the clue indicates the treasure will be." She glanced at him, catching the soft, appreciative smile—but like all of his smiles, it didn't last long.

"The Fountain of the Lost," Roth echoed. "Interesting."

"What is?" she asked curiously.

"I think it's interesting the largest treasure trove known to Erithenian history would be stashed in Wyne, let alone this fountain."

"But that's where the clue points to."

"I'm not saying it doesn't," Roth said. "What I am saying is I don't think the treasure is here at all because there's nowhere to hide it."

"How would you know?" Riley snapped back, suddenly feeling defensive. "You've never been to Wyne."

"Just because I've never been here doesn't mean I'm wrong."

She rolled her eyes, fixing her attention, instead, on the bustle of the docks.

Faeries scurried about, making deliveries and loading up their ships with goods as their captains shouted at them to hurry their asses up. One dodged a pelican swooping in front of them, the bird's eyes only for the fish in the water. Seagulls perched high above on ships, squawking, as though they were the ones giving the orders.

Brock's ship, still enchanted by Roth's magic, approached a pier with a mermaid sitting at its edge. The water faerie rested on her elbows, her brown skin bare to the heat of the sun. With her head tilted back, eyes closed, her long mint-green hair grazed the wood beneath her, while shimmering emerald and golden scales swished the lapping waves below.

Taking Alonzo's sword and the dagger he'd given her, Roth tucked them safely away below deck with the other weapons he'd "borrowed" from Brock's armory, while the ship docked and anchored itself.

The goblin was horrible for many reasons—not keeping his money on his ship being one of them—but because of him, they were able to sail to Wyne and acquire weapons. But that didn't mean they were willing to risk drawing the attention of the Avernii Guard—even if they were considered "welcomed."

Still, Riley tucked a knife into her boot—Roth might be a living, breathing weapon, but she certainly wasn't—and slung her bag across her chest, wishing the bird were carrying the heavy thing as Roth stepped onto the gangplank after it had magically positioned itself. She followed him, and at the bottom Roth extended a hand for her to take down the last few steps.

She eyed him with an arched, curious brow. "How very gentlemanly of you," she said, accepting his hand. Wanting to feel his skin against hers, knowing it would be the only contact she would get from him.

Once her feet were on the pier, Roth held her hand a moment

longer than needed before he let go, swiping his thumb smoothly over her knuckles in one quick motion.

"I'm surprised you didn't call me 'old bird,'" he teased.

"That's because you didn't let me finish my sentence. You're very gentlemanly, *old bird*."

Roth rolled his eyes, groaning. "That's better than 'stubborn, old bird.'" Riley opened her mouth, and he held up a hand. "Don't."

She grinned.

They walked through the cobblestone streets of Wyne, passing floating restaurants and gardens on the canals as they went over bridges, the railings decorated in vines blossoming with tiny flowers, on their way to the royal garden. Giant lily pads leisurely drifted down one of the canals, carrying the smaller of the woodland folk while they drank tea and ate honey cakes under umbrellas.

Riley took in the sweet scents of the bakeries and the spices coming from the restaurants, all making her mouth water. They passed a place with outdoor seating beneath an overhang of turquoise and rose-gold leaves from trees. The silver trunks grew against the wall of the building, and the branches stretched out to create cover from the sun. Elven sat at their tables, chatting. A few glanced at them, gaping at the pretty bird next to Riley, and she did the same.

The red tint of his wings was visible under the bright sun, letting everyone nearby know who walked among them.

Roth was unaware of the gasps, the pointing, the stares of fear and awe. He was too busy taking in the sights around him, the smells Riley was admiring herself.

There was a faint smile on his face as they came to a quaint, pastel pink stand selling fruit. The owner, a faerie with hummingbird wings, tidied the area around her stand.

Roth paused in front of her, startling the poor faerie half to death. She looked at him with wide, shimmering green eyes, but he didn't meet them. He looked past her, at the small crates filled with strawberries.

Riley peered up at him, to the berries, and back to him. "Did you want one?" she asked. "I'm sure it would be okay if you tried one."

He shook his head, a slight dip to the corners of his mouth. "No, that's all right." To the faerie, he said, "I'm sorry for startling you."

He began walking again, but Riley looked between him and the strawberries curiously. He paused and glanced over his shoulder when he realized she wasn't beside him.

"Riley?" She kept her curious gaze trained on him. "You coming?"

After a moment, she nodded, following him.

THEY WALKED down a set of stairs, painted to appear as stained glass and lined with pots of different flora, and over the largest bridge to the courtyard of the domed palace.

Ravens circled the domes, each one a different shimmering color of the rainbow with gilded suns standing tall at the peaks. Statues of elven, water folk—a symbol of Avernii's union with the sea—and pegasi stood sentinel from the rooftops. Cranes in flight were carved into the marble walls above arches painted with whale pods and schools of fish. Marble pillars, tall and short, lined the perimeter, decorated with intricate lines swirling into little suns and waves.

Following Riley through the pearlescent gate, Roth's eyes widened, taking it all in as he quickly discovered the courtyard of the palace was, in fact, the royal garden.

Flora, ranging from roses to peonies, lilacs, and sunflowers, surrounded them, but among the ordinary grew the unique and vibrant. Violet birds with wings outstretched burgeoned next to flowers with yellow centers and translucent petals. Next to a statue of a selkie shedding her skin grew flowers of the ocean, the petals that of sea anemones. And with each passing step, the kaleidoscope roses changed colors, holding every shade imaginable in one flower.

Courtiers mingled in their elegant gowns and suits, sitting on stone benches while they gossiped. Fanning themselves, the lords and ladies curled their upper lips into sneers and crinkled their noses in disgust, spotting the human among them. Either Riley didn't notice or she ignored every one of them.

But Roth didn't.

Welcoming city, my fucking ass, he scoffed to himself.

Flaring his wings slightly, he crossed his arms and stared down every single one. They took one look at the aileron and turned away, ducking their heads. Giving him and his human companion a wide berth.

Only one was foolish enough to stare at Riley, drool sliding from his mouth, his sharp canines protruding. Roth merely stepped out from the shade of a shrub shaped into a rearing pegasus and let the rumors of his wings speak for him. The lord tucked his lion tail between his legs and ran.

Roth smiled darkly, watching the man run for his life, as Riley stopped to observe the dancing ballerina flowers, allowing a ladybug to crawl onto her finger before setting it onto the nearby rearing pegasus shrub. His smile warmed at the sight.

"So, now that you've seen some of the city," Riley said, watching the ladybug, "would you say it's the most beautiful place you've ever been?"

Still smiling, Roth considered her question for a moment. "No," he answered finally, "it isn't."

She turned to him, confusion in her eyes turning skeptical. "You're not just saying that because you want *me* to owe *you* an apple rose, are you?"

"I'm not just saying that for an apple rose," he answered, chuckling. "I truly don't believe this is the most beautiful place on the continent."

"Then where?"

"Home."

"Paladon?"

Roth's lip curled into a sneer, mimicking the courtiers. "No, the Scyathan Mountains."

Without needing to look, he knew Riley was chewing on her bottom lip, not sure if she should ask her question, but after a moment, she said, "Why did you leave for Paladon?"

Roth didn't know how to answer. Like most of his past, it was complicated, and if he could, he avoided talking about it.

So, he ignored the question, saying, "Wyne's views might not be as good as Scyathan, but by the smells wafting from every restaurant and bakery, I imagine the food is better." He thought of the ripe, red strawberries.

Out of the corner of his eye, he saw the twist of her lips, but to his surprise she didn't press. There was a hint of understanding in her gaze, like she knew of his desire not to broach the subject.

Riley hummed in agreement. "The food is good, but Kararhys has the best desserts."

His brows shot up. "You've been to Kararhys?"

Although Avernii and its ruler were welcoming to all, it didn't mean the other kingdoms were, Bilyndria being the least. Because of the High King's presence in Kararhys, it made it the most dangerous city for a pirate. To venture over one of the bridges into the city would certainly mean death if one wasn't careful.

"It was before I met Mara," she explained, shrugging. Before she'd become a pirate, she didn't add, but she didn't need to. Roth saw it in her eyes.

And just as she had asked him, he said, "Why did you leave?"

She looked away from him, back to the ladybug that had flown from the pegasus's tail to the tip of one of the wings. She avoided his gaze, and he knew she didn't want him seeing the answer. Not without her permission.

Suddenly, he felt guilty for asking. Whatever her reasons might have been for leaving, if they were at all similar to the way his past made him feel, he regretted dredging those feelings up inside her.

Gently, he said, "You don't have to tell me if you don't want to."

She didn't.

HIDDEN BY A CANOPY OF WISTERIA, the Fountain of the Lost stood in the center of a seven-pointed star carved within white stone. Water poured from five tiers, the middle held up by rearing pegasi, the tips of their outstretched wings locking them together. Water spurted from carved stars on the rim of the fountain in intervals, into the open mouths of the pegasi.

Riley took her boots off and pulled her leggings up to her knees. "Keep watch," she said, jumping into the fountain, the water splashing and halfway up her calves. The jets from the rim sprayed her back and sides.

"What are you doing?" Roth asked, a slight rasp to his voice.

He couldn't help but remember the night he'd read to her and the way she'd casually asked if she could join him for a swim. He had wanted nothing more, but it couldn't happen. It would've only led to him questioning his actions, and he couldn't afford to do that.

But the swim he'd taken by himself, and the ice wrapped around his soul, did little to dull the heat within him. Even his daily morning meditation didn't douse the fever. It barely brushed the surface of the storm within. So, he kept his distance, hoping it would help, but the potential for calamity only grew every day.

It needed to be near her, to feel her. Any part of her. He would settle for her hand, her arm. A sweep of his fingers trailing over her back, through her hair.

But because he had to, he would continue to keep his distance as best he could. No matter how much the storm grew within.

Roth took a shuddering breath, burying the building heat, as Riley scowled at him over her shoulder.

"I'm searching for clues," she said.

He snorted. "Do you really think the treasure is here? Or more specifically, in that fountain?"

Her scowl deepened, and a determination to prove him wrong appeared in her eyes. "I guess we'll find out," she said. "Now, if you could turn around and keep watch?"

He crossed his arms. "Why can't you keep watch?"

"Because you don't know what we're looking for," she explained, circling the inside of the fountain, her eyes narrowed in concentration.

"Neither do you."

Riley paused, opened her mouth, and closed it. She pursed her lips. "Just turn around and keep watch."

Roth smirked.

Turning, he did as asked, making sure no one intruded. A couple approached the archway of the canopy—most likely to pay their respects at the fountain to the lives lost during the Terra War—but took one look at the aileron and scurried past to a marble gazebo.

A statue of a naked woman stood in the center. Patches of scales crawled up her legs, stopping at her hips. Ringlets fell past her shoulders, draping over one of her breasts. Her round face was solemn as her right arm stretched out before her, her palm up, fingers curled. As though beckoning onlookers to break her free of the stone from which she'd been carved.

Roth could almost feel her pain, his legs itching to move to her. To free her.

As he admired the woman, Roth listened to Riley searching for clues, the water splashing around, and every so often, he heard her mumbling to herself. He watched the elven couple move on from the gazebo and woman, when he heard the water stop flowing behind him and a gasp from Riley. He turned around just as Riley jumped out of the fountain, wet from head to toe.

But no water flowed from the fountain.

Riley backed away until she bumped into Roth. He braced her, hands on her shoulders.

The ground rumbled beneath them, and they heard gears turning. Stone panels of the seven-pointed star collapsed into the earth, revealing stairs spiraling into the dark depths below.

They both stared, wide-eyed, at the secret entrance.

"What did you do?" Roth asked, marveling at what they had just discovered.

Riley shrugged, Roth's hands going up with the movement. "I figured out there was a pattern to the jets of water and closed the pegasi's mouths in the correct order."

He'd never noticed the slim gap in the carvings before, and his eyesight was as keen as a hawk's. How in the fucking hells had she?

They approached the hole, Roth angling himself in front of Riley. He wasn't going to chance anything crawling up the stairs. But nothing of the sort happened as they descended into the unknown.

CHAPTER 23

Reaching the bottom of the spiral staircase, they discovered a stone near the root-covered wall controlled the panels of the star around the fountain, after Riley stepped on it and it sank into the ground, closing the panels.

"At least we know that's our way out," she murmured into the darkness and pulled an object out of her bag.

Pressing a button on it, she blinded Roth with sudden light while his eyes were adjusting. Blocking the light with his hand, he held in his snarl and decided not to tell her he could see in the dark as well as any owl; she had plenty to tease him about already.

They began their journey through the winding tunnel. It was carved from stone, but that didn't stop roots from forcing their way between the cracks. Unlit torches lined the walls, but with the object Riley held, the torches didn't need to be lit.

"What is that?" Roth asked, gesturing with his chin to the source of the light.

"Flashlight. I got it on one of the trips with Mara and Jasper to the mortal world."

It reminded him of glowing, floating solasta orbs, but only the nobles could afford those. If Riley had pulled one out of her bag, Roth would've assumed she—or Mara—had stolen it.

"Thankfully," Riley continued, "I haven't had the chance to use this very much, so the batteries shouldn't die on us."

"Batteries?" Roth's forehead creased. "What are batteries?"

"Magic."

He glanced at her, ducking out of the way of a dangling root in the ceiling. "I didn't know you had magic in the mortal world."

A smile played at the corners of Riley's lips like she knew something he didn't. "Have you ever been there?" she asked.

"No," he answered. "I haven't seen a lot outside of Paladon."

"Why is that?"

Because King Torryn doesn't allow us to leave. It was on the tip of his tongue, but instead, he shrugged, saying, "It's complicated."

Riley hummed with understanding, but she couldn't possibly understand.

Could she?

They rounded a corner and found themselves surrounded by—

"Why are there so many skeletons in the walls?" Riley asked, horrified.

Within the stone, skeletons slept peacefully in their little crevices. Flora grew around every one of them, looking like the garden above. Even without the proper nutrients, the plants thrived. They grew out of eye sockets and open mouths, within rib cages and along spines.

Roth didn't answer Riley. He had an inkling where they were, but the tunnel continued on, and he couldn't be sure just yet.

Rounding another corner, the skeletons watching them, they came to a large, open room. The beam of Riley's flashlight skimmed the space, revealing stone sarcophagi scattered throughout. Vines with leaves and budding flowers grew around them and through cracks where they broke out from beneath the lids.

"*Okay,*" Riley said, sounding on the verge of hysteria. "*Where are we?*"

"Catacombs," Roth replied, turning in a circle, taking in the crypt. It was as he suspected. "These must be the lives lost during the Terra War, and the king had nowhere else to put them." So many had died, it didn't surprise Roth that King Jorah had had to turn to mass graves and bury the fallen wherever they'd had space. Ailerons had had to do something similar, building a necropolis within the Scyathan Mountains.

"That explains the name of the fountain," Riley realized.

She moved within the room, observing the skeletons and flora growing around them. "How are these plants here?" she asked, observing a sarcophagus with blooms as blue as sapphires growing from it.

"It's what happens when faeries die," Roth answered. He felt a soft, golden petal from where it grew out between ribs, leaving a shiny gold streak on his fingers. "The land gives us life, and when we die, we give back to it."

After faeries are either killed or choose to transcend, their souls move on to the Elysian Fields. While their bodies are left behind, they flourish with new life instead of decaying. They become one with the earth. First their flesh, and lastly their bones.

"I think that's what the garden is," Roth went on. "The dead. I wouldn't be surprised if every flower, every tree in the city came from them. There were so many deaths during the war, and Wyne suffered the most after the giants made a surprise attack."

Brushing her fingers along a silky green leaf, Riley said, "I never thought death could look so . . . beautiful."

"The flora grown from our bodies is always more vibrant than anything natural. Sites of the worst battles are nothing more than the vibrant colors, mimicking the city above."

"It's why Wyne looks like a rainbow."

He nodded.

But he would never forget the first bloom from his first battle. It hadn't been bright and beautiful like a rainbow, but grim to match the devastation in the burning village. A tulip had grown from a gaping wound in a child's chest, who had still clutched his mother's hand. It had been the same tint as his wings—and it had been the first time he'd hated the color of them.

"What are we looking for?" Roth ground out, pinching his eyes shut. Trying to make the gruesome images and the sour taste in his mouth go away. If they didn't, he would be on the verge of shutting down.

It always happened.

He would be there physically, but mentally, emotionally . . . He had gone months without uttering a single word. No one knowing what he'd been thinking. What memories had haunted him. His friends and family had known he was in a dark place, but they hadn't *known*. And neither would Riley if he let himself wander there again. She had gone through enough already. The last thing she needed was to lose the last person she had left and not know *why* she'd lost him when he was living and breathing beside her.

For her, Roth would rise above and out of the darkness.

"I don't know," Riley answered, shrugging. "I would say something pirate-y, but there are so many damn plants, I can barely see anything el—"

The word died on her tongue, and Roth looked at her, curiosity finding its way to the surface. "What is it?" he asked.

She stood by a sarcophagus with running gazelles, but her focus and beam of light were on a different one near the back corner of the crypt. "Do you find it odd nothing is growing from that one?" Riley asked.

Roth tilted his head, first noticing no plant life grew from the sarcophagus. "You're right," he mused. "That is odd."

Riley gasped. "Did you just agree with me?" Shock lined her face in the glow of the flashlight.

He rolled his eyes. "Don't let it go to your head."

"Too late. I'm already envisioning 'Riley Was Right' embroidered on a pillow. In the corners are red-feathered wings, and on the back is the grumpy-ass face you're giving me right now."

Leveling a glare at her, Roth walked to the sarcophagus in question, ignoring her snickering.

Riley appeared beside him and ran a finger over the stone lid. "No dust," she said, rubbing her fingers together. "Someone's been here recently."

She crouched, shining the light on the side. "Look." She pointed at the flecked paint. "A dragon."

The beam of light danced along the painted landscape of mountains. A river flowed between the two largest peaks, pooling at the base to create a hidden lake—and hovering over that was a large dragon. Its massive, taloned, black wings stretched wide; it had two legs and no arms, but Roth knew from experience those wings could be just as destructive and deadly.

"Wasn't Lothaire's insignia a dragon?"

"Yes," Riley answered, sounding giddy. "I hope this will lead us to another hidden room and the treasure is there." She looked Roth square in the eye. "Because then you would have to tell me I was right."

He gave her a withering look. "If the treasure is here," he drawled, "I will get you as many apple roses you can eat in one sitting."

Her eyes went round. She lifted her head to the high, root-covered ceiling. "If there are any gods listening," she whispered, "please let the treasure be here."

Roth couldn't hold back his smile as he shook his head.

Riley circled the stone sarcophagus, running her hands over every inch of it while she searched for another clue. She cursed when she came full circle. "There isn't another button like the fountain."

"Maybe it's on the inside."

Riley stiffened. "I'm not getting inside that thing."

"Who said you have to?"

"I thought you were implying I should."

Roth snorted, shaking his head. He braced his hands against the lid and pushed. Grunting from the weight, he moved it ajar enough to see inside.

His brow furrowed. "It's empty."

She peered in, shining the light on the empty space. "Well, that explains the lack of plants," she said softly. Roth could almost hear the cogs turning in her mind as she puzzled through everything—

Approaching footsteps sounded from nearby, and it was then Roth noticed the other tunnel connected to the crypt, opposite from where they'd come in and shrouded by a veil of fiery-orange flowers.

Roth cursed to himself. If the tunnel was connected to the palace, the approaching footsteps could belong to royal guards.

With wide eyes, Riley turned on her heels, as if to run to the tunnel they had come from, but there was no time. Whoever was coming would be pulling back the veil of flowers soon.

Roth picked Riley up, hearing a tiny squeak. The flashlight clattered to the ground.

"What was that?" asked a deep voice.

The footsteps came faster, louder.

Roth cursed to himself, nearly dropping Riley on her ass on the hard stone in the empty sarcophagus as he placed her inside and grabbed the flashlight, tossing it inside with her.

He glanced at the tunnel and saw light growing brighter, brighter, brighter.

They were nearly upon him.

Quickly, Roth climbed into the sarcophagus atop a wide-eyed Riley and slid the lid into place as quietly as he could, right before a hand poked through the veil of flowers.

CHAPTER 24

Stone scraped against Riley's skin through her clothes.

While the aileron hovered over her, fidgeting against their tight quarters, she wondered why the fountain had to lead to a crypt.

She wanted to smack Roth for shoving her inside the sarcophagus, but she understood. Whoever was down there with them had been approaching quickly, and if they'd been found out, who knew what they would've had to do to make it out of there.

"It was probably a rat," said a feminine voice outside of the sarcophagus. It held authority—power—but when she added, "King Jorah," Riley's eyes widened further, and she thanked the gods her and Roth had not been caught by the *king*.

But there was still a chance they could be—especially if Roth wouldn't stop fidgeting, as if he were trying to get comfortable. Riley wanted to point out they were in a sarcophagus, and it wasn't as if she were exactly cozy either.

Roth tried to give them as much space as possible, holding himself up by his arms, his knees next to either side of her hips, and his hands braced on either side of her head. On her chest, her flashlight illuminated the small space, and she saw how scrunched he was. She didn't know how he'd fit. His wings—even tucked in as tight as they were—

took up a large amount of space, and they didn't have a lot to begin with. The talons scraped against the stone lid—

"Did you hear that?" a deep voice said, and Riley assumed it belonged to King Jorah. "Do you truly believe that's a rat?" he asked his companion.

Riley could almost hear the eye roll as the woman drawled, "We're in a crypt. There are bound to be rats down here."

Footsteps scuffed against stone, coming near.

Riley glared at Roth, telling him with her eyes to stop fidgeting, but he couldn't, not while he held himself above her, forcing his wings against the lid. She knew why he gave them this space; it was the same reason why they had been avoiding each other on Brock's ship. But Riley rolled her eyes at the notion anything was going to happen between them in a sarcophagus. There was no way in all the gods-damned worlds she was going to get it on with him—with anyone—inside a space meant for a corpse.

Just as the footsteps stopped outside of their hiding place, Riley wrapped her arms around Roth's waist and pulled him flush against her. His body snuffed out the light from the flashlight, and the last thing she saw was his wide, surprised eyes.

They held their breath as they waited to be found.

After a moment, King Jorah said, "Perhaps you're right."

Riley counted the king's footsteps while he walked farther away, and only when they were sure they wouldn't be caught did they exhale in unison. Riley resisted the shiver from Roth's hot breath against her ear. His chest pushed into hers from its release, and her limbs grew heavy, relaxing the slightest beneath him.

"Tell me what you want and be on your way," King Jorah said, his deep voice slightly muffled by the stone. "I'm risking a great deal by talking to you."

Riley tried to focus on the king's words instead of the wet, earthy scent of Roth. It was all she could smell, and it filled her lungs—not that she was complaining.

The woman clicked her tongue. "You should think before speaking to me in that tone, *boy*."

Riley's brows rose, and even in the darkness, she knew Roth's did as well. For anyone to speak to a king the way this woman did, let alone call him boy, would mean severe punishment—and then execution.

The crypt was silent, promising more death than it already held, but the king grumbled, "My apologies."

Gods, Riley thought, *who is this woman?*

The woman scoffed, and there were footsteps moving away from them, toward the king. "You know what I want—what she wants," the woman said. "I'm here for an answer."

"And if I do this, what do I get in return?"

Riley nearly snorted but didn't hold back her eye roll.

Once a faerie, always a faerie; they couldn't resist a godsdamn bargain even if the world was crumbling to ruins around them.

"You won't lose what you hold most valuable in your heart and soul," the woman said, her voice dangerous.

Riley rolled her eyes again, the only movement she could risk without making a sound. *Most valuable*, Riley thought, mentally snorting. *It's probably a gem or a horse.*

King Jorah stuttered, "You—how—"

"Yes," the woman purred, "we know about your daughter."

Riley's head jerked to the side, in the direction of the voices; she wondered if she'd heard correctly.

With her head in that position, her nose rubbed against Roth's stubbled jaw, and his lips brushed against the spot between her eyebrows. Her skin hummed from the touch, and it took all of her willpower not to lean into it. She considered moving her head back to the position it had been in, but . . . she was finding it rather difficult. The logical part of her brain argued with the part overwhelmed by the scent of him, wanting more.

"So, what's your answer?" the woman asked impatiently. "Which do you value more?"

Riley and Roth held their breath once more. The former had no clue as to what this woman wanted, but surely this daughter—one he kept a secret—was worth more.

Sighing with defeat, King Jorah said, "I'll need to retrieve it before I can give it to her. All I ask is she be willing to wait until I can do so."

"She is," the woman said, satisfied with his answer. "And if you try to find a way out of this, you know what will happen—and it won't just be your daughter who will pay the price. Your entire kingdom will fall."

A deadly silence stretched through the crypt, wrapping its clawed fingers around not only King Jorah's throat, but Riley's and Roth's, too. The woman's words weighed heavy.

"Once you have it," the woman continued, as if she hadn't just threatened the life of the king's daughter and his entire kingdom, "wait for the appropriate time to give it to her, and then you'll no longer need to fret for your daughter's life."

Riley's stomach churned at the way this woman nonchalantly threatened innocent lives.

"What is the 'appropriate time'?" King Jorah asked, a slight tremor to his voice. There was a lot riding on his capability to retrieve whatever it was this woman wanted.

"When the bitch of the sea is finally gutted like the conniving fish she is."

Riley's eyes widened. She bit her tongue to keep from gasping.

This woman, and whoever she was working with, was plotting to murder Jasper's mother. Did he know? He must. He once mentioned his mother's spies were everywhere: in the lakes, the rivers, ponds. Wherever there was water, she had operatives.

"So, the rumors are true," King Jorah said. "There will be an assassination attempt on the Sea Queen." He mumbled what sounded like a string of curses. "I thought it was just gossip spread by bored courtiers, but I guess I shouldn't be surprised it isn't. Or that she is willing to go to these lengths to get what she wants," he added with a laugh, the falseness of it settling over the crypt.

"And never forget that, *boy*."

Outside the sarcophagus, a set of footsteps grew closer before disappearing down the tunnel they'd appeared from, and soon the other set dragged along.

Riley and Roth waited—never breathing, never flinching—before he shifted atop her, lifting himself, allowing the light of the flashlight to illuminate the sarcophagus again. His cheeks were flushed, and she didn't doubt hers were, too. She wiped her clammy hands on her leggings as he shifted the lid—

"Stop," Riley said, almost shouting.

Roth paused, a crease in his brow. "Why?" he asked. "They're gone."

"I know," she said, "but . . ."

Her heart beat wildly behind her breastbone. She pointed the light on the inside of the lid, and there, the next clue to Lothaire's treasure shimmered.

CHAPTER 25

Standing at the edge of Grendelwyn Forest, they stared into the depths of one of the hells—which one, Riley didn't know. The sun shined brightly over the tops of the trees, but no light pierced them. Only the path lit by the glowing blue of the wisps in hanging lanterns showed the way through the abyss.

The dragon from the sarcophagus had been painted flying over a tower guarding a lake this time, near a devastated town in a forest with monstrous, almost demonic creatures roaming the streets and hiding behind buildings of what could've been the town square with a well at its center. Above the painting, inscribed with what appeared to be blood, were the words:

> *Dive into darkness to ascend into light,*
> *Find the four, but fear the three,*
> *Ignite the flame to illuminate your fate.*

Roth had cursed when they'd found the clue, immediately knowing what town the painting depicted, and had said: "*If I were going to hide a treasure, I'd pick the most dangerous place in this world, too.*"

Riley had done the same, cursing the clue as he had, but not due to the painting. No, she had cursed the clue because the treasure hadn't been in Wyne, as Roth had predicted.

Lou pulled on the reins Riley held, almost taking her arm with the movement. Riley tried to soothe the horse by stroking her tan neck, but the mare was wiser than her company. She would not go past the forest's border and let the darkness claim her. *Fools*, the mare seemed to say with every snort and lift of her head.

"Let her go," Roth said, never taking his eyes off of the forest. "She'll draw more attention to us once inside." He paused, then added, "If we haven't drawn attention to us already, that is."

That wasn't a comforting thought.

Begrudgingly, Riley let the mare go. Lou galloped in the direction they had come from, and Riley gripped the strap of her bag across her chest, mumbling, "I just lost good coin."

"You stole the horse," Roth reminded her dryly, his eyes searching the trees while his hands rested on the hilts of the swords they had gone back to retrieve from Brock's ship. As if he waited for a demon to slink out of the darkness.

Roth had grumbled when Riley had stolen Lou from a stable in a town outside of Wyne, but it had been the only way she was going to travel to Grendelwyn Forest. She had refused to allow him to fly them to the next location of their treasure hunt, and he had refused to ride Lou. Riley assumed it was because of how close they would be. After arguing how they would travel, they'd come to an arrangement: he would fly, and she would ride. Riley hadn't been able to stop the disappointment she'd felt—she'd liked the thought of their thighs touching, her back bumping against his chest, his breath caressing the crown of her head, taking in his petrichor scent—but once again, she'd understood why they shouldn't.

Riley retorted, "But I was going to sell her once I no longer needed her."

Roth gave her a sidelong glance, knowing she was lying, but it hadn't always been a lie. At first, she'd intended to sell the mare, but it hadn't taken long for her to fall head-over-heels in love with Lou, ready to take the horse to the ends of the world with her. With Roth flying,

Lou had become her sole company. Her chest tightened as she watched the mare become a galloping dot in the distance.

"It's for the best," Roth said, trying to reassure her, a hand on her shoulder.

She rolled her eyes, nearly snorting. She remembered the arched, sardonic brow he'd given her when she'd named the mare Lou, the way he'd looked at the horse with disdain; he couldn't wait to be rid of the majestic creature. She looked from the disappearing mare to the hand on her shoulder, then to Roth, but he wasn't focused on her; his eyes were still on the forest.

"You don't have to do this," Riley offered.

She knew what lurked beyond the tree line. Roth had told her the previous night, when they'd made camp, of the demons within. That they would try to gain her attention, lead her away from him, and make a meal of her after having some fun. Witches roamed within the wicked woodland, cast out by the faeries, and water spirits ruled the streams and lakes, waiting to lure their next victim to their doom. And if they survived the witches, the water spirits, there were still the creatures with no names, no depictions, to contend with.

Those were the monsters to be scared of—the ones none lived to tell the tale of.

Riley suppressed a shudder. Just thinking about what prowled the forest made her almost wet her pants.

Roth frowned, his brow creasing. He glanced at her. "I know."

She waited for him to turn around, telling her good luck, but he never did. He remained by her side with his hands on the hilts of his swords, ready if a demon risked the sunlight.

Riley didn't know what would happen if they went beyond the darkness, but right now the sun was her best friend. If they lost the light . . .

She swallowed.

Death, she thought. *That's what would happen.*

There were stories of travelers who camped too close to the forest, and the darkness crept beyond the tree line and the demons with it.

"You should turn around, Roth," Riley told him.

He looked at her then, his face scrunched with stubbornness. "Why would I do that?" he asked as if she'd made the most ludicrous suggestion.

"Because this forest is evil and dangerous," she said, pointing out the obvious. "I know you had your reasons to come with me—whatever they may be—but I don't think killing yourself is worth it. The chances of surviving this are—"

"Stop," he interrupted, holding up a hand. "I know what the chances are, and I'm still willing to risk them."

"Why? What reasons could be worth your life?"

"I want you to get Mara back," he blurted. "And if you have a shot at that, you have to take it, along with all the help you can get."

She stared at him, dumbstruck, and he took a deep inhale before letting it out in a long stream, as if he needed to steady himself before he spoke again. And despite the steadying breath, when he did speak, his voice was quiet, tentative.

"I know what it is to lose the ones you love." His eyes darted away from hers, finding a spot in the distance over her shoulder. They glazed over, as though the faces of those loved ones flickered to life in the spot he stared at. "To have every ounce of joy ripped from you," he continued, his voice hitching. "And eventually, you accept you'll never be the same again. That you'll never get that joy back. I don't"—he paused, swallowing to wet a dry throat, before his eyes could finally meet hers again—"I don't want that to happen to you."

Riley was stunned and—

She didn't know what other emotion pulsed through her, spreading outward from her chest to her fingertips and toes. It was unfamiliar but . . . welcoming.

He was doing all of this for her? To ensure she wouldn't become him, unable to find the ability within himself to smile because he'd lost too many?

She wanted to tell him it was too late. She'd already lost her joy. It had walked out on her a long time ago, with no sign it would ever return. But instead, she found herself saying, "You barely know me," her voice cracking.

He tucked strands of hair behind her ear, his thumb brushing over the curve. His hand fell to her shoulder and down her arm, until he turned it over, sliding the glove down to reveal the dragonfly there. His thumb traced the long scar. "I know enough," he said roughly.

Riley's eyes watered, and she blinked the tears away before they could fall. Before Roth could see how much his words affected her and the truth of what had happened to her three years ago.

He released her arm with one last featherlight stroke against her scar, sliding her glove back into place, and turned back to the forest as his hands fell to his swords.

"Wait," Riley said.

He turned to her with a questioning look and watched as she moved behind a nearby bush. When she returned to him, she gave him a nod.

"Okay," she said, "now I'm ready."

Roth stared at her, unmoving, and Riley worried he was reconsidering joining her inside the abyss.

When he moved away from the forest, she sucked in a breath, thinking he was abandoning her, but he stopped in front of a tree, his back to her. He made a tight circle with his finger, and her brows rose as a smile grew.

She turned around, snickering into her hand.

After a moment, Roth reappeared by her side, and she couldn't help but wonder how he'd managed to get those godsdamn tight leathers off when her eyes slid down of their own accord and found no buttons.

"Ready?" Roth asked, either ignoring her blatant perusal of him or oblivious to it.

Riley blinked, her eyes finding his.

The twitch of his lips suggested he knew all too well what was going through her head. Her cheeks flushed, and she nodded. But mentally, she gave him the middle finger.

The quiet, yet raspy chuckle he let out was the only sign the message was received. Loud and clear.

THE FOREST WAS DARKER than the cave on Obsidian Island, if that was possible. Although the lit path shielded them from the monsters, Riley knew they were surrounded. Her skin crawled, and the instinct to run was almost as choking as the darkness appeared.

The black was thick and moved as if it were a living entity. It swirled outside the light of the wisp lanterns and curled around trees. A thought occurred to Riley and grew: *What would happen if it touched my skin? Would it eat away at me like a disease? Or would it take hold of me? Turn me into something else? Something* inhuman?

She shivered, not wanting to find out.

It had been daylight when they'd entered, but with the thick coverage of the trees and the darkness, there was no way to know what time it was. It felt as though they had been walking for hours, long enough that the sun had gone down—but for all Riley knew, it could have been only an hour.

They traveled in silence, listening to the rustling alongside them. The growling and the clawing and the shrieking. By the time they reached an unlit portion of the path, Riley was in a cold sweat, thanking the gods she had relieved herself before entering.

Looking at the darkness in front of them, she asked, "What do we do now?" She didn't bother to try to hide the fear in her voice; she knew Roth was aware by the way he would squeeze her hand or his wing would brush over her skin as they walked. Small touches to reassure her he was still there. That she was not alone.

"Do you still have your magic glow-stick-light?" Roth asked, whispering.

"Flashlight," she murmured, reminding him.

She dug around the books before pulling it out. She clicked it on, and the darkness scattered and slithered away like snakes to reveal the lit path on the other side. Riley's eyes widened, watching the darkness dance around and test the edges of light from her flashlight. "I've never seen the dark do that before," she whispered.

"Neither have I," Roth whispered in turn.

His words didn't comfort her as his touch had.

"I guess we keep going?" Riley suggested.

About to take the first, terrifying step forward, Riley was stopped by Roth's hand on her shoulder and his soft voice. "Wait, I think . . ." His hand shifted from her shoulder to the hand holding the flashlight. He moved them, scanning the side of the path, causing the darkness to move again, but where the light vanished from, the darkness crept in again. Where the light landed revealed another wider path.

A road, Riley realized.

"That must be the way to the town of Yenmoor," Roth said quietly. "And why some wisp lanterns are missing."

Choosing a wisp lantern for himself, Roth held it up. It bathed the two of them in a soft blue light, and with Riley's flashlight to move the darkness in front of them, they were well-equipped to travel the unlit road.

Although the darkness was as thick as a wall, they caught glimpses of pale limbs as the monsters scurried back into the safety of the black. Riley's heart beat faster within her chest. They looked . . . *human*, but as if they crawled on all fours.

The only thing keeping Riley from running was the hand that every so often rubbed the spot between her shoulder blades.

"Remember the reason you're here," Roth murmured behind her. "Remember Mara."

Riley tried, but it wasn't easy. Every time something growled beside them, every time she saw pale skin disappearing into the black, every time the darkness tested their shield of light—it made all thoughts of Mara vanish.

"What's your favorite color?" Riley asked softly into the silence.

She knew it was a stupid question, but it was all she could think of to ask. She needed to be grounded before the fear overwhelmed her and her survival instincts took over, commanding her legs to run back to safety. She knew Roth couldn't keep his hand on her back, not with the surrounding danger, but she needed to be reminded he was there and had not abandoned her. She needed to hear his voice.

As if he sensed this, Roth murmured without hesitation, "Anything but red. You?"

An image of red-tinted wings flashed in her mind. "Red," she answered, and she could almost hear his eye roll from thinking she was just saying that because he didn't like the color. She wasn't; his wings were beautiful. Thinking of another, she added, "And sea green, but with gold."

"'Sea green but with gold'?" he asked, as if he couldn't fathom where this answer had come from.

She felt her cheeks flush. "You have very pretty eyes," she admitted, her embarrassment stark in her voice.

He laughed softly behind her, her hair doing little to block the puff of hot air. "You've mentioned that before," he said, amused.

Riley racked her brain, searching her memories for when she might have told him this, but couldn't remember. She shrugged, moving on to her next question. "Morning or night?"

"Morning."

"Normally, I would answer night," Riley said, "but I might be rethinking that." After this, she never wanted to be in the dark again.

Roth grunted his agreement.

"What's your favorite food?"

"Strawberries."

Riley almost spun on him, but thought better of it at the last second, realizing she would be redirecting the light. "That's why you stopped and stared at the crates of strawberries in Wyne," she said. Her brows narrowed in confusion as she frowned. "Why didn't you try one?"

"My vow," was all he said. As if it answered the question, but it only created more.

Before Riley had a chance to ask him to elaborate, the small town of Yenmoor began springing up on either side of the road.

It was nothing more than web-covered ruins. The trees and brush grew within and around the rubble. Broken glass shimmered under Riley's flashlight.

They made their way past the ruins of the town, following the patches of light coming through gaps in the cover of the forest, where the road led them to what once was the town square. Riley moved the flashlight across the space, finding a stone well at the center, completely intact. Not one stone was out of place.

"That's weird," she murmured. She walked toward it, thinking of the sarcophagus in the crypt; it had been the only one without plant life growing from it, and it had held the next clue to Lothaire's treasure. She thought if the sarcophagus had been the answer before, surely the intact stone well, surrounded by ruin, was the next.

"Stop," Roth said, nearly shouting. He wrapped an arm around her waist and tugged her to him.

"What is it?" Riley asked. Her heart was beating so fast inside her chest, it wouldn't surprise her if it stopped.

"That's a faerie ring."

"A what?"

He had her move the beam of light slightly. On the ground, circling the well, were white-capped mushrooms oozing a thick black discharge; white threads of webs linked them together. "A faerie ring leads to another world," Roth said. "To one that could be far worse and more dangerous than the one we're currently in. And by the way the darkness seems to be seeping from the depths of that well, I'd say we're getting a glimpse of what we would be walking into."

Riley blanched, watching the darkness climb its way out of the well —and pale, clawed fingers grasping the edge from the inside. As if the demon waited for an unsuspecting victim to come along and make the mistake of stepping inside the circle, as Riley had almost done. If it hadn't been for Roth . . .

Her hand rested over her racing heart. "I thought"—she swallowed hard—"I thought it led to the next clue. Like the sarcophagus. It's the only thing still standing."

"Just because the outside appears to be strong and unbroken, doesn't mean the inside will be whole as well." He threaded his fingers through hers, leading her away from the door to hell.

"But what about what it said above the painting in the sarcophagus?" she reminded him. "'*Dive into darkness to ascend into light.*' What if we're supposed to dive into the well?"

He shook his head. "I don't think so. We already dove into darkness by entering the forest and taking the unlit road. Don't forget, in the painting, the dragon was flying above a tower near a lake just outside the ruined town. I think we need to find that."

She would have closed her eyes, smacking her head with her palm, if she wasn't, currently, in hell. It should've occurred to her, but it hadn't. She could've led them to their deaths if he hadn't been paying attention, and if she had, because of something as short-sighted as walking into a faerie ring, she would have never forgiven herself.

"Come on," Roth said, "let's go find a long-lost pirate's treasure."

CHAPTER 26

The road through Yenmoor curved around a small lake to a moss-covered stone tower. Fortunately, the trees stopped a distance away from the edge of the lake, causing the darkness to end as well.

They blinked from the bright sun, but within hours it wouldn't be there to protect them from the dangers within the forest. Roth prayed to fucking hells it wasn't going to be a cloudy night and they would have the moonlight to shield them.

Riley clicked off her flashlight, shoving it back inside her bag, but Roth hung on to the wisp lantern in case they found themselves back inside the darkness. Riley's flashlight helped but wouldn't be enough.

He pointed to the tower. "That's probably the one from the clue."

They stopped at the threshold and looked up. The structure stood well above the tree line, and without having to look, Roth knew Riley was working up the courage to climb it.

"You can stay here if you want," Roth said. "I can go up there and look around and let you know if I find anything." Although he didn't like the idea of leaving her at the bottom by herself, he didn't want to make her do anything she didn't want to either.

"But you don't know what to look for," Riley said, her voice shaky.

"I think we've had this conversation once before."

"And did that stop me from looking for clues?"

"No," Roth answered, adding, "but you were looking in a fountain, not a tower."

Riley faced him. "I need to do this, Roth. For Mara, I need to climb the stairs to the top and find the godsdamn treasure."

He searched her face, her eyes, and saw only determination. She was afraid but resolved to get her best friend back, even if she had to face her fear of heights. If she stayed at the bottom, he didn't doubt she would wonder if he'd missed something.

She walked through the threshold, and he followed. She paused in the middle, looking up. The tower somehow seemed taller on the inside, with its spiraling stairs crawling up the edge of the walls. Riley swayed, and Roth placed his hand on her shoulder, steadying her.

"If at any point you'd like to turn around and go back down," Roth said, "there is no shame in it. I'll look, and I promise I will search every inch of this tower."

Riley tilted her head back and peered up at him. "I know," she said, placing her hand over his. "But I can do this."

He gave her a small, encouraging smile, and with a pat of her hand on his, she took the first step.

Around and around and around, they walked up the spiraling, stone steps.

Up and up and up.

The only sounds were their footsteps and Riley's breathing becoming heavier the farther they climbed, passing broken windows along the way. There was no railing to hang on to, and Riley resorted to skimming her hand along the wall, over the rough stone and spongy moss. She paused more and more the higher they went, resting her forehead against the cool stone wall. Every time she stopped, trying to be rid of her vertigo, Roth patiently waited, squeezing her shoulder and rubbing the tension from her back until she was ready again.

At the top, three large brass bells hung in the open archways, with a fourth, the largest of them, in the center. Beside each archway was a crank for the bell it was connected to, leaving the fourth mysteriously without a way to ring it.

"*Find the four,*" Roth murmured to himself before he said louder,

"The bells must be the 'four' from the riddle." He observed the bells in turn. "Well, we found them," he grumbled. "Now what? Do we light them on fire or something if we're supposed to '*Ignite the flame*'? Or maybe just one? The part after finding the four was '*fear the three.*' So, which three are we supposed to be afraid of?"

A breeze swept in from the archways, ruffling his feathers. He waited for Riley to respond, and when she didn't, he found her pressed up against the stone in the corner at the top of the stairs, shaking and slick with sweat, her arms wrapped around herself. "Riley?" He went to her, tilting her chin up; terror laced her hazel eyes. "Do you want to go back down?"

She shook her head fervently. "I'm not leaving until we figure this out. Besides, I'm not sure I can get back down, even if we did," she added, trying to force a note of lightness to her voice. As if to convince him she wasn't as afraid as she truly was, but it didn't work.

"Okay," Roth said, sighing. He understood her determination, but that didn't mean he wasn't at war with himself. He fought the instinct to scoop her up and carry her back down. "Do you know what we're supposed to do next?" he asked, going back to the bells.

"Is there a dragon on any of them?"

"It's probably not going to be that again. It's too obvious."

"Okay, but when you find one, I'm going to say I told you so."

Roth gave her a dry look over his shoulder, hoping they wouldn't find another dragon.

He searched the bell in the center for any clue, while Riley remained in the corner, unable to move. When he didn't find anything, he moved to the next one in the closest archway to Riley, before going to the next.

"Stop!" she shouted.

Roth whirled, unsheathing his sword. His eyes darted around the tower, but he spotted no danger. "What is it?" he demanded, eyes narrowed. "What's wrong?"

"The lantern," she answered. He had all but forgotten he still held it in his other hand. "There was something on the bell as the light passed over it."

Sheathing his sword, Roth passed the wisp lantern over the bell. There, in the blue glow, was a drawing of a woman, bare of clothing, sitting in a chair while she held a length of thread in her hands before her. She appeared as though she were scrutinizing the thread.

The corner of his mouth lifted as he looked at Riley. "That doesn't look like a dragon to me."

At this, Riley straightened, and her arms unfurled themselves from around her waist to cross over her chest. "There are still two more bells, old bird," she pointed out, a hint of the strong, brave Riley he had come to know and admire shining through. "My bet is one of them has a dragon."

"I guess we'll find out."

Roth moved to the next bell. He ran the blue glow of the wisp lantern over the front of it, and like the first, a naked woman appeared, but this time she stood, a spindle in her hand, weaving thread from the bundle at her feet. His smile grew an inch. On the final bell, a third naked woman stood, a ball of thread at her feet. In one hand, she held the spindle, and in the other was a pair of shears, poised to cut the floating thread before her.

Looking over his shoulder at Riley, Roth grinned. "No dragon."

She rolled her eyes. "We don't know what the one in the center is yet."

"There was nothing there."

She pursed her lips.

"Admit it, Riley—I was right."

Her chin rose. "I will admit nothing until we either have the next clue or find the treasure here."

"Of course, you're going to be stubborn," Roth muttered.

"Takes one to know one."

He sighed. "Well, these must be the 'three.' And the riddle was right to warn us to fear them. These women are—"

"The Fates," Riley finished for him. Roth looked at her with surprised brows. "My father loved folklore," she explained with a shrug. "He read whatever he could get his hands on, watched documentaries, listened to podcasts. I would've loved to see his face once he found out it was all real," she added absently, longingly.

Roth hadn't a clue what those last two things she'd mentioned were, but it didn't matter. He felt his legs nudging him forward to comfort her. And he would have, if she hadn't shaken her head lightly, shoving away the pain, and said, "Since they appear to be out of order, I'm assuming we're supposed to ring them—not burn them"—she gave Roth a pointed look—"in the correct order."

Going along with this idea, Roth said, "Okay, so, Spinner, Allotter, Inflexible."

She nodded. "Wind the crank for the bell in the center archway, then the one closest to me, and lastly the one on the other side."

Roth arched a brow at her, about to ask why she couldn't, but reminded himself not to be fooled by her change in demeanor. She was still frightened to move from the corner, and he didn't blame her. With the wind howling through the archways, it felt as though from one strong gust, he could fall through one of the openings.

Moving to the bell in the center archway, as Riley had instructed, he wrapped his hands around the crank handle. "I'd cover your ears," he suggested, and she brought her hands over her ears. She nodded, ready for the noise. After he wound the handle, the bell slowly lifted backward in the air, and when he reached the crank's limit, he released the handle. The bell swung forward, and the clapper struck the brass. Bringing his hands to his ears, Roth grimaced from the clanging.

The image of the Spinner shimmered and glowed. The thread began to move with the woman's hands, spinning it around and around.

Roth's eyes widened slightly as his brows inched higher. They were on the right track.

He moved to the crank closest to Riley and the stairs, repeating what he'd done with the other. Covering his ears again, he watched the image of the Allotter glow and come to life as the other had, moving the thread through her fingers while measuring the length meticulously. He moved to the final crank and covered his ears one last time. He watched the Inflexible appear, her shears slicing through the thread, ending a soul's time on earth.

Above him, he heard a crackle of flame and looked up in time to see the cause of it. Like a lit fuse, light sparked and traveled across the stone ceiling, drawing a dragon's taloned, membranous wing, then its body. It curled around, closer to the rope in the center holding the fourth bell up, to create the head.

Staring at the glowing dragon, Roth muttered, "You've got to be fucking kidding me."

Riley had been right—there was a dragon.

It ended with flames bursting from its mouth, catching the rope in the center. It sparked down it, heading toward the bell, and once it reached the brass, it glowed hot. With the magic guiding it, the bell lifted backward from an invisible crank and released.

Roth gritted his teeth against the noise and covered his ears again, while he watched the stone ceiling around the rope melt away. The bell slid up into the ceiling, disappearing, only to be replaced by a wooden ladder.

As the ringing ceased around him—but not in his ears—Roth peered up, trying to get a glimpse of what they could be climbing into. He waited for Riley to gloat about the damn dragon, but it never came. For a moment, he wondered if she was teasing him, but he had truly lost his hearing.

He turned around.

"Riley?"

She wasn't in the corner where he'd last seen her; she wasn't in any of the corners. He turned in a full circle and rubbed his eyes, hoping she would magically appear when he opened them again, but she didn't.

Roth swallowed.

What if she fell through an archway?

He stopped at the edge of each one, holding his breath as he looked over. He released a heavy sigh of relief when he didn't find her prone body sprawled on the ground below.

She probably went down the stairs to get away from the noise, he told himself. It had probably been enough to get her to move. But would she leave the tower without knowing what the bells revealed?

While he descended the stairs, his thoughts spiraled with him.

What if the noise attracted a demon not affected by the light? What if this demon dragged her into the darkness? It could be tearing into her right now. Sinking its teeth into her skin and feeding on her blood or bones . . . or both.

But he heard no screams.

Maybe I've gone deaf from the bells, he thought. *Or maybe the demon tore out her vocal cords so she couldn't scream.*

By the time he reached the bottom, Roth was panting and in a cold sweat.

A chilling fog settled in, blocking out the remnants of the sun. The darkness slithered beyond the tree line, and if Roth hadn't been clutching the wisp lantern, he would be the darkness's next victim. It mixed with the chilling fog, and rime froze to the ends of Roth's hair and brows. His face stung from the bitter cold.

"Riley?" Roth called out, his breath a puff of air. He didn't care if he was bringing attention to himself. Riley was out there in the freezing fog without a cloak while demons surrounded her, waiting to pounce on her if they hadn't already.

A sour taste was in his mouth at the thought. Bile rose up his throat. And although he was trying to convince himself a demon hadn't sunk its claws into Riley, she never answered his call. The wisp lantern rattled in his hand while the frost crawled along his bare skin, coating him in it as the air chilled further. It threatened to freeze his eyes and mouth shut. His lungs burned. He couldn't breathe. His chest heaved as he tried to gasp gulps of air down, but it was no use. He choked on the fog around him, his fear.

Stop it, a calm, steady voice said within him. It was the fighter, the survivor. The warrior. *You're hyperventilating. You need to breathe. Riley needs you, but you are of no use to her like this.*

The warrior was right; Roth couldn't find and help Riley if he couldn't breathe—couldn't calm his mind.

Breathe, he told himself. *One breath at a time. Focus.*

He inhaled, counting to ten, and released, counting to ten again. He began walking. Searching for Riley—breathing as he did. Focusing his mind on the task at hand and turning it into a blade, like the ones sheathed at his waist and back.

Boots splashing, Roth came to the edge of the lake. He held the lantern higher in front of him. The fog had thinned and the chill had vanished, but the cloud still hovered. Still blocked enough sunlight for the darkness to remain around him.

He searched the water, but found no disturbance.

There were creatures who lived in the lake and would gladly feast on a human.

Could she have been pulled under?

There was only one way to find out.

Setting his shoulders in resolve, Roth placed the lantern at his feet and sucked in a deep breath, ready to take the plunge for Riley—

His eyes snagged on the water—on his reflection. It stared back at him, blood coating his hands and face.

He lifted a hand to his cheek, and the reflection mirrored his movements—but when he swept his fingers across his brow, they came away clean. No blood. But the reflection's brow . . . There was a smear through the crimson.

"Is it worth it?" Roth's reflection asked.

Roth brought his fingers to his unmoving lips, and his eyes widened as he watched his reflection's hand remain at his side.

"Is sacrificing their lives worth it?" his reflection asked, his sea-green eyes earnest. "If you continue down this path, all the blood you've wiped from your hands will mean nothing. The lives you'll lose—*you'll sacrifice*—their blood will forever stain you. Nothing you do will change that." He splayed his arms, showing the blood dripping from them. "*Is she worth this?*"

Skin paling, Roth gaped at his reflection. He couldn't breathe again, but it was because of a whole new fear. "I-I— She's—"

Roth didn't get to answer.

Within the fog, a woman sang. It was the most beautiful voice he had ever heard, and her song—it was the one within his heart and soul, melting the remaining ice that had formed around the storm. The melody was the eye—his center. The calm to his raging, torturous soul.

It was all he wanted.

All he *needed.*

The fog dispersed completely, letting the sunlight scatter the darkness away, as if it knew Roth needed to find this woman with the mesmerizing, angelic song.

He needed it in his mouth. It was the air to help him breathe, to give him life. She was the oxygen his lungs screamed for.

Yearned for.

He needed to taste the words on his tongue, down his throat. Feel them scrape against his teeth. He needed her to explore every inch of his mouth. Of his body. Needed to merge with this mysterious woman.

Become one.

Nothing else mattered.

Nothing.

In the lake, the woman stood, the water up to her hips, with her arms outstretched to him. She was the one Roth had waited centuries for. Searched for all of his life. She was his heart, his soul. *His everything.* She was his and he was hers, and there was no one in all the worlds who could keep them apart.

The woman's song caressed his skin, creating goose bumps. He couldn't take his eyes off her naked, moon-pale body. Her fiery hair glowed in the remaining fragments of the sunlight, illuminating her face —she was the most breathtaking woman he ever had the honor of looking upon.

His lungs began to fill with air once more, her song filling them. He needed to draw closer to her. *To fill his lungs completely.*

Water splashed at his ankles, his calves—through his reflection screaming a warning to him—as he drew nearer, and she stepped away from him, arms still outstretched. The woman sang her heavenly song while the water drew up to her waist, her breasts. Until all that remained above the surface was her head.

The water splashed around Roth as his boots dragged through the mud of the lake's bed, him following the woman farther. When the water was up to his thighs, the woman's head disappeared. "Wait," Roth said, reaching out a hand to her.

No ripples were left in her wake. No evidence she existed—except for her song, rising from the depths. Calling for him to follow her home.

Home.

It was what Roth had yearned for for centuries. A place that made him feel at peace with his past and banished all worries of the future.

A spark ignited deep within him—a crackle of energy. It smelled of earth and citrus and vanilla and—

A woman's ear-splitting scream pierced the forest, the clearing, the lake.

Roth's eyes focused, widening. "Riley," he breathed. He had forgotten her. How had he forgotten her? He looked around, realizing he was thigh-deep in the lake, and wondered how he had gotten *there*. He turned back to the forest. "Riley!" he yelled, flaring his wings.

He began making his way back to the shore. He had to get to her. Needed to save her before it was too late and she was gone from his life forever—

His feet snagged below the water, and he thought he was tangled up in branches or weeds, but it was so much worse.

Moon-pale hands gripped both of his ankles.

Roth turned in time to see the rusalka's sharp-toothed smile and icy blue eyes before she dragged him under the water with her . . . and finally filled his lungs with her watery song.

CHAPTER 27

In the tower, while Roth turned the final crank, Riley's body moved on its own, back down the spiraling stairs, without her telling it to do so. She tried calling out his name, but nothing emerged from her mouth. Her heart thundered beneath her breastbone, and her head spun as she took one step at a time down the stairs.

Across from the entrance to the tower, a pair of pale, almost skeletal boys wearing loincloths waited for her. In each of their bony hands was a wisp lantern to keep the darkness away. The boy to her right, with thinning, dark hair, beckoned her to come, to follow. And no matter how hard she tried, Riley couldn't stop her legs from moving her forward, into the safety of the blue glow surrounding the boys.

Follow my changelings, a woman said, and the children, standing on either side of Riley, took her hands and led her into the forest.

Riley tried moving her eyes—tried to get a glimpse of who spoke—but not even they would obey her.

With the darkness circling her once more, a chilling fog crept in, freezing her down to the bone. Ice crystals formed on her exposed skin, and if her body had been cooperating, she would have shivered, her teeth chattering.

As she moved deeper into the forest, Riley heard her name.

ROTH!

His was a scream on the tip of her tongue. A desperate, heart-wrenching plea—but no sound passed her unmovable lips.

Shh, my child, the woman soothed, her voice like a grandmother's. *I'm in control now.*

A chill swept down Riley's spine, but she didn't shiver as the hairs on the back of her neck rose. The woman's voice wasn't beside her—it was inside her mind, telling her what to do. Commanding her body to follow the changelings holding her hands.

Impossible, Riley thought.

This was nothing like when she'd lost control over her body to the tune of an enchanted flute. She was fully aware of what was happening to her. And it couldn't be compulsion magic, not only because she couldn't be compelled, but because the only faeries around were the changelings. They hadn't said a word to her.

The only answer she received was the woman cackling inside her head.

They moved from the road down a small path, hidden behind broken buildings. It would be easy to miss, covered as it was with thick cobwebs and hidden by branches, and unless one shined a light on it, the darkness made it impossible to see.

They stopped in front of a gate. The razor-wire fence on either side kept not only the small critters caught within from going inside, but Riley imagined the demons stalking within the darkness as well—and gods only knew what the fence was protecting. Atop the nearest fence posts sat skulls of varying sizes and species, but some were notably *human.*

The changelings led Riley through the gate and past the skull-lined fence posts, stopping when the earth rumbled and shook. As if something very large stalked their way. The vibrations shot through Riley with every earth-trembling step.

Is it a giant? she wondered. Although they'd been killed off and erased from existence during the Terra War, she couldn't help but wonder if the woman in her head was a giantess and walking toward her in the darkness.

Guess again, child, the woman answered.

But Riley didn't need to. The legs moved into the blue glow from the wisp lanterns. At first, she thought they were two tall trees walking, their roots dangling, but upon further inspection, she saw the talons at the ends of the so-called roots and the trunks were a shade of yellow.

Bird legs. Riley gasped inside her head.

Abruptly, they halted; they crouched, lowering themselves, and like a bird sitting in its nest, the legs disappeared—but it wasn't the body of a bird Riley stared at. A hut sat in its place. Branches piled under it, as if it sat upon a giant bird's nest, and mixed among it were bones.

Since being taken, Riley had seen a lot that shouldn't be possible, but never *this*.

Still holding Riley's hand, the changeling on her left with thinning, snow-white hair pushed back the wooden door and led them inside. The overwhelming stench of rotting corpses, spices, and herbs slapped Riley in the face as a fire roared to life beneath a cauldron in the hearth, and little wisps of flames winked into existence overhead from the candelabra made from ribs.

Riley would've gasped—or possibly vomited—if she were able while she took in what her eyes saw without being able to look around.

Herbs and severed limbs hung from the ceiling. Intestines were strung up from the mantle over the hearth like sausages. The circular table in the center was cluttered with twigs, unlit black candles, more bones—of critters, faeries, and humans alike—crystals, and an obsidian bowl in the middle, carved with two crescent moons and a pentacle between them. One of the wooden legs of the table had been replaced with a leg of flesh, as if the original wood had broken and that was all that had been on hand. Mice nibbled on the remnants of the foot and skittered away into small holes at the bottom of the walls.

The changelings unstrapped the sword from Riley's waist and the dagger at her thigh, placing them in a woven basket in the corner holding a broom, a large pestle, and various weapons that were both sharp and polished and dull and rusty. They took her bag, emptying the contents into a glass-doored armoire carved with a swirling pattern, next to the basket with other trinkets—belongings—safe from thieves.

Riley's body vibrated with anticipation while she waited for the woman in her mind to make an appearance, but there was no one else in the hut with her and the changelings.

Soon, child, soon, the woman reassured her. *Take a seat at the table while you wait.*

Riley prayed to the gods it was the table beneath the candelabra and not the one against the left wall, with carving knives and saws hanging above it—but there was a disfigured, bodily-shaped lump already occupying the space, blood dribbling through a hole in the surface into the bucket beneath.

With the woman guiding her legs, Riley walked past a cot against the wall, opposite the butcher table, to the chair in front of the hearth at the circular one. She sat down, her back to the cauldron, its contents bubbling and emitting a foul stench. From her spot, she could see from the corner of her eye that the blanket covering the cot had been woven from fine threads of . . .

Oh, gods, that's hair, Riley realized.

And in between the armoire and butcher's table were shelves with jars filled with organs, teeth, bones, flesh-covered fingers and toes, eyeballs . . . *tongues.*

A scream crawled up Riley's throat and lodged there.

There, there, child, the woman soothed in Riley's mind, *no need to get upset.*

My ass, there isn't, Riley thought back harshly.

The woman laughed.

By the door, the changelings shifted, their heads tilted as if they were listening to something—or *someone*—outside. It wasn't long before Riley heard what they did.

Sweet humming drifted through the open door from beyond the threshold. Every hair on Riley's body rose as the sound floated closer, until a hunched, frail, elderly woman with knee-length gray hair and wearing tattered rags hobbled through the threshold.

She padded past the changelings to the shelves with miscellaneous body parts, her crooked fingers landing on a jar filled with red liquid, and she handed it to the changeling with snow-white hair.

"There you go, my darlings," the crone cooed. The changeling gleefully gulped down half of the jar's contents before handing it to the other. "Now," the woman said, "run along. You've earned it."

The changelings smiled, revealing spindly, spiked teeth. Their mouths were stained crimson, and the one with dark hair licked at the blood with his pointed tongue. Their sunken, dark eyes began to glow as they left the hut, leaving Riley alone with the witch.

Sighing, she went to the disfigured lump on the table, taking a bowl and a spoon. She hovered over what looked like the head and, with her spoon, dug in. There was a sickening sound as she carved into whomever it used to be. "I am delighted to have come upon a human in the forest," the crone said, dropping an eyeball into her bowl. "It has been so very long since I have had the sweet, pleasurable taste of human." She dug back in for the other eye. "I've been trying to make this snake last, but alas, he's going bad." Shrugging, she added, "He wasn't very tasty—nagas are the delicious serpents—but I'm not one to waste food." The other eye plopped into the bowl, and if not for the control the witch had over Riley's body, she would have vomited.

While the crone hobbled past Riley to her cauldron, bowl of eyeballs in hand, she noted the woman's eyes, milky and unseeing. *She's blind.*

"Yes, child," the witch said. "I am—but that doesn't mean I don't *see* everything." She looked pointedly at Riley, who darted her eyes away.

Riley blinked, realizing she could move. *Maybe what this woman did to me is weakening.*

The crone dumped the eyeballs into the cauldron. "My magic is not weakening," she scoffed. "You move because I allow it, Riley Hayes."

Riley's head whipped to her. *How does she know my name?*

"You may speak aloud if you wish," the crone told her. She scooped the contents of the cauldron with a ladle, bringing it to her lips. She slurped and found it lacking, her nose crinkling.

Riley watched the woman go to the shelves beside the hearth with spices and oils and sniff a few before she found the one she searched for. "How do you know my name?" Riley asked, her throat dry. And although she could speak and move her head, the rest of her body remained paralyzed.

The crone sprinkled the spice into the cauldron and stirred. "I am a witch, child," she explained, "as old as the Mother of All. I know everyone's name, and I know all of their futures, too." Lifting the ladle to her lips once more, she nodded, satisfied, and began stirring again.

"You can see the future?" Riley asked skeptically.

"I may be blind—a steep price to pay for the Sight—but I can see all the golden threads of possibilities attached to you." The witch turned to Riley, ladle in hand. "The threads connect like a spider's web, and at its center is you." With a crooked finger, she tapped the center of Riley's chest.

Riley frowned at the finger. "So, this is my future?" she asked, looking from the gnarled finger to the crone's blind eyes. "To be eaten by a witch?"

The witch smiled, her few remaining teeth black and yellow. "It is one of them," she answered. With her fingers, she pulled on an invisible, golden thread. "Or perhaps, you would prefer this future? Your handsome knight coming to save you." She clicked her tongue. "It's too bad he's indisposed at the moment, finding the woman of his dreams." The witch cackled, her head thrown back, before choking on her own spit.

Watching the crone hack and cough, Riley curled her upper lip in disgust, but the witch's words crashed down on her, hard. What had happened to Roth? And who was this woman of his dreams?

Regaining her composure, the crone cleared her throat, her focus finding Riley. She arched a quizzical brow and reached out tentatively to another unseen strand. She set the ladle on the table, amongst the clutter, and with both hands, her fingers began sifting through the air. "Curious, child, very curious. Beneath the top layer is a hazy mist."

Riley frowned, arching a dry brow. *This witch is crazier than I thought.*

"If you had the Sight, child, you would not be thinking that about —ah, what is this?" The witch pursed her lips in thought. "Leaves," she mumbled. "And a . . . vine?" The witch reached out and made a tugging motion, as if she were pulling on this invisible vine enshrouded in a hazy mist. Her eyes widened, she gasped, and there was a flash of light—

The witch screamed as her milky eyes burst into flames.

CHAPTER 28

Roth struggled against the rusalka's grip dragging him down, down, down, to where her home—her grave—lay beneath the lake.

He'd been trained, like all ailerons, to stay underwater longer than most, but his lungs screamed for air as the rusalka's song filled him. Claiming him, as she did with all her victims.

His dagger and short swords had been lost to the lake in his attempts to escape, which had only enraged her. She moved swiftly through the water, avoiding obstacles as only one who knew the area intimately could. The pressure of the water and the velocity of their movement had disabled him immediately. His arms were heavy and useless, trailing behind him.

Black crept in around the edges of his vision. His head felt light and airy, and it was all he could do to stay awake.

He had to stay awake.

Weeds slipped over him, threatening to tangle him up, but the rusalka moved too quickly. The slimy foliage clung to him, wrapped around his arms, his waist, his neck, as they were ripped free. Smooth sludge slipped through his fingers, and he realized it was mud. The rusalka pulled him along the lake's bed.

Rocks sliced across his cheeks, cut up his palms, his knuckles. Sharp, pointed sticks poked through the sediment, stabbing at him but unable to find his flesh through his leathers.

As the rusalka whipped through the water, Roth's fingers found a smooth rock embedded in the mud. He clung on, hoping it would halt the spirit from dragging him farther through her grave. But as it slipped free, he realized what he gripped was not a rock.

It was a skull. And the stabbing sticks were ribs.

The skull's empty gaze stared at Roth, screamed at him this would be his fate, before it slid through his grasp and spiraled through the water back to the bottom.

The bones of the murdered slapped against his face. They snatched at his arms, his hands, as though they, too, tried to drag him down—as the dead had always done to him.

The black at the edges of his vision overwhelmed him, and the pain in his lungs was unbearable. It grew harder to resist it, to run from Death.

The fight within him was slipping away with every mind-bending turn the rusalka took. With the last ounce of air leaving his lungs, Roth thought of Riley and every single soul he had failed.

CHAPTER 29

The witch collapsed to the floor, her blind eyes gone, leaving behind charred, smoking sockets. Her skin sagged more than before, appearing almost like melting wax, and she smelled of cooked meat.

Riley gaped, wide-eyed, at the deceased woman. *What just happened?*

"You killed her," said a light, boyish voice, sounding just as in shock as Riley felt.

Riley leapt from her chair, knocking it over. She looked down at her hands and legs in surprise before her eyes widened further as she took in the sight of the changelings, still holding their wisp lanterns. They were no longer skin and bones, but two healthy, young boys, their glowing eyes the only feature setting them apart from appearing completely human.

How was this possible?

Before they'd left the hut, they'd been walking skeletons wearing skin suits, and now they looked ready to wrestle like young boys did. Even the pallor of their skin had a rosy tint to it.

As they stood inside the doorway, their heads leaned toward each other, as if they were oppositely charged magnets.

"I didn't," she told them, holding out her hands placatingly. The changelings exchanged looks; they didn't believe her. "I swear, I didn't kill the witch," she said again, urgently this time. "She pulled on a future —that's all! I swear, *I didn't do anything.*"

But the changelings didn't listen. They crept closer, rounding the table. Riley backed away, her hands still raised in surrender. She nearly tripped over the fallen chair, and when her calves hit the edge of the cot, she fell back, her hands gripping the rough, woven blanket made of hair. The dark-haired changeling crept closer to her, while his brother hung back, examining the witch's body.

Heart beating wildly in her chest, Riley pleaded one last time. "Wait, please—"

The white-haired changeling spat on the witch and kicked her lifeless body. Riley blinked, trying to process why he would do that when he had helped the crone.

In front of her, the dark-haired changeling held out his hand. "Thank you," he said in his light, boyish voice. Around his mouth was still stained with blood, but his smile was thoughtful, genuine. Albeit somewhat terrifying with his spiked teeth.

Warily, Riley eyed the changeling's offered hand. "I don't— I don't understand," she said, her voice shaky.

"You are not the only one the witch controlled," the dark-haired changeling said. "Thank you," he repeated, reaching his hand out farther. Trying to show Riley he truly meant her no harm.

She worried her bottom lip, looking between the outstretched hand and the changelings. A heavy weight settled in her chest as the changeling's words sunk in. She knew how it felt to be there, watching as your body did what it was told but not as you commanded. To feel the sting of what you'd done to yourself as the one who'd made you do it laughs, their eyes big and fascinated while they took it all in, wondering what they should make you do next. She knew what it was to be a puppet and wish for the strings to be cut away. To be free once and for all.

"I'm Ilyas," he said as Riley accepted his help. "And that's my twin, Iyan."

Iyan looked at her with frantic, glowing eyes. "We must hurry," he said. "Your friend won't last long against the rusalka."

Riley tensed. *Oh, gods—Roth.*

Iyan went to the armoire and began taking her items back out, stuffing them inside her bag as she asked, "What's a rusalka?" She knew it had to be *very* bad if Roth wouldn't last long against it.

"A water spirit," answered Ilyas. "She lures men into the lake to drown, as she did."

Swallowing, Riley remembered the witch's words: *"It's too bad he's indisposed at the moment, finding the woman of his dreams."* She took a deep breath. "Okay, how do we stop it?"

The changelings exchanged a look and turned back to her. "We can't," they said in unison.

"Only avenging the rusalka can stop her," explained Iyan.

"How do you do that?" Riley asked.

They looked at each other before Ilyas answered, "By bringing her murderer to the lake and drowning him. It's the only way her spirit can be set free."

Okay, Riley thought, frustrated, *that's not going to happen.* But it wasn't going to stop her from getting Roth.

She took her bag from Iyan and went to retrieve her dagger and sword from the basket with the large pestle. "I'll need to borrow one of your lanterns," she said. "I'll give it back after I get Roth . . . Or if I don't survive, it should be by the lake," she added.

That's not going to happen, she told herself. *I will get Roth back, and we'll leave this godsdamned forest together—treasure or no treasure.*

They could always return another time. They knew where the tower was, but at that very moment, Roth was her priority. Mara was gone, but he was still alive—as far as she knew.

The stubborn, old bird had grown on Riley. He knew more about her than most and had been the first to make her feel deserving of love in a long time. He saw her—*truly saw her*—and hadn't abandoned her after so many who had come before him had. Riley wasn't about to give up on him. Not after all they had been through together. Not when he meant so godsdamned much to her.

Iyan placed a hand on her arm, slowing her as she buckled her sword belt around her hips. "You don't need to borrow a lantern," he said. "We will take you to him."

Riley looked between the changelings, grateful for their help—even though she didn't think she deserved it.

"Thank you," she said and buckled her dagger to her thigh. "Lead the way."

Exchanging another glance, the changelings smiled, showing their spiked teeth. In unison, they spoke in another language, the words rhythmic, like an incantation.

And when the words ceased, the hut shot into the air, rising to its feet. Riley's stomach dropped. The hut took its first step, and she lurched forward, catching the corner of the butcher table. She clung to it despite the blood and what was left of the body on it, as the hut with bird legs crashed through the forest.

Pots clanged, the cutlery on the wall rattled, and the knick-knacks in the armoire rolled about, but nothing moved from its place, as if magic held it still. Even the changelings remained where they were, at the center of the hut, in front of the circular table, standing as if the entire place weren't colliding with trees outside. And like the inside, the outside must have been magicked as well to prevent damage. Otherwise, they would be under a pile of ruin.

Minutes passed, and the hut came to a jolting stop.

Before letting go of the table, Riley waited for the world to stop spinning and made sure they weren't about to go for another ride. Her grip loosened. Her arms and fingers were sore from gripping the wood too tight, but other than that, she was in one piece. Using the edge of the table, she stood on wobbly legs and gasped.

She stared, wide-eyed, at the broken body before her. At the carved-out eye sockets, the absent lips, and chipped fangs. Both legs were missing, and the left arm had been chopped to the elbow. On the right arm, scales had been peeled away, making the roaring tiger tattoo on the bicep nearly unidentifiable.

Riley's body trembled. Bile rose from her stomach. She whirled and vomited on the wooden floor.

"Oh, gods," she rasped. "Nathair."

She might have wanted the snake dead—wanted him to suffer—for killing Mara, but no one should be treated like *that*.

A small, pale hand rested on her shoulder. "Are you all right?" asked Ilyas.

With the back of her hand, Riley wiped her mouth and nodded. "How long has he been here?" she asked.

Iyan answered, "Almost a week."

That meant Grimsley had almost a whole week's head start, Riley realized. But like Nathair, Grimsley might not have made it out alive.

That's not going to happen to me, Riley told herself.

Setting her shoulders with determination, Riley went to the door and opened it. She squinted into the setting sun, watching the remnants of the fog dissipate. But before she could take her first step outside, the changelings grabbed her by the arms and yanked her back. She yelped as her ass connected with the floor.

Terror overwhelmed her determination. The changelings stood over her, and she thought this was it. They had tricked her into trusting them, and now they were going to kill and eat her.

But they didn't.

They held her down while the hut dropped to the ground, preventing her from knocking her head into the ceiling as her feet would have left the floor. After the hut settled into its nest of branches and bones, the changelings helped Riley to her feet. She dusted her ass off as she walked out of the door, staring at the lake.

Somewhere, down below, Roth was either fighting for his life or . . .

Not allowing herself to consider the alternative, Riley dropped her bag and took off her boots. She unstrapped her sword, praying to the gods she would find him in time.

CHAPTER 30

Bubbles floated up from Riley's mouth, as she was desperate for air. Surfacing for the third time, she swallowed as much oxygen as her lungs would permit before she dove again, searching for Roth.

Below the surface, it was nearly as dark as inside the forest. She could have passed over Roth for all she knew. She hadn't come upon his body floating in the water and didn't know whether to consider it a good sign or not. She wouldn't feel better until he was in her arms, breathing and awake. Telling her he was all right and they could finally leave this godsforsaken forest. But every time she surfaced without a trace of him, every time she scoured the lake with her hands and legs, hoping to brush against him, the unfurling bud inside her shriveled more and more as the shadows came out of their crevices, testing the dying whirlwind of warmth.

He's dead.

The words forced themselves out—the shadows pouncing on the chilling heat—and Riley slapped the thought away. *Roth isn't dead*, she told herself. He's too stubborn to be—

A heavy weight wrapped around Riley's ankles, pulling her down. Her insides lurched from the velocity, and the pressure was crushing.

She tried reaching for her dagger at her thigh, but the force kept her arms pinned above her head—

Abruptly, Riley stopped plunging through the water. She bobbed back and forth in place like a buoy in the ocean, her body smacking into a solid mass on her left. Reaching out, she felt hard curves, and her fingers grazed softness, almost silky like—like *feathers*.

Hoping it was him, she felt around for Roth's face—and pulled her fingers back when she found the talon at the apex of his wing. Riley's heart somersaulted in her chest, but the warmth in her soul was nearly gone. She found his neck and wrapped her arms around him, thanking the gods she'd found him. Thanking whatever had dragged her down to him. She had found him, and it wasn't too—

She jerked back, denial and horror stirring in her stomach. With her arms around his neck, she felt something was missing. There was no beating of a pulse against her skin, and with her lungs first starting to burn with a yearning for air, she began to shake.

She couldn't be too late. They were supposed to leave the forest together.

But there was still a sprinkling of warmth left inside her, protecting the fragile new life.

Riley searched Roth's body for the source holding him down. Her hands traveled the length of his torso, then his legs, until she felt thin, soft strands wrapped around his ankles, keeping him in place.

Unsheathing her dagger, she cut through them, releasing Roth. His body began to drift away from her, and she scrambled to cut herself free. But the heavy weight holding her in place was much stronger and thicker than the soft strands that had held Roth. It was taking too long to saw through her thick bindings, and the more she tried, the tighter they became.

Riley couldn't see Roth, but she reached out, hoping to catch him before she lost him again. It had been a miracle she had found him floating at the bottom of the lake next to her, and she didn't know if another would occur if he drifted too far. Her fingers grazed his leathers, but the murk of the water made him slippery. He floated out of her reach.

A moon-pale woman with glowing copper hair swam out of the

darkness toward Roth. She caught him effortlessly in her arms, his head resting between her breasts. Her nails over his unmoving chest grew into needles, and her eyes like icicles bored into Riley.

"Mine," the rusalka snarled. "He's *mine*."

Like hell, he's yours, Riley wanted to snarl back.

Lungs screaming as loudly as the rage within her, Riley's eyes illuminated with newfound power, and the rusalka jerked back with Roth, her arms still wrapped firmly around his chest. Riley spurred herself forward, forgetting about the thick bindings holding her in place—but instead of holding her down, they propelled her forward, guiding her to Roth and the rusalka.

The rusalka swiped at Riley with her needlelike nails, catching the ends of Riley's hair as she bent backward. Riley's bindings wrapped around her torso, jerking her back, keeping her out of the rusalka's reach. With her dagger drawn, Riley cut through the water, mindful of Roth. Her blade nicked the rusalka's cheek. The water spirit screamed, not in pain but anger. The glow around the rusalka brightened, and her nails lengthened further as she bared her sharp teeth. She lifted her arm, readying to cut Riley down in one swipe.

Riley's eyes widened—but not from the bloodthirsty glint in the water spirit's cold eyes.

In the bright glow of the rusalka, a thick root emerged from the bed of the lake and wrapped around the water spirit's wrist. The rusalka cried out, the sound an ear-splintering wail, as the root continued to twist around her wrist, tighter and tighter, until Riley thought her hand might be sliced off.

Loosening her grip on Roth, the water spirit slashed at the root around her wrist with her other hand, and—

The lake's bed began to shake as the earth began crumbling away, swallowing water. Root after root shot out, wrapping around the rusalka.

Riley surged forward, hands outstretched to catch Roth, taking advantage of the distraction—but she didn't have to. Another root emerged from the bottom of the lake, wrapping around Roth's waist, and brought him to her. Despite her lungs constricting in her chest, she felt like she could breathe once he was safe in her arms.

The rusalka struggled against the thick roots clamped tight around her as they dragged her into the depths below. Enraged, she screamed and slashed at them, but it was no use. They pulled her down into the earth, and the ground began closing in around her, silencing her screams, until the lake's bed appeared undisturbed.

Eyes wide, Riley stared at the spot where the rusalka had disappeared. She shook, but not with fear—with anger and bitterness. She knew who controlled those roots, knew who had brought her to Roth. Even as the one around her ankles slithered up her legs and around her waist, stretching out to Roth to bind them together, even as it carried them to the surface—Riley hated the person behind this aid. She knew she should thank him, but as she breached the lake's surface, sucking air into her lungs in gasps, she would never be able to forgive him after everything he had done.

The root, still wrapped tight around Riley and Roth, brought them to shore, and Riley spat at it as it slithered away, back into the lake.

Dragging Roth from under his arms through the dirt, Riley set him down by the hut. Droplets of water coated his face and fell from her nose to his as she knelt beside him. This felt all too familiar to her, but Roth had been the one bringing a drowning Riley to shore.

Burying her anger and bitterness, she tilted his head to the side, opening his mouth, willing any water to escape. Pinching his nose shut and tilting his head back, she breathed puffs of air into his lungs before she brought her hands to his chest and started compressions.

One, two, three, four, five . . .

She repeated the pattern twice before the panic was nearly as overwhelming as the shadows encroaching on the vulnerable bud within, the warmth no longer there to protect it.

"This is not how you die," she said thickly as tears trickled down her cheeks. She started compressions again. "Do you hear me, stubborn, old bird? You are not dying today."

Mouth upon his, Riley breathed air into Roth's lungs again. His chest rose, but not on its own. She drew back and cupped his face, searching for any sign he hadn't gone to the Elysian Fields, where he would stay for the rest of eternity. "Don't leave me, Roth," she said softly.

But he was already gone.

Riley wrapped her arms around Roth and rested her forehead against his chest. Her tears rolled down her cheeks and dropped onto his wet leathers as she sobbed.

Within her soul, the shadows had regained control of their barren wasteland. They toyed with the bud before they would inevitably rip its roots out from the dirt and throw it into the chasm with the monsters below. To let them suck the remaining life from it.

As the shadows consumed Riley within, it wouldn't be long before the sun's protecting light vanished, and the darkness of the forest would slither and gather beyond it.

But Riley was ready for it to devour her. There was no fight left in her.

Mara was gone, Jasper was somewhere under the sea, and Roth . . .

A sob tore from Riley's throat.

Roth was dead.

He would never roll his eyes again as she teased him, never try to make her blush while she read a steamy book. She would never hear his rough laugh again, see his smile that made the corners of his eyes crinkle. And there would be no one to soothe her when she was having a rough day and remind her how worthy she was and would always be.

In this moment, clutching onto the remainder of Roth, Riley felt a piece of her glass heart break. But it went deeper than that, down to what made her *her*, as if a part of her had faded away.

Distantly, as she waited for the darkness to sweep in and consume her, Riley smelled the faint stench of burning embers. She turned her head and opened her eyes, finding Iyan rubbing Roth's neck with his hands. Riley blinked a few times, wondering if her tear-filled eyes were playing tricks on her. "What are you doing?" she asked, wiping her nose with the back of her hand, her voice rough from crying.

"He's too cold," Iyan said without so much as a glance at her, continuing to rub Roth's neck. "He needs to be warmed before he can come back. This salamander oil should do just that."

Riley sat up, first noticing the small glass vial filled with clear liquid as Iyan let a few drops fall on his hand. He moved to Roth's hand, rubbing the oil over every inch of exposed skin. By Roth's feet, Ilyas had removed his boots and was doing the same as his twin: rubbing the oil into Roth's skin.

Holding out her hand, Riley said, "Let me help." She didn't understand how this was supposed to work. Roth was gone—but the changelings seemed to believe otherwise.

That was enough for her.

Iyan let a few drops spill onto Riley's outstretched hand. Where the oil touched, her skin warmed. She rubbed her hands together, letting the oil spread, before she took Roth's other hand and mirrored the changeling. And when his hand was coated, she gently placed his hand at his side and began on his head. Her fingers worked the oil into the skin behind his ears. On his earlobes and to the tips. They traveled to his brow, his temples, along his sharp jaw. They were soft against the tender skin of his eyelids and the groove between his nose and upper lip. And when they reached his cheeks, Riley jolted back, eyes round.

She gasped.

The hair on her arms stood up straight, and her skin tingled from her fingertips to her chest. There had been a spark—a small shock of electricity. It was the same she had felt between them the day they'd met. When their skin had made contact for the first time.

"He's ready," said Iyan. He corked the glass vial, sitting back on his heels, his brother doing the same. Gesturing to Roth's chest, he said to Riley, "Try again."

Riley didn't hesitate. She tilted Roth's head back, pinching his nose shut, and breathed into his mouth once more.

"Come back to me," she whispered.

Pumping his chest with her fists, she began to count. And each count held a word—a prayer.

Live.

CHAPTER 31

Roth gasped for air as his body spasmed back to life. He coughed up water from his lungs, and his head was turned to the side, helping him expel the liquid.

What happened?

A weight fell on top of him. Hands wrapped around his neck, pulling him close. A familiar voice, shaking with sobs, said into the crook of his neck, "You came back." Her voice was full of relief as her fists clenched in his damp hair.

Opening his eyes, he saw a dragonfly curled under his head and he breathed easier. She was alive, and safe, and held on to him as though she thought she would never be able to again.

It all came back to him in a rush: Riley missing from the tower, finding himself in front of a lake, being pulled into that water by a rusalka . . . drowning as the water spirit dragged him along the lake's bed.

Roth realized then, Riley had lost him the same way he'd feared of losing her.

Resting a hand against Riley's waist, he hugged her tighter against him. She squeezed him in response before pulling back. She smiled at him. Her lips were as bruised and sore as his felt. From the aching in his chest, he knew she had been trying her damn hardest to revive him. He thought one of his ribs might be cracked as he slowly sat up.

Roth lifted his heavy, aching arm, tracing her smile with the tips of his fingers. He caught a tear on her jaw with his thumb before it could fall and let his touch travel delicately along her jaw, her cheekbones, and to her brow. He wanted to memorize the feel of her soft, rosy skin. The freckles dotting her nose and cheeks. The tiny golden flecks of wild-flowers in her eyes.

But he also wanted so much more.

He wanted to know every little thing that made her the woman before him. The adventures she had been on with Mara's crew. The years in Erithena before they'd met. What her life had been like before she'd been taken. He wanted to know about her world. To be able to go there with her one day.

To kiss her with no reservations. To know the feeling of her bare chest against his and how perfectly their bodies fit together.

He wanted to experience *life* with her—and all the wonders, joy, and hardships that came with it.

Slowly, tentatively, Roth took the leap of faith for the second time in his life, closing the distance between them.

RILEY INHALED SHARPLY, holding her breath, and with wide eyes, she let his lips brush against hers. There was a question in the whisper-soft touch, one he had already answered for himself.

Do you want this?

She answered by deepening the kiss, her eyelids fluttering shut. He sighed against her, the tension in his shoulders leaving as her hands traveled over the strong muscles covered by his leathers. They slid up to his nape, where her fingers laced together.

The kiss was warm and tender but far too brief as Roth pulled back. But it said more than words ever could. It was a promise Roth would not abandon her. No matter the danger, the cost, he would stay with her. That he cared for her more than his vow and was willing to break it. Everything he did—yoga on the beach, reading under the stars, traveling across kingdoms for treasure, risking an evil forest—it was all for *her*.

The spark from their touch ignited within her, and the warmth flooded her with new and impressive force, driving the shadows back. The scent of rain poured over the barren wasteland of her soul. Clouds unleashed droplets of water, replenishing the earth, all while the warmth swirled around its precious bud, letting the droplets in. And from that rain, that warmth, the bud bloomed, giving life to a rose with petals of pure starlight.

Resting his brow against hers, Roth cupped Riley's cheek. "I thought I lost you," he said softly, hoarsely.

A surprised, rough laugh escaped Riley. "And I thought I lost you."

They remained like that, brows together, breathing in each other's scents and committing them to memory. Reveling in the feel of their shared breaths against their skin, with the knowledge they were both alive and together again. Until a shadow loomed over them and small fingers tapped on Riley's shoulder.

Startled, Riley jerked back. She glared at Ilyas. His brother shifted on his feet, watching the forest. She had forgotten about them after Roth had taken his first breath, coughing up the remnants of the water.

"What?" she snapped. She hadn't meant for the edge in her voice . . . or maybe she had. He had interrupted the moment she was having with Roth.

Unfazed by her tone, Ilyas said, "The sun is almost gone, and the darkness is sweeping in. If you want to live, you'll need to be on your way."

And with that, the changelings left for the safety of their home and the horrors within. It wasn't long before the hut stood from its nest, exposing its bird legs.

Riley silently thanked the changelings for helping her save Roth. She watched the hut disappear into the forest, the sound of trees falling as it crashed through them fading the farther it got.

"I have a lot of questions," Roth murmured, "but I don't know which one to ask first." He stared, eyes round, at the spot the walking hut had been.

Riley smiled, chuckling softly. She got to her feet and helped Roth to his. "I'll answer as many of them as I can, but first I think it's time we leave this godsdamned hellhole behind."

"Agreed."

Her smiled turned teasing as she arched a brow.

He laughed, shoulders shaking with the sound. Smiling, he said, "I told you not to let it go to your head."

"And that's immediately where it went." She returned his grin. "What else did you expect?"

"Nothing less, I suppose." His wide grin crinkled the corners of his eyes. If she had her camera with her, she would have taken a picture of him and tucked that smile close to her heart.

Gods, I almost lost that smile forever, she thought.

Riley bent over, picking up her discarded boots. "The changeling was right," she said, putting them on. "The darkness will be on us soon if we don't leave. I can't believe I'm about to ask this, but can you fly us?" They only had her flashlight to keep the darkness at bay, and that wouldn't be enough.

"Yes," Roth answered, his brows pinched in confusion, "But what about the treasure? The tower?" He trailed off, shock washing over his features as his eyes looked beyond her. "What happened?" he asked, his voice a mixture of surprise and sorrow.

She turned and gaped. Where there should have been a moss-covered tower, a pile of collapsed stone sat in its place, the water lapping over the crumpled ruins.

"I don't know," she began, but then she remembered the earth shaking, the roots coming forth from the lake's floor. *It must have brought the tower down*, she realized. And the trail to Lothaire's treasure and the scroll with it. Her fragile heart was already nearly in pieces, and seeing the fallen tower—the last hope she had of bringing Mara back—shattered it.

Riley fell to her knees, staring at the destruction. She barely felt Roth's arms wrap around her as he knelt behind her. Barely heard his apologies whispered into her hair.

Inside the hut, she had told herself she would leave the forest with Roth whether it meant finding the treasure or not. They could come back when it wasn't getting dark. When it was safer. At the time, her adrenaline and fear had allowed for her to be all right with that decision, but facing the reality of it now was devastating. To know—*truly know*—Mara was gone for good.

Riley could have knelt there for hours, but the darkness had other plans.

It closed in fast as the sun retreated, slithering beyond the tree line and over the grass. Snarls and growls drew closer by the second.

Roth cursed, and his arms and warmth vanished from around her. But she never moved. Not as Roth put his boots on, as he strapped her sword across his back between his wings with his remaining one, as he slung her bag across his chest. Not as he cupped her face, telling her to rise.

How could she when she had never stopped falling?

Roth didn't give her a chance to figure out the answer. He gathered her in his arms, pressing her tightly against him, and spread his magnificent crimson wings before the black claimed them.

CHAPTER 32

Riley's body ached. Her lungs were tight and heavy as the dreaded feelings flooded them slowly. The voice was back, telling her it was her fault they'd lost the trail to Lothaire's treasure. That if she hadn't run three years ago, Mara might still be alive. But even as they overwhelmed her, she wouldn't tell Roth those thoughts—there were more pressing issues to worry about.

Dawn was on the horizon as they traveled to Misthaven, the nearest town. Roth had informed Riley it wouldn't be much longer, but that had been an hour ago, and she thought he wouldn't last another as his eyelids drooped. They couldn't land, not with Grendelwyn Forest still beneath them. Their only hope was to reach the town of Misthaven, safe from the dangers of the forest.

Riley gripped her hands tighter around Roth's neck. She refused to look anywhere but his face, every so often catching a glimpse of dark crimson in the light of the rising sun. After Roth had picked her up and flown them away from the darkness, it hadn't taken long for the cool air to knock her out of her daze—but not enough to drive all the thoughts and emotions away. Once she'd realized the only thing preventing her from falling to her death was Roth's strong wings and arms, she'd clung to him like a cat stuck in a tree. Her nails bit into his skin, but he didn't wince or cry out. The only sign he felt it was his clenched jaw, but he never said a word.

Roth's hands tightened around her waist and under her knees. Riley wondered how sore his arms were from carrying her, but he showed no sign of fatigue from her weight; if anything, his arms seemed to hold the most strength after flying all night. As though even if his wings betrayed him and they fell, he would not let her go.

Stretching his neck, he sighed heavily. "When is your birthday?"

Riley slowly blinked at the question and realized he was asking to help stay awake. That he was doing the same as she had in the forest to stay grounded. He needed to hear her voice more than the wind whipping over them.

Clearing her throat, she shoved the voice in her head away, focusing all of her attention on him. "It's in the sixth month. In my world, it's called June," she answered, her voice still raspy despite clearing it.

Frowning, Roth asked, "Which day?"

"The thirtieth."

His frown deepened as his eyes filled with sadness when he figured it out. "You spent your birthday on that island? Just days after . . ." He trailed off, unable to finish.

But he didn't have to. Riley knew what he meant. That it was just days after Mara had died. And she'd spent her birthday on a deserted island, with no one but an elusive bird. She'd spent it alone, staring at the waves, wondering if she would ever be saved. Wondering if she *deserved* to be saved.

"I'm sorry," Roth said, dragging her out of her thoughts. "If I had known, I would've . . ."

"What? What would you have done? We were stuck on an island."

"I would've done something," he said softly. He sighed through his nose, the words almost disappearing on the wind before she heard them. "I shouldn't have left you alone."

In her soul, a patch of barren land became green with fresh grass as the warmth spread beyond the starlight rose.

"But you're here now," she said with a small smile.

His face softened as he brushed a kiss to her forehead.

She rested her head against his shoulder. "What about you?" she asked. "When is your birthday?"

"The first day of the first month."

Riley hummed thoughtfully. "I'll start planning the party now."

Her favorite smile stretched across Roth's face. "I'm sure you will, and knowing you it'll only have apple roses."

She clicked her tongue. "Nonsense, it'll have cake, too. And I'll even make sure it's strawberry, with strawberry frosting, decorated with strawberries."

"I don't think that's enough strawberries."

"You're right," she said, nodding. "The cake needs to look like one too."

Roth laughed. The kind that made his whole body shake and had tears sliding down his face. It was the kind that warmed hearts and made one realize how lucky they were to have this person in their life—and Riley felt just that. Warm and so godsdamned lucky to have this stubborn, old bird catch her during one of her hardest times. That through it all, he was still beside her.

Riley dislodged her nails from Roth's neck and wiped away the tears of laughter sliding down his cheeks. Smiling, she said, "My turn. What's the language you occasionally mumble in?"

Still laughing, he asked, "Afraid of what I've been saying about you?"

"No," she said, her eyes narrowing at him. "Not until this moment."

He grinned. "It's Scyathan, my native tongue."

"I didn't know ailerons had their own language."

"Not many do."

She wondered how much the world truly knew about ailerons; it couldn't have been a lot if they believed Roth to be a monstrous Crimson Knight, when she knew him to be someone completely different.

"Your turn," she said. "Next question."

His face bunched in thought, until a slow, mischievous smile stretched over his lips. She couldn't help but think she was going to regret indulging him to keep him awake. From the wicked gleam in his eyes, she wondered if she should let them plummet to the ground.

"What's the most embarrassing thing to happen to you?" His smile turned almost smug as she glared at him.

He was evil, pure evil. Hitting the earth with a *splat* was sounding like the best course of action.

Riley coughed, not saying a godsdamned word. Her throat became sore; from the wind, she assumed. She rubbed at it. "If you honestly think I'm going to answer that question, you've lost your mind," she said.

Chuckling softly—*evilly*—Roth's smile went wide. "How about this?" he suggested. "You tell me, and I will owe you an apple rose."

Brow arched in intrigue, she countered, "A dozen."

"Six."

"Deal."

His smile and the flash of gold in his eyes suggested he'd known she would agree to those terms.

Sighing heavily, her lungs aching with regret, Riley said, "When I was eight, I ran into a tree."

Roth's eyes flicked to her, skepticism dancing in them. "You ran into a tree," he said flatly. She nodded. "That is the most embarrassing thing to happen to you?" She nodded again, clearing her throat. "I don't believe you."

She feigned a gasp. "I can't believe you don't think I ran into a tree," she said as the pressure in her lungs built.

Shaking his head, Roth said, "No, I believe you ran into a tree. I don't believe that's your most embarrassing moment."

"It is."

"Liar."

She was absolutely lying. But she wanted those apple roses while keeping some of her dignity.

Avoiding eye contact to ensure Roth wouldn't see he was right, Riley opened her mouth to argue—but no words came out as her lungs constricted and spasmed, hard.

Her eyes widened with panic, and her heart beat wildly in her chest. She gasped, trying to suck down air. The slow flooding picked up speed, but it wasn't those dreaded feelings filling them.

"Riley?" Roth's voice was sharp with concern. Worry etched his brow, his eyes.

Coughs racked her body, and he held her close, his thumbs sweeping over her knee and waist, trying to calm the ever-rising panic in her blood.

And then she vomited. Bursts of water spewed from her mouth—but as she dispelled it, her lungs refilled.

Fingers clenching tighter around her, Roth cursed and beat his wings harder, driving them forward faster.

Riley didn't understand how or why this was happening to her.

I'm drowning while flying in the arms of a bird, she thought, her vision growing darker by the second. She wanted to laugh at the thought. Only in a magical world would that happen.

"Hold on, Riley," Roth said, his voice fading. "We're almost there."

We were almost there an hour ago, she wanted to argue, but the water wouldn't stop. Her lungs screamed for oxygen.

As she felt life fading away—as the newly born starlight rose began to wither—Roth brushed his lips against her temple, whispering, "Stay with me."

CHAPTER 33

"Help! I need a healer!" Roth yelled as he landed in the middle of the street in Misthaven. His legs wobbled beneath him, but he commanded them to stay strong for Riley's sake.

Images of Riley sinking to the bottom of the Gorsium Sea wouldn't stop invading Roth's mind. The first time she had drowned, he had been able to bring her back—to breathe life back into her. He had a feeling, deep down, it wouldn't work that way again. That she was already gone, only a flicker of light left within her, and it would take magic he didn't possess to bring her back to him.

Trickles of water still seeped from her mouth, despite her heart no longer beating behind her breastbone. The feeling of her cold skin against his slithered down to his spine. He began to shake from the chill, from the creeping finality of her life.

Roth stumbled through the street, pleading with whomever he passed to point him in the direction of a healer, but they all shrank back from him, from his crazed, thunderous eyes. Only one was brave enough to point down the street.

His legs burst into action, sprinting down the road, shouting for the healer. He held Riley tighter to him, not wanting to jostle her, even though she no longer breathed.

But that would change soon—it had to. He couldn't lose her, not when he'd finally chosen her. He'd broken everything for her.

Everything.

He knew he didn't deserve her, but she was worthy of life. And if she didn't live, then what was this all for? He couldn't go back to the way things were. To take another vow of abstinence—of penance—felt like taking one step forward, two steps back. But not only that, he was going back on his own advice.

"Everyone is worthy *of saving."*

He had said that to her on Brock's ship, when she'd thought herself to be nothing. And if everyone was worthy, didn't that include him? Didn't that mean he deserved to live, too? To be happy?

Forcing the prickling behind his eyes to go away, Roth sidestepped a small child playing in the street, shouting with all the might of his lungs and soul, "Healer! I need a healer!"

Rounding the bend four buildings down, a dark-skinned woman in white robes rushed to him, sprinting as fast as her legs would allow. She raised her hand, flagging Roth down, and his heart swelled with hope— with the possibility he could hold on to the first sprinkling of joy he had felt in a century.

And where the storm resided, tendrils of clouds drifted farther down, finding a small barren path, coming upon a forest as thick as a jungle. It twisted through foliage until it found what it craved, wrapping around the flicker of light, encasing it in its safety.

CHAPTER 34

The scent of lavender coated the room, relaxing Riley as she woke to a pair of unfamiliar hands running a damp cloth over her bare skin. She would have been alarmed if she hadn't seen what the woman wore—only a healer donned white robes covering them from their nape to the floor. They were cinched at the waist by a golden chain embedded with turquoise, showing the curves of her hips.

Riley swallowed, wetting her dry throat. "What happened?" Her voice was hoarse, as if she hadn't used it in days. The last thing she remembered was vomiting endless water in Roth's arms while they'd flown over Grendelwyn Forest.

She tried to sit up, but a dark brown hand settled on her shoulder, preventing her from doing so.

"Don't," the healer said, as soothing as the lavender oil on her skin. "You need your rest. You were poisoned by a rusalka," she added. The veil healers wore was missing, showing the thick, luscious, dark curls falling past her shoulders.

Riley blinked. "I was what?"

"You were poisoned."

"I don't understand." Riley's eyebrows scrunched. "*How?*"

"Her nails," the healer explained. "If they break your skin, her poison will enter the body, and you will die a watery death as she did. And you found out the hard way you don't have to be underwater for it to work," she added, bringing the cloth over Riley's arm.

Riley licked her dry, chapped lips. "But she didn't make contact with my skin; she only caught my hair."

"It doesn't take much," the healer replied. She brushed strands of Riley's chestnut hair aside and ran a thumb over the healthy skin above her breast. "She got you here—barely—but it was enough to get into your bloodstream. That's why it took so long to take effect, but eventually it'll still cause you to drown."

Settling deeper into her pillows, Riley blew out a shaky breath. "But you healed me? That's why I'm still alive?"

The healer nodded, her curls bouncing. "The magic in my soul sensed you before I heard your friend's shouts. It told me I would need to act fast if you were to come back. I had trouble doing so, but luckily you chose life over death." She gave Riley a soft smile, her dimples appearing beside her full lips.

The small gesture calmed Riley, although she just learned she had *died*. But because of Roth, this healer had been able to bring her back.

"Thank you, um . . ." Riley realized she didn't know the healer's name. Did healers give out their names?

The healer's smile grew. "Melissandra," she said, adding, "but you can call me Mel. Everybody does."

"Thank you, Mel," Riley replied with a small smile and looked around the room, hoping to thank Roth, too, but he wasn't there.

A plush beige chair was on the other side of her bed. It was dirty and smelled like the lake in Grendelwyn Forest. As if someone who had been covered in the foul odor had sat there far longer than they should have, embedding the stench within the velvet.

The door across from the bed, leading to the bathing chamber, was open, showing no sign of her old bird.

"He's still here," Mel said, dipping the cloth in the basin of water on the nightstand. She wrung it out and dragged it gently over Riley.

"Where is he?" Riley asked, sitting up, ignoring Mel's earlier advice.

"I sent him to take a bath," Mel explained, pushing Riley back down on the bed. She wasn't finished cleaning her. "He was stinking up the entire room." She crinkled her nose in disgust. "He was making it hard to concentrate while I tried to heal you, but he insisted on staying until you were well. My chair is completely ruined thanks to him. Now, I'm going to have to throw the damn thing out." She sighed, adding longingly, "I loved that chair."

Riley's brows inched higher. She had never heard a healer speak the way Mel did, nor as much. They were quiet folk, focused on their work. They usually only spoke when they were giving their patient aftercare instructions, if they required them.

Mel went on, "He is very loyal, your aileron, and incredibly stubborn. I damn near had to drag his ass out of this room and into another to clean himself up, all the while hoping he didn't pass out in the hallway." She shook her head, dragging the cloth over Riley's abdomen. "He was even too stubborn to close his damn eyes."

Riley smiled. "That sounds like him."

Dropping the cloth into the basin, Mel got to her feet, carrying it into the bathing chamber. "He had the audacity to growl at me when I tried to pry you out of his arms," she said from inside. "He only let me once I reminded him I was there to help, but he refused to let go of your hand. He held it the entire time, whispering lovely things against your fingers—sometimes filthy, dirty things, but he was sweet."

Riley's face heated as she smiled to herself. *Filthy, dirty things?*

Mel walked from the bathing chamber, snapping her fingers once. A pile of folded clothes appeared in her hands, and she handed them to a gaping Riley.

"I thought faeries couldn't make things appear," Riley said in awe.

"When you've been alive as long as I have, you learn a thing or two," Mel quipped, winking. Like she had tricks hidden up her billowy sleeves and she was the only one who was able to do them.

A thought occurred to Riley as she pulled her arms through the long sleeves of the pine-green shirt, the fabric light for the autumn weather setting in. Sliding the tawny pants on, she asked, "Can you make an apple rose appear?" It was magic Roth had told her he couldn't do, and she had craved one ever since being denied.

Mel smirked. She snapped her fingers and an apple rose appeared on the nightstand beside Riley.

Riley gasped, snatching it up. "You're a goddess," she said, taking a bite of the dessert. Her eyes rolled into the back of her head as she chewed.

Mel laughed, her midnight-blue eyes sparkling with tiny stars. "I'll give you and your dessert some privacy. If you need anything, I'll be downstairs." She snapped her fingers once more and disappeared, along with her ruined velvet chair.

Riley stared at the vacant space. Mouth full, she mumbled, "Thank you."

Finishing her dessert, she licked her fingers clean of the caramel and saw to her needs in the bathing chamber. Once done, she padded barefoot out of her bedroom in search of Roth.

She didn't have to search long; his room was next to hers.

He wasn't in bed asleep, but in his bathing chamber, lying in the white clawfoot bath with the water up to the rim. His back was to the door, and his wings drooped on the tiles. With his head bowed forward, he snored lightly as his arms rested on the rim of the tub.

A small smile found its way to Riley's lips as she listened to the soft purrs emanating from him. Wanting to let him rest, she turned around—

Water splashed, and instead of seeing Roth emerge from the bath, his body thrashed from side to side from an invisible attack. His snoring turned into grunts as his head was thrown back, cracking against the edge's hard surface, and his hands held a white-knuckled grip on the rim, the leather cuffs at his wrists digging into flesh.

Riley rushed to his side. His eyes were clenched shut and his jaw was locked. But there was nothing amiss. No evil force attacked him.

It was a nightmare, she realized.

Whatever hell his brain was conjuring, it forced the veins in his neck to bulge. He could have been reliving a thousand different nightmares he had faced back in the war, or it could have been a recent event. Whichever it was, Riley needed to get him out of his mind and back into safety.

Her hands cupped his face. "Roth, wake up, you're dreaming." Her words didn't reach him as he continued to thrash, splashing water onto her fresh clothes. "Roth," she said, louder this time, "you need to wake up. Whatever you're seeing, it isn't real. It isn't happening —Roth!"

It all happened in the blink of an eye—he was in the water, her hands holding his face, and then he was standing. Her body twisted around, his large hand coming to rest on the top of her head as his other one wrapped around her neck. As if he were going to snap it.

Gasping for air, she tried to scream, but there was no sound. Nothing came out of her mouth. She couldn't breathe. She clawed at his hand, his arm, trying to get him to stop, but he wouldn't.

In the mirror on the wall, Riley saw his eyes. They were dull and dazed, his pupils dilated. He was still asleep, fighting his nightmare.

BLOOD COATED EVERYTHING: the ground, buildings, trees . . . Roth's hands, his face, his tongue. It was a memory of a battle in a small village. Everything was the same except for one thing.

Riley. She was there, hanging in a tree by her neck, alongside the other humans of the village, strung up not by giants but elves. He cried out, scrambling to get her down, but someone grabbed his wing, keeping him from her. He turned, finding it was himself—the reflection from the lake within Grendelwyn Forest, drenched in blood—holding him back. And behind his doppelgänger were his people.

He recognized every aileron. Some had perished in the war, while the others were still alive, counting on him to do what had to be done—but he couldn't. He couldn't go through with it.

"There has to be another way," he pleaded to his reflection. "I know there has to be."

"You would choose her after everything I've been through?" a woman said, voice all too familiar. Roth could see her copper hair weaving through the crowd as she made her way to the front. She towered over the others, but that wasn't what made her stand out—it was the absence of wings. She bared her teeth. "After everything *we've* been through?"

Others made their way to the front of the crowd to stand next to their general—all missing their wings, all female.

From the corner of his eye, Roth spotted hair so fair, it could have been white. Hair he had run his fingers through and knew smelled like berries in fresh snow; a scent that would stay with him for as long as he lived. It was engraved in him, just as citrus and vanilla was becoming.

Roth's general gestured from the female ailerons standing beside her to the fair-haired woman standing to her right—but Roth made sure not to look her way, knowing he would only see a ghost, for she did not live like the general speaking to him.

"We have sacrificed *everything* for sanctuary, and now you would risk it all for *her*?" she spat. "Is this how you achieve penance for your wrongdoing? Is she truly worth our *lives*?"

Roth hesitated. He knew what he should say—knew what they were all counting on him to do—but the words wouldn't come out.

After learning how Riley saw herself, how she felt undeserving of love and saving, he couldn't fathom going through with it. Because like the dragonfly inked on her arm, she must shed her skin and leave behind the shell of hurt, loss, and anger to become the magnificent creature she has always been. Roth had set out to show her how worthy she was of love and life in a world determined to make her believe the opposite, and it tortured him the world was winning.

So, no, he couldn't go through with what he was supposed to do. He would find another way to keep his people from danger, but he couldn't leave Riley when she had lost everything in the blink of an eye. It would tell her she was worthless and nothing, like she had always believed herself to be, and she deserved so much more—more than him. But she had him, every part. Until his last breath, his heart and soul belonged to her.

"I'm sorry," Roth said. It was all he could say before his general unstrapped her spiked mace, stained with the blood of their enemies, and attacked.

CHAPTER 35

Riley kicked back with her bare feet, connecting with his shin, and when that didn't work, she tried using the vanity to push them into the bath, but her legs weren't long enough. She dug her nails into his hair, finding blood and a bump where he had knocked it against the rim of the tub. She tugged, hard. His grip around her neck tightened, and his nails made shallow cuts in the tender skin. Small beads of her blood pooled at the openings. In the mirror, she saw the moment he smelled it; his nostrils flared, his pupils constricting, becoming sharp with clarity.

Eyes widening, he gasped, releasing Riley. He shoved her off to the side, away from him, and she fell to her knees on the hard tile, rubbing at her neck, coughing. She sucked air into her lungs as her body shook.

Looking over her shoulder, Roth stood with his hands braced against the vanity, his head bowed, eyes shut tight, and jaw clenched. His bare chest heaved as he breathed heavily. The strength in his wings vanished, letting them droop down to the tiles and rest against his wet, naked body.

Riley couldn't stop her gaze from going to the massive scar covering his entire torso. The pink, raised skin spread out like branches over his chest and arms, stopping at the top of his hips. The branches had small needles, like that of a pine tree, and were of varying lengths. They traveled up and over his shoulders and onto his back, and at the center, between his wings, was a large patch of pink, as if the injury had started there.

Approaching slowly, Riley grazed the tips of her curious fingers against the raised skin of his arm. Watching her, he stiffened but didn't turn her away. He let her explore, starting at his shoulder to where they stopped just above the leather cuff at his wrist, over his chest and down, feeling every ripple of muscle beneath the scarred skin. It was awful and yet beautiful somehow.

A perfect imperfection.

The mark told a tale, and just like her scars, his were proof he had survived something horrid and painful. She wondered what could have made such a mark on his skin, one that would cause him to hide it from her. He had refused to get the compass tattooed on his wrist, had never removed his leathers on the island under the blaring sun. They had spent weeks together, never parting from each other's sides, but just like his wings, he had been too ashamed to reveal it to the world—to her. She felt it in his stiff body, the way he couldn't look her in the eye, and it stirred something deep inside her. She wanted to know him inside and out, and this blemish on his skin wouldn't keep her from wanting that. It wouldn't keep her from wanting *him*.

Ducking beneath his arm, she stood in front of him, turning his face to hers. He closed his eyes as though he couldn't bear to see what hers said back to him. Hers spoke volumes; they said everything she couldn't, and he always saw, never ignoring the truth of what lay within her soul. If he wouldn't look, then she would show him the only other way she knew how.

She brought her lips to the center of his chest, over a particularly thick branch laced with small pine needles. She trailed kisses over the painful memory, his breathing becoming heavier with each soft touch of her lips, until he tilted her head back and looked into her eyes. What he saw there brought him to tears.

Standing on the tips of her toes, she kissed the stray drops away as he closed his eyes again and wrapped his arms around her waist, drawing her against him, her hands flat against his chest. He buried his face in the crown of her head, pressing a soft kiss to her hair, and she leaned farther into him, her forehead resting against the thick branch at the center of his chest. His wings found their strength and wrapped them in a cocoon of feathers.

They held each other in silence, and time stood still. Roth breathed her in deeply and sighed contentedly. A smile pulled at the corners of Riley's lips before she did the same, breathing him in as she'd done by the lake after he'd come back to life. But this time she didn't revel in it. Masking his wet, earthy smell was a burnt, rotten one.

Riley crinkled her nose, recalling Mel's words and remembering Roth had been asleep when she'd found him. She realized he must have fallen asleep before he could bathe. "You smell like a lake full of sala-mander oil," she mumbled against him.

Roth's lips curled into a smile against her hair and his shoulders shook as he chuckled roughly, breathing puffs of warm air against her scalp.

Briefly feeling his fingers press into her skin through her shirt, Roth unfurled his wings from around them, tucking them behind him. Riley wanted their warmth and promise of safety back as time began to move again. She buried her face deeper into his skin, trying to block out the sunlight streaming in through the window, showcasing the small town of Misthaven and farm fields beyond, covered in a thin layer of fog. But the smell of the lake only became worse, and flashes of Roth's prone body tormented her.

Riley listened to the steady rhythm of Roth's beating heart, reminding herself this was real, before pressing her lips over that spot and begrudgingly stepping out of his embrace. Wanting to give him his privacy, she turned for the door, but as she took one step out of the bathing chamber, his hand caught her wrist gently. She looked back over her shoulder.

So much had happened to them inside Grendelwyn Forest, and those events had brought them closer, made them realize how impor-tant they were to each other. But Riley had never imagined she would be able to see through Roth's eyes what he was thinking, as he could with her.

But there, in those sea-green depths, were the horrors from his nightmare, the pain he had felt—and the apology for what he'd done to her. He laid it all bare for her to see. Let his vulnerability show, as he had with his scar. And in his eyes, she saw one word.

Stay.

CHAPTER 36

Stiffly sitting on the edge of the tub, Riley examined the glass bottles filled with scented tonics for washing hair on the small table in the corner with all of her concentration.

As Roth had moved for the water-filled bath, she had become painstakingly aware of his nudity and had averted her gaze to the ceiling. This was not the time to be gawking, even if she really, *really* wanted to.

Water splashed behind her as Roth scrubbed himself clean. Her eyes wanted to betray her and sneak a peek over her shoulder, but she wouldn't allow herself to do so.

Picking up one of the bottles, she uncorked and sniffed it. Jasmine overwhelmed her senses, and she hummed her approval. She set down the scented tonic and picked up another, smelling lavender. It reminded her of Mel, and she instantly craved another apple rose. She regretted not asking if the healer could make a whole plate appear. Saliva pooled in Riley's mouth at the prospect.

A foot tapped at her back, splattering water on her shirt, where it soaked through to her skin. "Riley," Roth said, getting her attention. His voice was hoarse, as if his nightmare still plagued him.

"What?" she ground out, arching away from his damp foot. Her throat ached from the hold he'd had around her neck before surfacing from his nightmare. She reminded herself to ask Mel to heal the bruising she knew must be there. Roth didn't need the reminder of what he'd done in his sleep.

"Where did you go just then?" he asked, his foot disappearing below the water.

Her cheeks flushed. "I was thinking about apple roses."

He laughed roughly. "That doesn't surprise me."

Shooting him a quick glare over her shoulder, Riley muttered, "Did you need something?"

"I asked you what a standing bath is," he said through laughter.

"What are you talking about?"

"The small passage I read from your book, inside the cave, mentioned something like a bath, but it wasn't because the couple was standing."

Riley twisted toward him. "You've been thinking about this since the *cave*?"

"I hadn't thought about it until now. Sitting in the bath made me think of it."

She stared at him, wondering how much of her world he knew if he had to ask what a *standing bath* was. Blinking, she sighed. "I think I know what you're talking about; it's called a shower."

"Shower," he repeated thoughtfully, testing the foreign word on his tongue.

Riley's lips twitched in amusement as she listened to him. "I think you'd like a shower."

He cocked his head. "You do?"

She nodded. Many things could happen in one, things that were much harder to do in a bath. But she didn't say that, even while she couldn't prevent her eyes from wandering. His legs were bunched, causing his knees to poke out of the water, but through the sudsy water, she could see everything. She bit her lip, her breath hitching. Feeling his eyes on her, she forced herself to look away. She picked up a different tonic. Clearing her throat, she said roughly, "I think you'd have to bend over, though, to get the water to run over your head."

"These showers must be very small if I would have to do that," Roth mused, his voice low.

Riley swallowed, humming a noncommittal answer. Her fingers rolled the glass bottle in her hands as she tried not to picture him naked in a shower, with water running over his bronze skin and down the curves of his muscled back.

Water jostled behind her, and she felt warmth hovering over her. Roth's scarred arm reached around, taking the glass bottle from her. He placed it with the other tonics, his chest leaning into her back. She didn't notice the water from his skin soaking through her shirt this time as she arched into him. She watched him move glass bottles aside until he found the one he wanted.

Placing his free hand on her waist, he offered the tonic to her.

She stared at the proffered bottle. "Feeling lazy?"

"I think you know that's not the reason."

If there had been any shred of doubt inside her that he hadn't meant that kiss beside the lake, it was gone now.

Taking the bottle, her heart fluttered in her chest, and in that moment, she forgot it had been shattered into sharp pieces.

Against the shell of her ear, Roth murmured, "And you can look anytime you want, dragonfly."

The hand at her waist seared into her skin, through the fabric of her shirt. Riley's fingers squeezed the bottle as her toes curled on the tiles. Dragonfly? Her whole body flushed with heat. He hummed when he noticed, pressing a light kiss to her jaw before relaxing in the bath again.

Riley found a small stool in the corner and positioned it behind him, where he leaned against the back of the tub, letting his wings sweep the tiles. Rolling up her sleeves, she sat down behind him and uncorked the bottle, breathing in a scent she had become accustomed to over the last three years. One that made her feel *free*.

She poured the ocean-scented tonic on top of Roth's hair and began massaging it into his scalp, scrubbing away the remnants of the lake. He leaned his head back, closing his eyes as her fingers worked the tonic through his hair. A low, approving rumble emanated from the back of his throat, causing her skin to tingle.

"Tell me more about your world," Roth said, almost purring like a content feline. "What was your life like?"

Riley's fingers paused as she chewed on her bottom lip, trying to decide where to start.

As if sensing this, Roth said, "Start with the best parts."

A smile spread across her lips; she knew exactly where to begin. "I had a twin brother," she told him. "His name was Liam, and we'd call each other Lee. Drove my mom crazy," she added, her smile growing.

The corners of Roth's lips curled up. "What was your brother like?"

"A goofball," she said fondly. Her fingers worked through Roth's hair again. "He loved to play pranks and make people laugh; he was good at that—making others smile. He was the only one who could cheer me up when I was having a bad day."

Until now. Now, she had Roth. Someone she'd thought she would never have.

"What would he do?" Roth asked gently.

"For our birthday one year," Riley started, "I was really sad. My best friend had moved away and wouldn't be there to celebrate. Liam told all of his friends there wouldn't be a party—if I didn't have my friends, he wouldn't have his; he was always doing things like that for me. Anyway, after my family ate cake and Liam and I opened presents, I wanted to be alone, but he grabbed my hand and pulled me out the door. He said we were going sledding."

Riley snorted, remembering. "It was a ridiculous idea. It was summer, but Liam grabbed the sled and we walked to a nearby hill known for sledding. At the top, we argued about whether it would work or not, and finally I got in the sled like he'd been telling me to."

"Did it work?" Roth asked, curious.

Riley laughed. "Not even a little. We just ended up rolling down the hill, giggling the whole time like fools." She grinned. "But it got me laughing and smiling like he wanted."

"It sounds like you ended up having a nice birthday," he said with a hint of a smile.

"I did." But her voice was sad, full of longing. "That was the last birthday we celebrated together before I was taken."

Roth was quiet. He took one of her hands and held it against his chest, swiping his thumb over the back of it in comforting strokes.

"I'm forgetting him, Roth," she said softly, thickly. Just like her mother and father, memories of Liam were fading away, and she didn't know what she would do when the final one was gone. "I don't want to forget Liam."

"You won't," Roth tried reassuring her, but it wasn't working.

How could he ensure that?

He pulled her other hand into his, setting it atop the other on his chest. She leaned into him, bringing her chest to his back between his wings, and rested her head on his shoulder. His wing brushed against her calf; it was a comforting gesture and helped dull some of the encroaching sorrow. But the scent of the ocean filled her senses, and it was as if she were back on Mara's ship, sailing wherever the wind took them.

Riley didn't want to forget Mara, as she was beginning to with her brother. She didn't want to forget everyone she had lost over the years, but it was happening. In time, they would only be a name to her. They would have no face, no scent, no voice. Only a name and the knowledge they had meant something to her.

Was that what it was like for Liam? Riley wondered. Did he forget her over time until she was only a name?

Her chest tightened, aching, and her body stiffened.

She was feeling nothing and . . . *everything*.

She had to get out of that room. Away from the ocean scent and the fading memories. From everything over the past twelve years she had been burying deep inside her.

Riley jerked back and out of Roth's embrace. She couldn't get words to form on her tongue, so she tapped his shoulders instead, letting him know she was done washing his hair. He dunked his head under the water, and she jumped to her feet, toppling over the stool.

She had to get out—before she was overtaken by those godsdamned feelings, the shadows.

But it was too late.

They were there, swarming her essence—her soul—where they always were and would always be. There was no getting rid of them. Only letting them overwhelm her or learning to live with them.

Riley fell to her knees outside the bathing chamber, doubling over, her arms wrapped around herself as sobs racked her chest, her throat. Tears poured down her cheeks with no promise of an end.

But it had to end—she *needed* it to. How else could she go on? How else would she be able to function day in and day out?

There was too much. Everything poured out of her at once, and she couldn't separate grief from anger, longing from loneliness. It was there, and it wouldn't stop.

It needed to stop.

She screamed into the abyss. *Someone, make it stop!*

ROTH CAME UP FOR AIR, finding himself alone in the bathing chamber. Stepping out of the bath, he grabbed a towel, wrapping it low on his waist, and heard a loud sob from outside the chamber.

He rushed to a fallen Riley and wrapped his arms tightly around her. Her body shook against him with each cry tearing from her throat. He tried to calm her, soothe her as he had done on Brock's ship, but what gripped her heart this time went much deeper.

There was more than just one emotion terrorizing her, and he could feel them—*all of them*. There were so many, he couldn't sort through them. Years and years of shoving everything down, and now they were coming back up full force.

There was no way to stop it. She had to ride it out, let it all pour free until there wasn't a drop left.

Picking Riley up, Roth sat down on the edge of the bed, setting her in his lap. Holding her close to him, he encircled them in his wings, blocking out the rest of the world. And as everything ripped free from her soul, he held her through it all, never letting go.

CHAPTER 37

Riley didn't leave the comfort of the bed, watching the sun go down, the moon come out, and the sun return—the only sign that days had passed.

She was in a daze, her head light and mind foggy; she couldn't function. All that was buried deep inside her still worked its way to the surface. She couldn't move, eat, or speak. No energy remained within her.

Roth never left her side, keeping her close and holding her tight. He ran a hand over her hair, rubbed her back, and rocked her in his lap. She felt like an invalid, but as it all came out of her with the strength of a tidal wave, she didn't care. All she wanted was to be held and soothed while she waited for the tears to stop.

And when she would get a short reprieve, Roth would coax her into eating, even if it was only a bite, and after she did, if her eyes remained dry, he would read to her as he had done on Brock's ship.

Until the next wave hit, and they would repeat it all over again.

A WEEK WENT BY, and the flood dried up, leaving Riley feeling . . . empty.

Hollow.

Whatever was left, it had grown roots, made her its home, and it would take a lot more to be rid of it.

She stared at the ceiling, watching the shadows from the lit candle dance. Roth's scarred, bare arm and crimson wing draped over her middle; his face nuzzled the crook of her neck while his light snores filled the room. The book he had been reading from was crushed beneath him; her old bird had fallen asleep mid-sentence during a sex scene, but Riley didn't fault him for it or tease him. He'd barely slept the last week, too busy taking care of her, and when he had, he'd woken drenched in sweat and breathing heavily from a nightmare.

The first night it had happened, Riley had tried being there for him but found it difficult. She could barely hold herself together for a minute without crying.

After tonight, it would be different. She could feel the fog in her mind thinning, but the lightness remained. It left her head feeling . . . blank. Devoid of despair and longing.

The grief, however, carried on. Her family and Mara were still *dead*.

As if he sensed that, even in sleep, Roth squeezed her impossibly close. She released a full-body sigh. His touch, his scent, even his snores filled her with some semblance of serenity.

She was grateful he was there with her. It had been hard after learning the fate of her family, especially Liam, and she knew she wouldn't make it through the loss of Mara without him.

The hardest part was the knowledge she would never have the chance to know the *real* Mara, the one who had existed long before they'd met. Before the faerie fruit and her father. The one Riley had come to know had been a fractured and broken girl, unable to escape her lies and cravings.

But there had been a time—a moment—when Riley had caught a glimpse of the real Mara.

On their last trip to the mortal world, they had gone to the beach, chocolate milkshakes in hand. They had sunbathed in the sand, while Jasper had scared Riley's fellow humans in the water, poking his head above the surface, his finned ears on display and golden-blue tail splashing.

The children had adored him, wanting to touch his tail and get photos taken with him; he'd had to dive under to get away. Unfortunately, not long after, he'd traumatized the children, strutting out of the water in his naked human form. Some women and men had whistled, liking what they saw, but the parents of the children had chased Jasper off the beach.

Riley and Mara had never laughed so hard, and Riley thought that was the first time she had seen Mara at peace. Drinking her chocolate milkshake, Mara had closed her eyes, soaking up the sun with a grin on her face. She'd been serene—*happy.*

Riley wanted to believe Mara was at peace and happy in the Elysian Fields. It eased her further to think her best friend wasn't suffering anymore.

Beside her, Roth moved his leg, stretching the limb across her lower half. Her lips twitched with the hint of a smile. She was slowly being buried beneath him, as if he couldn't get close enough to her.

She watched his eyes dance beneath closed lids and waited, wondering if he would wake from another nightmare. Bringing her forehead to his, she closed her eyes, wishing him good dreams. The warm air he breathed onto her skin sent shivers racing down her spine and raised goose bumps over her arms.

In the pile of shattered glass where her heart used to be, pieces lifted, found each other, and melded back together.

She knew it would take time to heal from the loss of her best friend, but she also knew she wasn't alone. She had Roth looking out for her. He would always be there to catch her when she fell—and with the help of his strength, she would rise.

Feeling his lashes tickle her cheeks, Riley opened her eyes and found him staring back at her. His own asked, *Are you all right?*

But they held so much more than that sole question.

The lone starlight rose, in the garden of her soul, was not alone anymore—dozens of red roses burgeoned and bloomed around the first. What she saw in Roth's eyes made her feel more alive and worthy than she had ever felt before. It was bright, and warm, and wonderful, offering her a new path in the webs of life.

With her eyes, she told him, *I will be.*

And she would.

She might be broken, but with a little help, and time, and care, she would be all right. Because she was still breathing, and she was not done living—not yet. Not when she had this realm-shattering, sky-splintering, wish-upon-a-shooting-star, beautiful new path lying beside her in all of his wondrous, perfect imperfections.

CHAPTER 38

Roth woke to the smell of pastries and an empty bed. A slowly building sense of alarm worked its way through him as he clawed at the cool, vacant space beside him, searching for Riley. He blinked away sleep crusted in the corners of his eyes and found her.

Sitting on the sofa with her legs tucked beneath her and a quilt over her lap, Riley read one of her books, using the morning sunlight streaming in from the window behind her. She wore a teal, long-sleeved shirt and black pants. Her damp, ocean-scented hair was tied back in a braid, draped over her shoulder, and he noticed the bruises on her neck were gone. Dark circles remained under her eyes, but the puffiness was gone. They were more aware and brighter than he'd seen in days. She looked lighter, unburdened.

Roth ran a hand through his tangled curls, sitting up. He sat on the edge of the bed and stretched, mindful of his wings near the fragile pot with an orchid on the nightstand.

He caught Riley watching him, her eyes traveling over the planes of muscle on his abdomen, following the branches of his scar to his wing, sunlight showing their true color. A soft smile fell across her face, and when she found him looking, she grinned. One he had only seen a ghost of before. He had seen her smile plenty of times before now, but this bright, crooked one was new. Genuine. It stretched to her eyes, making the tiny golden wildflowers shimmer in the fields of green.

"Good morning, old bird," Riley said. It had been just over a week since she'd used her voice, and there was a hint of hoarseness beneath her light, feminine tone, but it sounded like music to Roth's ears.

He smiled, his heart dancing to the melody of finally hearing her speak again. The corners of his eyes crinkled, and Riley released a small sigh of contentment.

He rose to his feet. "Good morning, dragonfly," he said, leaning down to kiss the corner of her mouth, but at the last second, she turned her head slightly, and he found her warm, slightly chapped lips instead. Her mouth curved into a smile against his. "Good morning, indeed," he murmured against her before kissing her again.

Sitting down beside her on the sofa, he noticed a plate of pancakes, a glass of orange juice, and a rather large bowl of strawberries on the table in front of them. Beside the meal was an empty plate and glass, with remnants of Riley's breakfast.

"Mel?" Roth guessed. Everything given to them since they'd arrived had been from the healer, including the softest pants Roth had ever had the pleasure of wearing. Only the gods could have created something so soft, and he was never taking them off again if he could help it.

Riley nodded. "I never would've guessed the healer was running a B and B, but I should've known, considering the room is so cozy with all the plush furniture, pillows, and quilts."

Furrowing his brow, Roth stopped mid-reach for a strawberry. "B and B?"

"Bed-and-breakfast," she explained, adding, "It's just like an inn, only homier."

Humming, he took a bite of his strawberry. Flavor exploded on his tongue; it had just the right balance of sweet and tart. He closed his eyes, groaning. It had been almost a century since he had allowed himself to eat his favorite food as part of the vow of abstinence he'd taken—it hadn't only been women he was abstaining from, but anything he loved and enjoyed.

Laughing, Riley said, "Do you want me to leave you alone with that big bowl of strawberries?"

Roth tried to flick her nose, but she brought her book up to block him. He settled for pinching her side instead, and she playfully swatted his hand away.

He ate a dozen more strawberries before diving into his pancakes. He froze, tasting—

"Strawberry pancakes," Riley said, smiling. "I told Mel you loved strawberries and needed a very strawberry breakfast. It's to hold you over until your birthday, when you get that cake," she tacked on with a wink.

The blood in Roth's veins heated, and his heart couldn't stop flip-flopping. It felt like a summer's breeze swept through him, smelling of roses.

Swallowing his food, he murmured, "Thank you."

"You're welcome," she said and went back to her book, letting Roth enjoy his "very strawberry breakfast."

It wasn't long before the pancakes were gone and the bowl of strawberries nearly empty.

"Are your wings red because your mother ate too many strawberries while you were in the womb?" She eyed him curiously.

Roth arched a sardonic eyebrow at her. "Did you really just ask me that?"

Riley arched a conspiratorial brow in return. "It would explain the obsession with the fruit."

He rolled his eyes, snorting. "I don't have an obsession with strawberries like someone I know has with apple roses."

She clicked her tongue. "It may be an obsession, but it's a healthy one."

"Says who?"

"Me."

Roth laughed, plopping another strawberry into his mouth.

"So, is that why they're red?" Riley asked again.

"No," he said, snorting. "That's not why." There were many stories about why his wings were crimson, but they all involved blood and brutality; no one had suggested *strawberries* were the cause. The corner of his mouth quirked up in amusement.

He waited for her to try to get an answer out of him, like everyone before her—she was the most stubborn person he knew, after all—but she went back to her book, content to give him as much time as he needed before he decided to tell her the story. A small smile spread across his lips.

One day, he would tell her how they'd become the color of blood, when he was ready to relive the pain.

Picking up the final strawberry in the bowl, Roth felt a sense of sorrow for not possessing the ability to pace himself. He stared at the berry, the corners of his lips curved down. His chest panged with longing.

While he wished he could have more, a knock came from the other side of the bedroom door. One glance at Riley told him she wasn't expecting anyone.

She set her book down on the table in front of them and sat up straighter, swinging her legs from the sofa as Roth replaced the strawberry with the knife from breakfast.

The door creaked open enough for a head with thick, bouncy, dark curls to poke inside. "Knock, knock," Mel, the healer, greeted.

Riley released a long breath as Roth set the knife back down on his empty plate. "Come on in," she said, waving the healer inside.

As Mel stepped in the room and closed the door behind her, Roth picked up his final strawberry again, biting into it, savoring the delicious taste of it.

"Sorry to bother you," Mel said with a sheepish smile. "I thought I'd check in. See if you liked the pancakes and if you wanted more." Her eyes went to Roth as he chewed the last of his strawberry. "Or, maybe you'd like some more strawberries, too?"

"I'm full, thank you," Riley said with a soft smile. "But I think Roth here needs all the strawberries you have in the building." She patted his knee, adding, "Maybe the town, too."

His mouth watered at the prospect of more strawberries, rather liking the idea of that after depriving himself.

Mel chuckled lightly. "Well, I don't know about the town, but I'll see what I can do." With the snap of her fingers, more strawberries appeared in the large bowl, along with more strawberry pancakes on Roth's plate.

He would've gasped if he hadn't already seen Mel perform this trick.

While Riley had been lost in her grief, he had gone to the healer, looking to her for help with Riley's broken heart, but there was nothing Mel could have done for her except make her as comfortable as possible as she'd gone through the hardest of times.

"That's all we can do," she had told him, handing him a tray of food she had made appear out of thin air for Riley. "Just be there for her, letting her know she isn't alone. And when she's ready, she'll come back to you."

And just as Mel had said, Riley had come back to him in her own time. But if he'd had to, he would've waited another four hundred years for her.

Roth smiled softly at the fruit and looked at Mel. "Thank you—and not just for the delicious breakfast."

"You are very welcome," she said, smiling back. "And I mean that; you both are welcome back here anytime. I had no idea pirates could be this behaved, not after the previous ones who stayed here a week ago." She crinkled her nose in disgust. "They were filthy and far too rude to— What? Why are you both staring at me like that?"

The strawberry Roth had been bringing to his mouth fell, hitting his bare foot before rolling under the low table as he gaped at the healer. Without glancing at her, he knew Riley was staring at Mel with the same shock flaring to life within him, followed by a string of *fucks*.

Beside him, Riley audibly swallowed her shock and curses. "What did they look like?" she asked, her voice as raspy as it had been when she'd greeted him good morning.

Mel considered her question. "Like I said, they were filthy. Covered in dirt and blood." Her lips puckered. "They destroyed every piece of furniture they brushed against—but they didn't ruin my favorite chair." She gave Roth a pointed look, and he avoided her gaze, looking up at the ceiling.

"Was one of them a lizard covered in thorns?" Riley asked, oblivious to the healer's glare she was shooting Roth.

"Now that you mention it," Mel said, wandering over to the edge of the bed to perch on, "one was. Nasty little bastard, that one, and definitely the captain. He shot orders at me like I didn't have anything better to do than constantly serve him and his crew while they talked in riddles. I have other patrons for fuck's sake! I was *this* close to pouring scalding tea on his groin." There was a wild, mad gleam in her midnight eyes.

Absently cupping himself, Roth made a mental note not to get on the healer's bad side—if he wasn't already for the chair.

"Did you happen to overhear what the riddles were?" Riley asked, a tinge of hope cresting her voice.

Humming, Mel's brow knitted in thought, a finger tapping the tip of her nose. "No," she said after a moment, shaking her head, her finger dropping to her lap. "I never paid much attention to the riddles."

Riley sagged into the sofa, the growing hope lost already.

"But," Mel said, and Riley perked up, "it sounded like they were heading to Kararhys."

Roth's stomach dropped, a brick taking its place, weighing him down.

Sitting on the edge of the sofa, Riley asked, "Are you sure?"

Mel started nodding, the movement becoming surer the more she thought about it. "Yes, they were. I remember because I was hoping they would get caught by the High Crown Guard and hanged. It's the least of what they deserve after the shit they put me through."

Riley beamed as she turned her attention on Roth. The way she looked at him, with her wide, crooked grin, made the storm within him want to calm for a beat, but all it did was stir and thrash, panicking like a caged wild animal.

He tried so damn hard to return the smile, the rare hope she felt. To make her believe he was beyond thrilled for her to be back on track to revive Mara. And if they were going anywhere else, he would be. He would be ecstatic for her. But he couldn't be, not when they would be going to the one place that would mean the end for them.

CHAPTER 39

After a grueling week and a half of traveling through the Misty Plains, the White Hills were finally on the horizon, a sign they would soon be entering the kingdom of Bilyndria. As they needed to be extra cautious in the High King's territory, Mel had gladly given them cloaks to hide their weapons and pirate insignias, and leather straps for Roth to hide his wings as he had on Obsidian Island. He had started to grumble about pinning them down again, but once Mel had handed them a bag of food for the road, strawberries included, he'd clamped his mouth shut and thanked her with a genuine smile.

Digging a strawberry out of the bag, Roth watched as Riley dug through her own, tugging out the pants from Mel—sweatpants from the mortal world, Riley had told him after he'd declared them to be made by the gods while he had shoved them into her bag. There was no way in fucking hells he was giving up such luxury. A few books followed before she found the one she had started in Misthaven. With the sun shining in through the few windows on the second level of the barn they'd decided to spend the night in, she would have an hour or two before the light was gone.

Riley sat back against a wooden beam, rolling her shoulder as she tried to massage the knots from carrying her bag, her free hand holding the book open to where she'd left off.

Roth took a bite of his strawberry, tossing the top aside, and scooted closer to her until she was no longer resting against the beam but his chest. His hands went to her shoulders, taking over for her. "You're too stubborn for your own good," he murmured against her hair. "I said I would carry your bag for you."

Leaning into his touch, Riley hummed. "Yes, but then you'd read ahead of me in the book. You can't deny your interest in it much longer."

He chuckled. She was right; after spending the majority of the trip listening to her tell him about the witch who fell in love with the king of one of the hells, his interest had been piqued. Growing up, he'd never had a lot of time to read, and if he tried to start now, he wouldn't know what to pick up first. But he was discovering he rather enjoyed the stories Riley liked—or maybe he just liked the woman who refused to be ashamed of her taste in filthy books.

Tilting his head down, he brushed his lips against her ear. "Then we better get reading, if I'm to carry your bag the rest of the way."

They spent what little time they had left of the light in each other's arms, stretched out against a pile of hay. With Riley's back against his chest, Roth read silently from over her shoulder, turning the pages back when she finished before him. Every so often, she would pause and turn to kiss him. His temple, his throat, his jaw—wherever she saw bare skin; it didn't seem to matter, as long as her lips could touch him. And he returned her kisses, eventually getting distracted by the column of her neck, grazing his teeth over a sensitive patch of skin and sucking lightly.

The book long forgotten and sun already set, she exposed her neck, giving him more access, and he nipped the tender flesh. She released a soft gasp, her eyelids becoming heavy.

A low, approving growl escaped him, his hand going flat over her stomach. With the taste of her skin on his tongue and the scent of her filling him, he would do this for the rest of their lives, if she allowed. Every cell in his body vibrated, and he grew hard as his blood pumped harder. It had been so damn long since he had been with a woman. He had had numerous opportunities to break his vow—but no one had ever come close to being as worthy as she was.

A bit breathless, Riley said, "Roth?"

He dragged the tip of his tongue over the curve of her ear. "Riley?" he murmured huskily.

"If I went home, to live in my world, would you go with me?"

He stilled, and he felt her body go rigid. Her pulse drummed in her throat.

He hadn't considered living in the mortal world before. Since she'd begun telling him about her home, he had wanted to go, but he'd never thought he'd stay forever. He had obligations here. Family and friends counting on him—

But he had made his choice.

Every nightmare he'd had since Riley had found him in the bath, he chose her. Every time. No matter what torture followed, he continued to choose her over and over again. He might've been still formulating a plan, trying to figure out a way to get everything he wanted, but one way or another he would keep everyone safe.

"Yes," Roth said softly. "I would go with you."

He felt her whole body sigh in relief. She traced her fingertips, lightly, over his leather-clad arm until they froze suddenly.

"You would have to glamour yourself," she said, hushed. "Hide your wings, who you are, from everyone."

"Yes."

She shook her head. "We're not going to do that, then. I don't want you to have to hide who you are for the rest of your life."

"I don't mind," Roth admitted. He was used to hiding, preferred it. Like the scar covering his torso, the color of his wings was an imperfection he shied from, one that made the world identify him as a bloodthirsty warrior. He'd never shown the world his scar to spare him from the tales they would weave.

Bringing his arm to her, she pressed her lips to the leather, sending a tingling sensation dancing over his scarred flesh. "I do," she whispered.

Gently, he squeezed her closer to him. The swirling storm inside his soul guttered out temporarily, and when it kicked back up again, it wasn't as strong as it once was.

"If we were to go live in your world," Roth said, "how would we get there? Navigating the rocks within the fog surrounding the whirlpool is dangerous. Only the most skilled sailors can do it, and even then, sometimes they don't make it."

The whirlpool, containing the tear between the faerie and mortal worlds, was located near the southern border of Dormirrius, in the Gorsium Sea—it was why more human slaves could be found in Paladon; the city was the first stop for any slave trader, knowing they would get the most from the lords and ladies there and, most importantly, from King Torryn. The treacherous waters surrounding the whirlpool were shrouded in thick, soupy fog and were known to house ferocious angulpers, making it a trek for only the most skilled—and insane—to try to make it to the other side, to kidnap humans to bring back and sell.

Riley's fingers tapped the back of his hand as her mind worked. "You make a valid point." Leaning her head back against his shoulder, she asked, "Want to start a pirate crew with me?"

Slowly, a curious, amused smile spread over his lips. "Sure," he said, playing along with this absurd idea. "I could be your first mate."

She scoffed. "You must be going mad if you think I'm going to make you my first mate. You have no idea what you're doing on a ship."

"Neither do you."

"Out of the two of us, who has spent the most time on one?"

"That doesn't mean you know how to captain."

"Agree to disagree."

Chuckling, Roth kissed her jaw. "What is this all about?" A thought struck him, and he lowered his voice. "Is this for Mara?"

"No," she admitted. "This isn't for Mara—I mean, it kind of is?" She sighed heavily, running a hand down her face. "I've being thinking lately," she started slowly, quietly. "What if I bring Mara back, but she's unhappy that I did?"

"What do you mean?" Roth asked gently into the back of her hair. "Why would she be unhappy?"

Riley chewed her bottom lip nervously. "What if she's happy now?" she asked, her voice small. "What if Mara's finally at peace in the Elysian Fields? How could I take that away from her? She suffered her whole life, at the hands of her father, his crew, her addiction to faerie fruit." Riley shook her head against Roth's shoulder, breathing in a shuddering breath. "I can't take her out of paradise, only to drag her back into hell."

Roth hummed, finally understanding she was trying to figure out what to do if she decided not to bring Mara back. Kissing her temple, he held her tighter to him. "I wish I could answer that for you," he murmured. "I wish I could guarantee Mara's happiness if you were to bring her back, but I can't. There's no way to know. But one thing I do know: Mara would want you to be happy. She would want you to live for yourself, not wondering what she would've wanted."

"Are you saying I shouldn't try to bring her back?"

"Not at all." Fucking hells, what was he trying to say? He took a deep breath, inhaling her citrus and vanilla scent, letting it clear his mind. "Whatever you decide, just know that I'll be by your side, supporting you the whole way. I want you to be happy, Riley."

The hand atop his began to tremble, and he laced his fingers with hers, squeezing, telling her she could trust him with whatever troubled her, all her doubts and fears. She licked her lips and closed her eyes, taking a moment to gather herself, before she said, "What if I don't know how to be happy, Roth, without someone guiding me? I feel so . . . *lost* without her—without anyone telling me what to do next. What if I choose the wrong path?"

"Then, you choose another, and when that one comes to an end, you go to the next—and the next and the next," he said, wishing he could protect her from the loneliness he could feel rooted deep within her. "You can choose whatever path you want—big or small, right or wrong—because that's the point. Exploring and living life to the fullest, and finding others along the way to walk those paths beside you."

"You make it sound so easy."

"It can be," he said, tucking strands of hair that had escaped her braid back behind her ear, "if you let it. What you're trying to do, bringing Mara back from the dead, is a big path—a huge one that takes you to the top of a mountain—and maybe, what you need right now is a little path that curves off from the current one but will still lead you back to it."

"What kind of little path?" she asked, curiosity layered within.

"What's something you've dreamed about doing for a long time? Something as small as visiting a little bookshop or"—Roth's lips twitched in amusement—"perhaps branching out and trying a dessert that isn't an apple rose—" He grunted as her elbow connected with his diaphragm. "So that's a no." He pinched her side in retaliation.

Riley giggled, swatting at his fingers. "Don't distract me; I'm thinking," she said between laughs.

Roth hushed, letting her think, but it took a lot more willpower than he cared to admit.

It wasn't long before Riley's eyes burst open, the fields of wildflowers glimmering with a dream long abandoned. She bolted upright, twisting in his arms to look at him.

Smiling, Roth asked, "Are you going to make me tickle it out of you?" He was hoping she would say yes.

Riley's arms immediately wrapped around her middle, covering her. "You wouldn't."

"Oh, but I would." He lifted his hands, wiggling his fingers, inching them closer, closer, closer.

"The Lunar Theater!" she squeaked. "I want to see a ballet at the Lunar Theater in Kararhys."

His hands stilled. "Really?"

She nodded, worrying her bottom lip, as if he might think her dream ridiculous. But why would he?

Reaching out, he smiled, tugging her closer until their chests met. Her arms wrapped around his neck, the tips of her fingers playing with strands of his hair. "I think that's a wonderful dream, dragonfly," he murmured, kissing her brow. A blush crept into her cheeks as she gave him a small smile. "And it's one that the path won't stray too far from the bigger one. We're already heading to Kararhys, so it works out perfectly. We can attend a ballet first and then find the next location for Lothaire's treasure in the city. If Grimsley got the riddle right, that is," he added, grumbling.

She stiffened in his arms. "I hadn't thought of that," she mumbled. "What if he didn't? I don't think I can live with that failure, Roth."

"Yes, you can, Riley," he said gently, sweeping stray hair from her brow. "I know you can. You're a lot stronger than you give yourself credit for. You have been through your own hell, and you're still here, fighting. With life, there is always pain, but there's also joy and hope and love, and the only way to heal is to live. To keep going, despite the obstacles thrown at you."

With the pad of his thumb, he wiped a fallen tear away from her cheek. "But, there is also a chance Grimsley was right," he said, "and Kararhys is the next location Lothaire is sending us to. Who knows, maybe the treasure is there?" He winked when she met his eye, a speck of hope in the tiny golden wildflowers.

"I hadn't thought of that, either," she conceded, her eyes staring at a spot beyond Roth's shoulder. Through them, he knew she was imagining finding the treasure, just as he was imagining the pure, radiating joy on her face while giving him a crooked grin, the Scroll of Desires in her hands.

"But," he said, and her eyes snapped back into focus, finding his, "there's only one way to find out if it's there."

She nodded slowly, and the surer she became, the faster her head moved up and down. "We keep looking for the treasure. And only the treasure," she quickly added. "We'll be risking enough looking for it in the High King's territory." Her shoulders bunched around her neck, guilt seeping into her eyes.

But it wasn't from the possibility of disappointing Roth—it was from disappointing Mara. That she had to stay focused, to not let her doubts and fears block the path to her best friend.

Roth understood, far more than she could ever realize. If she knew what had really brought them together on Obsidian Island, she would never speak to him again—fucking hells, she might try to kill him. But that didn't matter anymore because in the end, he would always choose *her*.

Giving her a reassuring smile, he said, "Whatever you want. It doesn't matter how high the risk; I'm with you—always."

CHAPTER 40

Shoving slices of honeyed ham into her mouth, Riley watched Roth's friend, Maurice, slicing cheesy bread across from where she sat at the table in his kitchen.

It had been a long few weeks of traveling to Kararhys through the White Hills, and by the time they'd crossed the southern bridge, over Moonfyre Lake and into the city, they'd both been exhausted. Riley had envied the slumbering fire sprites in their lampposts lining the cobblestone streets, wishing she were fast asleep and tucked away in their warmth.

As they had traveled farther north, the nights had become chillier. Other than the cold, the trees turning colors was the first sign autumn was approaching. Riley had huddled closer to Roth as they'd walked through the streets of the different districts, passing the occasional carriage and handsy, albeit clumsy, couple still out at the ungodly hour, making their way home to the Gentry District from whatever revel they'd attended that evening. Eventually, they'd found their way into the Trading and Market District, where Maurice's tailor shop was and the apartment he occupied above it, somehow managing to avoid drawing attention to themselves.

The High Crown Guard was everywhere, watching and waiting to catch a thief—or pirate.

Maurice finished cutting the cheesy bread, sliding it toward Riley. She reached for a piece at the same time Roth did, and his knuckles brushed her skin, sparking heat low in her belly.

Since the barn outside of Bilyndria, they had shared the occasional kiss, but they never went further than that. The closest they had come was when Roth had her back pressed against a tree while he explored her neck with his lips, but a family of woodland folk had passed by, the children pointing and asking their parents questions. It was safe to say Riley was frustrated—and embarrassed—and after that incident, they hadn't tried again. But right now, she might've wanted to get Roth naked and do filthy acts with him, but more than anything else, she wanted a steaming hot bath.

She took a bite of the bread, and the cheese melted on her tongue. Closing her eyes, she groaned. She could feel all eyes on her, but she was too wrapped up in the cheesy goodness to give a damn. The bread was a *very satisfying* substitute until she could act on her other needs.

Maurice laughed softly, a left dimple appearing. "I take it you like the bread."

Riley smiled. "What gave it away?"

Although Maurice's smile was bright and awake, his face told a different story. Dark circles were beneath his narrow, angular brown eyes that curved up at the outer corners, and his golden skin was pale. His long black hair was knotted into a messy bun at his nape, as if it were all he could manage after being woken up in the middle of the night by an incessant pounding on his back door.

His long, thin fingers wrapped around a steaming cup of fennel tea, bringing it to his lips. As he took a sip, Riley got the sense they were intruding. She whispered to Roth, "I think we should go somewhere else."

Roth opened his mouth, but Maurice beat him to it. "Nonsense, it's no problem. Anything for a brother."

A warm smile crept along Riley's lips. She had no idea they were so close or that Roth had anyone besides her. She'd once thought maybe everyone he loved was gone, but knowing she was wrong sent a different kind of heat fluttering through her.

She couldn't possibly thank Maurice enough. They were already risking a lot by showing their faces in a city hell-bent on killing those with the mark of a pirate.

Without realizing she was doing it, Riley tugged on her left sleeve, even though the tiger was well hidden already. Roth settled a hand on her knee, squeezing lightly, and she glanced at him. Words were in his eyes.

You have nothing to fear from Maurice.

How do you know that? she asked with her own.

Because we're not the only ones in hiding.

Riley furrowed her brow, trying to sort out what that meant, when Maurice clapped his hands together.

He stood. "I have some clean clothes set aside for you. These, well" —he looked them up and down—"I'll just have to incinerate these disgusting rags."

Riley frowned and looked at the clothes she wore. They were still the teal shirt and black pants from Mel, but they were now covered in dirt and smelled like a stable from sleeping in their fair share of them on their journey, unbeknownst to the owners. Roth was no better, somehow managing to smell worse than her, leaving her wondering if he'd slept in horse shit one of those nights. He'd managed to smell like wet earth after a rainstorm on the island, but after weeks of traveling, they both smelled like Calydonian boars.

Roth shook his head. "Oh, no. I'm not falling for that. The last time someone borrowed the clothes you made, they ended up—"

Riley slapped a hand over Roth's mouth. "I think what he means to say is, thank you." She felt his teeth nip at the skin of her palm, but she didn't budge. "Do you mind if we turn in? It's been a long few weeks, and he stinks." She yelped when his teeth sunk deeper and removed her hand. To Roth, she mumbled, "You do kind of stink."

"And you smell like roses," Roth retorted flatly.

She flicked his nose.

Maurice chuckled. "Of course." Standing, he gestured for Roth to follow him. "Sorry to say this, brother, but—"

"Then don't," Roth retorted, knowing where his friend was going.

"—you smell like you were recently birthed from a boar's ass, realized it was a lot cozier up there, and decided to crawl back in, only to be shitted out later."

That was an image.

Riley snickered into her hand.

"What about her?" Roth asked.

Maurice clicked his tongue. "Please, Roth, I'm a gentleman. I would never say a lady has a foul odor."

Riley lifted her chin, shoving a piece of cheesy bread into her mouth.

He looked back at Riley. "You'll have to wait your turn to bathe, though. I only have one bath."

She gave him a thumbs-up, unable to speak with her mouth full of deliciousness.

Roth shook his head, bending down to kiss one of her chipmunk cheeks. "You also smell of citrus and vanilla," he whispered in her ear, making her shiver. "And I never knew how much I craved them until I couldn't get enough of you." His teeth grazed the curve of her ear, and she swallowed a gasp.

Pushing at his chest, she said breathlessly, "Go take a bath, stinky, old bird."

Roth grinned at her as he followed Maurice out of the kitchen, and only when he was out of sight did Riley get up and splash some cool water on her face.

After showing Roth to the bathing chamber, Maurice returned. He took the dirty dishes from the table to the sink and began cleaning them. Feeling guilty watching him clean up after her, Riley went to his side to help, and after a minute of going back and forth about whether she should because she was the guest, Maurice gave in.

Taking the cup Maurice had washed, Riley dried it. "Thank you for letting us stay here and for the fresh clothes," she said.

"Whatever Roth asks of me, I will give. I owe him my life," Maurice replied, washing a plate.

"Did you two fight in the war together?" Riley asked, taking the plate when Maurice was done and drying it.

He shook his head. "I was born after the war, but I know Roth from training in King Torryn's army."

"You're from Paladon?"

"Yes."

The answer was strained, and Riley wondered if she should press the issue. Roth had never spoken much about Paladon, but she knew it must not be as magical as the city wanted one to think if he'd left for an island home to vicious faerie pirates.

They cleaned the rest of the dishes in silence, and as Riley turned around to sit back at the table, she saw a small head with dark, straight hair poking through the doorway. The girl's eyes—the shape of them identical to Maurice's—widened. Riley and the girl gasped at the same moment, before the girl vanished.

Riley held a hand to her chest, feeling her heart pounding within her rib cage. "Who was that?" she asked.

Maurice chuckled quietly, his brown eyes warm. "My daughter, Evelyn. She must have heard us from her room and wanted to see what all the fuss was about." He pulled out a chair for Riley. "It's been a few years since we've had company. I'm sure she's curious to meet you. Especially someone willing to accompany Roth."

Riley's brows inched higher. *So, Roth is stubborn with everyone he's close with.*

She took the proffered seat. "It sounds like you know him well."

"He got Evie and I out of Paladon safely, along with a few other ailerons."

"You're an aileron?"

He nodded.

Riley never would have guessed. With his missing wings, he looked like any other elve.

"Why did you leave?" she asked. Her stomach twisted as she wondered if she wanted to know the answer to her question.

Maurice furrowed his brows. "Roth didn't tell you about the Rule of Rebirth?" She shook her head, and he blew out a long breath as if preparing himself. "His royal fucking pain in my ass decreed a new law almost a century ago, allowing the godsdamned removal of an aileron's wings if they acted out of line. But in his fucked-up mind, he considers it a rebirth."

He shook his head, mumbling something in Scyathan, the same language Roth would sometimes speak, before continuing, "Rebirth started with the females, after the king's consort tried to escape, flying under the cover of night."

Riley's eyes were wide. "There's a Queen of Dormirrius?"

"Technically, no, there wasn't a *queen*." Maurice's mouth formed a thin line. "King Torryn named Talia as consort only, giving her no authority whatsoever. It was a fucking mockery, really. Talia was one of the best fighters in the Terra War. She was strong, beautiful, and was more honorable than most of our elders. But not only that, she was merciful. More often than not, the stories from the war are of her trying to save those who couldn't defend themselves—on both sides—and she continued to show mercy to those in Paladon who fell to the injustice under Torryn's rulership." Maurice's hands clenched into fists. "Torryn made sure to strip every last ounce of that from her by the end."

"What did he do?" Riley's voice came out in a whisper.

"Before she was shot down with arrows trying to escape, he would beat her, fuck with her head by locking her away in a room with no windows for days on end. Then, he would act like the perfect husband, as if she should be grateful for all he had given her. He did all kinds of tortuous shit to her. It pained us—most of all Roth—to see everything he did to her and not be able to do a damn thing without it being 'treason'." Maurice took a deep breath. "You're either loyal to him or you're his enemy. There is no in-between. And he made sure to remind everyone of that.

"Torryn brought Talia before his court and army shortly after he'd given the order to put arrows in her wings, but it was long enough for an infection to set in. I guess with what he had planned, there was no point in removing them."

Maurice trembled, the memory stark in the shadows under his brown eyes, and when he spoke again, there was an underlying rage he was trying desperately to keep caged.

"He made every last fucking one of us watch as he had her wings removed." Maurice bared his teeth. "The bastard isn't even aileron, but he *knows* how sacred our wings are to us. And he made Roth do it, forcing him to make the ultimate choice: loyalty to his king or his betrothed—who had been stolen from him. Roth was never the same after," he added, sighing heavily. But the slight tremor remained in his body.

Riley gaped.

The horrors Maurice had told her were too much to comprehend. The things King Torryn had put Talia through just so he could . . . what exactly? Instill fear into his kingdom? Show his power?

But that wasn't all she was reeling from.

Roth had been *engaged.*

Although Riley assumed Roth had past lovers, she had never imagined he had been betrothed to one—that would go on to become a fucking *king's consort.*

Gods, she must have been magnificent, Riley mused to herself. Just from what Maurice had said about her, Talia sounded like someone to look up to and admire.

A heavy weight dropped into Riley's stomach. She was nothing like Talia. She was a pirate, and a terrible one at that. She didn't know a godsdamned thing about sailing or running a crew. All she'd done was sit back and watch as Mara got herself into more trouble, Jasper trailing after her, trying to clean up her messes. And if she wasn't doing that, she'd been fucking Jasper.

How in the hell does Roth feel anything *for me?*

Roth had been engaged to a woman the King of Dormirrius had deemed worthy enough to steal away.

The trauma he suffered from, Riley realized, was not only from the war, but from the king's actions. Having to cut the wings from the woman he *loved* would have devastated his mind and soul.

Riley shuddered.

Roth's actions over the past few months began making more sense to her. The way he had looked at her when she had told Grimsley she would do anything he wanted if he didn't hurt Roth's wings; he'd been shocked and grateful, but there had been a hint of shame in his eyes. She hadn't recognized it then, but now the emotion was unmistakable. Riley had barely known him and had willingly offered to do anything in exchange for the safety of his wings. He had been given the same choice years before and regretted the decision he had made.

Maurice went on, "Not long after Roth removed Talia's wings, she killed herself. She couldn't live with the disgrace and betrayal it had brought her, but Torryn"—he spat the name—"never cared, making it fucking law—the Rule of Rebirth—that anyone could remove an aileron's wings if they were believed to have *misbehaved* in any way deemed plausible. It really just gave the shitheads of Paladon an excuse to cut their wives' and daughters' wings off to control them."

Riley felt sick. She could feel the food she had just eaten threatening to come back up. She had no idea life in Paladon was so cruel.

Does the world know? Does Darrow?

Her hands fisted at the thought the High King knew of this cruelty but chose not to do anything about it. The sickening feeling worsened.

But it wasn't only from the removal of wings and Darrow.

Every time Roth's eyes drifted to her forearms, she could see it affected him. Made him clench his jaw and fists. From the beginning, he'd been determined to make sure she knew she mattered, not only to him but the world. She knew he cared about her, but now she wasn't sure if it was only due to her scars and his past.

Riley tried shoving away the feeling of worthlessness that had been creeping up her throat, but hints of it still remained. She worried that no matter how hard she tried, it would always be lurking in the shadows.

She frowned as Maurice continued, "After men began following Torryn's lead, the female ailerons in his army rose up against him, starting a rebellion. It didn't take long before they started losing their wings, too."

He shook his head. "This last century has been so fucking difficult for ailerons, but especially the women. They have fought for their right to freedom, and while some lost their wings, others lost their lives. It wasn't long before the men—who'd lost their sisters, their wives, *their daughters*—fought back, but it only ended the same." Staring at the table, he gestured to his wingless back.

He blew out a breath.

"So we ran instead, taking as many ailerons as we could, always going back until we're all safe and free. That's what Roth did for Evie and me five years ago. He got us out with a few others, taking us across the Chysos Sea. But it seems like the more we go back, the more of our people we need to save."

Gods, she'd had no idea how bad it was. If she had known . . . *If I had known, then what? What could I have done?*

Quietly, she asked, "What happened to Evie's mother?"

Maurice's face became solemn. "She died shortly after giving birth to Evie. It's just been us for fourteen years."

Riley reached across the table, to where Maurice sat, and took his hand, squeezing. "I'm sorry. I-I shouldn't have asked."

He shook his head, waving his other hand. "It's okay. It took me a while before I could say Gideon's name, but eventually it got easier to talk about her without shaking."

"Did she . . . ?" Riley started.

Sensing her question, Maurice shook his head. "Gideon wasn't aileron, but even if she had been, I would've never made her go through the rebirth process—and I certainly didn't force Evie, either."

"Who did?" Riley asked softly as dread coiled around her insides.

His lips curled. "Captain Jarrek." His eyes darkened with more hatred than there was before. "I was chosen as the palace tailor after King Torryn found out about the work I was doing for others in secret. I was godsdamned lucky he didn't punish me, instead using my talents," he added, running a hand down his face.

"During a fitting with Jarrek," he said with a sneer, looking as if he'd swallowed acid, "there was an . . . incident. Evie hadn't meant to, but"— his hostile eyes flicked to Riley—"Jarrek is a cruel, cold-blooded man. He's known as 'the Carver' throughout the armies in Erithena, and h-he—"

Maurice began to shake, and Riley squeezed his hand harder.

He tried again, swallowing down his wrath. "That fucking monster *carved* up my little girl—not only taking her wings but her voice, too. *She was three years old.*"

Riley's other hand went to her mouth to stifle her gasp as dread pierced her insides, making her feel sicker than she thought possible.

Fucking monster was right. Who did that to anyone—especially a *child*? What he'd done wasn't right. *None of it was*—for Maurice and Evie, for Roth and Talia, and for every single aileron.

"I'm so sorry, Maurice," Riley consoled. It was all she could think to say—because what else could be said?

He squeezed her hand, the only acknowledgement he gave that he'd heard her, and then let go.

They sat in silence for a long while, the heaviness of their conversation hanging in the air over them like a dark cloud, before Maurice stood and showed Riley to the bathing chamber, giving her a clean nightgown to wear.

"There's a spare room at the end of the hall you can stay in," Maurice said, his voice cracking slightly. "Roth's probably already in there."

As he walked away, he stopped, looking over his shoulder. "I've known Roth for centuries—before and after Talia's death—and I never thought I'd see the day when he was happy again." A small smile spread across his lips, despite all he had told mere moments ago. "I'm happy he found you, Riley."

Clutching her folded, clean towel and nightgown to her body, she said, "Me, too." After he disappeared into his own room, she whispered, "More than you could ever know."

QUICKLY AND EFFICIENTLY, Riley scrubbed herself clean of the horrors Maurice had told her, wanting to get in bed as soon as possible.

Leaving her hair free from her leather tie, she pulled on the silk, lilac nightgown. The neckline dipped low, showing the swell of her breasts, and the hem stopped mid-thigh. If she bent over, it would be exceptionally obvious she was not wearing undergarments.

Padding down the hallway, she found the spare bedroom Maurice had told her she could stay in with Roth. The aileron had already found it and was lying on his stomach on the floor next to the bed, with one of the pillows tucked under his head.

"Why are you on the floor?" Riley asked from the doorway. Her eyes traveled the length of his body, from his bare torso, showing the branches of his scar, to his lower half snugged in too-small pants. They hugged his ass perfectly, showing off the glorious curve of it.

Her fatigue instantly vanished, replaced with damp heat.

Eyes closed, he answered, "My wings won't fit. It's a rather small bed, and I thought I'd try being a gentleman and let you have it."

He wasn't wrong; it was a rather small bed and both of them wouldn't be able to fit with his wings. But she was determined to make it work. His presence beside her was something she had gotten used to, and she wasn't about to give that up.

She climbed on and patted the remaining space. "Get your pretty, round ass in this bed before I have to throw you in it."

He chuckled from his spot on the floor. "We won't fit."

Riley peeked her head over the edge of the bed. "I can think of some *positions*," she purred.

Smirking, he rolled onto his back, his wings pinned beneath him, but he didn't seem to mind. She sucked in a breath, and he grinned, seeing exactly where her eyes had landed.

The too-small, too-short tan pants he wore showed the outlines of his hard muscles and harder cock, and his hips didn't allow them to be buttoned all the way.

"Why are your pants so small?" The question came out low and thick, but she had to know.

"Because after I made a fuss about wearing anything from Maurice's shop, and I managed to convince him to have the pants from Mel cleaned instead of burned to ash—a feat I am incredibly proud of, mind you—he shoved a pair of his own pants at me." He added with a grumble, "He's much shorter and leaner than I am."

Riley snickered into her hand. "Clearly, but I'm not complaining." She bit her bottom lip. "There is another option." He arched a brow, waiting. "No pants at all," she said, winking.

Roth's smirk turned primal. "I didn't want to be presumptu—"

The words died on his tongue as he got to his feet and froze. It was his turn for his eyes to travel the length of her, seeing her for the first time in the revealing nightgown, as she knelt on the bed before him.

"You are a masterpiece sculpted by the gods," he complimented, his voice smoky.

She bunched her hands into the silky fabric. "If you're saying this now," she said, dragging the hem of the nightgown up with the tips of her fingers, "what will you say when I don't have a stitch of clothing on?"

His eyes blazed with lust, and his pants strained with the bulge beneath them. Her arms were ready to snatch the pillow from the bed, using it as a shield in case the buttons popped off, flying at her.

She smirked, curling her finger. *Come here.*

CHAPTER 41

Roth claimed her mouth with fervor, igniting a spark of heat so deep within him, the sun blared through the storm, widening the eye.

A fever swept over the room, as if an invisible fire roared to life in a hearth.

Riley's fingers laced through his curls, bringing him closer as his hands found her hips and did the same. His tongue swept over her bottom lip, tasting and savoring, as his fingers glided over her smooth skin. He cupped her ass beneath the nightgown, and a soft gasp escaped her. With his tongue flicking over hers, he scooped the sound up and swallowed it whole with a groan. She shivered, moaning, and his strong fingers dug into soft, plush skin.

The sound reverberated loudly over the room, over him. It travelled straight to the storm within his soul, colliding with it.

But whereas the caress of her moan sent a thrill through his blood, he felt the opposite from her. She stilled, her fingers clamped tight in his hair, and he pulled back, brows drawn together and worry etched into his thunderous eyes.

"What's wrong?" he asked, breathing heavily. His voice was rough and thick in a sultry, cloudy haze.

The heat in the room stuttered, chilled ever so slightly.

Riley licked her swollen lips, and Roth darted his eyes to them instantly, wanting to suck on the full bottom one. A bit breathless, and with a hint of anxiety to her voice, she asked, "Can you enchant the room to be soundproof?" His thunderous concern vanished, turning into misty bewilderment. "I don't want anyone to overhear," she explained, her cheeks turning rosier than they'd already been.

The corner of his mouth lifted. "As you wish, dragonfly." He closed his eyes in concentration, letting his faerie magic course through his veins. It took only seconds before he felt the spark of magic washing over the room, its walls, windows, and door. His eyes opened and he said, "Done," before leaning in to pick up where they'd left off, but she held him at bay.

"Are you sure?" Riley asked.

Smiling, Roth kissed her nose. "I'm sure," he said confidently, adding, "but I guess we'll just have to find out."

His lips crashed into hers before she could object, and all it took was the soft, wet slide of his tongue to sweep away any objection.

They explored each other's mouths, their hands roaming over flesh and feathers, trading gasps and moans. Their hips rolled against one another, sending shivers of bliss racing through them.

Roth worked his way down Riley's neck, kissing the dip in her throat deeply before trailing open-mouthed kisses down between the valley of her breasts. His hands slid to her shoulders, and he fingered the thin, silky straps, debating how much trouble he would be in with Maurice if he snapped them with his teeth. Not liking his odds, he dragged the dainty straps down her arms. The nightgown pooled at her waist, leaving her exposed to the heated room.

With a shuddering breath, Roth raked his gaze over her. And to his surprise—and adoration—she didn't balk from it, didn't shrink and try to cover herself up. Within her eyes, he saw—no, he *felt*—how comfortable she was with him to be this vulnerable with him. He had seen her at her worst, and it hadn't changed a damn thing about how he felt toward her. It never would.

Seeing her like this fueled all of his hunger and desire and—

Roth breathed in a shaky breath, realizing just how strong of an emotion he was feeling. One he vowed to never feel again. But it was there, and it was overwhelming, taking him over, and Riley didn't shy away from it as he thought she might. She arched her back, gravitating toward it, wanting more.

Roth's hands found her waist, squeezing gently before sliding up. His thumb brushed along the undersides of her breasts and traveled back down to her waist. Reverently, he lowered her onto her back and slid the nightgown past her hips, her thighs, until it was gone completely.

Placing his hands over her knees, he spread her legs, exposing her to him, slick with her need. His breaths became rapid, his grip on her tightening while his thumbs drew tight circles in the hollows behind her knees. His cock throbbed against the abrasive fabric of his pants.

All at once, the air seemed to be sucked from the room and outside. All was silent, as though the wind itself held its breath.

Swallowing hard, Roth committed every inch of her bare body to memory.

"Sculpted by the gods indeed," he declared roughly. His voice was barely recognizable, even to himself. Gone was the stubborn, old bird she always called him. Now, it was time to introduce the seductive, almost sinful man that had been buried deep within.

Slowly, the air poured back in, and the wind tapped lightly against the window as Roth crawled onto the bed, between her legs, dragging his mouth and tongue along her bare skin from her navel to her breasts. He sucked on the plump flesh before sinking his teeth down lightly, remembering how on their island, she'd told him he would beg for more of her love nibbles, but right now, in this moment, all he wanted to hear was her begging for more of *his*. She gasped, arching into him, her fingers tangling in his hair once more. He licked the spot he'd bitten, kissing it lightly before turning to her other breast, doing the same to hear her soft gasps.

Riley moaned as Roth kneaded her breast while he sucked on her nipple, licking and grazing them with his teeth before he moved to the other. When he finished doing as he had done to the first, he kissed her, hard and deep.

Roth sucked on her bottom lip and pulled back, propping himself on his side above her, a devilish grin forming. He cocked his head. "Did you know everything created by the gods was worshipped—is still worshipped?" he asked, his voice pure sin.

"What are you talking about?" she asked breathlessly.

His devilish grin crinkled the corners of his eyes, and she sucked in a breath. "I've never worshipped anything made by the gods," he said. "Even our sacred mountain back home." His lustful eyes traveled down the length of her before finding her own, filled with the same desire. "Until now," he declared. He dragged his hand, gingerly, over her bare, flushed skin, following the path his eyes had taken. "I'm going to worship you so thoroughly that by the time I've finished, my name will be the only word you know."

His eyes bored into hers, and her next breath lodged in her throat, as if she had forgotten how to breathe, how to speak. All that came out of her was a small squeak close to a whimper. That sound—fucking hells, he was going to do more than just worship her.

Roth's sinful sea-green eyes never left hers, the gold streaks flashing as he dragged a finger through her slick folds. Her mouth formed a small *O* in a soft gasp, her eyes widening, and he had to remind himself to breathe, to control his impulse to bring this moment to the end. Her hands gripped his shoulders, and when he pressed his thumb into her clit, her nails bit into his skin. His cock twitched against her thigh, his breaths shallow.

Through the haze clouding his mind, Roth could have sworn he heard the closed door and windows rattle, the pictures knocking against the wall while a soft, warm breeze caressed their arms, their legs, settling between them, but he didn't lose focus for long. How could he when he had his hand between the legs of the woman he loved?

Two fingers swept down either side of her center, his thumb still applying pressure. He let each pass of his fingers, each press build tension within her that had her chest rising higher, higher, higher. She lifted her hips, wanting that mind-numbing pleasure to explode within her, but he didn't want this to end. Not so soon.

He pulled his fingers away from her, immediately feeling a sense of loss from not touching her.

"Why did you stop?" Riley snarled, not sounding at all like herself. Unless she were a feral wolf, fighting over its first meal in weeks.

And for her, that was exactly what this was, but for him—it was so much more. And he wanted to savor every waking minute of it.

Slowly, a smug grin stretched across his lips as he heard the demand in her voice. Heard just how much she wanted him. "Because you're trying to speed this up," he said, his voice a caress, "and I've dreamt too many times of this moment to have you come in seconds because you're too impatient." He settled his hand low on her belly, gently applying pressure, and she relaxed under his touch, lowering her ass to the bed once more. "Now," he murmured in her ear decadently, "close your eyes and let me do exactly what I've always dreamed of doing to you."

She groaned, shivering, and it made him want to throw everything he had just said out the window, wanting nothing more than to push inside her in one quick motion and fuck her into oblivion. But before he could say, "Fuck it," Riley did as she was told, her eyes fluttering shut.

The hand on her abdomen rubbed smoothly over her, and beneath his touch, he felt her wriggle ever so slightly, but she didn't goad him to go faster. She remained as still as she could. His hand traveled lower, goose bumps popping up in its wake as it moved across her hip to her outer thigh. He pinched the flesh there, and a small squeak escaped her.

Grazing his lips over the sensitive spot of her neck, just below her ear, he murmured, "I don't want you to be shy. I soundproofed the room, remember?" A soft groan left her as she turned her face into him, her eyes still closed. He chuckled low, pressing a kiss to the corner of her mouth. "Patience, dragonfly. I'll have you moaning a sweet song in no time."

"Just wait until it's *your* turn, pretty bird," she said, frustrated, her breath hot against his mouth. "Teasing you has become a hobby of mine, one I take immense pleasure in."

He nipped at the tip of her nose. "I don't doubt it."

Roth shifted over her to kneel between her legs, and Riley's hands slid from his scarred shoulders, falling to either side of her head. He brought his other hand to rest on her inner thigh, rubbing tenderly. Her breasts rose and fell with every shaky breath she took.

Up and down, his hands ran the outer length of her legs, lifting them to his shoulders. He brought his lips to the sensitive skin on the inside of her ankle, brushing them featherlight before nipping. She gasped, her toes curling beside his head. Small tremors rocked her, and his mouth curved into a smile against her.

Gingerly, Roth set her legs down on the bed on either side of him, bent at the knee. Taking care to apply the perfect, mind-melting pressure, he moved his hands up her inner thighs and down again after reaching the apex. He did this once, twice, three more times before spreading her legs wider. Riley shivered as he bent down to her. His shallow breaths washed over her center. He hesitated, knowing there was no going back after this. One taste was all it was going to take; he wouldn't be able to stop. His vow would forever be obsolete.

"Roth," Riley said, the word a strangled whimper. "*Please.*"

Suddenly, with stark clarity, Roth knew he had broken his vow long before this moment. He would give this woman anything she wanted. Just as he had been doing since he'd hesitated that day on Obsidian Island, outside the fighting pit. His body, heart, and soul—they were all hers.

Growling, he granted her wish. His tongue licked up her center, and Riley gasped, her fingers digging into the blankets beside her head. A half-groan, half-growl vibrated through him.

He reached her clit and sucked her into his mouth. She moaned, arching. He wrapped an arm across her middle to hold her down, while soft strokes brushed over her pulsing core. He dipped his tongue inside her, and she cried out, begging for *more*.

This time, Roth didn't stop—he gave her exactly what she wanted.

Still gripping the blankets with one hand, Riley found the crown of his hair with the other. And as Roth did dirty, wicked things to her with his mouth and tongue, she hung on to him as if her life depended on it. She writhed and squirmed, and he smiled into her, holding her tighter—

Her back bowed from the bed, her nails scraping his scalp as release found her. She cried out his name, and he groaned, giving her only a moment to recover as his tongue left her center, finding that pulsing pinnacle he craved so dearly.

Two fingers plunged inside her, curling against that glorious spot. Riley gasped and moaned and babbled incoherently. Her hips moved against him to match the thrusts of those two digits. She constricted around his fingers—

"*Roth!*" She came undone even more thoroughly than the last. Her body convulsed with pleasure, arching away from the bed. He continued moving his fingers within her as she rode out the orgasm overwhelming her, slowly bringing them to a halt.

Roth pulled his fingers from her as Riley relaxed beneath him, every muscle loose.

Her fingers still in his hair, she guided his mouth to hers, groaning from the taste of herself. He smiled as her other hand trailed fingertips down his chest, feeling along the thick, damaged skin and over the muscles of his abdomen, past the sprinkling of dark hair and the buttons of his tight pants. They skated over his hard length, palming him.

He inhaled sharply, going still.

It was her turn to smile.

Her hand moved, and he hissed into her mouth. His hips rolled, giving him a taste of the friction he craved. Her smile grew. She slowly dragged her hand up and down the length of him, and he groaned. So good—fucking hells, it felt so damn good.

But it had been too long. His brows pulled together in concentration, his closed eyes pinched tight. The muscles in his neck strained as his swollen lips parted. He sucked down tight, shallow breaths. Her hand alone was going to undo him.

Riley's lips drew back, pulling away, but she didn't go far. "Tell me, pretty bird," she purred sensually, "in your dreams, do I have my hand around your cock like I do now?"

Roth nodded.

"Have you lost your words?" She nipped at his bottom lip.

"Yes," he ground out, "you've had your hand around my cock many times."

She hummed approvingly. "What about my mouth? Do I slide my tongue over you and suck you until you come?"

"Yes." The word was so strangled, it was more of a half-groan, half-grunt.

She hummed again, bringing his hand between her thighs to cup her. "But I bet it's *this* you love the most. Taking you in deeply, clenching tight around your—"

"Riley," he rasped, his breathing rapid and uneven, "*stop*."

Her hand stilled as he snatched his away from her center.

In the silence of the room, the wild drumming of her heart was deafening. Each beat asked: *What did I do wrong?*

Nothing, he wanted to tell her. *Absolutely nothing*. But no words would come out, not when he was trying so fucking hard to prevent the night he'd longed for from ending so soon.

It was as though time had frozen along with her as she waited for him to explain what she'd done. And finally, when he could make his throat work, through gritted teeth, he said, "If you keep that up, I'm going to come in these damn pants and not that beautiful pink cunt of yours like I've dreamt about for months."

She breathed a surprised laugh.

The hand that had been stroking him slipped away.

Riley's fingers fumbled for the buttons on his pants, but before she could reach them, Roth lifted himself from the bed. He stood before her, knowing there was no way he would ever have enough of her as he took all of her in again.

Roth's deft fingers pulled at the buttons. She swallowed thickly, staring as he shimmied out of the tight pants with slight difficulty, propping herself up on her elbows. Her beautiful hazel eyes dilated as she took in the sight of him. Absently, she sucked her bottom lip into her mouth, biting it.

"Any harder and it's going to bleed," Roth said, hushed.

After a moment, as if it took a second for his words to sink in, she licked her lip, scooping up a droplet of blood on the tip, but she didn't take her eyes off him.

"You're staring," he said. Smug satisfaction mixed with the decadent roughness of his voice.

Cheeks pinking, she met his eyes. "You're nice to look at—dazzling, actually," she added, flashing him a small smile.

The corners of his lips twitched, and he glanced down at himself before meeting her eye again. He arched a sardonic brow. "I'm dazzling?" he asked dryly.

Her smile grew into a crooked grin, and his breath snagged in his throat.

She did the same as he had, looking down at his cock, but she didn't stop there. Her eyes wandered over every muscle in his body, head to toe, her fingers bunching the blankets as she lingered on his thighs. But when she reached his scar, his wings—her gaze softened. The fingers gripping the blankets loosened and twitched, as if they wanted to touch him, to trace over the lines marking his body with her lips as reverently as they had in Misthaven.

His wings flared slightly, and she met his stare. "You're perfect," Riley breathed.

The storm in his soul flickered, slowly petering out into a dreary drizzle.

Frowning, Roth's eyes darted to the floor, unable to meet Riley's gaze. "I'm far from that," he said softly, his voice too small to be recognizable as the warrior he was supposed to be—the one he never wanted to become.

How could something as disfiguring as the scar on his skin and the wings the color of blood be declared perfect? How could he—a man with the reputation of unmerciful violence—be said to be anything more by this stubborn and impossible, strong, fierce, and beautiful woman? She was worthy of love and joy more than he would ever be.

It was why he'd made the vow of abstinence. All of his wrongs, his mistakes added up, and they had cost him everything he loved. He didn't deserve anything that brought him happiness, certainly not Riley.

His wings—strong enough to carry them the distance over Grendelwyn Forest to safety—fell an inch.

A hand so much smaller than his, so much gentler than he deserved, cupped his cheek. He wanted to lean into the touch, to grant himself a sense of comfort, but he wouldn't allow himself that—his vow might be broken, but its remnants couldn't be shed from him completely. That would take time.

Riley knelt before him on the bed, but still he couldn't meet her eye. She lifted his chin, but he averted his gaze, landing on the wall over her shoulder.

The tips of her fingers glided over his jaw, his brow, his temples, his lips. "I don't think you've looked in the mirror lately," Riley said, the awe in her voice unmistakable, "because, from where I'm standing, you're realm-shattering, sky-splintering, wish-upon-a-shooting-star beautiful." But underneath the awe, he heard the emotion he had run away from. And with it, the storm within stirred to life again—but it wasn't one of mayhem and destruction. It was a summer storm, breathing life into the world again.

Slowly, a small smile spread across Roth's lips, and he lifted his gaze to her, finally seeing all that her voice held. Bashfulness swirled around the golden streaks of lightning in his eyes. A soft chuckle fell past his lips, the sound holding bewilderment and the love he could no longer hold at bay.

"You might think I'm all of those things," he said, "but I'm certainly not sculpted by the gods." He gave her a pointed look.

Biting back a smile, she lowered herself back onto the bed, propping herself up on her elbows once more. She scoffed, waving a hand in faux dismissal. "Well," she drawled, "we can't all be."

Roth's gaze traveled over her, taking in inch by inch of bare skin. The bashfulness in his eyes disappeared as they went up, up, up, becoming engulfed by dark, hungry desire. "Indeed," he murmured. Ravenous eyes met hers.

A low rumble rolled across the night sky beyond the window. A light pitter-patter tapped against the glass as the heavens opened up, letting droplets fall on the land below.

Roth's eyes flicked to Riley's chest, where her breasts rose rapidly with every sharp, tiny breath she took. At his sides, his hands clenched and unclenched, while his wings twitched as he remembered how the night was going to end—how he wanted it to because she was worthy of being the one to break his vow with. Her own eyes became heavy, her legs spreading ever so slightly.

That was all it took for Roth's weight to be back atop her. His mouth crashed into hers. Light rippled across the clouds within him from the feel of her tongue caressing his. Her fingers tangled in his hair, cupped his nape. She arched into him, and he needed not just more of her, but all of her.

He guided himself to her, nudging against her entrance, and she gasped. Looking at her, he braced himself on an arm next to her head. The tip of him rubbed against her, sliding up and down through her slick folds before slowly pushing inside her.

Every coherent thought leapt from Roth's mind as he felt her around him. Her fingers curled tighter in his hair, and her nails made crescent moons in his skin at his nape. A breathy moan escaped her as she clenched around him.

Fucking hells. Halfway inside her, he stilled. His other arm came to brace himself on the other side of her head, and he buried his face in the crook of her neck. Breathing heavily against her, he trembled.

"I need to confess something," he said roughly into her skin.

Tensing beneath him, she asked, a slight tremor to her voice, "What is it?" Her whole body was clenched tight, as if she were worried.

A groan vibrated out of him, against her skin, and she gripped him tighter; it then turned guttural. Fingers dug into the blankets beside her head.

Looking at her, his face tight with concentration, he ground out in one big rush, "I might not last long."

Surprise washed over her, as if she had expected something worse.

Her feet ran down the length of his legs, the arch fitting perfectly over the curve of his calves, the soft touch tickling the hairs there. Prying her hands free from his hair and skin, she wrapped her arms around his neck and purred, "Then, it's good faeries are very . . . *vigorous.*"

His throat bobbed. She was going to be death of him.

Before she had time to blink, Roth's hips moved. The air rushed from the heated room as he found himself seated wholly inside her. Their moans echoed around them.

He stilled above her, shuddering, his breaths stilted as he gave himself time to cool his blood long enough to not spill inside her right then.

Golden streaks lit up his eyes as he pulled out slightly and thrust back in. His mouth parted on a loud moan, and Riley gasped, her hands going to his shoulders, fingertips digging in. The only sounds in the room were their building groans and skin slapping against skin.

The room grew hotter and hotter; wind rattled the windows while the pelts of rain became stronger, picking up momentum.

Roth's body was wide awake, more than it had been in so long, with an ache growing stronger by the second. Riley wrapped her legs around his waist, mindful of his wings, and with the lift of her hips, his next thrust went deeper, finding that hidden spot. She clenched tight around him, gasping. He tensed.

It was too much—more than he remembered being possible.

Roth's head kicked back as he cried out, shuddering. He came inside her, the barreling shock and sensation of release rocking through him as his hips rolled slower, slower, until they came to a stop.

Riley slid her hands down his back, over his wings, the tense muscles relaxing beneath her fingertips. Outside, the wind calmed to gentle strokes as soft as the fingers caressing his back.

Panting shallowly, his lips found hers; the kiss was soft and sweet. She kept her legs wrapped firmly around his waist, as if she didn't want him to go anywhere, and they both smiled. His shoulders and back began to shake slightly with soft laughter.

"I forgot what that felt like," Roth murmured, bringing his forehead to hers. He breathed a laugh. "How could I have forgotten?"

Still smiling, Riley bit her lip. "I'm happy I got to help remind you. To be here with you."

"Me, too," he said gently. He kissed her nose, her cheeks, along her jaw before bringing his lips to the center of her brow. "There's no one else I would rather have with me."

Riley's hold tightened around him, her walls constricting around his length, and he groaned, hardening inside her.

She licked her lips. "Round two?" she said, a bit breathless.

The summer storm within turned wild, craving. Needing to consume and devour every last moan and gasp from her delicious lips after finally, *finally* getting a taste of sweet release after being starved of pleasure for decades.

Roth looked at her, and she sucked in a breath. Her toes curled against his waist as he nodded, his throat bobbing. "This time, though, when I fuck you"—he chuckled low, rough, while shaking his head—"and I mean when I *really* fuck you, I'm going to have you screaming my name, just like I had you doing when I used my mouth and hands on your beautiful pink cunt."

She swallowed. Her hands left his back and braced against the wooden headboard behind her. With her own hungry, wild eyes, she said, "Then what are you waiting for, pretty bird? *Fuck me.*"

There was no holding back this time; no worries he wouldn't last long. He was a man hell-bent on hearing her cries of pleasure. And oh, did she give him what he wanted to hear as he fucked her with wild abandon, driving her into a babbling, moaning, blissful mess.

After she came, crying out his name, his own release followed close behind. Roth sat up, drawing her onto his lap so she was straddling him. He held her close, their damp chests flush against one another, as his hips rolled slowly, giving her time to find her way back to him before he started all over again. She wrapped loose arms around his neck and kissed him thoroughly until she was ready for him to wind her up again, only to have her unravel, screaming his name until it was all that she knew. Until *this* was all they knew.

CHAPTER 42

With sleepy eyes, Riley watched the sunlight creeping in through the window while Roth's soft lips glided over her shoulder. She was curled on her side, her back against his chest and their legs tangled together, tucked within the safety of his protective arms. A crimson wing draped over them; the soft edges of feathers tickled her skin. She couldn't help but notice they fit perfectly together. As if from the beginning of creation, they'd been meant to find each other and put one another back together after being fractured into a million scattered pieces.

Roth bit down gingerly on her damp skin, giving her a love nibble. Her mouth stretched into a lazy grin.

"You look thoroughly worshipped," he murmured against her, lips curved up into a gloating smile. "Would you agree, dragonfly?"

She swallowed and licked her lips. "I would," she said hoarsely, her throat sore from the night's events. She could, without a doubt, say her earlier frustrations had been unabashedly tamed from a vociferous roar to a tranquil purr.

"Would you say *too* thoroughly?" He kissed the tender skin he nibbled on. "I know I got . . . carried away." He breathed a rough laugh against her. "I guess that's what happens when you don't have sex for as long as I did. Even after hours of having you, I find myself craving more." He dragged a finger down her arm, and goose bumps erupted in its wake.

Riley had had an inkling it had been a while. After Maurice had mentioned the events with Talia and the Rule of Rebirth beginning nearly a century ago, one could only assume that was when Roth had taken his vow. But if he thought he had gotten carried away, then she had as well. Some time ago, he had kissed her, telling her to get some sleep; instead, she had flipped him on his back, pinning his wings beneath him, and showed him just how much better real Riley was than dream Riley. After that, they'd given up trying to get any sleep before the sun came up.

Turning her satisfied smile on him, Riley said, "No, I wouldn't say *too* thoroughly." She felt a shift in him beside her, a light tension. As if he worried she hadn't enjoyed the night as much as she'd made him think. But gods, she had to admit her old bird was not out of practice, even after all those years. Dragging a lazy finger along his wing, she added, "But I'm not complaining, either."

She should be exhausted, yet she found her body waking up, ready for more. She didn't understand it, needing more and more of him. With Jasper, she had barely ever lasted half the night, attaining blissful, sexual heaven in so many naughty—sometimes kinky—ways. But with Roth, it was as if she would always be left wanting more. Craving him as one did faerie fruit until the end of their days. And she knew he craved more as she did; she could feel his arousal digging into her backside while he drew swirls from her shoulder, around her breasts, and to her navel.

The corner of Roth's mouth lifted in smug satisfaction. He looked damn near ready to pat himself on the back. Even his wings appeared pleased, the one draped across her fluttering, feathers flaring slightly.

Riley didn't hold back the eye roll she gave him. "Abstinence has made you so humble," she said flatly.

Chuckling, he pressed his lips softly to her temple. "You go nearly a century without sex and see if you can stop yourself from being immensely pleased when the one you're courting tells you you've still got it."

Her brows slowly inched to her hairline. "'Courting'?" she asked innocently. He scratched the back of his neck, unable to hide the growing shade of pink on his cheeks. She couldn't stop her teasing, crooked grin. "Old bird, are you and I courting?" She gasped sardonically, a hand going to her mouth. "Are we going to go on a first date?"

It was his turn to roll his eyes. Shifting onto his back, he groaned. "Fucking hells, you're insufferable." His wing left her, draping over the side of the bed and onto the floor, mimicking an arm dangling over the edge.

Unable to help herself, she cackled lightly. She enjoyed teasing him as much as eating apple roses. It was inevitably turning from a hobby into an obsession, one she had no plans in the future to ever break.

A chill swept over her from the sudden loss of warmth from his wing, and instinctively she scooted closer, until she lay on top of him. As if it were a reflex, his hands and arms wrapped around her, while his legs entangled with hers; his wing came across her again, giving her the warmth and comfort she sought. She loved being wrapped up in the protection of his arms and legs, cocooned in feathers. She burrowed her face into his chest, deeply inhaling his petrichor scent—it might as well have been pixie dust she was snorting, as a rush of weightlessness settled in her limbs and head.

During her time with Jasper, she had done this many times. Lying atop him, trying to conjure up the airy sensation gliding through her now. But no matter how tightly she'd held the Sea Prince, he had never held her as tightly in return, like she'd wanted. Hope had always filled her veins that one day he would wake up and decide she was the adventure—the treasure he sought so fiercely, he'd left his home under the sea to find it—and he would tighten his grip on her, never wanting to let go of his precious gem. But as the days had worn on, it had become clear her hopes were as fantastical as the world she lived in, and eventually the feeling was foreign, almost invasive.

She didn't want to go through that again. Not with someone that if she lost him, would have her bring worlds crashing down around her with a raging, sorrowful scream. And *that* scared her more than anything.

The tips of Roth's fingers lightly danced up and down her spin, sending a shiver cascading through her.

"Roth?" she murmured into his chest. Her fingers poked at the soft skin of his pectoral, and she felt the muscle twitch.

"Yeah?" His chest vibrated beneath her, and she nuzzled him with her nose.

"All jokes aside, do you—" She swallowed, trying to get the damn butterflies to stop fluttering. She focused on his beating heart. "Do you want to court me?"

Although she couldn't see his smile with her face buried in his chest, it didn't matter; it was clear in his voice when he said, "Yes, Riley, I want to court you. If you'll allow it."

She smiled against him. There was no stopping the butterflies now. The warm, fluttery sensation in her chest bounced around, slamming off the stone guarding her repairing heart—where it struck, a dent was left in its place, a small crack in the center.

Roth's own heartbeat grew rapid.

"I guess I'll allow it," Riley mumbled teasingly.

He laughed, the sound deep and husky. The movement of his chest and abdomen lifted her with it, and she couldn't stop herself from joining in.

The fingers dancing along her spine landed on the low dip above the curve of her ass and pinched lightly, only making her laugh more.

Through giggles, she planted an open-mouthed kiss on his chest. Her teeth bit down lightly, giving him a love nibble, and his laughter subsided. Feeling the press of his erection against her stomach, hers vanished along with his. Slithering up the length of him, her peaked nipples dragging along his skin, she reverently kissed the damaged flesh.

His hands slid to her ass, cupping the plush, soft skin as she took a detour from his collarbone to nip at the point of his ear before she moved back down again. His fingers dug into her.

With the tip of her nose, she grazed over his sharp jawline, the abrasive stubble barely registering as she breathed in his addictive scent. She kissed his jaw, featherlight, moving to his cheekbones, his temples, his brow, his nose. She brushed her lips over the corners of his mouth before meeting his own soft lips.

The room faded away as time stood still. In this kiss, there was no urgency; it was only them and this moment, slow and passionate. Their hands glided over damp skin, tangling in each other's hair. Quiet gasps were exchanged as tongues caressed. Teeth grazed lightly over bottom lips before gingerly sucking.

Roth rolled them over gracefully in one fluid motion, never breaking the kiss with Riley. Her legs instinctively wrapped around his waist, and her fingers traveled over the planes of his shoulder blades, feeling the muscles ripple under her touch. She brushed over his wing, and feathers stroked her thigh in response. Her toes curled, and her fingertips dug into his back. A shiver raced down her spine.

Hours could have passed, but in the heated room, time was meaningless. All that mattered was their mouths, hands, and breaths. The warmth and weight of their bodies moving against one another. The beating rhythm of their hearts syncing to create a harmonious melody.

Guiding himself, Roth's hardness prodded at Riley's slick entrance. They sighed into each other as she welcomed every inch of him. As if they hadn't been truly able to breathe until they became one again.

But this time was different from the others. They weren't searching for one release after the other. It mirrored their everlasting kiss—slow and passionate. Gentle. As though if they went any faster, harder, they might wake up to find it was all a wet dream.

But this moment—this harmony she felt slowly tying them together —was as real as the scars on her flesh and the memories of loss and heartache they'd left behind.

With one hand gripping her thigh, Roth slid his other arm under her head and curled his fingers around her shoulder, holding her tighter. Each kiss, breath, and gentle stroke of his tongue, each heartbreaking, tender roll of his hips—they spoke as loudly as his eyes ever did. As if he were whispering into her very soul, telling her: *I won't abandon you. I'll follow you—be by your side down whatever path you take and through any and all worlds—no matter the risk. I choose you, dragonfly, because you are worthy—you are so damn* worthy.

She could feel it then, the warm dot in the dark sky of her soul. It flared to life, growing, until it was as bright and large as the sun. The desert land became illuminated in the shining light. The grass surged outward, sweeping across the barren expanse, and in the center of the roses, a blue iris grew. Giving a promise of hope that one day her soul would be filled with renewed life—one of overwhelming love and ever-lasting joy.

But despite the roses and the lone iris, she was afraid of losing every-thing when this moment ended. Because it would have to end, this feeling—it always did. Every time she grabbed ahold of hope, or love, or joy, it always eventually slipped through her fingers.

She couldn't let it—the eye-crinkling smiles, the soft kisses, the protective embraces, the still-forming bond, the promise of a *future*—she needed it all to last forever. Because just as the land needs the sun to flourish, so too will it always need the rain.

She breathed him in, every ounce of wet earth she could fill her lungs with. It filled her heart and soul, flowed through her veins. It became a part of her—became as necessary as breathing to live. It was all she could do to prepare herself for the end as it crept closer, closer, closer.

And when Roth broke the kiss, dampness coated his cheeks, his jaw —but they weren't his tears. Riley didn't know the moment she had started to cry; she hadn't felt the droplets sliding down her face, but she felt them then in that moment as she looked into those striking green eyes, seeing everything they had to say: *This never has to end. This can be our beginning—and our future.*

Riley breathed in a shaky breath.

In the ever-growing garden of her soul, new irises grew, becoming a field of red and blue. Blooming with renewed hope.

The end drew nearer, and a small sob escaped her.

The hand at her thigh lifted, and Roth held it out before her, an offering. With his eyes, he said: *Together?*

Still holding on to him with one hand, she interlaced the other with his. *Together.*

Their hands landed above her head; his grip tightened around hers. Their eyes never left each other's as they watched the other draw closer. The hand at her shoulder pulled her impossibly closer to him as he picked up the pace, driving his thrusts deeper, bringing them to the brink of this moment.

Together, they went over the edge, diving into their beginning—and their future.

Riley shattered under its force. It drove right into the center of the dented stone guarding her still-mending heart. Right into the tiny crack. And from that formed newer, larger ones, stretching across the stone as if it were as breakable as her fragile glass heart. And like her glass heart once had—the stone shattered, crumbling away into dust. The soft, warm breeze from deep in her soul rose and swept the ashes away, where they would disappear forever.

And that was okay. She didn't want the stone anymore. The walls had been placed there to protect herself from further hurt. But in doing so, they'd never truly allowed her to find what she had always wanted. Because a life without pain was the same as one without joy and love. One could not truly live without experiencing the other. One could not find joy and love without planting the seeds of hope.

CHAPTER 43

A robin stood on the slightly dirty, white windowsill outside, its head tilting in tiny, stilted movements. Its bright, rusted belly was dull in the late-morning shadows as it hopped a few inches forward, toward the glass. It moved its beak, singing a little song as it peered inside, watching another, much larger bird stretch his limbs and wings.

Curled on her side, Riley smiled. It wasn't every day she awoke to a bird watching another bird do naked yoga. A sight she would gladly watch, knowing her day was about to become as agonizing and discouraging as the ones leading up to it.

A week had passed since their arrival in Kararhys. Each day, they searched the districts for possibilities that could lead them to Lothaire's next clue or the treasure itself, and each day they went back to Maurice's apartment empty-handed. But that didn't mean they ended their nights in disappointment and frustration. Every night since the first, they'd spent in each other's arms, making love. It was a future Riley was more than happy to have.

Stifling a yawn, she watched Roth slide from tree pose into eagle, his arms twisting together while his leg curled around the front to the back of the other. He balanced gracefully on one leg, and she admired his thighs again, remembering how she'd shamelessly ridden them until she'd come last night. A flush settled over her cheeks. The corners of her mouth twitched up in amusement as she noticed, between his thighs, he was suffocating the life out of his arousal.

"Is that really the best pose you should be doing right now?" she asked teasingly. His eyes flicked to hers momentarily before staring straight ahead again—at a painting of mountains under a blanket of stars and constellations with a small girl standing at the base of the tallest mountain with broken, almost featherless wings at her back— concentration straining his brows. "The reason I ask," she said, "is it looks like you might break an important appendage, one I rather enjoy."

His mouth quirked, a crack in the mask of concentration he wore. Without a word, he disentangled his limbs and stood, his arms relaxing at his sides in mountain pose. Blood flowed south again, showing off his erection. "Better?" he asked as smoothly as asking about the weather. The corner of his mouth was lifted in unabashed smugness.

Sitting up, she tapped her chin in faux deep thought while admiring him. His gaze slid down to where the blankets gathered at her waist and up a few inches to her exposed breasts. She could have sworn the low growl that came from him sounded like the rumble of thunder from a distant storm. But there was no mistaking the dark, stormy look in his eyes. Her finger stilled on her chin.

How was it possible he was still ready to go another round after last night—and all the ones before? She knew faeries possessed more stamina than humans, but Roth was insatiable.

"I suppose so," she said, dropping her finger. She tilted her head. "But you know what would be even better?" She gripped the blankets and tossed them aside, revealing the rest of her.

His arms began to tremble beside him, his hands fisted at his sides. Every muscle strained and quivered in his body, and it looked as if he were nearly about to pop a blood vessel in his neck. He shifted his legs with restraint, keeping them from leaping on her.

She grinned, bracing herself with her hands behind her. Her arms were still slightly shaky from keeping her head from smacking into the headboard that first night—and every night since—but she willed them to remain strong.

Closing his eyes, he inhaled deeply, then exhaled. Repeating the motions once more, he said in one long rush, "As much as I would like to, I don't think we have time for that."

She frowned, looking out the window. "Isn't it late morning?" They still had plenty of time to think where to look next for Lothaire's treasure, although the more they found nothing, the more frustrated she became. Her head would near split in half if she continued to think as hard as she had to for an idea of where to search next, and the more she did, the less she could come up with. A little release from her mind was exactly what she needed.

Minutes passed before Roth answered, as he waited for his body to cease shaking. He dragged a hand over his face and opened his eyes. "It is," he said roughly, "but if I get in that bed with you—or within arm's length of you—we won't make it to the ballet tonight. And I don't want you to miss experiencing a dream of yours because I can't keep my cock in my pants."

"To be fair, though," she retorted, tucking her hair behind an ear, "those pants Maurice gave you can barely contain your cock. It was only a matter of time before it broke free."

He chuckled softly. "I hate those fucking pants," he declared, his hands going to his hips.

"I love those fucking pants."

"Of course, you would," he said, rolling his eyes.

She grinned, but slowly, as she realized what he'd said, fell away into confusion.

Ballet?

From the smile spreading on Roth's lips, she knew he could see questions swirling around in her head. "Was wondering when you were going to realize what I said," he whispered.

"I don't understand. We're here for Lothaire's treasure, not a ballet, remember?"

"And we still are," he placated, holding up his hands. "We'll continue looking, like we've been doing, but I think right now we need a break from it. Other than sex," he quickly added when she opened her mouth. She closed it, pouting. "I think attending a ballet would be just the right thing to clear our minds. We can keep looking tomorrow, but I think tonight we should go do something fun, because I would like it if my head didn't explode from the frustration building inside it, and I know you would, too."

Roth was right. Hadn't she just been wanting a release from her mind? She was losing it trying to think of where Lothaire could've been sending them within Kararhys. There were too many possibilities, too many fucking districts to search—all while trying to remain discreet from the High Crown Guard or anyone who might report them. But most importantly, if she couldn't think, it meant Mara would stay dead longer.

"So," Roth said, "what do you think, dragonfly? Go to the ballet with me?"

Slowly, a grin stretched wide across her lips. "Okay, old bird, I'll be your date to the ballet."

He beamed, grinning back.

"How long until it begins?" she asked.

"The Autumn Equinox Ballet begins at twilight, and it should end just before midnight and the beginning of the Autumn Rite," he informed her. "Which is good because it may be hours before you try on all the dresses Maurice selects for you from his shop."

She might have groaned if there hadn't been a spark of excitement inside her. There had been times during her trips to the mortal world when Jasper had had to physically drag her and Mara away from stores in the mall after hours of trying on different clothing. She imagined Roth needing to do the same: hoisting her over his shoulder, not giving a fuck if what she was wearing was all wrong. It would get torn to shreds anyway, after the ballet was over.

Roth must have seen the imagery playing out in her mind because his laugh was dark with wicked delight. "And risk Maurice's wrath for shredding one of his masterpieces?" He shook his head, clicking his tongue. "Even I am not that foolish. My appendage you rather enjoy wouldn't only be broken—it would be missing altogether."

"That seems a rather dramatic reaction."

"Only because Maurice is a very dramatic, foulmouthed man."

She grinned. "My favorite kind." Roth scowled, almost as dramatic as the man he was describing, and she laughed. "But he's got nothing on stubborn, old, pretty birds," she added with a wink.

Roth rolled his eyes and retrieved his wonderfully tight pants from the floor. "You should get ready before he drags you downstairs to try on dresses." With some difficulty, he pulled them up, hopping for good measure. Riley's lips curled back between her teeth, holding her snicker in, as she watched him button his pants halfway, grumbling as he did about Maurice needing to put on weight and grow a few more inches.

"What will you be doing?" Riley asked.

"Finishing your book before you."

Chuckling at her look of betrayal, he went for her bag discarded by the door and bent—

The distinct tearing of fabric filled the room; it seemed to echo, bouncing off the walls before fading into a silence wrapping around them. Even the robin at the window fell quiet, shocked.

Riley's eyes widened as her mouth fell open, and she watched as Roth turned as red as a strawberry. "You—" A tiny giggle burst past her lips. She slapped a hand over her mouth and tried again, the words muffled. "You just split Maurice's pants."

Slowly, Roth faced her, his own wide eyes filled with horror. "Don't tell him," he pled, mortified.

She snickered into her hand. "I think he's going to find out when you return them to him with a hole in the ass."

He grimaced. "Fucking hells, he's going to castrate me," he said distantly as his hand absently cupped his groin.

Rolling her eyes, Riley got to her feet and slipped a lacy turquoise nightgown on.

She didn't doubt Maurice was protective over his creations, but she didn't think the man would *castrate* Roth for splitting his pants. He might be dramatic, but he didn't seem *that* dramatic.

Reaching the door, she stopped to take one last look before going to the bathing room down the hall. She grinned crookedly. "Just as I said," she started, patting his rear. "Damn fine ass."

He looked over his shoulder, shooting lightning bolts at her as he swatted at her hand, and she left the spare room, head thrown back, cackling.

She called back to him, "This is what happens when you try to finish my book before me."

RILEY GRIMACED IN THE MIRROR.

It was quite possibly the worst dress she had tried on yet. The bright golden bodice fitted tightly to her waist, the curved neckline made her breasts appear more plump than usual, and the short, puffy, gold-and-black striped sleeves made her arms rest awkwardly at her sides. But the skirts . . . Oh gods, they might have been the worst part. Multi-layered and alternating between gold and black, they were covered with what appeared to be soft, furry hair and, even without a hoop, managed to take up a large portion of the alterations room in Maurice's tailor shop below his apartment.

"I look like a bumblebee," she grumbled. And with the silver gossamer, almost translucent, shimmery cape flowing at her back from the bodice, appearing as insect wings—there was no mistaking her for anything else. All she was missing was antennae poking out the top of her head.

There was the sound of bursts of air somewhere behind her, and although she couldn't see anything through the mirror because of the godsdamned dress, Riley was certain it was Evie snickering to herself from where she sat with her legs crossed beneath her on the cream chaise lounge, drawing in her sketchbook.

"I should just go to the ballet in one of the nightgowns," Riley muttered. There was a part of her that truly wondered if she was better off doing just that. It had accomplished exactly what she'd hoped Roth's reaction would be when he'd seen her: stunned into silent, dark hunger.

Maurice clicked his tongue from somewhere. "You do that and you'll give the gentry the impression Roth paid you to be there with him."

She scoffed. "More like *compelled* me to wear the nightgown while accompanying him for the evening." To make a mockery of her in front of the noble faeries of Kararhys. Little did they know, she couldn't be compelled into doing anything she didn't want to.

There was shuffling while Maurice waded through flowing, bright gold and black. His silky black hair fell past his shoulders, and his lean build could be seen beneath his half-buttoned, white shirt and dark blue pants. He stood in front of the mirror, his dark brows pinched tightly, a finger tapping his chin and the tip of his tongue sticking out of the side of his mouth. After a minute of careful scrutinizing his work, Maurice said matter-of-factly, "I really don't see what the fucking problem with this dress is." His hand waved dismissively in the air. "What's wrong with looking like a bumblebee?"

Riley gave him her best you've-got-to-be-fucking-kidding-me look, and they stared at each other for a long while as she wondered if she truly had to answer that—the dress spoke for itself. Maurice was the first to look away, and a swell of pride rushed through her. If she had been competing against Roth, they would've been standing there all night and missed the ballet.

Maurice grumbled what sounded like a string of curses in Scyathan before sighing heavily. "Well, I suppose, if I must"—he gave Riley a pointed look—"I'll find something else."

Riley rolled her eyes as he left the room. *Dramatic* was definitely one word to describe Maurice.

Using the fabric of the skirts, she bunched them up beneath her and sat down. Even if the dress was ridiculous, it did, at the very least, make a comfortable, makeshift pillow to sit on. She looked around the room, contentedly listening to Evie sketch behind her.

A few framed paintings covered the walls; they ranged from dancing women in fancy dresses to a sunset over a field of lavender. They were all meant to dredge up feelings of hope and happiness, but that wasn't what caught Riley's attention; it was the style of the art— the brushstrokes, the shadowing. They were done by the same hand who had painted the framed artwork on the walls in Maurice's apartment.

Riley swiveled herself around with some difficulty to face the girl drawing, as content as could be. "Did you paint these?" Riley asked, indicating the paintings.

Evie looked up from her sketchbook. The tip of her tongue stuck out of the corner of her mouth while her dark brows pinched tightly together on her heart-shaped, golden face. Her amber eyes regained focus on Riley as she realized she'd been asked a question. The girl nodded, the tip of her tongue slipping back between her lips. Riley couldn't help the smile growing on her face. Not only did Maurice's daughter have his artistic talent, but also his mannerisms.

"They're beautiful," Riley told her. Evie gave her a simple smile and nod of thanks, but not before Riley saw the slight dip of the girl's mouth, the sadness in her eyes. "You don't think they are?"

Before answering, Evie looked at the paintings around the room, her face falling more with each pass. A shoulder lifted and fell, and Riley saw it then—why Evie didn't believe these works of art weren't beautiful—as she glanced at the drawing in the girl's lap. Of the eerily similar girl on the paper, her mouth sewn shut, the needle and thread dangling past her chin. The sadness and loneliness in the girl's eyes while she stood in the middle of a crowd. The inability to be heard and therefore seen, despite being surrounded by others.

The paintings on the walls might have been bright and cheerful, but they were not what the artist felt. It didn't depict the world she knew; the ones on the walls were false, an image to alter a patron's mood into buying more. But the ones on the walls of the apartment above were the truth. They showed the world Evie had grown up to know, one of hurt and despair and silence. The one in the spare room of a girl with broken wings staring at the highest mountain before her was the truth of what Evie felt day after day.

Perhaps it was the sadness in the girl's eyes, or knowing all too well what it felt like to be unheard and unseen and alone, or the growing bond with Roth and the reminders she was worthy. Maybe it was all of these reasons that made Riley scoot closer to the girl, place a hand over her arm, and say, "You are not alone, Evie. No matter what the voices tell you, you are never alone. And as quiet as it may be, you do have a voice, and believe me when I say, you are heard."

Evie stared wide-eyed at Riley, her lower lip wobbling as she hugged her sketchbook close to her heart. A tear slipped free.

Riley caught it with the pad of her finger and felt compelled to continue. "I know what I'm saying may not make any sense now, but someday I think it will. For now—and this is something I'm working on myself—whenever the voices tell you you are alone, try to remember the only one forcing you to be alone is yourself and list the people in your life. Prove those voices wrong. Because I know, even after meeting you just days ago, your father loves you more than anything in all the worlds, and he would *never* abandon you. He does see you, and he does hear you —you are his world, Evie."

More tears slipped down the girl's cheeks, and Riley squeezed her arm, offering her a portion of the furry skirts to wipe them with. Evie laughed softly, the sound nothing more than puffs of air, and Riley gave her a small smile. Releasing a shaky breath, Evie wiped away the tears sliding down her cheeks before they could fall from her jaw onto her drawing and only add to the sorrow of it.

"I know what I told you is a lot to take in, and I hope I haven't upset you too much," Riley said, a nervous feeling flaring in her chest. "That wasn't my intention. But I also hope you know you can add my name to your list." Evie's mouth parted in shock. Riley added, "And Roth, too. I'm more than sure he would tell you to add his."

Slowly, Evie nodded, her breathing uneven. She stared at the drawing in her sketchbook of herself with her mouth sewn shut. The tips of her thin, pale fingers brushed over the stitches. Her jaw clenched as her mouth became a tight, thin line, and abruptly she turned the page to a blank one, tearing it out. She handed the parchment to Riley, along with a slender piece of graphite, before picking up her own and beginning a new drawing.

Riley didn't utter another word, understanding Evie needed the distraction as she put the graphite to the blank parchment and began to draw. Minutes passed before Evie tapped her arm. Riley looked up at her and recognized her scrunched brows as confusion. Evie tapped the drawing and tilted her head, asking in her own way what it was.

"It's Roth," Riley answered. She could see why Evie wouldn't recognize him. She wasn't an artist like Evie by any means . . . and his body was a bird's. "See," she said, pointing to the head. "That's his stubborn face." She smiled as Evie's head tilted back in breathy laughter, her shoulders lifting.

"All right, you two," Maurice said, sweeping into his alterations room, holding a dress behind his back. He looked as pleased as could be with himself, until he saw his daughter with laughter lighting up her eyes. The smugness melted into warm adoration and pure love and joy.

Riley felt a pang of longing in her chest. It had been too long since a father had looked at her the same way.

She swallowed, reminding herself although she didn't have her family any longer, it didn't mean she was alone.

Clearing her throat, she asked, "Did you find a dress that doesn't make me look like an insect, Maurice?"

His warm brown eyes slid to her. "Hm? Oh, right," he said, blinking. He shook his head slightly. The smugness was creeping back into his features as Evie smiled at him, waiting to see what new masterpiece of his creation he had for Riley to try on. He revealed the dress from behind his back. "It's okay, you can admit it," he said, his chest puffed. "I'm a fucking genius."

With the back of her hand, Evie hit Riley's shoulder lightly as she never took her eyes off the dress, as if she were saying *that's the one* with every light tap. But Riley barely registered it as her breath caught in her lungs, and she said the only thing that came to her dazzled mind, "Oh."

CHAPTER 44

Chatter filled the air as gentry made their way inside the Lunar Theater of Kararhys, all dressed in elegant attire for the ballet. Servants, faerie and compelled human alike, took fur coats and carved canes topped with gemstones at the door before making their way to a section in the back of the theater, where they were forced to stand for hours as they waited on their masters.

Riley's stomach tightened. She should feel safe with an aileron by her side, but how could she as the tiger on her arm almost throbbed, reminding her of its presence as she passed one High Crown Guard after another? If they happened to see it, if her sleeve happened to inch high enough and they arrested her . . . She resisted the shudder raking against her bones.

After making their way through the arched doors with the phases of a silver moon carved above them, her arm tucked through Roth's, Riley glanced at him beside her, hoping he hadn't noticed the shift in her emotions. Her eyes first landed on the silver embroidery of his black tail-coat suit. Where it buttoned down the center, the silver threads traveling up to the collar were made to appear as wispy clouds sprinkled with little stars. With his wings, he looked like a bird flying through the clouds under the cover of a starry night.

A half-growl, half-whimper came from the back of his throat, causing her eyes to finally find his, and thankfully, he was as distracted by her clothing as she was by his to notice the change.

Hunger had settled in his eyes since she'd descended the stairs from Maurice's apartment, and they wandered over every inch of her now from the bottom up. It was somewhere around the hundredth time she'd caught him looking since they'd left Maurice's.

Smirking at Roth's blatant lust, she asked innocently, "Is something wrong with the dress? Is there a tear in the fabric I don't know about?" She made a show of looking for a flaw, her fingertips running lightly over the diaphanous material.

Riley reveled in the desire she had hoped to see in Roth's eyes as they traveled up the long black skirts where a slit revealed her right leg almost to her hip, and his pupils dilated when they reached the top. The sheer fabric of the top and the dress's only sleeve were covered in black feathers. The farther up they traveled from her waist, the fewer there were. Thankfully, they were thicker around her wrist and forearm, covering the Roaring Tigers' insignia, before fading as they climbed up her arm. And there were just enough feathers to cover her breasts and hide the peaked tips from Roth's hungry eyes.

His gaze never wavered from her dress. "I've done a thorough search," he said, leaning in close, "but in order to make sure there are no flaws, I'd have to examine it closer." His voice was smoky, seductive.

She shivered as her eyelids fluttered shut, crimson sparkles sprinkling down from her lashes. Black, outstretched wings grew from the corners of her eyes, flecks of red sparkling within the feathers, and her lips were painted ruby, all courtesy of Evie. Riley couldn't line her eyes with kohl to save her life, and after she'd put the feathered dress on, she'd asked Evie if she would help. The girl was an artist with natural talent, and she'd been more than ecstatic to draw with the kohl for her. She had banned Riley from looking in the mirror as she'd worked until she'd deemed it all right, and Riley's heart had nearly stopped beating within her chest. Just as it did now.

"How close?" she asked Roth, a bit breathless.

"*Very.*"

Riley bit back her groan as they were ushered inside to their seats. She stumbled, her heart nearly stopping for a whole new reason.

Dangling from the ceiling and illuminated by floating solasta orbs were white moonflowers, their star-shaped centers a dark violet. The walls were painted a midnight blue with sparkling stars, and the columns were carved to appear as flowing silver water, mirroring the lake surrounding the city. The two upper levels and balconies floated on plush clouds with dim solasta orbs bathing them in a sensual glow. Matching the walls, the seat cushions were a midnight blue, trimmed with silver. And front and center, the stage floated on the grandest of clouds, the orchestra tucked within the bottom layer.

Taking it all in, Riley wondered if she hadn't had been afraid to look anywhere but at Roth when they had escaped Grendelwyn Forest, if this was what he felt like when he flew, what it was like to be among the clouds and the stars.

They were ushered to a small section off to the side of the theater, where the chairs had lower backs, accommodating Roth's large wings. Other faeries were already seated, and one by one, they turned to stare at Roth. The true color of his wings was masked by the dim lighting, but there was no hiding his heritage. Murmurs and whispers began, and they only increased once they saw the human on the aileron's arm. Riley ignored them all, too enamored with the fantastical beauty of the theater to care what they thought.

With wide, dazzled eyes, she gasped softly as the back of Roth's knuckle swept down her bare arm, and he leaned in, whispering into her ear, "I never knew feathers could be so maddeningly seductive before tonight." The tips of his fingers slid over the silver feather comb pinning her hair back above her ear. With her chestnut curls tamed to smooth waves and gently swept to one side, her collarbone and shoulder were left exposed to Roth's achingly gentle touch.

Her breathing turned shallow as she searched her memory for any door on their way to their seats that might've been a closet. Since she'd awoken in the late morning, they hadn't had any alone time. Roth had been gone for most of the day, running the errands Maurice had given him for splitting his pants—although this idea had formed after a lot of convincing from Riley to not castrate Roth like he wanted to, just as he had predicted.

Riley brought a hand to her mouth to help stifle the growing laughter from the memory. This wasn't the first time throughout the day it had found its way to the forefront of her thoughts, and Roth had ignored her snickers every time. Except this one.

"I'm definitely not finding a closet with you now," he said, straightening beside her. He smoothed a hand down the creases of his waistcoat. "You have officially killed the mood."

She burst out laughing, unable to contain it. Others looked her way, but she continued to ignore their stares as she dabbed at tears welling in the corners of her eyes, careful of Evie's work. "Imagining your ass peeking through the ripped seam is worth it every time," she said through laughter.

"At least one of us enjoyed that experience," he replied dryly.

"Tell me," she continued, mirth turning her grin crooked, "would you say that was your most embarrassing moment?" He tilted his head, considering, and slowly shook it. "Really?" she asked, surprised, almost stunned.

"I would say that was the second most embarrassing thing to happen to me."

"Okay, now you *have* to tell me what the first is." She crossed her right leg at the knee, exposing it further.

With a secretive grin, Roth's hand landed on her bare knee gracefully, as though this was something he did all the time. "Never going to happen, dragonfly."

"I wouldn't sound so confident." She walked two fingers down his thigh and back up. Leaning over, making sure to press her breasts against his arm, she purred in his ear, "I know many ways to get my pretty bird to sing for me."

He squeezed her knee as he inhaled sharply. His pants shifted as he hardened against her fingers. Huskily, he said, "If that is a challenge, then consider it accepted."

Riley leaned in farther, wanting to start this challenge straight away. Her lips met his in a whisper of a kiss. There were gasps of shock and grumblings of disapproval from those around them, but they paid them no mind. Not when this kiss held all the promises of what she would do to make her pretty bird *sing*.

The solasta orbs dimmed, and Riley broke the spell. But not the promises it held.

Her heart beat wildly behind her breastbone as her blood hummed with excitement. Roth's fingers drew idle circles on her knee; it had a slight calming effect on her. Enough to keep her from fidgeting and her leg from bouncing. But when the shimmering silver curtain drew back, as if it were a waterfall dividing, she couldn't stop herself from leaning forward in anticipation and that crooked grin from emerging.

THAT CROOKED grin was going to be the death of Roth.

A calm had settled deep within him from it, and as he watched it grow as the music began and the dancers glided fluidly on the stage, telling a story, there was a flutter within the calm, spreading through him. His eyes traveled over the angles of her face, the wings Evie had done, halting momentarily on her lips, the shade he thought he could never love again—but red had never looked so beautiful before. He counted each and every freckle on her nose, cheeks, and exposed shoulder. And before he realized it, he was smiling. One that crinkled his eyes so much, they were almost closed—but they had never been more open.

They landed on her dragonfly tattoo and the scar beneath.

Since the day she'd rolled up her sleeve to show him the tattoos he would have inked on his skin, he'd wondered what had made her feel so worthless and unwanted to make her choose to disappear from the world.

And although her scars had been a reminder of the mistakes he had made in the past, they were also a second chance to show this incredible woman how much she was worth saving.

Roth never imagined joy would find him again, his soul broken and consumed by the very storm that had given him his scar, but here he was, the happiest he'd ever been. And it was all because of *her*. She reminded him of what life had to offer. Every piece of herself she gave to him, he tucked into the eye of the storm of his soul, letting it become his center.

His calm.

And he would do the same for her.

He never wanted her to believe what the shadows whispered to her from within the dark. Never wanted her to place the edge of a blade against her skin again. He would remind her day after day if he had to that she was worthy of life. That it was calling her name. Screaming for her to live because no matter the hard times, when you least expected it —*joy would come.*

CHAPTER 45

Despite the late hour, they weaved through the crowded street of the square in the Temples of the Gods District. The Autumn Rite for the goddess, Mab, was to begin at the stroke of midnight, the beginning of the autumnal equinox, but that didn't stop faeries from beginning the celebrations early.

The smell of sweet wine and an almost spicy incense was in the air. Children raced each other in a game of tag; they threw colored powders at one another, occasionally missing and hitting a sacred statue of the gods or a couple dancing to the music. Chimes hung from trees, statues, and the temples, all ringing in time with the soft breeze while couples drew closer on the amber, marbled steps and shadowy alcoves of Mab's temple.

Riley held on to Roth's free hand, the other carrying a pink box as he used his wings to shield them from the flying colored powders—if they returned to Maurice's apartment with splotches of bright yellow, orange, and red on his designs, not only would Roth be castrated, but she imagined the tailor would come up with a considerable punishment for her as well. He navigated them past the square to a garden tucked behind the temples, away from the celebrations that were sure to get out of hand.

While the gardens and landscapes of Wyne were a vibrant kaleido-scope of a rainbow, the garden behind the Temples of the Gods in Kararhys held a certain whimsical ambiance.

Whispers from tiny, winged faeries came from behind a statue of a naked woman who had antlers poking from the top of her head and through her flowing hair. Vines with tiny flowers crawled up her left leg and curled around her waist to her right, outstretched arm, where a rose bloomed in her open palm—Aiyana, the goddess of earth, Riley real-ized, and she suppressed a sudden shudder.

Autumn leaves gathered on their own, forming stags walking through the grass. They walked near the spiraling, stone path, lined by an array of colorful flowers in full bloom—thanks to the powerful god magic, gifted to the High King, keeping them alive during all seasons—that branched off from the main one Riley and Roth walked. The stags bent their heads here and there as though they were eating.

One, with a large set of antlers, spotted Riley and Roth. It lowered the front half of its leafy body until it appeared as if it were kneeling and bowed its head. Riley squeezed her eyes shut, shaking her head slightly. She had to have imagined it. Opening her eyes, she saw that she had, and the stag was merely trailing its head along the ground like the others.

Cypress trees lined the main walkway they traveled on. It was made of mosaic tiles, creating swirling vines of roses that led into a tunnel made of the same flower, each one a different shade. It appeared as though they had sprung to life from the tile to create the tunnel itself. Butterflies with glittering wings fluttered from rose to rose, lighting the path within the tunnel. They stopped once to allow Riley to catch one on her finger. Her grin turned into a fit of giggles as she looked at Roth and found his eyes crossed while he stared at a butterfly resting on the tip of his nose.

Emerging from the tunnel, they were met with a turquoise pond with lily pads and croaking frogs. But Riley's focus was solely on the patch of land in the center, where a towering weeping willow stood.

Stepping stones created a makeshift path through the water to the willow, and with her hand still in his, Roth led her from stone to stone as dragonflies zipped and darted by.

Still holding on to the pink box, Roth released her and pulled back the curtain of leaves and branches. "After you, dragonfly."

"You're still a very gentlemanly old bird, I see," she teased, giving him a wink and a smile to match her tone, but it all vanished as she stepped behind the curtain.

She gasped.

Twinkling lights crawled up the twisting trunk of the willow, and fireflies floated through the air, their lights winking in and out of existence. Tiny, winged, naked faeries lounged on branches and the stone bench in front of the willow, carved with stags in a forest.

With her lips slightly parted, Riley turned in a slow circle, taking it all in.

"How did you know this was here?"

Roth joined her beneath the tree, letting the curtain slide back into place. His eyes lit up almost as bright as the twinkling lights around them. "Maurice told me about it," he said, his voice reflecting his awe.

"Really?" Riley asked, surprised. "Even after you split his pants, he told you about this place?"

He gave her a small, amused smile. "Yes, even then. Maurice told me about this place when I asked him if he knew of somewhere . . . private and as beautiful as the company I would be in."

Her cheeks flushed as he passed her and sat down on the stone bench. He set the pink box down beside him and patted the space on the other side, giving her the smile she adored so much. Breath hitching, she sat in the spot he'd patted as he crossed a leg, his ankle resting on his knee, and draped an arm across the back of the bench. His fingertips played with a feather on her sleeve.

He opened the box, and saliva pooled in her mouth as the scents of cinnamon and apple wafted up. She breathed them in, snatching an apple rose. She nearly ate the dessert whole before Roth had a chance to pick up one of the strawberry lemon cheesecake croissants he'd gotten for himself. He stared at her with raised brows.

"What?" she said around a mouthful before swallowing.

"You've got caramel on your face," he teased, thumbing the sweet, sticky substance from the corner of her mouth. He brought his thumb up to his lips, but before he could place it inside his mouth, she caught his hand, bringing it to her own. She sucked the caramel greedily from his thumb, sliding her tongue over the pad. "If you keep that up," he murmured thickly, his eyes dilating, "we're going to have a repeat of last night, and the night before that, and so on."

"You make it sound like that's a bad thing."

A smile played on Roth's lips as he leaned in, but before he could close the distance, a high, feminine voice asked, "What happened last night?"

A tiny, naked, and plump faerie with dark brown skin fluttered from her perch on the willow to Roth's arm. Her tiny freckles, sprinkled across her nose and cheeks, were the same shade as her magenta ringlets, and her wings mirrored the fireflies' floating around them. She glanced back and forth between Riley and Roth, waiting.

Roth scratched the back of his neck, a silent plea in his eyes for help, while Riley snickered into her hand. He could stand before an orc with a deadly smile on his face, but when a tiny faerie inquired about their sexual activities, he turned into a nervous baby bird.

Seeing this, the faerie giggled, her hands covering her mouth. "Naked things happened, didn't they?" She arched a knowing brow.

Roth avoided the faerie's knowing look, shoving a croissant in his mouth as Riley said, "Yes, they did."

Giggling, the faerie's wings fluttered, floating her to eye level with Roth. She hovered there for a moment, a finger tapping her chin, assessing, before prying his lips open to observe his teeth. She poked and prodded at his face, and when she was done, she glided to his soft curls atop his head and rolled around in them, whispering, "So soft," over and over.

All the while, Roth glared at Riley while she tried desperately to contain the laughter bubbling to the surface, but not once did he try to stop the faerie. He only shoved another croissant in his mouth and chewed. If Riley didn't know any better, she could've sworn there was a part of him enjoying the feel of the little faerie rolling around in his hair.

"If you think his hair is soft, you should feel his feathers," Riley said to the faerie. Roth halted chewing. His glare could wither and freeze the roses they'd passed by earlier, but it only made Riley snicker more.

The faerie popped up from his hair, and once her eyes landed on his wings, she squealed with glee. She flew to one, disappearing behind it. Giggles floated up from behind.

Roth resumed chewing, but with his eyes, he said: *You're insufferable.*

Grinning, Riley asked the faerie, "What's your name?"

The faerie poked her head through Roth's feathers, giggling, her magenta eyes bright. "Giselle," she said, wrapping herself in feathers. She nuzzled her face against them. Roth's cheek twitched, as though her nuzzling tickled. "What's yours?"

"Riley."

"That's pretty."

"So is yours."

"What about him?" Giselle asked. She unfurled herself from feathers and used her wings to propel herself to Riley. "What's his name?"

Riley gave him a moment to answer, but his withering glare remained trained on her while he took another bite of his croissant. "Roth," she told Giselle.

"Roth," Giselle repeated dreamily as she floated onto Riley's shoulder, her chin propped in her hands. "A fittingly handsome name. You wouldn't happen to have a brother, would you?"

Riley's smile faltered for a moment. Did Roth have a brother? Or siblings, for that matter? If so, were they still alive? She had told him about Liam, but she realized he'd never spoken of his family. After what Maurice had told her of the Rule of Rebirth, perhaps whatever family Roth had left had fallen victim to the cruel, horrendous law.

Roth's glare disappeared, softening as memories flickered in his eyes while he swallowed his croissant. "I'm afraid I don't have any brothers, only sisters."

"As disappointed as I am you don't have a brother," Giselle said, almost pouting, "sisters are good, too." She winked, twirling a ringlet around her finger.

Riley's mouth gaped slightly. "*Sisters?*" she said, her brows rising in surprise. "As in more than one?"

"Yes." Roth tilted his head as a hint of a smile played on his lips. "Two of them, actually."

Two sisters. All this time, Roth had sisters and he hadn't told her. What else didn't she know about his family? About him?

She picked up an apple rose, taking a large bite. She let the sweet taste of caramel wash over her, dissolving the questions forming in her mind.

"Are they as gorgeous as you?" Giselle asked.

Roth laughed softly. "They are far more beautiful than you make me out to be." He thumbed caramel from the corner of Riley's mouth, smiling as he sucked it clean, a delightfully sinful gleam in his eyes.

"They must be something else." Giselle sighed dreamily, absently reaching out, taking a tiny fistful of the apple rose Riley held to her mouth.

Riley resisted the urge to swat the little faerie away from her precious dessert, reminding herself she had four more in the pastry box; Roth had gotten her the six apple roses she had bargained with him for in exchange for her most embarrassing moment—he didn't need to know she had lied through her teeth at the time of her *confession*.

The tiny faerie closed her eyes and moaned as she chewed her bite. She reached for another fistful, moaning again. Before she could take more, Riley shoved the rest of the apple rose into her mouth.

Heartbroken from this sudden betrayal, Giselle pouted and fluttered from Riley's shoulder to Roth's hair; she flopped down, disappearing into the curls, but her sobs could be heard from within.

Riley slumped against the back of the bench, her features falling while she listened to the tiny faerie weep. Roth shook his head slightly, giving her a disapproving look, and she sighed. "Giselle, would you like one of my apple roses?"

Giselle poked her head out of the front of Roth's hair, wiping her nose with a fistful. "Really?" she asked, her voice small but hopeful.

Nodding, Riley lifted the box of pastries to the faerie while ignoring the shock on Roth's face. Giselle grinned and glided down to the proffered box. Her arms stretched wide and hugged an apple rose before she whispered, "I know this is scary, but it's only out of love that I eat you." With those final words, she dug in, devouring the thing one tiny bite after another.

Riley chuckled softly and was surprised to find Roth smiling adoringly at the faerie.

She set the box back down on the bench. "What are your sisters like?" she asked Roth, picking up another apple rose while maneuvering around a sprawled-out Giselle, her belly round and full and face covered in caramel and crumbs.

"They're both younger than I am, but that doesn't stop Kalliope from teasing me endlessly," he said, taking a croissant for himself. "I'm terrified to put you two in the same room. My ego would suffer greatly from that." Riley grinned as he bit into the pastry, chewed, and swallowed. The smile forming on his face was warm, soft. "Amaya's shy at first, but once she warms up to you, she shines as bright as the stars above."

The love for his sisters was as stark in his eyes as it was in his voice, and seeing it, hearing it, melded more pieces of Riley's heart back together. Her grin softened, mirroring his.

Finishing his croissant, Roth reached for one of the last two remaining apple roses. Riley smacked his hand away. "What do you think you're doing?"

"What does it look like?"

"It looks like you have a death wish."

He huffed an almost surprised laugh. "You really do have an obsession."

"I never said I didn't."

"So, you'll let Giselle have one but not me?"

From the box, Giselle said sleepily, "We have a deep and profound connection. Admit it, you're jealous."

The corners of his mouth twitched as he shook his head. "I have to say I'm disappointed. I thought you trusted me more than this."

"This has nothing to do with trust," she volleyed, crossing her arms. He took advantage and tried to swipe an apple rose again. She caught him by the wrist. "I like you, Roth, but I'm afraid I'm going to have to hurt you if you take one."

"You like me," he echoed, grinning.

Giselle's giggles floated up from the box before she made kissing noises.

Riley rolled her eyes. As if that hadn't been made clear earlier. "Was that the only thing you heard?"

"I don't think I've ever met anyone so violent when it comes to dessert."

"You should meet my sister, Fiona," Giselle piped in, followed by a yawn.

Roth smiled, chuckling softly at the little faerie as his wrist twisted in Riley's grip. His fingers wrapped around hers and his thumb slowly rubbed circles. Her next breath lodged in her throat as he stroked the sensitive skin. She bit her lower lip, drawing his eyes to her mouth. He licked his lips. Her skin felt so, so, tight as he continued rubbing circles. His eyes slowly traversed her features before sliding down to her breasts; his mouth parted slightly. She crossed her legs at the knee, clenching her thighs together as heat pooled low in her belly.

All thoughts of the apple rose vanished—until Roth brought it to his lips with his free hand.

Eyes wide, she gasped. "Ass. You distracted me on purpose." She released his wrist, yanking her own away from him. The heat instantly vanished. Smiling, he chewed. "I can't believe you did that." She glared at him as he shoved the rest of the dessert into his mouth.

Licking the caramel off his fingers, he asked innocently, "Something wrong?"

She glared at him as she took the last apple rose before he could think to steal it from her. "Ass," she repeated.

A thought occurred to her as she chewed. "Tell me, is your baking as *extraordinary* as your cooking?"

His eyes narrowed slightly. "Why do you want to know?"

"I'm deciding whether or not it's worth it to have you bake me the apple roses that were taken from me—and more."

"Sorry," he said with a hint of mirth and a smile playing on his lips. "I'm afraid my baking is worse than my cooking." She frowned, disappointed, and finished off her treat, savoring the finality of it. "Now, you tell me something," he said as she licked her fingers clean. "Why the ballet? You never said."

"You never asked."

"I'm asking now."

She hesitated, unsure if she wanted to dive down to that part of herself.

"Please?"

And that was all it took for her to crack open a part of her she had buried long ago.

"I've loved dancing for as long as I can remember," she said with a ghost of a smile on her lips. "My mother put me in classes at a very young age, and I worked my way up as I got older."

She paused, steeling herself, her eyes darting away from him. As if sensing the difficulty of what came next, Roth placed a hand over hers, squeezing reassuringly. Telling her with the gesture that she didn't have to relive the past if she didn't want to, but if she chose to, she didn't have to go through it alone.

Taking deep breaths, she continued, "After I was taken, it was hard for me to adapt to my new reality. It was my love of dancing that got me through a lot. It was a sense of normality in this new world, and the more I found out about it—the crueler it became—the more I danced.

"One day, a guard found me trying to teach myself ballroom dancing in my room, and instead of punishing me, he told me I shouldn't watch my feet so much. That I should trust in my abilities." The ghost of her smile was back. "He taught me in secret after that day. He was the first and only friend I had during my captivity, but that friendship still wasn't enough for him to risk sneaking me to the Lunar Theater. I begged him every day to take me there—I even told him I wouldn't try to escape, that I would go back to my prison willingly if he just allowed me to see a ballet—but he never did. I understand the risk he would've been taking if he had, and in the end, I'm glad he never took it. Seeing a ballet was not worth the risk of losing my one and only friend."

She blew out a deep breath after expelling a story she had never told another living soul. "So, that's why the ballet," she said, finally able to look at Roth. "Because dancing has always been the one constant in my life, and I might have had that bit of normalcy taken from me a few years ago, but I won't let that stop me from enjoying the one thing I have always loved to do."

"And you shouldn't," Roth replied softly, brushing his thumb over her knuckles. "In fact . . ." His brows knitted together, as if he were contemplating his next words, his next move. He blew out a soft breath, mumbling, "Fuck it," before he got to his feet, stood before her, and held out his other hand. "Dance with me," he said, conviction stark in his eyes.

Behind her breastbone, Riley's heart did a little dance of its own. "Really?"

He knelt before her, placing his hand on her knee. "Really," he said, grinning. He placed a fist over his heart. "And I promise, you will make me look incompetent—and if I've learned *anything* about you these past few months, you're going to enjoy watching me trip over my own damn feet."

She laughed. "I would enjoy that immensely."

"Then do me this honor," he pled, taking her hands in his. He leaned in close, brushing his lips whisper-soft against hers. Her eyelids fluttered shut as he whispered, "Dance with me, Riley Hayes."

SHE TWIRLED AROUND and around to the beat of her own heart. Her pulse sang the notes of the melody within her chest. It was a realm-shattering, sky-splintering, wish-upon-a-shooting-star, beautiful song. One full of renewed life. It was exhilarating, liberating.

Tiny faeries in the willow sang, while one slumbered, surrounded by pastry crumbs. Notes of instruments floated on the wind from the not-too-distant square, but she didn't notice any of it, lost to the song within and the man she danced with.

He'd exaggerated the limits of his skills, and although there was room for improvement, he lifted her flawlessly in time with her song, not missing a beat. Not once did he waver as he spun them around, nor did he step on her toes—or his own.

Grin on his face, he guided them around the patch of land in the center of the pond, his eyes locked on hers, as if they were the only ones under the willow. If she concentrated hard enough, they were back on their little island in the middle of the Gorsium Sea with no one but each other. As it should always be.

In her blossoming soul, in the garden burgeoning from the warmth in his steady eyes, she found her beginning—and her future. It had been walking beside her for months. Listening to her weeping soul and catching her when she fell. Reminding her she was *worthy*.

The roses swayed in time with the music as they reached the crescendo. Her dance partner did his best to keep up with the maestro conducting the orchestra within her soul. And with every rising note, he spiraled into that grand finale—that *future*—with her, never letting go.

CHAPTER 46

After hours of dancing, it wouldn't be long before dawn was on the horizon. The Temples of the Gods District flourished with celebrators. Newcomers brought their offerings for the Autumn Rite to Mab's temple, placing them on the amber, marbled steps wherever there was space, the area overflowing. Soon, they would be spilling onto the streets, but never to the other temples. It wouldn't be wise to cross another god.

With Riley's arm tucked through his, her body pressed against him as they wove their way through the ever-growing crowd, Roth watched her eyes dance over the different temples they passed, taking in every minute detail of the different seasonal gods represented in the square. He couldn't wipe the smile from his lips. It reflected the long-lost joy blaring through the dark clouds within him.

It had been so long since Roth had last danced. With the vow of abstinence he'd taken and the violence of the war before that, he couldn't remember the last time he had felt so free doing something other than flying. It had been the only form of happiness he had allowed himself, and even then, it had never felt the same knowing there were brothers and sisters of his out there who could no longer experience it.

The light shining through the clouds within his soul dimmed, but not enough to go out completely. How could it, when the woman nestled against his side radiated all the joy he could've hoped for?

Without allowing himself to think about his actions, Roth leaned in, placing a tender kiss on the crown of her head. "Riley," he murmured against her hair, "I—"

"Look!" Riley gasped, cutting off Roth's declaration. He didn't allow himself to feel the sting of disappointment as he followed the finger she pointed.

The ominous temple was darker than night, as though it absorbed the light from the spiked metal torches positioned near the top of four pillars guarding the black stairs. It was made completely from drakenite stone, mined from the Aztalon Mountains that had been breathed into existence by the god of fire himself.

"Look at the pillars!" Riley shouted over the din of the celebrations around them. "Dragons!"

Snaking up the four pillars of the drakenite temple were dragons. Unlike Beldir, the god of fire, these dragons had long, slim bodies, and their arms and legs were shorter. On their winding backs, they were missing wings, and on their heads, in place of their horns, were antlers of a stag. Two long wisps of hair swirled from their snouts.

Roth nodded, trying to show as much enthusiasm as he could muster. But within, it was as though a giant sat upon his chest. Dread settled within him, burying him under its heavy weight. He hadn't realized they had made it to the main square within the district, representing the first gods created by the Mother of All.

For days, Roth had been trying to lead Riley away from this place until he was ready, knowing it would be where Lothaire wanted them to go. But he hadn't yet devised a plan to keep everyone he loved safe without risking losing one or the other—or worse, both.

But there, before him, was Beldir's temple. The very being Obsidian Island was rumored to have grown from and the starting point of Lothaire's treasure hunt. It seemed only appropriate that a pirate with a dragon emblem would lead them here. The god, after all, was the first of the dragons.

The light within Roth dimmed further as Riley tugged on his arm, leading him up the drakenite steps of the temple. But there was still a beam of hope left within that he would figure out a way to save them all.

RILEY'S SLIPPERS glided over the smooth drakenite floor without a sound. A veil of swirling steam rose up, as though it came from the very depths of the Abyss. It shrouded the temple's entrance, and once through, Riley halted, breathing in a sharp gasp.

Silver water carved out a path along the perimeter, the steam rising from it curling and winding its way through the air. The shimmering water was striking in contrast to the dark stone surrounding it. If it wasn't for its glow and the hanging, large bowls of flames above them, Riley had the sense it would feel as though she were trapped in a tomb of unending darkness.

With Roth by her side, Riley swept forward, her black skirts trailing through velvet-soft red petals littering the floor. A shiver skittered down her spine as the hairs on the back of her neck rose. The sudden sense of being watched overcame her, and from the way Roth subtly angled himself in front of her, she knew he felt it too. Her eyes darted around, scanning upward she found the source.

From perches set into the alcoves of the vaulted Gothic ceiling on either side of the temple, six statues of dragons sat, peering down upon them. Each one a sentry to guard their powerful, fallen god. Glittering light from the flames reflecting off the crystal chandeliers dangling from the center of the vaulted ceiling danced along the pillars they balanced on. Each one was carved to appear as though they were made up of dragon scales.

Riley's nerves began to settle. But with Roth still angled in front of her, his wings tucked in tight behind him, ready to dismantle whatever threat might be lurking within the shadows, she knew not to let her guard down.

They stalked through the red petals leading toward the back wall with a large, circular, stained-glass window, housing the main attraction of the temple.

The mighty dragon statue, completely made of drakenite, stretched from one wall to the other. Its large, powerful wings reared back, while its deadly tail curled down and around to the front of the steps leading to the dais it crouched on. Sharp claws broke the surface of the drakenite, indicating just how dangerous it was to cross the god of fire. And within its open, snarling maw was the silver-blue Undying Flame of Beldir, casting a massive shadow of the dragon and its eight horns on the wall behind it.

Each footfall up the stairs was eerily silent, candle flames flickering this way and that as they passed. And when they reached the dais, Riley didn't dare breathe at first. From afar, the dragon was intimidating; up close, it made every survival instinct she possessed scream at her to run.

If her fear was this overwhelming in the presence of a statue, she didn't dare think about standing before a real one.

In the center of the dais, the dragon curled protectively around an altar. Wax gathered and trailed over the sides from the lit candles in the four corners and center. Smoke wafted from recently lit incense, and around it, the petals were piled high, creating a barrier of sorts. One that had the appearance of pooling blood.

Riley cocked her head, seeing a shade of color that didn't belong among the crimson. Taking careful steps, she buried her hand in the petals, searching, while Roth remained at the edge of the dais, acting as her own sentry. Her fingertips grazed something hard among the velvet-soft petals. Pulling it out, she peered at the object, losing her ability to breathe all over again.

But it wasn't fear that gripped her heart—it was hope.

The teal and silver threads were dirtier than the last time she'd seen them, and the tiny gold beads had flecks of blood mixed with the dirt. But the golden tiger charm dangling at the center of the bracelet was as pristine as the day she had given it to her best friend for her birthday. As if someone had taken the time and care to clean it.

Riley had thought she would never see the bracelet again, just as she'd thought she would never see the owner. Running the tips of her fingers over the woven threads made tears well up in the corners of her eyes.

Questions raced through her mind about how it had made its way to Kararhys when it should've been at the bottom of the Gorsium Sea.

Hope was as dangerous as it was fleeting. And from the hope she couldn't shake, the biggest question of them all flashed brightly before her.

Without turning, Riley asked almost as softly as their footfalls, "Do you think she could be alive?" Her voice threatened to crack, but she held it steady. "That maybe the magic within the compass didn't work?"

There was a moment of silence. Then Roth spoke just as quietly, his breath warm on her exposed shoulder as he peered at the bracelet behind her. "No, dragonfly, I don't."

"But—"

"I saw what happened with my own eyes. The compass couldn't find her because she no longer breathes."

"Then, how is this here?"

Roth hummed, thinking over her question. She stared at the bracelet, waiting for him to answer.

"Grimsley," he said into the quiet. "There are cruel beings in this world, doing wicked deeds for their own gain. But then, there are the monsters. The ones who delight in their sinful ways and find pleasure in the suffering of others. They look down upon their prey and smile at their pain. But when the suffering ends, they need something to remember the moment by, a trophy if you will."

Riley sniffled, wiping the tears from her eyes. "And you think Grimsley kept Mara's bracelet as a trophy after she died."

It wasn't a question, but Roth answered, "Yes," the word full of sorrow.

"How can you be so sure?"

"I know someone like Grimsley," he said, the sorrow digging deeper into his rough voice. "He always kept—" Roth cleared his throat. "There will always be monsters. No matter what world you find yourself in, they will always find a way to come out of the shadows to terrorize those who live in the light."

Riley had an inkling whom Roth spoke of, remembering what Maurice had told her the night they had arrived in Kararhys. The things Roth had witnessed and gone through over the centuries were horrifying. She hadn't a clue how he was still as together as he was—or perhaps, like the well they'd found in Grendelwyn Forest, the outside might appear unbroken, but within there were only ruins and darkness.

With a gentleness no one but her knew the Crimson Knight possessed, Roth turned her to him and took the bracelet. "Don't lose what little hope you have left, dragonfly." Wrapping it around her wrist, he clasped it above the compass. "Hold on to it and use it to rise from the darkness of despair."

Riley swallowed the sob rising in her throat. She took a deep breath, letting her grief wash over her without drowning in it, and allowed herself to take hold of the hope flowing alongside it.

Standing up straighter, she lifted her chin. "What do you say, old bird? Ready to find a dead pirate's treasure?"

He flashed her a grin. "Lead the way." He stepped aside, gesturing for her to do so.

Picking up her skirts, her chin still held high, she gracefully slipped on the red petals and nearly tumbled down the stairs on the side of the dais. Roth cursed, reaching around her waist, but not before she managed to grab ahold of a long, thick chain hanging from the ceiling. It gave under her weight, as a rope connected to a bell might.

Within the silence, the sound of stone grinding and moving made them freeze. They searched for the source of the noise.

"Look up there," Roth said, steadying Riley on her feet. He pointed to the opposite end of the temple, to the farthest dragon statue perched high above. "I don't remember its head turned this way, do you?"

"No," Riley said, "I don't." She looked at the other statues lining the temple above and noted how they remained staring at the points below them.

Roth's arm slipped from around her waist as he walked to the other side of the dais, where another chain hung in the shadows. He gripped it, looking to Riley in question.

She shrugged. "I don't see the harm in it."

"You say this now," Roth drawled, lifting a brow, "but when that enormous dragon statue comes to life, I'm going to have to strongly disagree with you."

Chuckling, Riley said, "Just pull the damn chain."

Roth did as commanded, and they watched the middle dragon

statue, on the same side as Riley, move its head to stare at the grandest one of all.

"Huh," Riley grunted. "If I didn't know any better, I'd say that *enormous* dragon is still a statue. Wouldn't you agree?"

Roth gave her a dry glare from across the room, and she could practically hear him silently calling her a smart-ass. She grinned.

They searched among the shadows for more chains, finding four. Each time they pulled on one, another dragon would move its head to look at the one on the dais. After pulling the final chain and the last dragon turning to its master, one more slid from the ceiling to land in front of the altar.

Standing before the new chain, Riley looked to Roth. "Together?"

He smiled softly and nodded once. "Together."

With their hands wrapped around it, they pulled in unison and watched the dragon before them close its snarling maw, snuffing out the silver-blue flame—or so it should have. The Undying Flame lit the statue from within, illuminating the words scrawled on its scaled body:

Destiny awaits, ye of fortune.
Look to the stars when the lights go dark,
for they will guide you to paradise.

Riley stared at the new clue, her head cocked to the side. Unlike the previous ones, this had no drawings to go with it, and she suddenly found herself wishing it did. It was from those they'd been able to decipher the next locations. Unless . . .

"This is it, Roth," she breathed. "'Destiny awaits.' This has to be where the treasure is."

Roth looked around. "Then, where is it?"

As if in answer, the dragon before them stood, revealing a gap in the drakenite floor.

Riley arched a brow at Roth, her lips twitching with mirth. "I'm going to take a wild guess and say it's down there."

He rolled his eyes. "Smart-ass."

CHAPTER 47

With her head ducked low, Riley held on to Roth's hand as he led them through the unlit, narrow tunnel. The poor, old bird was hunched over, nearly bent in half with his wings tucked in just to fit within the tunnel. From what Riley could tell without being able to see a thing, they were headed down an incline, traveling farther within the large island Kararhys had been built upon. The longer they walked, the damper it became. Her satin slippers squished on the uneven terrain, and she couldn't help but wonder how much trouble she would be in with Maurice for ruining them.

"I see some light up ahead." Roth grunted, preventing Riley from conjuring up all the ways Maurice might punish her. "We're close."

Behind her breastbone, Riley's heart hammered away. Her nerves and excitement threatened to force the muscle through her rib cage. This was it. Soon, she would have Mara back.

The cramped tunnel widened the closer they came to the light ahead. With every step, Roth was able to unfurl his wings more and straighten his back, until he stood tall, taking the first steps into the round, dimly lit room with Riley right behind him.

Beneath Riley's damp feet, soft, glowing silver light faded in and out with a familiar movement, one she had grown accustomed to over the last three years. It glided as waves might over the ocean. The movement entranced Riley, and she could almost feel the rocking of the ship in her bones.

Above, stars sparkled as brightly as they did out at sea, reminding Riley of a moment she had spent not too long ago on the *Tigress*, under the stars, with Roth.

The entire room was meant to appear as a ship under the cover of a starry night. There was even a helm in the center. But the four floor-length mirrors with arched, shining silver frames didn't belong. They hung on opposite walls from each other, creating a cross.

"So," Roth said, dragging out the word, "which mirror do you think leads to the treasure?"

She looked at each in turn, excluding the one they had just emerged from. Across from them, a skeleton sprouting foliage sprawled half in, half out of the mirror. "Not that one," she said, gesturing to it with her chin, and Roth grunted his agreement.

"That leaves two options."

Withdrawing her hand from Roth's, Riley went to the helm in the middle of the room. In the center of it was a compass, with the letters *N, W, S,* and *E* lining up with the mirrors.

"It looks like we're to choose either the west or the east mirror," Riley said as Roth came to stand beside her. His mouth became a tight, thin line as his brows scrunched in thought. "I can see you think I'm wrong."

His eyes slowly shifted to hers, a ghost of a smile playing on his lips. "I do."

"Care to elaborate why?"

The smile came into fruition. "I'm just thinking about the clue left behind on the dragon. '*Look to the stars when the lights go dark, for they will guide you to paradise.*' I think we're supposed to follow the stars."

Riley's head nodded slowly as she thought about it, and the more she did, the more she thought he was right. Sailors used the stars to navigate the sea; Mara had taught her that the first week on the ship. Looking up at the ceiling full of stars, she remembered what Mara had told her as they'd gazed up at the field of glittering lights all that time ago. "'If you're ever lost and alone,'" Riley said softly, "'the North Star will keep you safe.'"

"The Mother." Riley's attention jerked to Roth. He searched the stars. "The North Star is also known as the Mother, named after the Mother of All. Ailerons were told something similar about it." He found her eyes. "It will always guide you home."

"Or maybe, in this instance," Riley said, feeling her hope flare wider, "to paradise."

Roth nodded. "We need to find it."

It took some time, and for Riley's eyes to cross more than once, but eventually they found it behind them, shining brighter and bigger than the others surrounding it.

"Well, that can't be right," Riley grumbled, placing her hands on her hips. "According to the compass on the helm, the North Star is in the south."

"Not to mention, that's the mirror we came out of," Roth added. "But it can't be the mirror pointing north based off the corpse dangling between whatever location it came from."

Riley took a deep breath, trying to clear her mind and piece together what they were missing. "Pirates use the stars to navigate the sea," she mumbled to herself, talking it through. She began to pace the round room, following its circular path. When she came to the flower-covered skeleton, she stepped around it, still feeling as though she were on a ship being rocked by the waves.

Abruptly, she stopped in her tracks. Her eyes shot to the ceiling, taking in the stars and the constellations. "That's it!" she nearly shouted. "Pirates use the stars to navigate the sea!"

"I know," Roth said, arching a brow. "We've covered this already."

"But that's just it." Riley threw her arms out wide, gesturing to the room they stood in. "The stars, the waves beneath us, the helm with a compass—we're on a ship!"

She saw the moment all the pieces came together within his eyes, a light sparking within them. "And if this is a ship," he continued almost distantly, "and the North Star is behind us . . ."

"We need to turn the ship to go the right direction," she finished. Her smile shined as bright, if not more, than the stars above.

Riley nearly slipped and fell rushing to reach the helm. She gripped two of the handles.

"Wait!"

She looked at Roth, her eyes wild with excitement. "I'm right, Roth."

"I know," he said. He jabbed a thumb over his shoulder, at the mirror behind him. "We should mark the one we came from, otherwise who knows if we'll find our way back."

He had a point.

She nodded and watched as he easily sliced the palm of his hand open on one of his wing's talons. After letting the blood pool, he smeared it down the side of the arched silver frame, over carvings of constellations and crescent moons. When he turned back to her, the wound was already healing from his faerie magic.

With their way back marked, Riley didn't hesitate a moment longer. She turned the helm.

Roth let loose a string of curses as they watched not just the wall of mirrors rotate, but the stars as well. He closed his eyes, tucking his chin close to his chest. His forefinger and thumb rubbed his closed eyelids. Riley didn't blame him; the whirling stars made her teeter back and forth. She might as well have been standing at the edge of a cliff, she was so dizzy with vertigo.

Every few seconds, Riley would halt the spinning, needing to recalibrate and find the North Star before turning the wheel again. She didn't stop until it lined up with the N on the compass in the center of the helm and a mirror was directly below it.

Letting go of the handles, she swayed on her feet, the world still tilting on its axis. Roth's hands found her waist, steadying her until he was sure she wouldn't collide with the floor.

He slid his hands away from her waist to have one take her hand, entwining their fingers. Facing the mirror under the North Star, he asked, "Are you ready?"

Every nerve ending within Riley tingled with excitement. She squeezed his hand and nodded. "I'm ready."

Together, they stepped through the mirror and were greeted by a splash. Riley's already damp foot sank ankle deep in vibrant blue water.

One glance over her shoulder told her they'd stepped into a small pool of the brightest blue she had ever seen.

"I really, really hope stepping into the pool takes us back to the mirror room," Riley said, walking up the slight incline out of the water, "and not for a swim."

"I don't know," Roth replied, following her, his hand still in hers. Mirth coated his voice. "I wouldn't mind going for a swim." His eyes danced with mischief. "We should probably undress before we test where the pool leads."

Letting go of his hand, Riley playfully punched him in the arm. She ignored the sound of his laughter as she stepped around a stalactite hanging from the ceiling of the cavern the mirror had led them to.

Roth trailed behind her as they navigated their way through the maze of stalagmites and stalactites, some piercing each other to form columns, to the light coming in through a hole in the ceiling. Within the rock creating the cavern were speckles of smooth black stone.

"More drakenite," Riley murmured, her soft words bouncing off the walls around them.

Roth ran his fingers over a large patch of drakenite within the wall. "We must be in one of the many tunnels within the Aztalon Mountains. It's the only place to gather the stone."

"And not a bad place to hide treasure."

The network of tunnels within the mountains would make it difficult for one to find treasure, not to mention the dormant volcano in the center of the mountain range.

Reaching the middle of the cavern, through the gap within the ceiling, stars began to slowly disappear as the sun tried to rise. And illuminated beneath them were untold chests and barrels littering the cavern. There was barely room left to walk among the greatest treasure trove known to Erithenian history.

Riley nearly tripped over her skirts sprinting to the nearest chest. She didn't hear Roth go to a barrel beside her—or his string of curses he let out—as she lifted the lid. Her lungs clenched with the breath she held, and—

—and they immediately plummeted at the sight of the barren chest in front of her.

She looked to Roth, hoping the barrel wasn't the same. He frowned, his lips tight, and gave her one shake of his head.

Closing the lid, Riley went to another chest, finding that one empty too.

They went around the cavern, searching every barrel and chest. Each and every one of them was as empty as the once plentiful field of irises within the garden of Riley's soul. The only items left behind were some measly coins, jewelry, and useless broken blades.

"It's all gone," Riley said softly, turning in a slow circle. "Everything's just . . . gone." She looked over at Roth, seeing him pocket a chain. "Do you think it was Grimsley?"

He shrugged. "Could've been. But it could've been someone years ahead of us. We'll never know."

A dull pounding in Riley's temples began, growing heavier by the minute. Blowing out a breath, she ran a hand through her hair. "This was all for nothing. Everything we went through over the last three months—we both had to be brought back to life! And for what?" she shouted, throwing her arms wide. "For fucking nothing!"

He shook his head. "That's not true, Riley."

"Mara's gone, Roth! She's fucking gone, and she's not coming back! This was my chance—my one and only chance to bring her back! I have nothing left!"

Roth jerked back as though she had slapped him. But the grief flooding Riley was too much for her to notice how much her words had hurt him.

She fell to her knees, not feeling the sharp ground slice into her flesh. She buried her face in her hands. Her shoulders shook with the sobs working their way up her throat and past her lips. Tears welled and slid through the cracks between her fingers, sliding down the back of her hands.

Roth knelt before her. His arms stretched out as though he were going to scoop her up into his arms, but she pushed him away.

"Don't touch me!" she screamed at him. "Just get away from me!"

She couldn't see him step back from her through the tears; she only heard his boots scrape against the rocky floor, him doing as she wished without a word. There was a twinge of guilt pinching her chest, but it was nothing compared to the grief she would inevitably drown in all over again.

Mara was gone.

The finality of that knowledge hung in the air before falling with an impossibly heavy weight. She rocked herself as she could feel the glass pieces—the ones that had managed to heal—threatening to shatter once more. She couldn't go through that pain again. *Not again.* It had taken so much strength to crawl back from the bottom, she didn't know if there was enough left in her to do it a second time.

"You're stronger than you know."

Roth's voice was so soft, Riley had almost missed what he had spoken around her sobs. Her hands dropped from her face into her lap. She knew all of Evie's hard work was smeared and destroyed, but she didn't care. Roth had seen worse from her just weeks ago.

"What?" she asked, now seeing the hurt that lay within his eyes. The hurt she had caused him.

"You are much stronger than you believe yourself to be, Riley," Roth told her again, louder this time, as though he didn't want her to miss a word he had to say. "This isn't the first time you've had to pull yourself up, and it won't be the last. There will always be hardships along every path you take. And every time they appear, every time you have to rise above them, you become stronger than the last. You have faced enough to make plenty give up, but you haven't. You're still here, fighting everything this world has thrown at you."

He crouched down in front of her, meeting her eye to eye, his arms resting on his knees with his fingers clasped together, still obeying her wish to not be touched. "You are the strongest person I know, Riley, and I know a lot of warriors."

She huffed a laugh, the sound coming out more like a hiccup.

"But that doesn't mean you always have to be strong. Sometimes strength means asking for help when you need it the most." His clasped fingers twitched as if he were trying, with all his willpower, to not reach out to her, to give her the comfort she had forced away. "You might think you have nothing left, but you have me. You don't have to go through every hardship by yourself anymore. When you need it, my strength is yours, always."

Riley turned her eyes up to the gap in the ceiling, watching the stars fade farther away, and wondered if Mara was among them. Another hiccup forced its way past her lips, but the weight—the one dragging her down, down, down—it lifted, and she could take large gulps of air again. And she did just that, inhaling deeply, gathering that weight within her, and letting it all go with an exhale.

Ignoring the pain in her knees and shins, Riley rose once more—on her own. But she knew she would need help along the way, and just as Roth had said, she didn't have to go through it alone.

Before she could hold out her hand in question, Roth slid his into hers, weaving their fingers together as he stood. He smiled warmly down at her. Through his eyes, she saw how proud he was, and for the first time, she knew she *was* stronger than she believed. Time after time, she'd risen from the pit of despair, and she would do it again. As many times as she had to because life was worth living, no matter how hard it became to do so.

"Come on," Roth said gently. "It must be nearly dawn over Kararhys. We'll get some much-deserved rest, dodge Maurice before he can flay us for the grime on our clothes, and eat tasty pastries."

A smile played on Riley's lips, but it never graced her face. He took her chin in his other hand. "One day at a time, dragonfly. The feeling of the loss will never completely go away, but it will start to heal in time. And I'll be there with you every step of the way."

Slowly, Riley nodded and wiped her eyes and nose with the back of her hand. She felt better knowing he would be there on the days she wasn't strong enough to rise on her own, offering her his strength.

"I don't know about you," Roth said, a playful gleam among the golden streaks in his green eyes, "but I'm ready to find out if we're about to go for a swim." He winked, and Riley couldn't help herself.

She laughed.

CHAPTER 48

Riley was asleep the moment her head hit the pillow, dried up tears leaving a trail down her cheeks. She hadn't bothered to put another revealing nightgown on—or wear nothing at all—and Roth was grateful for it. The damn thing would surely torment him, and he wouldn't get any sleep—not that he planned on it. He had somewhere else to be.

He slipped Riley's damp shoes off her feet before curling his body around hers, soaking in her warmth and breathing in her citrus and vanilla scent. Wrapping a wing over them, he felt his heart flutter as she nestled farther against him within the safety of his arms.

He had been nervous to bring her to Kararhys, worried she would be spotted by a High Crown Guard and recognized as a pirate, but no one had. Roth wasn't going to give Riley up without a fight, and the only way they would take her was over his mangled corpse.

His eyes drifted to the window, past the roofs of the other shops in the Trading and Market District, past the elegant trim of manors in the Gentry District, to the emerald spires in the distance. To the castle on the hill, enshrouded in a forest of greenery. His throat felt dry.

A looming, dark cloud hovered over the woman he tried so hard to protect, to remind that she was worth more than she believed. It threatened to take her away from him, but he wouldn't allow that to happen. No matter the consequences.

They would leave in the morning and never return to this city—they wouldn't be able to, not after what he was about to do. Until he could ensure her safety once and for all, Riley would always be in danger. Even with him by her side to protect her, there would be others who would come for her—she was lucky he had been the first.

But he knew where they would flee to, not that they had any other choice. Once his deceit was discovered, no one would be foolish enough to take them in. Save for his people—he hoped. Most hadn't welcomed him home in decades after the turmoil he had caused them, but his family, his friends, they would welcome him and Riley with open arms, no matter how much he thought he didn't deserve it.

Roth waited until Riley was deep in slumber before slipping out of the bed. He tightened his leather cuffs around his wrists; if things went poorly, he would need his armor.

Taking one final look at the woman he would give up everything for, he kissed her lightly on her temple before leaving the apartment to go to the person who had started him on this path from the beginning.

CHAPTER 49

Roses danced in a circle, their leaves interlocking them together.
Instead of beneath a willow on a patch of land in a pond,
Riley stood in the middle of a field, watching the roses dance around her
and Roth. Fireflies twinkled around them—

No, not fireflies.

Stars.

Clusters upon clusters floated around them, creating a sea of
galaxies. It was like nothing Riley had ever seen before. Even on the
ocean, under the blanket of the night sky, she had never witnessed
anything like *this*. There was no sign of grass beneath them. Only the
sparkling light floating at her knees.

Roth's eye-crinkling smile was as bright as the starlight around
them. Still clad in her black feathers, Riley observed he wore the black
tailcoat suit from Maurice, but it was as if magic possessed it. Real
clouds drifted from the collar, swirling around them. They caressed the
dragonfly tattooed on her arm. The clouds circled up her arm to the
back of her neck, stroking her there. She shivered; it felt like fingertips
sliding along her skin. Her eyes fluttered shut from the touch as she let
the wispy cloud tendrils work their way over every inch of her bare skin,
until her body was warm and loose. Her lips parted.

"Dance with me, Riley Hayes," Roth said, low and seductive.

Riley opened her eyes.

With a hand outstretched to her, he remained grinning.

The words were enchanting coming out of his luscious mouth. They smelled like wet earth and would lead to an evening she would never want to forget. They would leave her feeling breathless and free. Liberated of all her unwanted thoughts.

The cloudy tendrils cleared away like smoke drifting on the wind.

"Dance with me, Riley Hayes," Roth repeated.

But instead of smelling wet earth, there was a foul stench in the air. Bitter and sour. Riley's brows wrinkled as she tried to figure out why the sudden change had occurred. It was as if the clouds were a curtain, and as they drifted away, it was pulled back to reveal the truth.

Roth closed the small distance between them. He ran his hands down her arms as the clouds had done and leaned in. "Won't you dance with me, Riley Hayes?" he murmured velvet-soft, brushing his lips along hers. He kissed the corner of her mouth.

She frowned. The kiss tasted of wet earth, like the clouds had smelled. As if the act were only to distract her from the bitter truth.

But what was she having trouble seeing?

Roth moved to kiss her cheek, then her temple, after each whispering, "Dance with me, Riley Hayes." And with each kiss, the wet, earthy scent drifted away, leaving a bitter, sour taste in her mouth. It filled her nose, her lungs, until her entire soul wreaked with the stench.

The roses dancing around them withered, their petals falling away until they were nothing but stems and thorns. The stars flickered out, showing the deadened earth beneath their feet, the weeds and dust, the cracks shadows slithered up through. They circled her ankles, stroking her flesh as the tendrils of clouds had done.

Light flashed in the sky, followed by a low rumble. Droplets of rain began to fall from the darkness above, nourishing the barren land.

But it was too late.

The shadows crawled up her legs, her waist. Her throat. Until they pried her mouth open and slid down, down, down. Filling her. Suffocating her with the bitter truth.

SHE GASPED, waking in the spare bedroom of Maurice's apartment. She was alone, the other side of the bed rumpled from where Roth had lain beside her. She could almost still feel the warmth of his body curled against hers. The wing he had settled over them. His wet, earthy scent clouding her thoughts and dreams. But it had vanished out of the open window, along with its owner.

She shivered as a cool, icy breeze swept into the room. Her insides began to sting, as if needles were trying to push their way through her body from the inside out. Her fingers wrapped around her arms and tightened.

She had forgotten roses had thorns.

The bitter truth remained, encasing her in its sour taste and stench. Although it might have been the shadows suffocating her, Roth had said it to her over and over.

Her jaw clenched as her fingers dug into the blankets beneath her.

He knew her last name when she had never given it.

CHAPTER 50

Riley sat on the bed, listening to the celebrations on the street, while Evie drew herself with dark, feathered, taloned wings soaring high over Kararhys, the castle's emerald spires, ivory walls, and thorny, flowered vines crawling up them behind her. The tip of the girl's tongue stuck out of the side of her mouth at times, her brows knitted in concentration.

The pain of losing Mara—of the knowledge Riley could never use the scroll to wish her best friend back to life—was still there, but watching Evie lessened the grief. It was a reminder that while Mara might be gone, there was still good in this world. There was still joy. Riley needed that small dose of happiness, especially after what the shadows had shown her.

Smiling, Riley leaned against a pile of pillows with her knees tucked close to her chest, reading a book written by a faerie known for her spicy romance novels. Things were getting noticeably steamy when the door to the spare bedroom opened.

Roth halted in the doorway, as if he weren't expecting to see Riley awake. He had been gone long enough for the sun to indicate it was midmorning but not long enough for Riley to get a decent amount of sleep since they'd returned at dawn.

After waking from her revelation, Riley had bathed and dressed in a simple gold tunic, bringing out the flecks in her hazel eyes, and black pants, both borrowed from Maurice's shop. She'd been surprised to find herself comfortable enough to roll her sleeves up to her elbows, showing off her pirate insignia, but she felt she could trust Maurice and Evie not to go to the High Crown Guard.

Riley met Roth's shocked expression with an uptilt of the corners of her mouth. The movement felt stiff and false, but the aileron smiled softly in return, not seeing through the mask. He moved to her side, leaning over her, and kissed her temple. "Good morning," he murmured against the curve of her ear.

She resisted the shudder traveling down her spine when his wet, earthy scent reached her.

"Good morning." Her voice sounded as lifeless as her smile had felt, but Roth either didn't notice or chose not to.

"Whatever you're reading must be extremely filthy," he whispered, his voice smoky. "Your cheeks are as red as my wings." He brushed a cool knuckle down her warm cheek.

She swatted his hand away.

He chuckled, thinking her action playful, but his touch made the bitter taste in her mouth unbearable.

Setting a small white box wrapped with green ribbon on the night table beside the bed, he sat in front of her, bringing her foot to his lap, and began rubbing the aches away.

She resisted the urge to kick him in the face—no matter how good it felt, the gesture made her skin crawl.

"So, I was thinking," he said while his thumbs applied pressure to the arch of her foot. "After we stock up on as many apple roses and strawberry lemon cheesecake croissants as we can carry, I thought maybe you'd want to—" The tips of his ears began turning a rosy shade. "I thought you'd like to meet my sisters." It all came out in a rush, as if there were no other way he could get the words to come out. "I'm going against my better judgement and risking putting you in the same room as Kallie," he tacked on with an eye-crinkling smile.

Riley's mind went blank from the reappearance of that smile she had learned to cherish.

"What do you think?" Roth was hesitant, almost shy, looking up at her through his lashes. "You want to go home with me?"

And for a brief second, it made her forget all of the realizations she'd come to in her dream—but it all came crashing back to her.

If he had asked her yesterday, she would have said yes—she would love to meet his sisters, to see how bright Amaya shined and tease him endlessly with Kalliope—but it was too late to make plans with him, no matter how appealing his intentions might seem.

Underneath all of the sweet and endearing ideas lay the bitter truth.

From the moment her eyelids had opened to an empty room, Riley had sifted through her memories, going over every interaction and conversation she'd had with him over the past three months, and not once could she recall telling him her name. She assumed he had picked up her first name from another in the crew. Most of the time, it was how anyone learned each other's names. But she'd only told Mara her surname, no one else.

She clenched her jaw, grinding her teeth, and she could have sworn the shadows nestled within her writhed and cackled with glee.

Her mouth became a thin line, and she closed her book, the sound holding a sense of finality to it. That this was the end of their beginning. There was no future for them. Only *this*. Lies and secrets.

"Evie?" Riley said, catching the girl's attention. "Do you mind giving Roth and me a moment alone? There's something we need to talk about."

Roth stopped rubbing the arch of her foot. He searched her eyes, looking for any unspoken hint what this could be about, but she would give him none.

Evie looked between them before slowly gathering her items. She scooted off the bed. At the door, she glanced back at Riley with a questioning look, as if she were asking if everything was all right. Riley gave her a small smile, letting her know she'd be fine, and Evie left.

"What's wrong?" Roth asked once the door closed. "This isn't about stealing your apple rose, is it?" He tilted his head, the corners of his mouth twitching. "You're not going to hurt me now, are you? If you are, please let it involve biting." He smirked. "Or spanking. I do love a good slap on the rear."

Riley's mouth opened, closed, then opened again.

He likes spanking? she thought. *Why didn't he say any—*

Pinching her eyes shut, she shook her head, clearing her mind. He was so godsdamned good at distracting her. She snatched her foot back from him, tucking it close to her once more. She tossed her book on the night table and arched a brow at the small white box he'd returned with. Her heart stuttered a beat when she realized the green ribbon was the same shade as his eyes, and the glitter was a sparkling gold—a combination she had embarrassingly mentioned was a favorite of hers.

"What's in the box?"

"That," he said, pointing to it, "is your birthday gift."

"My birthday was almost three months ago."

"I know." Smiling sheepishly, he gestured to the box again. "Open it."

No matter how many somersaults her heart did beneath her breastbone and how much her curiosity prodded at her, she refused to do that.

She crossed her arms. "I'm going to be perfectly honest with you; I don't want any fucking gift from *you*." He flinched, his wings shifting. She ignored the hurt that flashed in his eyes, focusing on the lies and secrets.

"What's your last name?"

He frowned. "I don't see how that's relevant."

She scoffed, not surprised by his answer. Faeries didn't make their surnames known to anyone. There was magic—and consequences—in trusting another with their true name. That kind of trust was unconditional and rare in this world. Some went as far as giving a fake first name in the case their surname was found out.

Through her teeth, Riley said, "It became fucking relevant the moment you knew mine."

He stiffened, his eyes glazed over as he sifted through memories, trying to remember where he had slipped up. His eyes slowly closed, the only indication he had realized.

"How do you know my last name, Roth?" she bit out. "Who are you?"

"I am exactly the man you've come to know."

She laughed harshly. "I doubt that. You've been lying to me since we met. Is Roth even your real name?"

His eyes snapped open, the gold streaks flashing across the sea. "Yes, my name is Roth. I never lied to you about that."

Outside, somewhere in the distance, a soft roll of thunder crept its way toward Kararhys.

Her eyes bored into his, searching for any semblance of a lie. Finding none, she said, "Fine, you never lied about your name, but you've known mine since before we met, haven't you?"

"Yes," he admitted, his voice raspy. "I knew before I sailed to Obsidian Island."

"How?" she demanded.

Roth licked his lips, swallowing. He hesitated. Riley thought for sure he wasn't going to answer her, but after a moment, he started, "Because I—"

Maurice barged through the door. His eyes were wide, wild, and his chest heaved while he panted. Sweat glistened on his brow.

Had he been running?

"You need to leave," he said. "Now."

In one swift movement, Roth bolted to his feet and tapped the leather cuffs at his wrists together. He went to their swords resting against the dresser, asking, "What happened?" But Riley barely heard the question as she watched his armor pour over his body like liquid night out of the leather cuffs, covering the suit he still wore from Maurice. In seconds, Roth looked like the aileron warrior he had been trained to be.

Riley gaped, transfixed by his sudden transformation.

"Riley," Roth said, grabbing her sword and dagger from the dresser.

"What?" she asked, dazed.

He gestured for her to stand, and she did without thought. She shook her head, forcing her mind to focus while he strapped her sword around her waist and dagger around her thigh, his hands making quick work of the buckles. "What are you doing?"

He checked to make sure the dagger was secure. "I'm making sure you have something to defend yourself with if it comes to that." Satisfied with his work, he stood from where he crouched before her.

Her brows furrowed. "Defend myself? Why would I—" The rest of her question lodged in her throat as she watched him strap his sword around his waist. "Roth, what is going on?"

"Didn't you hear Maurice?"

She shook her head but didn't mention it was he who distracted her. Again.

Looking around for the tailor, she asked, "Where is he?" He had disappeared without her notice.

"He went to get our cloaks and my straps."

"We're leaving?"

Roth nodded. "The High Crown Guard is searching the districts for two pirates who were spotted last night in the Temples of the Gods District."

Through the window, flickering light jumped across gray clouds growing nearer by the second.

Riley sucked in a sharp breath. How had they been found out? She had been so careful to make sure the tattoo was covered. She should have known coming to Kararhys would never work. That they would be discovered.

Maurice charged through the open door of the spare room, Evie in tow, her eyes frantic and full of fright. Riley went to her while Maurice helped Roth strap down his wings. She wrapped her arms around Evie and whispered, "It'll be okay," into the crown of her head. But Riley didn't know that. What she did know made her stomach churn: if Maurice and Evie were found harboring pirates, they would be hanged as traitors. She squeezed Evie tighter to her.

"Both of you should lie low and wait for things to settle," Roth said to Maurice, buckling the straps over his chest. "I don't think anyone knows we stayed here, but I don't want to take that chance."

Maurice nodded and turned to his daughter. "Sweetheart, go pack a bag. Quickly. We need to be out of here in the next five minutes." Evie squeezed Riley in return one last time before turning on her heel, doing as her father had told her without question.

"Good luck, brother," Maurice said, clapping a hand on Roth's shoulder.

Roth did the same and spoke to Maurice in Scyathan. The features on his face shifted as he did. But while his eyes told her what her ears could not decipher, she didn't look, no matter her curiosity. There was a reason why he'd chosen to use their native tongue. What he had to say to his friend, his brother, was meant for them and them only. It didn't matter how angry she was with him; she wouldn't take that away.

A smile slowly stretched across Maurice's lips as he replied, the strange syllables rolling off his tongue. And when he finished, Roth held out his other hand between them, wearing his own small smile. But instead of taking it, Maurice snorted, pulling him in for a quick embrace.

On his way out of the room, Maurice stopped in front of Riley, handing her her cloak. "It was a great pleasure to meet you, Riley," he told her. "And while only the Fates know our future, I can only hope our paths will cross again." His arms stretched out and he reeled her in for a hug as he had with Roth. In her ear, he whispered, "And if our paths don't align in the stars, thank you for giving me the gift of my daughter's smile again. I have missed it with all my heart and soul."

Riley's breath caught in her throat as Maurice pulled away. It lodged there, making it impossible to speak. All she could do was nod, the shock she felt from his words stark on her face as he left them.

It took her a moment to recover, to remember her surroundings and the impending threat closing in on her, but once she did, her legs propelled her into action.

Quickly, they gathered their things. Riley slung her bag across her chest and hastily buttoned her cloak at the neck, while Roth frowned out the window, looking at the darkening sky. He turned to her, lips still turned downward. "Are you ready?"

"I am."

CHAPTER 51

They hurried out of the spare room, down the apartment stairs, and to the back door of the shop.

Opening the door, Roth looked around, making sure no harm awaited them, and stepped into the alley.

The temperature had dropped since their night out. A chilling wind swept over Riley, settling within her bones, as she took one step and hesitated.

How did she know he wasn't leading her into a trap? If he had been keeping secrets from her all this time—vital secrets, such as knowing who she was since before they'd met—how could she trust him? Maybe she should take her chances by herself.

A streak of lightning crackled over Moonfyre Lake, illuminating its silver waters, and a loud clap of thunder followed, vibrating through the buildings.

"I might not have told you everything, Riley," Roth said, seeing her thoughts through her eyes, "but I never lied." She cursed herself for forgetting to hide her fears, to guard her heart. "You can be mad at me right now for all I care—you have every right to be—but trust in me to keep you safe."

She scoffed. "*Trust you?*" She shook her head, crossing her arms over her chest. "How could I ever trust you again when you have told me nothing?"

"I know you want answers—and I promise, you will have them—but listen to what I am telling you now: all I care about at this moment and every moment after is *you*. Please, don't be stubborn and come with me."

He held out his hand, an offering. Letting her know it was her choice. She could go with him, trust in him again to always keep her safe, or take her chances alone with the High Crown Guard.

No matter how much she didn't like it, the choice was easy.

Riley placed her hand in Roth's, and a spark—identical to when they had first met—shot through her, snuffing out the chill in her bones. "This doesn't mean I'm not mad at you."

"I never thought it did."

They made their way through the alley, the Autumn Rite celebrations becoming louder as they drew near. Riley tugged down the sleeves of her shirt, not taking any chances even with her cloak concealing her arm.

Roth halted at the end of the alley. He leaned forward, peeking around the building, and frowned. "Shit," he murmured. "They're everywhere."

Riley peered around him while using him as a shield. The guards were out in droves, their ivory armor glittering in the soft glow of the fire sprites as one by one, they came to life with the clouding sky. There were more guards roaming the streets than she had ever seen before, during her stay in the city all those years ago. Some rode on horseback, eyes scanning passersby, while others meandered into shops—but all looked for them.

Swallowing, Riley backed farther behind the spice shop, the smells glorious and mouth-watering. Her stomach growled, reminding her she hadn't eaten anything other than apple roses, and that had been hours ago.

Peering up, she saw the fast-approaching thunderhead looming on the horizon, promising destruction as deadly light flashed within, ensuring they wouldn't be flying their way out of the city.

"What do you think we should do?"

Roth followed her, hiding her from view with his solid build. "Either stay in this alley and wait for the guards to disperse, all the while praying to fucking hells none come here before then, or we can try to blend in with the crowd and leave through the gates."

She shot him a withering look. "I don't like either of those."

"There's always the sewers."

"I hate all of your ideas."

A patrol stopped on the other side of the street, the captain pointing to their alley. They converged, weaving through the crowd as they crossed the street.

"Fucking hells," Roth cursed. "New plan." He glanced at Riley. "Don't stab me for this."

"Wha—"

She was cut short by the press of Roth's lips against hers. Her eyes flared. But as the guards came closer, she understood why. To anyone else, they were just another couple careening toward the throes of passion during the Autumn Rite.

But this kiss . . . it devoured drop after drop of anger she felt.

Soon, there was only the music of the streets beating in time with her heart, the slide of his lips against hers, the soft prodding of his tongue. Her hands came to his chest, feeling the racing drum beneath. Her blood sang, a song she had almost lost weeks ago, and although she was still mad at him, she couldn't deny it was a melody she wanted to keep.

His hands slid down her sides to grip her hips, pulling her flush against him while pressing her back into the cool, coarse brick behind her. She could feel him, hard and wanting.

This kiss didn't only devour her, but him as well.

He dragged his hand from her hip to her thigh, wrapping it around him, pressing his arousal more roughly against her. A soft gasp escaped her into his mouth, and he groaned, gripping her tighter—

The captain of the patrol yanked Roth back by his right ear, seething at the roaring tiger tattooed behind it. "Pirate scum," he said through clenched teeth.

But the hand on Riley's thigh was already moving, unsheathing her dagger there in the blink of an eye.

Roth twisted, and the blade sliced into the captain's throat. Lightning illuminated the blood gushing from the wound, coating his ivory armor and the weeping willow crest at its center. Gurgling, the captain grabbed his throat as he collapsed to his knees, but Roth was already moving to the next guard, his sword now drawn with Riley's dagger in his other hand.

Dropping her bag, Riley whipped her own sword free and pounced. She probably looked near feral with her teeth bared and eyes wild. The guard's shouts became lost in the rolling thunder, and he couldn't release his blade before she was upon him, driving her sword through the gap in the armor on the side, past his rib cage. She punctured his lung, but she didn't give him another thought as she moved on to the next guard.

And the next.

And the next.

And the next.

Day became night as the dark, ominous thunderhead caught up to them. The wind stirred, picking up speed as it began to rain.

Roth's cloak was torn free, lying in a puddle of crimson next to a disemboweled guard. He was already halfway through them and covered in blood. If any of it was his, Riley couldn't tell. She didn't allow herself to think about it as she ducked a guard's blade, thrusting her sword into his armpit. She imagined she looked as Roth did, covered in blood, but it wouldn't be there long. The rain would wash it away.

Riley stepped back from the guard, pulling her blade out, and drove it into his head from the bottom of his chin. She kicked at his armored chest, forcing the weapon free.

Taking a step back, she didn't see the fallen guard behind her; she stumbled, falling to the ground. She gritted her teeth at the impact, unaware of the other guard closing in on her, their sword lifted, ready to cleave her in half.

Her eyes widened, and she gasped as a preternatural growl surged forth from the blur of black-leather armor.

Roth stood before her in an instant, and the guard's sword cut across his chest. A scream tore from Riley's throat just as a loud quake of thunder rattled through her—but he didn't fall. The blade never pierced his armor, and he didn't falter as he severed the guard's head from his body.

Riley watched the head, mouth agape, roll until it reached the back wall of a candle and incense shop. The guard's headless body dropped to the ground with a *thud*.

Staring at the head, Riley listened to the rain clink against fallen steel, the sound masking the celebrations beyond the alley. But nothing covered that growl again.

It rumbled from deep within Roth's chest as a flash of light flickered through the dark clouds, and Riley turned her gaze to the aileron standing between her and the last remaining High Crown Guard. His wings were flared slightly, shielding her.

There was a static in the air as Roth stared the guard down. The hairs on Riley's neck stood on edge while she watched the guard's face contort into alarm.

There was a resounding *crack* across the sky, and a bolt of lightning struck the earth. Thunder drowned out the screams coming from the next district over.

Roth took one step forward, and the guard turned on his heels, running from the carnage that had taken his brothers, into the packed street of celebrators.

Helping Riley to her feet, Roth asked, "Are you okay?"

She nodded. All things considered, she could be much worse. If he hadn't stepped in front of her when he had . . .

Across his chest, where the sword had cut him, there was a fine tear in the leather, but shallow enough to not see flesh beneath.

Riley drew in a shaky breath. "Thanks."

"You don't have to thank me, Riley. I would do it again in a heartbeat."

Blinking rain from her lashes, she looked into the eyes she loved so much, and it took her breath away, seeing the truth of his words there. Despite his secrets, he truly did care for her.

Roth went to her bag against the spice shop's wall and handed it to her. "We need to leave before the guard comes back with reinforcements."

She slung her soaked bag over her shoulder. "Reinforcements. Right."

Roth cleaned off her dagger with a damp scrap of cloth he found by the trash before returning it to her thigh sheath, and he quickly did the same with their swords.

Riley steeled her nerves, and they left the river of blood behind and weaved through the crowd the guard had disappeared into. They tried to blend in as well as they could, but Roth's wings made things far more difficult.

"Make your way to the Pleasure District," Roth nearly shouted in Riley's ear so she could hear him over the music and surrounding faeries, undeterred by the rain and rumbling warnings of danger. "There's a place we can—"

"There they are!"

It didn't take long for the guard to swiftly return with reinforcements.

"Fucking hells," Roth muttered. He grabbed Riley by the hand, tugging her toward another alley. "This way."

She followed without hesitation as the rain started coming down in sheets.

Shrilling winds swirled, slapping the torrential rain against Riley's cheeks, plastering her hair. She couldn't see a godsdamned thing.

Holding an arm above his eyes, Roth could just see the opening to the other alley through the downpour. "There!" he shouted.

Roth squeezed his hand tighter around Riley's, making sure it didn't slip free as they shoved through the crowd, finding it difficult to find a path through them. Fortunately for them, the High Crown Guards were having the same difficulty.

Roth growled low, exasperated. "Move!" he shouted, but it wasn't until he spread his powerful wings wide, knocking faeries out of his way, that they did as he commanded.

Reaching the alley, they sprinted through the backstreets, Riley doing her best to keep up with Roth. The backs of shops whirred by them as the rain drenched everything.

Crack after *crack* sounded, rippling across the sky, as whips of energy burst from the clouds, striking the ground. Everything they touched, burned, and anything that breathed, died. The winds grew stronger, ripping lampposts from the streets. They toppled over, crushing what lay beneath them. The glass shielding the fire sprites shattered, and the rain extinguished their flames forever.

But the High Crown Guards never ceased their pursuit. Riley glanced over her shoulder, seeing their ivory armor in the distance.

Roth skidded to a halt, and Riley bumped into his back with an *oof*.

Before them was a high brick wall—the line standing between them and the Pleasure District—and it was one they couldn't cross without flying.

Strong hands scooped Riley up. Roth held her close to his chest and spread his crimson wings. They beat at the air, lifting them a foot, two, three—

Roth cried out, his face contorted in pain. They fell the short distance back to the cobbled, stone street.

Groaning, Riley cursed, splayed out beside Roth. A pounding started in her head where it had knocked against the ground. She rubbed at the forming bump, but stopped as Roth clambered to his feet. She saw what had hurt him—what had caused his mighty wings to falter.

Arrows protruded from both of them.

Riley looked up, into the rain, and saw them then—archers stood on the rooftops, their bows lifted and enchanted arrows nocked, ready to loose on him again, but this time they wouldn't be aiming for his wings. She sucked in a sharp breath as she sat up.

"Stand down, now!"

Swallowing, Riley couldn't tell which archer spoke, but she knew not to go against his command. That if they didn't listen, they would find themselves bleeding out in the alley—but, as if all logic was knocked out of him, Roth ignored the archer, moving in front of Riley. He drew his sword, taking a step toward the pursuing High Crown Guards.

Static buzzed over Riley's skin as pressure built in the alley. It sent a tingling sensation through her veins and into her soul. It skipped over the field of roses and irises, finding the starlight rose in the center, joining the whirlwind of protection.

The guards, who had been chasing them, blocked their exit with swords drawn.

"Stop! Or it will be the last step you ever take!"

But Roth kept approaching.

Enchanted arrows split through the storm, searching for their target. Roth cried out, but it wasn't at the new arrows piercing his outstretched wings—it was for the one his wings hadn't been able to block from its intended target.

Riley screamed when the arrow tore through her left shoulder. Tears welled in her eyes and fell down her cheeks. The scent of blood filled her nostrils as it seeped through her soaked shirt. Pain burned through her, but it didn't compare to the white-hot fury pulsing from Roth.

A low snarl tore from Roth's throat as thunder and lightning struck as one. Streak after streak crashed down wildly upon the earth behind the guards, blocking their only exit—and trapping them in with the Crimson Knight.

It didn't matter that arrows littered Roth's wings. He was a warrior, and he wouldn't stop until the battle was won or he died trying.

Roth jerked toward the High Crown Guards with deadly intent—

The building pressure in the alley popped, and blinding light surged forth from Roth's chest.

CHAPTER 52

The storm within Roth's soul crackled and whirled with his wrath, a pressure tightening in his chest. It was as though someone had their hands wrapped around his insides and squeezed until he couldn't bear it any longer.

Roth heard Riley gasp as bolts of energy released from his soul.

Lightning, Roth realized. *That's* lightning.

It struck the rooftops, shooting from one archer to the next, wrapping them up in its fury as it went. Their screams faded away as one by one, they fell to the ground. The High Crown Guards jumped back from the archers' charred remains, their mouths falling open as smoke wafted from their bodies.

Gaping, Roth took in the sight of what he had just done. He shook his head, not understanding what had happened—what was still happening.

Lightning rippled down his arms and hands. Startled, he scrambled back a few steps. He shook them out, hoping the crackling light would disperse—but it didn't. It danced on until it covered the whole of his body. He could feel it along his torso and around his toes. It tickled his ears and slithered through his hair.

He sucked in a sharp breath as he waited for the pain to set in. A kind he had felt centuries ago and bore the mark of on his flesh. He waited for the stench of his burning flesh to join the archers'.

But it never did.

His mind caught up with his eyes, and he realized his skin remained untouched. Where the lightning traveled over his body, his skin tingled with the energy and his bones vibrated. The arrows in his wings turned to ash, and he watched the arrowheads fall to the ground. This should have been enough to calm him, but his panic only rose. His body began to tremble.

The storm in his soul swirled, and the wind gathered leaves and trash into the air.

Breathing heavily, Roth lifted his gaze from the nightmare dancing along his body and found something far worse. His ears popped as a tornado came whirling down in the distance, over Moon-fyre Lake.

"I-I don't understand," he stammered, backing away. "Wh-what's happening?"

His wings bumped into something solid. Pain lanced through him from the puncture wounds, but he barely felt it through the panic he was drowning in. Jumping back, he found that the something solid was Riley.

"Your eyes." She gasped. "They're glowing."

He took a step back. "Impossible." He shook his head, moving farther away from her. "That's impossible."

Wasn't it? But even as he wondered this, he could feel the storm within was connected to the storm happening above.

The wind howled in his ears, even as it howled in his soul. Crackles of light joined the whirlwind, bouncing around within its deadly center.

Roth kept backing away from Riley. He didn't want to hurt her and thanked fucking hells he hadn't already. But he had forgotten about the High Crown Guards trapped in the alley with him—and they had forgotten about him.

Distracted by the raging funnel of destruction, the guards didn't realize Roth was there until it was too late. They scrambled back, but there was nowhere to run—not from the storm's wrath. It sought vengeance, and it would have it. The lightning rippling over Roth's body pounced. The guards nearest him screamed in agony before they fell silent, the scent of burning flesh coating the air.

Taking in the chaos he'd caused, Roth fell to his knees before the fallen guards, but those who still breathed didn't dare go near him. No one was brave enough to approach the vulnerable aileron—except for one.

Roth didn't see her, couldn't hear her over the storm, but he knew she was there, approaching slowly. "Don't come near me!" he shouted at Riley. "I don't want to hurt you!"

"You won't!" she yelled back.

Before he could say anything, she was in front of him, taking tentative steps. Her hands were raised in front of her as though she were trying to coax a frightened animal to her.

You won't hurt me, her eyes told him.

The faith and trust he saw within them made him shake his head. *You can't know that.*

"You didn't before," she said, pointing to the wound at her shoulder. "I should look like those guards, but the lightning didn't hurt me. It didn't touch me, only the arrow."

He didn't understand how it was possible—but he didn't understand how any of this was.

Kneeling before him, Riley reached out slowly.

Roth trembled the closer her hand came to his, the lightning popping over him like wood in a fire, but when her fingers grazed his, the lightning skittered away up his arm. He barked out a surprised laugh and found her grinning back at him.

She moved her other hand along his, and just like the other, the lightning danced away from her touch. As though it knew she was the one person in all the worlds to never harm. The farther she slid her hands up, the more the lightning retreated.

Inching closer until her knees met his, Riley weaved her fingers into his hair and brought her forehead to his. Roth took a deep breath, letting her scent wash over him.

All at once, the lightning disappeared. The rain paused, and the swirling funnel vanished. The gaps between lightning strikes grew longer by the second, and the powerful winds settled.

Cupping his cheeks, she said, "See? You didn't hurt me."

His lips curved into a smile, but it wasn't there long. The High Crown Guards moved in now that the storm had turned into a light drizzle. Riley's hands disappeared from his skin as a guard shackled them behind her back, but her forehead remained against his.

"I'm sorry," he murmured.

Her breath was hot in the small space between them. "Me too."

There was no need for reassurances, no need for pretend. They both knew how this was going to end.

Roth felt the familiar burn of iron at his wrists. He bared his teeth, sucking in a sharp breath. But the smell of his burning flesh was lost among the charred remains of those who had perished from the storm's wrath—from his fear.

"That was quite the light show you just put on, Crimson Knight. Was it all for me?"

Roth went rigid at the sound of the light, almost feminine voice. Tendons in his neck strained, and a muscle in his jaw popped. His upper lip curled back in a snarl. "*Jarrek.*"

Riley jerked back from Roth and looked over her shoulder at the approaching tall, lean elve with golden-brown skin—the Carver.

Jarrek wore the same form-fitting leathers as Roth, and a scar cut diagonally across his face from the top of his bald head through his right eyebrow, and to his left ear. Roth had always thought it was a damn shame Maurice had missed the Carver's eye when he had given him that scar, but the mark never failed to give Roth some semblance of satisfaction—and hope that one day the Carver would meet his torturous fate.

"I was wondering when I would see you again," Jarrek said, stopping behind a stiff Riley. He clamped his hands on her shoulders, and she cried out as blood seeped from between his fingers. His grip was tight, keeping her in place despite her wriggling.

Roth snarled, trying to get to his feet and lunge at the Carver, but High Crown Guards held him. They slammed him back down to his knees, holding a sword to his throat.

"If I didn't know any better," Jarrek said close to Riley's ear, "I'd say he missed me."

Roth growled low, and he could feel the storm within begin to surge once again—

Magic like he had never felt before shot through him from his wrists. It dove down deep, engulfing his soul. The storm writhed against it, but it was as though a barrier had been placed around it, caging it in like a wild animal.

Jarrek quirked a brow. "Did you really think there wouldn't be primordial warding on your shackles to keep you in check after the performance you just gave?"

The Carver's fingers dug into Riley. "I want you to watch closely," Jarrek told her. "The second act is about to begin."

With the jerk of his chin, Jarrek commanded two guards forward. They each held an iron cuff, and when they reached Roth, they placed them at the base of his wings. Just as his armor cuffs had, liquid poured from the iron ones. It flowed over his feathers, seeping into the wounds left from the arrows, and within seconds, his wings were encased in iron.

Pain overwhelmed Roth's senses. The iron seared through the muscle of his wings, determined to find the bone beneath. Feathers melted away into nothing.

The storm within his soul roared, rattling its cage, but the warding keeping it trapped only intensified. The more the storm struggled—the more Roth struggled—the stronger the warding became.

Crying out, Roth fell on his side, pinching his eyes shut. Through the painful haze, he could hear Riley screaming his name, telling him to focus on her voice. He did as she said, focusing on her. He cracked his eyes open, feeling the tears fall without his permission.

"I'm sorry." Riley gasped through her own tears. "I'm so sorry."

Behind her, Jarrek still held her in place. He clicked his tongue. "Well, this is not as satisfying as I was hoping it would be." He sighed, finally releasing his grip on Riley.

"Take them to the castle dungeon," Jarrek ordered the guards. His clementine eyes snagged on Riley's arms before they met Roth's. A cruel smile stretched across his face. "And tell the High King to erect the gallows. He has a pirate to hang."

EPILOGUE

The gods were angry—or at least, one very powerful god was.

The storm wreaking havoc on the Trading and Market District of Kararhys could be seen from miles upon miles away, even from the safe distance of the sloping hill Mara stood on, watching the calamity unfold.

She wished she could spark just an ounce of that destruction. Strike down those who dared look at her wrong. Fuck, she'd be happy to hit the thorny thundercunt pissing on a tree behind her with a hailstone the size of a pebble if she could.

Maybe that's what I'll wish for instead, when I finally get my hands on that fucking scroll, she thought. *Power.*

The thought sent a shiver of pleasure racing through her veins.

Then, she would force her enemies to kneel before *her*. Make them beg for their pathetic, wretched lives before she sent them to hell—because those like her didn't go to the Elysian Fields. They had a special place reserved in the deepest, darkest crevices of the Abyss.

There was an overwhelming part of her oozing soul that dreaded when her day would come. When she found herself in the Abyss, not a speck of light to comfort her as the dark devoured her whole. But she knew it was where she was meant to be. That the Fates had written her this future long before she'd been conceived, and no one gave a damn to rewrite it.

Riley certainly hadn't.

Mara's wrist felt lighter than ever, with nothing to weigh it down anymore. She was surprised to find herself feeling more and more liberated after she'd left the bracelet behind to rot—as she had been.

She chuckled bitterly to herself. The image of Riley in that ridiculous dress she'd seen her wearing while she'd walked hand in hand with that fucking aileron in the Temples of the Gods District in Kararhys flashed before her. How she had looked at him with doe eyes and smiled. Truly smiled at him. One she had never seen for herself in the three years she had known her. It was at that moment, Mara realized Riley wasn't coming for her. That her best friend had abandoned her. Left her to die at the hands of the thorny thundercunt.

And for what?

For *him*?

They had been through thick and thin together. She had saved Riley's life more times than she could count. But once that traitorous aileron's cock had come out, Riley had left her to *rot*.

Setting her jaw in resolve, Mara watched as a tornado swirled and came down from the sky near the city, over Moonfyre Lake. She could almost hear the screams from those who resided there as the angry funnel of wind and destruction tore through their happy, perfect lives—and gods, did she fucking love it.

The leather collar around her neck, etched with the elven language, tightened at Grimsley's command. Done relieving himself, he pulled on the leash tethering him to her, ordering her to move, to follow him around like the dog he had treated her as for the last three months.

One day, he would regret his actions. One day, she wouldn't be wearing the abhorrent collar. One day, the wild creature she was would be let loose, and he would beg for the mercy he didn't deserve, just as her father had.

Mara lifted her chin, the marred skin at the center of her throat still raw from when Grimsley had burned the tiger away with a hot blade. She vowed to herself that when she found and killed the one responsible for stealing the treasure from her—when she found what her soul desired most—all who had hurt her, humiliated her, betrayed her would fear the power of her wrath. She would take her future into her own hands and rewrite the whole godsdamned thing. And she would be a god.

ACKNOWLEDGMENTS

Before I thank those who helped make this book a reality, I'd like to apologize to you, the reader, for leaving you with that cliffhanger. I am sorry . . . kind of. *maniacal laughter*

JoAnn, I don't even know where to start. A simple "thank you" doesn't come close to the amount of help and support you've given over the years. You've been there since the beginning when this book was only an idea about a young woman stolen from her family. You know of every idea that's been scrapped, altered, too ridiculous to do, and what's to come (the one you're dreading is still happening, but I'll replace that chapter with wholesome fan fiction in your copy). And then, there are the chapters and ideas that wouldn't exist without you that helped make this book what it is today. Riley and Roth—especially Roth—are as precious to you as they are to me. I know I'm not the kindest to them (and that won't change anytime soon), but I promise you can have them when the series is over and never let anything bad happen to them ever again.

Sandy, you were the first to read and critique OL&D (back when it had one of the many different titles). I'm so glad you liked it and that I was even able to surprise you! You've read so much you can spot a plot twist/foreshadowing a mile away! Thank you for taking the time to go through all of my questions and help brainstorm ideas to change and rearrange scenes.

Madi, you were the one to suggest self-publishing after reading OL&D and encouraged me to follow that path. I'm not sure I would've tried if it hadn't been for your enthusiastic comments throughout the manuscript, so thank you.

Family, thank you so much for your love, support, and encouragement. It's surreal to finally share this book with you all after years of talking about it. Dad, I especially wouldn't have been able to make this dream of mine happen without your help. Love you!

P.S. I hope you skipped Chapter 41. If not, I'll see you when I'm no longer uncomfortable to show my face. :)

Emma, I'm so grateful for your support and friendship. I loved sharing this book with you and what's to come over the last few years. Your "What!? OMG"s help keep me going. Thank you.

Niki, I couldn't have made it through the last few years without you. Every time I mentioned giving up, you always encouraged me to keep going. Thank you for always being there for me and giving me a safe space when I need it the most.

PPL Fam, thank you for all your support, encouragement, and enthusiasm throughout the writing and publishing process. It's been a blast to share it all with you along the way.

Shout out to Noah and Norma for editing this book. There would be so many unnecessary commas if it weren't for you. Madi can attest, as she gave up pretty quickly trying to get rid of all of them for me.

Moonpress aka Bianca, you did such a kick-ass job with the cover!!! I truly can't express how much I love it! You're pure magic, and I can't wait to work with you again!

Rena, the map is amazing!!! I love all the little details, especially the swinging dead faerie! Thank you so much for your hard work, but especially for your patience when I was incredibly indecisive.

Lastly, but certainly not least, I'd like to thank you, the reader (after a *very* sincere apology ;)), for making it this far. You support me by merely holding this book in your hands, and for that, I could never begin to repay you. I hope you loved this book as much as I enjoyed writing it. Riley and Roth are very near and dear to my heart. They are on a long journey of self-love and self-forgiveness. And that is not an easy thing to come by on your own! Which is why I'm telling their stories. They say writers put themselves into their work, and I did just that. Their struggles mirror some of my own. I know I'm not alone on this journey, and I wanted those out there—the Rileys and Roths of the world—to know it, too.

You are not alone. <3

ABOUT THE AUTHOR

Abigail R. Schieber has been trying to escape into a fantasy world since she was a child. Although she never acquired that magic, it didn't stop her from dreaming up her own. The moment she realized she could write those worlds into existence, she wanted others to be able to join her in them.

She lives in Wisconsin, surrounded by cows and the occasional coyote. If she's not writing or dreaming up worlds, she can be found in another author's world or binging *The Office* or *Parks and Recreation* again. But most likely, she's snuggling her very fashionable and sassy tuxedo cat, Louie, against his will.

© Crystal Berry, 2025

CONTENT WARNING

- Explicit language
- Depictions of grief from loss of a friend, parent, sibling, and partner
- Blood and gore
- Consensual sexually explicit scenes
- Sexual assault (mentioned)
- Use of the word "rape"
- Physical assault
- Substance abuse
- Emotional abuse
- Depression
- Attempted suicide (mentioned) and suicidal ideation
- PTSD
- Kidnapping and captivity of a minor (mentioned)
- Slavery